BROKEN RINGS

GIBSON MARRS

To Shawn,

All The Best !

RTP
Research Triangle Publishing

Published by
Research Triangle Publishing, Inc.
PO Box 1223
Fuquay-Varina, NC 27526

Jacket design by Micah Sanger

Library of Congress Catalog Card Number: 95-72491

ISBN 1-884570-37-2

Printed in the United States of America
10 9 8 7 6 5 4 3 2 1

For Cary

ACKNOWLEDGMENTS

Amanda Maple: loving sister and indispensable editor.

Floyd Harris and Bonnie Tilson: professional editors and extraordinary talents.

Linda McDaniel and Amelia Farley: esteemed prodders.

Peggy Kerr: valued reader and critic

Sharen Tetuan, Tara Howard, Carmela Evans, Katy Tiller, Kelly Johnson, Jeri Meredith, and Michelle Ouellet: diligent and faithful staff

Liz and Dave Anderson: wise, methodical, innovative publishers.

Heidi Romero: everlasting inspiration.

This story is a work of fiction told with fictional characters and staged in settings, some of which are real. The factual information regarding the 1996 Olympic venues was gleaned from the lucid reporting of Prentis Rogers, Maria Saporta, Melissa Turner, Gail Hagans, Shelia M. Poole, Bert Roughton, Jr., Bill Hendrick, Ron Martz, John Harmon, Sonia Murray, Betty Parham, Ken Foskett, and Michelle Hiskey, writers for *The Atlanta Journal-The Atlanta Constitution.*

The author gratefully acknowledges their expertise and research not only in reporting the monumental events leading up to the 1996 Summer Games, but also in portraying our daily comedy and tragedy with the talent and skill that has established the *Journal-Constitution* as a national institution.

ONE

Maria Cortez flashed her nervous mahogany eyes up at the clock. 5:34. Two more fleeting minutes had passed. She quickly returned her focus to the hem of the tattered second hand dress. Furrowing her brow, she intently guided the fabric through the pumping steel jaws of the sewing machine.

In spite of the autumn cool, her palms were wet and the back of her modest cotton blouse had become a sticky second skin. Maria could imagine her mother standing at the kitchen door, peering down the empty alley behind their stucco ranch house, conjuring visions of her only daughter kidnapped by a crazed maniac or injured and deserted on a Miami sidewalk by a merciless drunk driver.

Breaking her word to her mother upset the thirteen year old more than enduring a Freddy Krueger flick or being left off the list for a classmate's slumber party. It was even worse than the red-haired boy in religion class finding out that she liked him.

The raging needle nicked the tip of her right index finger and a grimace distorted her angelic face. But quickly checking that the needle had drawn no blood, Maria resumed her frenetic pace. Through the open windows of the deserted parish hall, sounds of the evening rush hour intensified. Automobile exhaust hung in the fall nip and mixed with the sweet familiar fragrance of votive candles flickering next door in the vestibule.

Every day for the last week, Maria had rummaged through the charity box in the church atrium, hoping to find dresses suitable for two second grade orphans in preparation for tomorrow's inspection by the archbishop. Late this afternoon, Mother Mary smiled, and two ragged floral prints appeared among the assemblage of putrid sweatshirts, ratty shoes, and mothball-smelling suits.

The frocks, though, sized for robust girls of nine or ten would have engulfed her small friends like kittens in a laundry sack. Now trapped by her good intentions, Maria felt God testing her character: either break the hearts of two innocent grade-schoolers, who at age seven had been rejected by their parents and abused by a state welfare system, or continue her sewing, tormented by the image of her worrying mother.

She wiped away beads of sweat with the back of her sleeve. An urban symphony of car horns and skidding tires crescendoed outside, accompanied by angry motorists chiding one another in Spanish.

Among the vehicles speeding through the busy intersection across from the church's wrought iron fence was a bright metallic blue 1970 Impala with shiny mirror-like chrome bumpers.

Another bead of sweat, this one rolling down Maria's temple and over her smooth bronze cheek, was brushed quickly away by hurried fingertips.

ONE OF THE BOYS in the back seat of the metallic blue low-rider had been in Maria's first grade class seven years

2

ago. His lean brown face had yet to sprout its first whisker. Hands shaking, the boy reached for a magazine of thirty-two rounds to clip into the bottom of the 9mm Uzi lying across his knees. He was determined to disguise his consuming fear from his older brother sitting at the opposite window in the back seat.

The driver, oldest of the four boys at twenty, spun the back tires of the car, wheeling it around the corner into Maria's neighborhood. The afternoon congestion of commuters returning to their homes—and the serenity they casually took for granted—interfered with the boys' pursuit of their assigned target, a small red pickup truck.

A sweaty black bandanna glued the driver's tangled dark hair to the sides of his head. His eyes showed no fear, no worry, no guilt, no life—void of emotion, they anticipated death as if it were imminent and certain destiny. Across his lap rested a Beretta submachine gun, barely cool from its last encounter, an easy kill the night before in an alley behind the warehouse where his gang assembled.

It's our turf, he swore to himself again. Fucker shouldn't have been there.

Next to him sat a boy of eighteen, the same age as the older boy in the back. All wore the same black bandannas.

No one listened to the Spanish rapping from the quad stereo speakers, but their hearts reflexively beat time with the dirge of bass notes.

Without expression, the older boy in the back seat faced his little brother with half-closed eyes. He cocked his head in a quick curt gesture as if to ask, "You okay?"

His younger brother stared back blankly and extended his right hand in a fist. In turn, the older boy made a fist with his left hand and tapped his brother knuckle to knuckle, tacitly reinforcing the blood tie binding them together.

The metallic blue Impala skidded around another corner as the driver raced the V-8 engine through the quiet neighborhood streets framed by green yards of even St. Augustine grass and clean sidewalks. Tall bent palm trees cast long shadows across the asphalt, feigning the bars of a giant jail cell.

The young boy felt sick to his stomach as a cold sweat broke out over his face.

MARIA LOOKED AT the clock again. 5:40. The second hand on the parish hall clock seemed uncommonly fast. Why couldn't it move this swiftly in algebra class? Her left foot tapped nervously against a crack in the terra-cotta floor.

The archbishop's review tomorrow would be the most important day in the history of the school. A decrease in contributions to the church was forcing the district council to consider adding St. Pius to a list of twelve other schools in the Southeast whose doors were closing.

Unlike Maria, who lived at home with her family and commuted to school with her brother, almost a third of the students at St. Pius resided in the church dormitory. Many had endured upheaval not once, but several times before their thirteenth birthday, and the horror of relocation threatened the fragile security offered by the caring nuns. To them, the shallow bond of brotherhood was as precariously thin as the porcelain face of the Madonna abiding in the church alcove.

Maria tried to assuage her friends' fears, even if it was by something as small and seemingly insignificant as altering dresses. If all the children looked and acted their best, perhaps the archbishop would be persuaded to keep the school open.

Under the faded pine, sewing table, the young girl tensed her right leg, then her left, then back again. Along the edge of the ceiling above the heating vents, soot from the decrepit heating system stained the pale chipped parish walls, where near one window, cracks in the masonry offered an array of footholds for a spider's lacy trap. The silvery threads, marvelously spun into fine symmetrical geometric shapes, shimmered in the scattered rays of fading sunlight that peeked through the dirty panes. Nearby, the ambivalent girl pushed herself even harder, never noticing nature's ageless muse for spellbinding children.

WHERE DID THE son of a bitch go?" The driver bent his head closer to the steering wheel, to see beneath the pink tassels fringing the Impala's interior ceiling.

"Turn down here," the boy in the passenger seat shouted, pointing to a side street on the right.

"No way, man. I would've seen him turn there. He's got to be ahead of us. Come on, man, where'd he go?"

In the back seat, the youngest boy whispered to his brother, "Who are we after?"

"Don't ask nothing, man," his brother said sharply. "We do what we're told. Just keep your mouth shut and your eyes open."

"What was the license plate number *señor* Miras gave us?" the driver yelled across the car.

"I thought you had the number, man," the other boy in the front seat said, his voice cracking under pressure.

"Damn it, man, do I gotta do everythin'? Look in the fuckin' glove compartment and read the number again. Shit!"

The boy riding shotgun hurried to obey.

The young boy in the back dug at the black vinyl peeling away from the padded door panel above the armrest. He burrowed his dirty index finger under the glossy plastic sheath and pulled another piece loose from the door. He had obeyed his older brother ever since their mother shot and killed their father five years before.

Between short shallow breaths, the youngest boy remembered how it used to be when he was little and the family was together: spending sunny afternoons playing basketball with his father and older brother, hearing his father's voice urging the boys on, showing them how to dribble between their legs. They had played on the asphalt court outside his elementary school, where in the first grade he had liked his teacher and had enjoyed hearing her read Rudyard Kipling and Robert Frost. But now, terrified by what he was about to do, the boy did not remember the cute brown-haired girl who had sat next to him in that class.

AGAIN, HER EYES GLARED at the indifferent timepiece.

The fear of disappointing her mother was winning the moral struggle over breaking her promise to the twins, but the image replayed in her mind of the twins bouncing on their toes and squealing with delight at the sight of the two pitiful dresses.

5:41. That's it, I've got to go.

THUD! A startling thunder exploded from the hallway.

Maria's heart jumped, and her foot reflexively lifted from the sewing machine pedal.

Just outside the door to the parish hall, a bound report, six inches thick, lay at Sister Mary Francis' feet where it had slipped from the top of a stack and crashed to the floor. Swaying under the imbalance, Sister Mary Francis teetered into the parish hall and slid the remaining logs of student attendance, textbook receipts, cafeteria inventories, and classroom supplies onto a table near the door.

"Maria!" the young nun said, peering around the pile of paper. "What are you still doing here all alone? Your mother must be beside herself with worry. Have you forgotten the time?"

As she drew close, the Sister saw that Maria was crying and gently kneeled down beside her at the sewing machine.

"Maria, what's wrong? This isn't like you. Tell me what's troubling you, child."

"Oh Sister!" Maria said, a tear trailing down her cheek. "I'm trying to finish these for the twins to wear for the archbishop's visit tomorrow, and it's taking me a lot longer than I thought. I know I should be home by now, but this is so important to the twins. Everyone is so upset about tomorrow."

A drop fell onto the threadbare garment.

"Maria, did you call your mother and tell her you were here?" The Sister, as well as the rest of the staff, was, of course, also under the same tremendous pressure. Yet her voice remained calm and comforting.

"I know I should have, Sister. But my father can be pretty strict and if he's home, he'll order me to leave right now. He just doesn't understand what this school means to all the other kids." The girl trembled as she spoke. More tears fell from the sides of her chin and spread fluidly across the dress, deepening the faded hues of the tiny wild flowers and roses to vivid hyacinth and crimson.

Sister Mary Francis surveyed the dresses, one lying across the sewing machine and the other slung on a table nearby. She rose to her feet and placed her right hand behind her head, speaking more to herself than to Maria.

"I think I should finish these for you and you should go home. Your mother is expecting you now and . . ."

"But you have so much to do, Sister," Maria protested, looking toward the stack of financial reports rising near the door to the room. "You can't finish these and get those ready for tomorrow. I don't want to be the 'cause of more work for you."

The nun sighed and glanced back at the reports, pondering the drudgery that would last late into the night. She rested her hand on Maria's shoulder. "Dear, stitching these hems will be a welcome distraction from a pencil and a calculator. We'll just call it one of the few legitimate instances for procrastination. . ." Then she glanced heavenward. ". . . Of which our Father would surely approve."

Sister Mary Francis' gentle smile warmed the faithful girl. Maria leapt to her feet and hugged the nun. "How can I ever thank you?"

"Do your homework and read a chapter in the Gospels and I'll be duly compensated," the nun said, returning the embrace.

Maria kissed the nun on the cheek and bolted out the door.

Sister Mary Francis called out to the hurrying girl, "Maria! Be careful going home. It's getting dark."

MARIE RAN DOWN Orchard Street toward the movie theater, barely slowing enough at intersections to let cars go by. Unwilling to wait for the flashing WALK sign, Maria darted away from the tired crowd on the street corner, causing a burly driver in a crusty brown Plymouth to skid suddenly at the green light to avoid squashing the skinny girl against his dented hood. Her long, dark brown hair streamed behind her as she kept an Olympian pace.

Maria's agility was a thorn in the side of Paul, her older brother, who had lost more than one race to his little sister. At sixteen, having his kid sister blow by him on a soccer field and score a breakaway goal in front of neighborhood friends was akin to having his dad drive him to the prom.

Maria scanned the street ahead, plotting a course through the jungle of pedestrians along the city blocks. Her lineless face was tense with anticipation. Her mother was a sweet, gentle woman who had emerged victorious over Castro and the strife he dictated in Cuba. Her plump face was unblemished and beaming, and when she stood at the kitchen counter preparing meals for her family, she cast an outline that was a little shorter but nearly as wide as the Sears refrigerator.

Her mother seldom had a harsh word for anyone. When the man next door got drunk and sent empty beer cans over the concrete block wall, Mrs. Cortez would calmly gather them into a plastic garbage bag for the recycling bin. She praised God every day for her two children, though she grieved to watch her bright and healthy sixteen-year-old son join a *crew* and trade a report card for a rap sheet.

Passing in front of the record store, Maria remembered racing Paul last summer along the same street. "Beat ya to Baskin Robbins!" Paul cried, running off ahead of his sister.

"Last one there buys", she screamed at his back.

"Sure squirt, you better have money."

Maria overtook her brother at the stone benches in front of Beaseley Drugs. Going into the ice cream shop, Paul caught up and grabbed his sister around the neck in a headlock. Rubbing his knuckles hard against the top of her scalp, he yelled, "Noogie patrol! Noogie patrol!" She hated that, just like Gilda Radner did on the old *Saturday Night Live* reruns. At least he was bigger.

Maria smiled to herself.

She tripped on an industrial, orange-colored extension cord running from the music store out to a lighted sign at the edge of the curb, but quickly regained her balance and resumed her pace. "Hey there young girl," shouted an old man. "What's the matta? What's the hurry? Why don't you slow down a minute. . ." His voice faded behind her.

She hurried by a seminarian handing out leaflets proclaiming, "Stop Gang Violence, Now!" and it reminded her of the priests who worked with Paul and tried to get him clean. Sometimes Paul stayed after school to talk with Father Morton and the other priests. The talks seemed to help. Then one weekend at a church retreat at the beach, Father Morton devoted all of his time to ridding Paul of his habit.

But something went wrong. After that weekend, Paul seemed angry. He would not talk to anyone, and his behavior and his drug abuse worsened.

Remembering her mother's ashen face from staying up late night after night while waiting for Paul to come home made Maria pick up her pace again. She darted around the corner at Pelican and started down Bayside Street, her house just six blocks away.

THE KNOCK ON THE DOOR WAS LOUD AND HARD.

Juan Cortez sat up quickly and glanced at his watch. His first thought was that his son was in trouble again, but rap music boomed from Paul's room at the back of the house, and Juan let out a breath of relief. He set down his mug and buttoned his sawdust-covered shirt as he headed to the front door.

"Juan, you've gotta help me. I'm in big trouble". He was pushed back abruptly by Jack Barton, his boss and owner of Barton Construction. Juan saw Jack's red pickup truck parked at an angle in the street, the right front tire perched halfway up the curb.

"Jack, calm down," Juan said. "What's the matter."

"They're going to kill me, Juan. They said if I didn't have the money by today they'd kill me. I just don't know what to do. I'm in a helluva mess, you've gotta help me."

"Sure, Jack sure," Juan returned. "Just calm down. Tell me what's going on."

Jack tried to sit, but was quickly back on his feet. To the pros of the construction business, Jack Barton was just a kid, tall and slender with a brown weathered face and stringy hair that fell over the collar of his shirt. He had started his construction company on his own, following a conservative strategy of low overhead and on-time completions. By staggering his jobs, Jack was able to maintain a positive cash flow and only purchased new land with cash.

His blueprint had worked, and those who knew Jack's business figured he would be a millionaire before he was thirty.

"Juan, I've screwed up big time." Jack nervously rubbed his sweaty chin against his shoulder, still trying to catch his breath. "You know with things going so well, I started building a house for Tina."

Jack's words grew clearer.

"Well, one thing led to another. First we had a Jacuzzi, then she wanted another in the guest bath. Then she wanted the marble entry extended into the kitchen, then into the den, and then onto the back porch. I mean, I started out figuring the place would cost me about eight hundred grand, and all of the sudden I was well over two million. I didn't know what to do, Juan. I couldn't tell Babydoll I couldn't afford the house. Right?"

Juan raised his eyebrows.

"Right, Juan?" Jack repeated, water rising in his red eyes.

Juan allowed a few slow nods, not so much in agreement, but for Jack to continue.

"I went to our regular banks, see, and all they saw was that Barton Construction had eighty-three houses under construction, all a hundred percent financed. They wouldn't extend me a dime over a million for my place." Jack again tried to sit, but couldn't stay still. "Well, a million got me along for a while, but I knew I needed more. A lot more."

Juan listened in disbelief. At first, he had been worried when Jack brought Tina back from a weekend in Vegas, but after getting to know her, Juan thought everything was okay.

Unexpected images from the past suddenly shot into Juan's mind: Jack sitting on the couch with four-year-old Maria on his knee. Jack beaming with pride at Paul's confirmation ceremony. Jack and Juan getting drunk after the company's first subdivision sold out.

Juan shook his head as Jack continued.

"A buddy told me about the Piedmont Bank who'd lend money with no collateral. So I went to them and they gave me all I wanted. They looked at our financial statements and said, 'No problem!' They were delighted to do business with such a successful contractor and they hoped we could work together on future ventures. They said they'd go as high as a million five if I needed. I thought my problems were over."

"So what's going on?" asked Juan.

"Those fourteen units in East Vinings didn't close and the Bridge's delayed Phase Two on the expansion of their beach house. Remember? Then the Chamberlain's place didn't finish on time 'cause that bitch kept changing her mind on lighting fixtures and granite tiles. Before I knew it, I'd missed two payments on my note with Piedmont."

"Okay," Juan said. "So you got a little behind."

"The first month I missed, no big deal. They sent one of their associates over to the office, some guy named Miras. A real bad-looking dude from somewhere in South America. Anyway, we talked about twenty minutes and I guaranteed him two payments today. Then I got a call this morning from Miras, saying if two payments weren't made by three o'clock, the bank would be cashing in on my collateral."

All color faded from Jack's face.

"I thought to myself, 'Collateral? What collateral?'"

Jack paused.

"Juan, it was an unsecured note."

The pieces began to fit.

"So I looked at my loan agreement and saw that my fifty-two hundred dollar down payment bought a three million dollar term life insurance policy on me with Piedmont as the beneficiary."

Jack stood silent for a moment running his hands through his hair. Then he started pacing the floor.

He stopped with a jerk and said, "Juan, I think they're going to kill me."

Juan rubbed his face with his callused hands. About then, his wife came into the room and cheerfully greeted Jack and offered them both a beer. She retreated immediately, seeing the grave expression on her husband's face. Her first thought was to inquire what was the matter, but she reconsidered and returned to the kitchen to wait for Maria.

After a long pause, Juan said, "Jack, nobody's going to get killed. They're just trying to scare you a little."

Juan's voice did not sound convincing even to himself.

"THERE IT IS!" the driver shouted, pointing to the red pickup truck parked at the curb.

He slammed on the brakes, skidding the bright blue car to a halt behind the truck parked in front of a light green stucco house. The dwelling resembled the others on the block, only with pale blue shutters and light gray asphalt shingles. A straight concrete walkway extended from the sidewalk directly to the front door, and beds of white pansies speckled with deep blue violet and bright yellow gold bordered both sides. In the setting sunlight, the flowers' colors seemed artificially brilliant against the deep green background of the mowed lawn.

The air was almost cold, but the young boy fumbling with the lever at the back door looked as though he had been swimming in his shirt. His eyes grew darker as his face blanched.

The driver got out of the car with his gun in hand. Each boy wore uniform sunglasses. The four knelt in front of the car like a pack of wolves, the youngest pushed behind the others by his brother.

"How do we know which one?"

The driver checked his ammunition clip and said, "*Señor* Miras said nail anyone the guy's with."

THEY WERE BOTH startled by the sound of tires screeching across the asphalt outside in front of the house. Juan stood up and peered through the blinds. There was a reflection off the windshield of the car, but he could see it was a metallic blue Impala with 'set-down' suspension for a low-rider.

Juan squinted to see the faces of the youths in front of the car, but he could not make out who they were.

He was about to call out to Paul to see if he knew any of them when a 9mm round crashed through the living room window and struck his face inches below his right eye.

The force of the blow knocked him off his feet and landed him against the couch on the far wall. In a blur, he struggled to his knees, not sure what had happened.

He looked down at his shirt and saw blood drenching his chest. He grabbed his head, throbbing like it had been hit by a sledgehammer. Blood flowed from his face, spurting between his fingers as he tried to apply pressure to the wound.

He turned to look at Jack, who ran toward the kitchen.

A barrage of fire from the submachine guns streamed through the front of the house. The bullets riddled the walls of the Cortez house like they were cutting through cardboard.

1 3

Jack was hit repeatedly in the back. His body made a thud against the floor as it rolled over against the baseboard. Juan crawled over the mangled body of his dead friend and screamed to his wife in the kitchen and towards Paul's room.

For a split second, the deafening sound of crashing glass preceded more bullets slamming the back of Juan's head and throwing him again into the couch.

At the sound of the gunfire, Paul bolted out of his room. The gunshots, together with the blasting stereo in his room, disoriented him as he entered the hallway leading to the living room.

Thirty rounds a second pierced the wall again.

Paul fell to the floor after being hit in the right calf. Hearing his hoarse screams in the hallway, his terrified mother yelled for him to come to the kitchen.

Leaving a bloody trail behind, Paul snaked on his belly toward the refuge of his mother.

On the floor near the doorway to the kitchen, Paul watched another succession of gunfire blow open the front door. He turned his head to see four Latino young men wearing jeans and dark tee shirts come into the living room of his house.

"Check out the cool walls, man!" one said, laughing at the blood splattered across the clean paint.

"Paul! Come to the kitchen! Now!" his mother screamed. She bent down to help her son, but one of the gunmen slugged her savagely across her face with the back of his arm, jamming her against the yellow Formica counter. Paul grabbed the man's leg, and tried to pull him to the floor.

Laughing at the boy sprawled on the floor, the gunman maliciously kicked Paul's wound.

Furiously, Paul reached up again and grabbed the gang member by the belt of his pants and jerked him to the floor. The gunman tripped over Paul's legs and landed on his back in the hallway. Paul pulled himself on top of the man and beat him in the face.

Unable to pry the Uzi from the young man's hands, Paul latched onto the weapon and threw his weight against the wall, breaking the gunman's grip. He quickly lodged the machine gun against his hip and fired down the hallway toward the living room. He did not realize the mad screams he heard were his own.

In seconds, Paul unloaded a mass of rounds through the hall, clearing the way for his mother's rescue. Before realizing it, though, he exhausted his supply of bullets.

Hot breaths parched his throat as he crawled back toward the groaning youth behind him and searched for more ammunition. In a back pocket was another clip which he seized to reload his weapon. He pushed the mechanism to release the used clip from the underside of the gun, but nothing happened. He pushed the latch again, but the clip would not release.

With fingers slippery with sweat and blood, Paul pushed on the latch and pounded the wedged clip against the wall in the hallway, smashing holes in the drywall with each blow. Finally, on the fourth jolt, the clip fell to the carpet. Looking up, Paul saw two other gunmen in the hall smiling like devils.

"What do ya think, Jose? Think he's got enough time to reload?" the tall one sneered arrogantly.

"Gee, man, I don't think so. I think he's in trouble."

Paul's hands trembled, struggling to insert the new clip with fingers numbed by fear.

Sitting on his knees in the hallway, he could feel the throbbing in his wounded leg. A few weeks ago he had sat in the identical place waiting to scare his little sister on Halloween.

His heart pounded blood to his head. "Get in there!" Paul cursed at the gun.

With a definite snapping sound, the clip found its place.

The two gunmen laughed at the sound.

"Party time!" one yelled.

Regaining her senses, Paul's mother struggled to her feet and rushed to the hallway just as the flash from the muzzles sprayed lead across Paul's chest and up his neck. His body twitched for a moment before becoming still.

Maria's mother shrieked and charged the gunmen with fists in the air, but never made it past the kitchen linoleum. With another fiendish hail of gunfire, her blood stained the bright yellow paint of the very room where she had ironed clothes, sewed shirts, and prepared meals for her family.

The entire attack lasted only minutes. The youngest one fired a cowardly round into each of the four bodies before running out the front door.

The same sound of screeching tires was heard again as the car sped away with four boys who would never become men.

MARIA PASSED MRS. COLONI'S bakery on the right where her mother sometimes bought croissants for special occasions, and then looked both ways before racing across Orange and turning into her neighborhood. The street lights were on, but the sun still cast a few fading rays of light against the lavender sky, the edge of the blazing dome disappearing below a gilded silhouette of pink stucco buildings and palm trees.

Maria came up the alley behind her house as she always did, fearing her mother would be angry with her for being late. She thought of telling her mother about the dresses for the twins as she climbed the back steps to the house.

At the top step, she stopped.

Something brown spotted the window of the kitchen door.

Her slender eyebrows pinched at the strange sight. Her mother always kept an immaculate house.

Maria turned the knob and opened the back door. Her knees collapsed and she threw up.

Two

The tiresome sound of honking horns persisted. Mark Townsend smiled and shook his head. What did these people think anyway, sitting on their horn is going to make the traffic move faster?

He rubbed his tired eyes. Reaching over to the radio and pushing in a James Taylor tape, he turned up the volume to drown out the line of drivers expressing their frustration. "How Sweet It Is (to be Loved by You)" hit the spot.

Friday afternoons were always the same in D.C., everyone heading to the hills for the weekend. The escape happened the same time, week in and week out, fifty-two weeks a year. It was a little lighter when Congress wasn't in session, but not much.

Mark wondered if anyone else shared his assessment of the weekend pilgrimage: humanity fleeing the malignant filth and sleaziness within the nation's hub of politics.

Only the diehards wanted to stay in town over the weekend, the caffeine-addicted political junkies, whose consciences had evaporated long ago between boiling-hot satin sheets or from scalding disclosures of sultry bureaucratic investigations. The corridors of Washington were filled with wild-eyed cannibals whose friendships resulted from convenience or influence.

Mark had seen it all from inside the White House.

It was scary. The people running the country were psychotic self-centered egomaniacs who worried about their own advancement infinitely more than the well-being of the citizenry who had entrusted them with the power to govern.

He leaned toward the dashboard, finding the chrome and black controls of the Pioneer cassette player, and fast-forwarded to "Carolina in My Mind," dreaming how it would be in two more weeks. At first, the decision to leave White House security after three years was difficult. Right now he could not remember why it had been so hard to decide.

About ten cars back, a bald heavyset man wearing a coat and tie got out of his sedan and climbed on top of the hood. He reclined against his windshield with his hands locked behind his head and his eyes closed.

Not a bad idea.

Initially, Mark had mixed emotions about moving back home to Atlanta. Although he had excelled during his years as the governor's security officer, comparisons with his father were inevitable—after all, no one could fill the shoes of the first four-star general from the state of Georgia.

The tape flipped over and James began singing about Mexico.

Through what medical science termed "instinctive delusions for self-protection," Mark tried to convince himself that he was not in competition with his father's ghost. Once, a government psychiatrist noted in Mark's chart a potential for psychological insecurity stemming from his father's fame. The doctor described Mark's ability to cope with his father's success as a healthy response, explaining to him matter-of-factly that evolution had selected a certain degree of self-delusion as a vital trait for survival in modern society. In other words, lying to oneself was tolerable if done so as an intermission from reality until one's character grew strong enough to accept accurate interpretations of the world.

We've come a long way since clubbing prey in the head for supper, Mark thought.

Another middle-aged man two cars ahead, dressed in an obnoxious Hawaiian-print shirt and white twill shorts, got out of his car and strolled over to a girl sitting in a red Miata in the next lane.

"Hello there, little lady . . ." Mark heard him say.

The young woman brandished exotic Mediterranean features and long dark hair, which she seductively tossed away from her face, curling locks behind her ears with smooth tan fingers.

Mark soon lost interest in the superficial passion and glanced down at his watch. He'd sat in the same spot for twenty-seven minutes. He sighed deeply, letting the air out in a slow stream. How unusual not to be in a hurry.

The tape began again at the beginning.

Mark scratched a dry scaly patch near his right sideburn. In the security profession, those who earned promotions packed a heavy dose of stress along with their 9mm automatic weapons. With the odd hours, irregular meals, and gallons of coffee, nervous disorders grew to become as much a part of the security team as fiber-optic cameras in fountain pens and radio transmitters in lapel pins. The pressure had left Mark with an advanced case of psoriasis, the secret service's red badge of courage. Cortisone ointments helped, but retirement was the only cure.

Mark was not movie star good-looking; he was appealing only to those women with the patience to see inside. Trouble was, his job rarely allowed a relationship to mature to the point where his outer layers of suspicion, caution, and intensity could be torn away.

He stood six feet tall, one hundred ninety pounds, with medium brown hair about the shade of suede pigskin; his hazel eyes, flecked with gold and green, were set a little too close together, exaggerating his concentrated demeanor. A uniform of traditional gray or blue suit, white shirt, and maroon tie camouflaged his cut physique, sculpted by daily trips to the gym—faithful lifting was as good for his mind as it was for his flesh and the sole reason psoriasis had not invaded more body surfaces.

Mark rapped his fingers over the steering wheel in excitement. He had paid his dues with grueling duty in the secret service after graduating from the FBI academy. At just thirty-four, he had already been head of security for the governor of Georgia, director of the White House security assigned to the vice president of the United States, and now was on his way to becoming second in charge of Olympic security.

A twinge of grief interrupted his episode of self-congratulation.

Whenever Mark was proudest of his accomplishments, deep regret and loneliness strangled his glory.

If only Dad were here to celebrate, too.

Respect and devotion were inadequate to describe Mark's emotional tie to his father, and yet feelings had been so hard to voice to the general. He never felt worthy of conveying his inner thoughts to a man who stared death in the eye, even after Mark had survived close encounters himself. Mark had never told his father how much he depended on their relationship, how much he yearned for reaching his father's unachievable ideal.

Tears swelled again as he remembered never having said, "Dad, I love you," . . . nor ever having heard, "Son, I'm proud of you."

The chance was gone forever.

Mark immediately choked off the emotion. Good soldiers never cry.

The car ahead advanced six feet. "Sweet Baby James" played a second time through the stereo speakers, and Mark stoically hummed harmony.

When the call came from Atlanta to apply for the deputy chief of security for the 1996 Olympic Games, Mark was not sure he was interested. In his field, joining the White House security team was the pinnacle of achievement.

Sitting in traffic, however, reminded him of the downsides of working in Washington, and he was glad he had taken the job. The money was good, and the danger considerably less. He would be responsible for developing the security strategy for the games and training officers for the field, not putting his life on the line every day in potentially hostile situations.

The public never knew about dismantling bombs during Middle East trips, or disarming seemingly harmless people during public appearances. Times were crazy, and the life insurance benefit for secret servicemen was growing in each new contract. Time had come to move on.

The lady in the car behind Mark slammed her horn. He looked in the rearview mirror and saw a scouring face above a red business suit shooting him the finger.

Tough day, Mark thought, and he put his car in gear and rolled forward a few feet before coming to a stop again.

SISTER MARY FRANCIS SHUFFLED her feet to Billy Joel on the radio while folding laundry on the second floor. She hardly endorsed the lyrics, but the rhythm matched her cheery disposition and she could not help singing along. The kids in the dorms were supposed to do their chores, including their own laundry, before going downstairs to the TV room, but Sister Mary Francis could not say 'No' tonight.

She really did not mind giving them a night off. Anxiety about the next day hovered in the air like static electricity, and everyone avoided touching the topic for fear they would shock each other.

She thought about the church losing the school. That would mean they would lose the dorms too, and the children would either be relocated to another church facility or be turned over to the Department of Family and Children Services.

Sister Mary Francis stopped singing.

Was it true? Do "Only the Good Die Young?"

She smiled to herself. "Gee, what would the bishop say if he heard me singing this?"

She finished the twins' jeans and tee shirts and stacked the folded clothes in two baskets to carry to the dorm rooms. With a thin and rather plain face, Sister Mary Francis looked her thirty-three years. The black cloth framing her temples made her caring blue eyes stand out and contrasted with her straight white teeth. A pale reddish birthmark followed the lower border of her jaw on the right side and disappeared beneath the cloth wrapping her neck.

A preschool nymph with a mess of short blonde curls bounded into the room and climbed up onto the table.

"What's jacking off mean?"

Sister Mary Francis froze with her eyes open wide, then smiled gently, continuing to methodically stack the clothes she had just folded.

"What makes you ask, Caroline?" the Sister replied nonchalantly.

The little girl crossed her arms across her chest in a huff. "Jaime was making fun of me downstairs. He said he saw Carlos in the bathroom jacking off. I asked 'What's that?' and everyone laughed at me. Sister, why did they laugh at me?"

Sister Mary Francis stopped what she was doing and directed her attention toward the child.

"Caroline, as you grow older, God changes your body in special ways . . . wonderful ways. But with those changes come new temptations that we have to learn to control."

The little girl's innocent eyes begged the Sister to continue.

"But, Caroline, it was not right for Jaime and the others to mock you that way. I'm glad you came to me with your question." The gentle nun picked the girl up from the table and set her on her feet.

"Now go on back downstairs and watch television for a few more minutes. It's almost bed time. Have you brushed your teeth?"

Caroline's eyes betrayed the lie she was considering. "Well . . ."

"Better get hopping, then," the nun admonished.

The child quickly pecked the nun's cheek before heading straightaway to an awaiting dry toothbrush.

Watching the little girl bound down the hall, the Sister pondered who Caroline would come to with her questions next time if the school closed. Who would be there for her when the frustrations and self-consciousness of adolescence forayed her childhood?

The nun rubbed her forehead and returned to the laundry.

Before taking her final vows and adopting the saintly name, Sister Mary Francis had been public school teacher Miss Elizabeth Gardner at Mendelson Elementary. Known for her kindness and understanding, she had attacked teaching with gusto the way she did everything else in her life at the time. Her proudest work had been with *at risk* students, those the system considered poor achievers and likely to drop out of school.

In spite of her disadvantaged group, Beth's students scored in the top percentile in the nation, a fact that caused a few elite members of the state Department of Education to visit Beth's class without mentioning why. They didn't seem to want to accept that plain old hard work, plus a dedication to hold afterschool and weekend workshops, or to pick students up in her own car, might be bringing about the high scores.

Yet the school board never knew Beth existed. Instead of focusing on what children were learning in school or on improving methods for assessing their mastery, the elected officials staged hours of debates on topics such as the merits of milk vendors and bids from bus chassis manufacturers.

But for all its waste in human potential, however, bureaucratic negligence never drove Beth from teaching. Personal tragedy did.

She lost the prince of her dreams in an accident in southern California after a late party following a business interview. Her fiancé lost control of his car and spun wildly through a congested intersection, smashing the ton of steel into an Aerostar van carrying a pregnant mother and two children.

The passengers of both cars died.

Beth had always been religious, and she sought comfort and answers in a monastery, where she grew in her faith and later felt the calling to become Sister Mary Francis.

The former public school teacher lifted the full laundry basket and landed it on a chair by the door. She crossed the worn hardwood floor to the window and reached above her head to close the drapes.

The sight of a young girl below on the steps of the church startled her. The girl looked familiar, but Sister Mary Francis was not certain.

She closed the drapes and hurried down the stairs. She pushed open the front doors and kneeled by the young girl.

"Oh sweet Mother of Jesus!" Sister Mary Francis gasped. "My angel, what has happened? Are you hurt? Maria, are you all right?"

Maria's sobs were quiet from exhaustion, and she could barely hold up her head. Sister Mary Francis pulled Maria close to her and hugged her for several minutes, caressing her long dark hair and slowly rocking her back and forth.

Blood saturated the young girl's clothes, and Sister Mary Francis' first horror envisaged Maria attacked and badly hurt, but instinctively, she realized that the pain was much deeper.

Sister Mary Francis held Maria at arm's length for a better view. The girl reeked of vomit and urine, and blood stained every part of her body. Without another word, Sister Mary Francis picked up the girl and carried her into the church.

After giving her a bath and finding her clean clothes for the night, Sister Mary Francis brought Maria hot soup and half a turkey sandwich. The distraught child ate a little and drank some Coke, but was really too tired to say much. Sister Mary Francis was able to piece together most of what had happened from the few sentences Maria offered.

Sister Mary Francis kissed the child on the forehead and tucked the blankets tightly around her shoulders before turning off the light in her small study. She took another look at the fragile body already asleep on the old, matted down pillow, and whispered a prayer before closing the door behind her.

"HELLO, YES, this is Sister Mary Francis at St. Pius Cathedral in Westside, and I need to report a shooting in our neighborhood."

"Yes ma'am. The address?"

"1455 Magnolia Avenue."

"Time of the shooting?"

"About 5:30 p.m."

"Were you present at the incident?"

"No, but I'm reporting what was told to me by someone who found the bodies. Maria Cortez."

"Could you hold a moment, Sister. I think we already have a report on this." A few seconds later the female voice returned.

"Sister, I do have a listing of this incident. Would you like to speak to the officer who was on the scene?"

"Yes, please." Sister Mary Francis looked at the clock above the archbishop's picture. 10:35. Before, the thought of policemen working at the precinct office late at night rarely crossed her mind, and suddenly she felt a uncommon surge of gratitude.

"Mrs. Francis?" It was another female voice.

"Hello, officer, this is Sister Mary Francis at St. Pius Cathedral."

"Oh, excuse me, Sister, I didn't realize you were a nun."

"That's quite all right, there's no way you could have known. I wonder if you could tell me about the shooting this afternoon. From what I understand, the entire family was killed. You see, the young daughter who lived there is a student here at our school and arrived in a state of shock this evening on the steps of the church."

"Is she there now, Sister?" asked the female officer.

"Yes. She's asleep in my study room."

"Is she injured?"

Touched by the gentleness of the officer's voice, Sister Mary Francis sensed genuine concern about Maria's condition.

"No, officer, not physically. Her body seems to be healthy enough. When I found her she was completely covered in blood, but I checked her closely after her bath and she appeared to be fine. She told me she was not hurt."

"Good. If you need any medical assistance, Sister, there is a county physician on call who will come to the church to examine the child."

"That's good to know, and I believe she should see a doctor tomorrow just to be safe. What can you tell me of this tragedy? It seems so senseless."

"Well, it's still pretty sketchy, Sister. We received a call from a neighbor, a Mrs. Elise Spokane, at 5:41 p.m. today, reporting she heard repeated gunfire in the Cortez house. She did not see the attackers nor could she offer a description of their vehicle. My unit arrived at 5:58 p.m. and found four dead bodies. One Juan Cortez, his wife, Miram Cortez, a male youth believed to be Paul Cortez, and one Jack Barton, all dead from multiple gunshot wounds.

"Sister, it was a real mess. There was no apparent motive for the attack. No apparent theft. My investigation thus far has shown Mr. Cortez to be a well-liked and respected neighbor, a good worker for a construction company, with no known enemies. The other man in the house, Jack Barton, was Mr. Cortez's boss at the construction company, and I'm still running background on him. The Cortez boy,

Paul, had been in trouble several times previously on misdemeanors and on a drug possession charge. My street sources have informed me that Paul was a member of the Black Demons, a street gang in this part of the city that has been connected with drug trafficking and possible gang violence. At this point, my best guess is that the Black Demons pushed another gang too far and the result was a tragedy for the Cortez family. I hope to know more tomorrow."

"I see," said Sister Mary Francis. "Why would they kill everyone in the house? Is that common?"

"Sister, nothing is predictable with gang violence," replied the officer. "I've seen worse, and none of them made much sense. I don't want to upset you further, but the truth is we rarely find the motive behind this kind of incident. Mind you, I'll keep trying."

"Oh, I'm quite confident of that, Officer. . ."

"Richardson. Alice Richardson."

"Well you've been most helpful, and I'll pray for your safety as you try to find the villains that have robbed this poor girl of her family," said Sister Mary Francis.

"Speaking of the girl, Sister, I'll have to notify DFACS of her location and status. I hope you understand," said Officer Simpson.

"I understand completely. I've had many dealings with the department before, and I'm sure we'll find the best place for Maria. Thank you again, officer, for your time and compassion. May God bless you." Sister Mary Francis hung up the phone.

THREE

Mark, damn good to meet you," Hank Powell said, extending his gargantuan black hand. "Knew your dad in the service. One of the finest men I've ever met. Said what he meant and meant what he said."

He patted Mark's shoulder firmly as he spoke. "I always knew I could count on the general. I couldn't wait to meet his boy. So how the hell are ya? How does it feel to be back home? Bet you're glad to be out of D.C., huh?"

"Haven't started missing it yet, Colonel," Mark said. "I saw Marvelyn on the way in. It's good to see her. She was like a second mom to me while we were in Europe. I didn't know she was still working."

"Doesn't she look great?" Hank agreed. His big smile stretched wider. "You know, I used to tell your dad I was going to steal Marvelyn from him, and I finally did. Everyone knew she really ran Europe when you guys were over there." Hank waved his hands in front of him. "Yeah, yeah, I know your dad got all the credit, but Marvelyn really did all the work."

The two men laughed easily.

Mark felt comfortable in Hank's office. With Marvelyn on board, Atlanta was beginning to feel like home again. Mark recalled his dad recounting Hank's exploits, describing him as an unsung American hero, with a list of accomplishments that read like a Tom Clancy novel. Hank commanded the unit that raided Libya in '88, and he had negotiated the release of forty-seven hostages in the past two years, alone. In a *Newsweek* cover story, his superior officer was quoted as saying, "The damn Iranians think the United States is the devil personified, but the bloodthirsty bastards still admire Hank."

The colonel's six-foot-five frame weighed between two-eighty and three-twenty, depending on the time of year, and his baritone voice resonated several decibels louder than most folks felt comfortable hearing. With firm muscles, he was in solid shape and did not look fifty-two, except for a gut that was a little bigger than when he was full-time brass. Retiring six months earlier, after a distinguished career in military intelligence in Europe, Hank had accepted the chief of security post for the 1996 Summer Olympics.

Seated behind his desk with his jacket off and the knot of his tie pulled down inches from his throat, Hank gave Mark the rundown on his plan for the security operation.

"There'll be at least one security official assigned to teams from each country," Hank began. "One or two assistants for larger delegations like Germany, China, Japan, and Russia. The security force will be made up of a combination of the Atlanta Olympic Council (AOC) employees and local police and sheriff officers on loan for the six weeks the athletes will be in this country. You'll act as the liaison with those groups and with airport security to plan added training for Hartsfield's staff and hire additional employees if need be."

Mark's trained mind quickly absorbed the details.

"Your other primary responsibility will be coordinating surveillance and intelligence with the FBI and the National Security Council in Washington. Olympic Games have a history of becoming targets of terrorism and political attacks. We're going to do everything we can to make sure it doesn't happen here."

Hank continued with his plans for the electronic support the security teams would have at their fingertips.

"The hub of the operation will be located on the Georgia Tech campus near the Olympic Village. We're renovating an oversized Winnebago as a mobile unit that will house a smaller but complete duplicate of all the communications network," Hank said, and then chuckled. "I'm trying to find a way to sneak a barbecue pit on board, but so far I'm striking out!"

Mark smiled.

"Anyway, the ship'll have all the relays for fiber-optic lines carrying video and digital signals, receptors of the co-axial cable television lines, twisted-copper telephone lines, and microwave dishes for infrared night surveillance signals. Data will enter computer banks for analysis, with reports spitting out every five minutes on the whereabouts of every athletic team." Hank paused a moment. "You've worked with a similar setup in Washington, didn't you?"

"Yes, sir," Mark replied. "Most of what you're describing is standard for White House security."

Hank nodded. "Pretty amazing stuff. Wish we had some of it when I was in Europe with your dad. Would've come in handy when we lifted the guys out of Syria, but then, you wouldn't of known about that one."

"I guess not," Mark said.

Hank resumed his description of the ID system for protecting the athletes and their coaches. "Identification badges with color photos will be issued for all AOC employees, security guards, athletes, coaches, judges, members of the press, television commentators, members of television crews, VIP's, members of foreign entourages, and volunteers. Microtransmitters impregnated along the bottom of each badge will be equipped to send an unique signal for each category of badge. The badge permits access to secured areas according to the wearer's designated security clearance. Wave receivers located throughout the village allow us to pinpoint the exact location of any badge within seconds through our ID LOK software."

Working with ID LOK again pleased Mark. The package automatically trips an alarm in the security control center if a badge is detected outside of its clearance zone. In high security locations, such as athlete housing, ID LOK would provide a cost-effective low-tolerance system of protection.

As Hank talked, Mark made several notes of improvements he could offer to streamline the organization and increase the sensitivity of the monitoring system. He had worked with the latest security advancements every day for the last five years. But he resisted the temptation to say much. Now was a time to listen.

Mark leaned back in the leather armchair across from Hank's desk and stretched his legs out in front of him.

"Hey, don't get comfortable," boomed the boss. "Let's go eat at Charley's. I'm getting hungry, how about you? Sound good?"

Mark had a blank look on his face.

"No way," Hank said, reading Mark's expression. "That's impossible. You worked for the governor all those years and you've never eaten at Charley's? Boy, where've you been?" Hank put his arm around Mark's shoulder. "Didn't you secret service guys ever take a break? Charley's got the best hash on the planet. Let's go. I'll drive."

"Leave your jacket here, son," Hank added, as they got up to go. "You wouldn't want to look out of place."

ON THE WAY DOWNTOWN, Hank talked almost nonstop, mainly about his kids. His oldest, Jerome, was in his second year at Tech as a Double-E major. Hank said that his boy was damn glad to be through with calculus. "But I don't know why. I never had any trouble with it," he said with a deep chuckle, leaning toward Mark.

His second son, Johnny, was a junior at J.T. Rowell High with the second-highest rushing average in the state for Quad-A. "He makes straight A's. Or no football." Hank punctuated the last two words with a determined nod of his head.

"You know, it feels good to be settled in one place. The kids can be confident dad's not gonna move them again next year. Before, Johnny never had a chance to see how good he was at playing ball. Now he can."

His third child was a girl, Felicia, an eighth grader at Hertwig Middle school. "Into music, just like her mom. Started playing the piano at about seven and hasn't stopped. She substituted at church four times this year after the regular accompanist's husband went into the hospital. Felicia likes to pull out a little Bach and Vilvaldi. Congregation loves it. I think Mrs. Arnold gets her feelings hurt, though, when no one misses her."

Hank turned the Buick into an alley two blocks from the capitol, and parked at an angle alongside a brand new emerald Mercedes, leaving the back of the car still sticking out halfway into the alley. Mark could barely squeeze out of his side of the car, his arm scratching against branches of an old holly bush peeking through breaks in a stonewall.

Hank noticed his new deputy eyeing the way he had parked the car. "Don't sweat it, son," he said with a slap on the back. "Bet ya lunch the Atlanta chief of police is at the next table."

Entering the shack, Mark surmised that the city building inspectors were also well-fed regulars. Most of the smoky light came from naked bulbs hanging overhead from frayed wires. Divided between them were groaning ceiling fans that wobbled, struggling to push the hot, humid air around the room. Open screenless windows welcomed in the outside, but the cooler air seemed to resist, held back by the savory billows pouring from atop the kitchen stove. Flies, on the other hand, eagerly took advantage of the invitation, and several darted from table to table.

The room accommodated about twenty unstable tables, covered with chipped and peeling turquoise Formica, each with four chairs around them. A few of the groups in the dining room had stolen chairs from other tables for an extra friend or two. No two chairs were the same. Some looked pretty new, the kind from a school lunchroom, and some were old wooden highbacks with all sorts of words carved into the seats and armrests.

The crowd, an interesting mix of businessmen and politicians in suits without coats, conversed with ordinary street folk of all sizes, ages, and colors. Steady chatter mingled with the rich smell of simmering tomatoes and ground pepper. The only pictures on the walls were a poster of Sid Bream smothered at home plate underneath a pile of elated Atlanta Braves and photographs of former mayors, congressmen, actors, and actresses who had eaten at Charley's sometime in the last twenty years.

Taking in a long deep breath, Hank exclaimed his delight, drawing out each word slowly as he roared, "Hallelujah! Straight from heaven!"

Mark looked down at a cricket skipping across the chipped brick-red paint on the concrete floor when he heard a male's voice in a southern drawl, "Hey, Colonel! Great to see ya. How are ya getting along over at the center?"

"Just fine and dandy, Senator," answered Hank. "I'm tickled pink. We'll have the world's best security organization up and running within six months. I'll guarantee you that, sir."

"With you at the helm, Colonel, I have no doubts."

"Nothing like Charley's in Washington, is there Senator?"

"Nothing close, Colonel. And I hate I can't stay. But I have to be back by tonight," said the junior U.S. senator from Georgia.

"Hope everything's okay, sir," Hank boomed back.

"Oh you know. Same ole, same ole. Group of bankers in Florida got their hands in some tills they shouldn't. The briefings are tonight for the hearings starting tomorrow. Looks like this scandal went pretty high up in some of the banks. It'll be another drawn-out ordeal with nobody winning, especially the taxpayers."

The senator shook Hank's hand hard, and turned to head out the door. He did not make it far before being stopped by three or four people trying to ask a favor or exert some influence.

Mark thought of the senator's words, "Same ole, same ole."

MARIA SAT UP in bed and stretched. She was uncertain of the exact time, but the sun shone brightly through the cotton pastel curtains, and the pink and blue and yellow cast gave the room a springtime air. She felt good, for a moment at least, before the haunting memory slowly returned.

She opened the door into the next room, and Sister Mary Francis looked up from the book cradled in her lap and smiled, "Hello, angel. You look much better today."

The softness of her voice soothed the young girl, and she returned the smile. "Have you heard anything from the police about what happened to my family?" she asked.

Sister Mary Francis beckoned Maria onto the footstool next to her chair and told her quietly but straightforwardly what she had learned from Officer Richardson. Maria wept as the nun relayed her news, but Sister Mary Francis continued until she had told Maria all she knew.

After completing the report, the Sister held Maria again for a minute and read to her a series of Psalms she had marked earlier that morning.

"I know I'll never understand what happened," Maria said. "But I thank God you were here."

"Maria, there's something else you need to know." Sister Mary Francis kissed Maria on the forehead before continuing. "The archbishop came this morning while you were sleeping and announced the school would be closing. Apparently the church has lost funds during the recession and can't afford to continue the school and the dorms for the children here."

"But . . . what's going to happen?" Maria asked.

"I'm leaving this afternoon to visit another church in North Miami to see if they can accept our children into their facility," the Sister said. "I'll be gone overnight. Everyone is pretty upset by the news, but I've assured them that we'll find a good and loving place for everyone. That includes you, too, Maria. I know you'll receive the very best care at any of our churches. Right now, though, I can't tell you where you'll be. We have a couple of weeks before our school is closed, so it's not something to worry about today."

MILTON, NEW HEAD OF OLYMPIC FORCE, read the front-page headline in *The Atlanta Journal,* ending several months of speculation about whether the eccentric philanthropist would be named the new CEO of the AOC.

Victoria Milton had worked side by side with the former chair to win the bid for the games, and her appointment surprised few within the inner circle of aristocrats. Now, as the chair of AOC, she would be wielded broad power during the ensuing months of preparation, promotion, and sponsorship solicitation.

Milton had proven her mettle. After witnessing the impact of the Seoul Games on the relatively poor host country, she became enamored with the idea of an Atlanta Summer Olympics and declared she would bring the games to her hometown. Nearly everyone guffawed and dismissed her vision as a complete fantasy, yet with the support of Georgia Tech, the powerful utility companies, several banks, Coca-Cola, and the state government, she succeeded.

Athens, as the birth site of the modern games, had been the world's overwhelming sentimental favorite to host the one hundredth anniversary of the Olympics. But when the selection committee made the surprise announcement live from Tokyo, "And the winning city is . . . Atlanta!" the entire metropolis erupted into unprecedented jubilation that rocked a city not known for accomplishments of national prominence, much less international fervor.

Only in the last decade had the rest of the nation come to recognize Atlanta as a player in corporate America. More than once during the '80s, Hartsfield International Airport passed Chicago's O'Hare as the busiest airport in the world, and later in the decade, several corporate giants, including UPS, relocated their headquarters to the South's emerging star.

Even so, national newspapers did not count Atlanta among Los Angeles, New York, or Dallas as a national power. Local civic leaders still flinched recalling the Democratic National Convention at the Omni in 1988, when the media had a field day interviewing illiterate county sheriffs in rural parts of the state, hardly leaving the city limits to uncover the country bumpkin image the South struggled to leave behind.

Several issues contributed to Atlanta's image problem as a city and Georgia's problem as a state. Northern and Western Americans viewed the South as backward, where technical innovations and social development arrived years behind the rest of the country. In terms of national education statistics, Georgia students routinely scored at the bottom of their peers on standardized test scores, where in primary and secondary grades, Georgia battled with South Carolina or Mississippi or some other southern state for the bottom rung of the nation's school ladder.

Georgia's social ills did not end with schools. The state's rate of infant mortality, teen pregnancy, high school dropouts, and inner city crime had all been at the top or near the top of national statistics during the '80s.

Having lived her entire life in the city, Victoria Milton recognized the image problem. Her father had been a railroad tycoon who, during the '40s, was solely responsible for transporting most commercial goods entering and leaving the state. He sent his daughter to Vanderbilt University for a liberal arts education only to watch her marry her worthless childhood sweetheart, who as an adult became a drunkard and rarely paid her a moment's notice. Eventually, Victoria returned his disinterest with neglect and managed her inheritance into a billion dollar fortune.

Victoria was a petite woman, just under five feet tall and weighing less than a hundred pounds. Her dyed red hair made her pale, chiseled face look even whiter, and her angled cheekbones and pointed chin accentuated the coolness of her thin smile.

But, her stature did not hamper action.

She was famous in corporate boards of directors meetings for ramrodding her own agenda. The United Way knew Victoria well not only for her significant annual contributions, but also for her persistence in molding the organization's policies to benefit needy children. And her motives for the Olympics were pure. The games were to save the disadvantaged children of the state.

A week after being named CEO, Victoria's picture appeared again on the front page of the paper standing next to the newly appointed finance director for the AOC, M. Caldwell Lockhart, a former president and CEO of Midland National Bank of Chicago.

In the article about his selection, Victoria expressed her appreciation to Lockhart for his willingness to come out of retirement to lead the billion dollar AOC operation. The accompanying photograph showed Lockhart to be in his early sixties, with gray hair worn in a crew cut, and a gentle smile more suited for a caring grandfather than a successful corporate financial officer, but both were true.

Just behind and to the left of Lockhart was a younger man in his late thirties with jet-black hair, dark skin, and dark eyes. He was also smiling. The article identified him as Andrew Janis, also of Midland National Bank, who Lockhart had appointed as his assistant.

The caption quoted Lockhart as saying, "I am proud to accept such an honorable position, and I dedicate myself to

work with other members of Victoria's team to make the
'96 Games the greatest in Olympic history."

Janis appeared to nod his head in agreement.

MARIA FINISHED READING her literature assignment, three
more chapters in *Moby Dick,* and prepared for bed. She was
becoming accustomed to the copious reading the nuns demanded. Maria's parents had placed her and her brother
in the Catholic school when Maria experienced trouble reading in the second grade.

The lack of phonics instruction at her daughter's public school concerned Mrs. Cortez, and after visiting several
private schools in the city, Maria's mother finally singled
out St. Pius because of the extensive reading list included in
the school's curriculum brochure.

The school was forthright about their expectations. The
student continuing at St. Pius from kindergarten to eighth-
grade graduation was required by signed annual contract to
have read and critiqued everything from *Adventures of
Pinocchio, The Secret Garden,* and *The Call of the Wild,* to *Diary
of a Young Girl, The Pearl,* and *The Story of My Life,* by Helen
Keller. The list included writings from different cultures
and touched on many issues facing society.

Maria's mother was impressed. She saw a close correla-
tion between St. Pius' high school students' extraordinary
verbal SAT scores and the extensive reading the school required.

Maria brushed her teeth and slipped on the extra-large
Miami Dolphins tee shirt she wore for a nightgown, then
she climbed into bed and read the Bible passages Sister Beth
had marked. Maria found a note in the Bible next to her bed:

> *You are in my prayers tonight, angel.*
> *Read the verses I've marked, say your prayers,*
> *and go to bed early. I'll see you*
> *tomorrow afternoon. May God bless you.*
> *All my love, Sister Mary Francis*

She reached over and turned out the light. She was nearly asleep when she heard a quiet knock on the door.

"Maria? Maria, are you asleep?"

"No Father, please come in." She sat up quickly in bed and smiled at Father Morton, giving the genial, elderly priest a hug as he sat down beside her.

"Thanks for coming to see me, Father. I know you've been so busy with the school closing and all."

"Oh, no. Please forgive *me* for not coming sooner, my child," the priest said, gently taking the young girl's hand. "How are you doing? Feeling better now?"

"Father, Sister Mary Francis has been wonderful," Maria replied. "I feel much better now that I'm here with you and the Sisters. Sometimes I almost forget what happened. But then the pain returns deeper than before. I wonder if it will ever go away."

As she spoke, tears dropped from her innocent eyes.

The priest reached out and wiped Maria's soft cheek with his fingers. "I know, my child. It is hard for us to understand the mystery of life and death. But, you must find the strength inside to go on with your life. I've seen this type of tragedy many times during my years in the church, and I know time is a great healer."

"Thank you, Father," Maria said quietly.

The old man smiled at the girl, his eyes amazingly alert for the late hour. "I didn't mean to disturb your sleep, Maria. Here, lie back and close your eyes, and we'll talk while you rest."

Maria laid back and pulled the warm covers up around her shoulders. As Father Morton continued to talk in a quiet soothing tone, Maria felt more and more relaxed. The pain of the last twenty-four hours slipped to the back of her consciousness, and she felt calm for the first time since the incident in her house. She slowly drifted into a peaceful, dreamy sleep and clouds of good memories began filling her mind.

She could see herself and her mother gliding about like in a silent movie. Their mouths moved, but they made no sound. In one scene, Maria was only eight years old and her mother showed her how to cut pieces of a dress pattern out of a paisley print material laid out on the kitchen table. They pinned the onion skin paper pattern to the material in a strategic way to give the best use of all the material. Maria's mother grimaced as she stuck a pin in her right index finger, and they both laughed. Maria's mother showed her how to align the pattern of the material so the sleeves would match the bodice. They carried the cut pieces to the sewing machine where her mother began a seam and let Maria finish it. Then to the next seam. Then to the collar. They finished with the buttons and the hem. Maria was thrilled. The dress was beautiful, and when she tried it on, her mother gave her a long hug. Her mother smiled as Maria turned 'round and 'round in front of the mirror admiring herself. Maria said she'd wear the dress to the church social next Sunday night. Her mother poked fun and said all the boys would be looking at her. Maria blushed and ran into her mother's arms again. Her mother brushed back the hair from Maria's face and kissed her forehead, telling her daughter how proud she was of her, how God had blessed her with such an angel. Oh, it felt so good. She longed for another hug from her mother. The touch of her hand. The caress of her fingers. Maria could almost feel her mother now . . .

She awoke with a start.

She was cold.

The covers were no longer around her shoulders, and her tee shirt had been lifted up above her chest. Maria gasped again and again, but could not catch her breath as she stared horrified at Father Morton.

Without a word, the man slowly stood up from the bed and went out the door, closing it forever behind him.

FOUR

Esther Clements poured liquid Egg Beaters from a bright yellow cardboard carton into the hot skillet on her stove and hummed along with the morning show on FM 90.1. A misfit of her generation, she liked public radio. The sounds of classical music, intermingled with NPR news, gently nudged her faculties awake without relying on a caffeine jump-start every morning.

Esther stirred the egg substitute with a wooden spoon. Her mother-in-law warned her on her wedding day, "You'd better like getting up early and fixin' eggs if ya gonna marry my boy. He always has a healthy appetite when he wakes up, and if he ain't got a full stomach by seven, there's hell to pay."

Esther had been happily married for nine years.

"Something smells good," Darryl said, sneaking up and wrapping his arms around Esther's growing waistline. "I'm hungry, woman, and not just for those fake eggs you keep feeding me."

"Now, Darryl," Esther began patiently, "You know the doctor says you'll be dead before you reach forty if you keep eating like you used to."

"I believe I'd rather *be* dead than keep eating them damn fake scrambled eggs every morning," Darryl moaned. Licking his wife's earlobe and blowing on her neck, he whispered, "Let's go back to the bedroom for a few minutes and leave the food warmin' here on the stove."

Esther smiled and put her hands over his. "Honey, after the spotting I had last week, Doc said no sex for two weeks. Just to be safe."

"That's okay, baby. We can figure out somthin'. Just have to use a little imagination. Remember when we were first dating back in high school?"

Esther slapped her husband's hands. "Boy! I should take some Clorox to your brain!" She turned around and placing her hands on his shoulders, guided him to the kitchen table, and sat him down at one of the four chrome tubular chairs.

"You didn't mind it so much back then," Darryl said.

"Quit your dirty talk and sit down and eat your food. It's time for you to go to work and all you want to do is mess around. I told my momma just yesterday that having a child won't be no problem at all 'cause I've been takin' care of a little boy for coming up on ten years now."

"Good grief, woman, I might as well die of cholesterol," Darryl groaned as he landed his elbows on the table and rubbed his eyes.

He reached over and pulled his wife up close to him, then onto his lap. "You know, I'm sure lucky to have you," he said in a gentler tone.

"You're damn right, you are. And you better not forget it when you're downtown rubbing shoulders with all those important businessmen . . . and their pretty secretaries."

"And I'll have you know I have another big meeting today, too," Darryl said proudly. "Some big rep from AOC is coming to my office this afternoon. Says they have a very interesting opportunity for my company. Says we might get to write some policies for the construction companies building Olympic sites."

"Sounds pretty important. Can you handle it?"

"Honey, insurance is insurance. It don't matter if the company works for the Olympics or not. Point is, AOC wants to work with local companies and they want it to look like they're spreading the contracts around with black businesses. That's why I applied to AOC last spring."

"Well, all the more reason to eat right," Esther said getting up from her husband's lap. "Besides, I can't raise this child by myself. He needs his daddy around to pitch to and to teach him about girls."

Darryl shook his head. "You mean, *she* needs somebody to take *her* to concerts and keep *her* away from boys."

"I'm telling you now, mister, this child is a son and he's going to be beautiful and brilliant and athletic and successful. And he is going to *love his momma!*"

During the three sonograms, the technician said she could tell them the sex of the baby, and Darryl wanted to know, but Esther's emotional arguments convinced her husband to wait until delivery day before learning if the nursery would become filled with pink-or-blue pillows, blankets, and pacifiers.

There was no doubt in Darryl's mind. He wanted a girl. He wasn't sure why, perhaps it had to do with the often tough time he'd had being his father's only son. Darryl's father had grown up in the Great Depression, when a single Idaho potato constituted breakfast, lunch, and dinner. Poverty's deep scar and the fight to become self-sufficient had made Darryl's father a principled man. He was famous for telling his children, "Never buy nothing you can't pay for with the money in your pocket."

If he had not abided strictly by all of his father's edicts, Darryl had stuck to most. Years ago as a newly established black businessman, conventional marketing techniques had proven ineffective against the invisible, yet formidable wall of prejudice, so Darryl built his own insurance market by doing something unheard of in the insurance industry, foregoing up-front profit in return for a long-term relationship with clients. After a few businesses purchased their liability, contents, and worker's comp coverage from him, Darryl did not quit. He watched their needs and rewrote their policies if the changes reduced premiums without effecting coverage, even if it meant a reduction in commission. He gambled that watching out for his clients would bring more business in the future.

And he was right.

Darryl's company became the second largest minority-owned insurance company in the southeast, and he was damn proud of it.

"MR. CLEMENTS, Mr. Simpson from AOC is here." The sweet, refined voice of Darryl's niece came over the intercom. He loved how the Bell South secretary training classes had given her confidence and enthusiasm.

"Thank you, Sylvia. Please send him in," Darryl said, slipping on his coat and straightening his tie. The emerald carpet and glossy-white baseboards reflected clearly in his black dress shoes.

"Mr. Simpson, it's an honor to meet you, sir." Darryl extended his hand as he stepped forward to greet his visitor.

"Pleasure is all mine, Mr. Clements," said Simpson, a bulging man in his late forties, with red bushy hair and white freckled skin. He entered the room like a hurricane. "What a great office!" he exclaimed. "I just get the biggest kick out of seeing family pictures. Is this all yours? Man, you must have a big family! Who are all those folks, anyway? Oh, look at that little tike! What a great picture! Did you take that? Oh look there, with the little league team. That's you isn't it? Did you coach? How'd the team do? I never miss a Braves game, how 'bout you? Boy do I remember the days of my little league team back in Warner Robbins. We were the brattiest bunch of kids in the league!"

Darryl wondered if this guy would ever shut up, fearing this appointment was just a token call on a black business-man. Darryl could never escape the thought he might be patronized because of his color. He despised affirmative action.

Darryl waited for the man to pause. "Yep, that's me with the kids," he interjected. "I coach for the Boys Club near my house. About our record, well, let's just say the kids had a real good time."

"And isn't that what it's all about," said Simpson. "Some folks just get too intense over a game that's just supposed to be plain old fun. I say if the kids aren't enjoying themselves, then the league isn't serving its function. I bet there's a whole host of youngsters who wish they'd never started play-ing baseball. Why, I bet bunches of young boys just cry their little eyes out over missing a fly ball or striking out in the bottom of the ninth. What d'ya think?"

Finally. Another breath.

"I think you had some information for me about insur-ing contractors?" Darryl asked, trying to gently change the subject.

"And aren't you right about that, too, my friend. Here I am going on and on about baseball, and we're supposed to be building the foundation for a couple of other games. Why, sometimes I almost forget what my job is."

With that, Simpson eased over to Darryl's conference table and spread out the contents of two huge black three-ring notebooks—several thirty-page documents detailing the specifications for the insurance needs for the construction about to commence for the Olympic venues.

In less than twenty minutes, and with even fewer pauses for air, Simpson delivered a nonstop monologue of remark-able breadth and insight to marvel anyone knowledgeable of the insurance industry.

When he finished, Simpson leaned back in his chair. "Our review board has studied all the applications and pre-liminary bids for insurance carriers and have chosen your company to oversee the policies covering this portion of the Olympic effort. The assistant director of finance, who chaired our review board, was particularly insistent on your firm's selection. While venue construction constitutes only one part of the overall insurance needs for AOC, we feel the construction portion represents one of the most critical aspects of the entire project. Your selection was unanimous from the board and was determined after thorough deliberation. Congratulations."

Darryl was speechless.

In his wildest dreams he never considered for a moment that he would be awarded all the policies for construction. He hoped for maybe one of the concession vendor's workers' comp, or maybe site liability for one event. But, coverage for all the construction?

Visions of contracts swirled in his head. What would this mean? Both vice presidents would need more help, and he would need to move up delivery on the fourteen new IBM-clone terminals. Hell, maybe he ought to go with IBM, their maintenance contract was better, and now he could not afford to have a station go down.

"Well, Mr. Clements? Do you accept?" asked Simpson.

"It will be my privilege, sir."

IN THE BUILDING COMMONLY KNOWN AS THE IBM TOWER, Mark finished an article in the paper about the new executive council appointments Victoria Milton made for AOC. Standard procedure for the security department dictated a file on each director on the executive council including background information and listings of present and former business and political ties.

The profiles on executive council members reported in the paper intrigued Mark, knowing in the back of his mind he would discover a wealth of facts no newspaper reporter could ever uncover. Mark's job was summarizing FBI and secret service analyses for each director for the purpose of protecting council members. Over the last five years, he had spent so much time reading the personal reports on VIP's that sleuthing networks of business people and their relationships had become a game. Everybody important knows the same people, sooner or later, and Mark enjoyed piecing together the puzzles of influence that ran the nation and the world.

The first name on the list: Caldwell Lockhart.

Mark's computer search of the FBI data banks showed information primarily from the social security office. References led him to the national directory of corporate boards, the alumni lists of Yale and Harvard, the membership lists from the American Bar Association and the American Bankers Association, all accessible through the secret service data banks.

Born: April 18, 1932, Asheville, North Carolina.
Parents: Harold and Elizabeth Lockhart, father was president of First Bank of Charlotte 1927-49. Father died February 5, 1978.

Caldwell attended Brighton School for boys until age 16; business degree from Yale, 1952; law degree from Harvard, 1955. Married Susan Myrl Fletcher from Boston, 1956; had two children, C. Lilburn, an attorney in Cary, N.C., and Brenda Lockhart Burber, an interior designer in Columbia, Ohio. Three grandchildren from his son.

Professional history: associate of Graber, Henderson & Fitch, Attorneys at Law, Boston, 1955-1961; vice president of operations, Metropolitan Life Insurance Co., Chicago, 1962-1970; vice president, Midland National Bank, Chicago, 1970-1978; president, Midland National Bank, Chicago, 1978-1991. Member of the Rotary Club of Greater Chicago, past national campaign chairman United Way, board of directors Campbell Soup Co., board of directors

Washington Post, board of directors Georgia Union Railroad, board of directors National Democratic Party.

Personal notes: drinks Chevas and water on rare social occasions, plays tennis three times a week, attends First United Presbyterian Church, likes deep-sea fishing, attends the U.S. Open tennis tournament every Labor Day weekend.

Mark read the printout. Sounds like he should run for president, Mark thought. But then, his first cursory inspection rarely identified glaring flaws in a person's past or showed points of vulnerability cunning extortionists might exploit.

Mark typed a few more commands and explored cross-referenced files among the attorneys suspected of mob ties, law firms associated with illegal activity, law firms representing clients suspected of illegal activity, banks suspected of mob ties, etc.

Nothing.

Mark entered the password for the IRS data banks. As expected, Lockhart's tax return was a hundred pages long, including the multitude of attachments, forms, amendments, extensions, and the like. He had real estate holdings in several states and two foreign countries. He traded on the stock exchanges in New York, London, and Japan, and owned mineral rights in South Africa and Belgium. Nothing out of the ordinary in Mark's view. After all, the guy did pay nearly three quarters of a million dollars in taxes in 1992 alone.

The next step, phone calls. Mark picked up the phone and dialed the number for the secret service office in Washington, D.C.

MARIA HUDDLED AGAINST A DUMPSTER in the alley behind the Publix in Orange Square, protected against the cold damp night air by a thin gray sweater she had grabbed on the way out of Sister Mary Francis' makeshift bedroom.

Pressing her back against the concrete block wall, she wedged herself between empty boxes that a few hours earlier had stored rolls of Scott toilet tissue. A cold breeze blew and a bright crescent moon shone against a black velvet sky.

She longed for a warm safe bed in her own bedroom.

In her own house.

With her own mother.

She cried, again.

The horrible reality of the last twenty-four hours hit hard. She desperately needed Sister Mary Francis, but could not go back to the church, not after what had just happened in the secrecy of the back bedroom.

Maria shivered from the cold creeping through the box shelter.

The scenes kept finding their way back into her thoughts, her house early yesterday evening . . . how her brother looked, and her poor father in the living room against the couch . . . how her blessed mother lay in an inhuman position on the bloodstained floor of a kitchen that had always been as scrubbed as an operating room.

How could this happen?

She had begun feeling better at the church with Sister Mary Francis. If only she could see Sister Mary Francis now. But she felt so dirty after Father Morton left, she had to get away as quickly as possible. The look on his face haunted her, along with an improbable mixture of guilt and agitation. She would never forget that look, right before he turned to leave the room. It was a look of judgment. *Almost like she had done something wrong!*

She squeezed her knees closer to her chest. Her head rested against her knees, and her hair fell all around the sides of her legs forming a fortress against the outside world. The muscles in her legs and back started to twitch, and dizziness swirled in her head, slowed a bit by closing her eyes.

Four roaches ran over and between her toes on their way to a smorgasbord awaiting them in the dumpster.

The sound of someone walking toward her heightened fear again.

The steps came closer.

She tried to not make a sound.

She held her breath, with thoughts that Father Morton had somehow tracked her down and was coming to scold her.

Someone pulled the boxes away.

Maria's heart stopped.

Her eyes opened wider.

"Well, well, well. What do we have here?" The dirty, wrinkled face of a toothless old man grinned down on the trembling child.

Maria froze, preparing herself to run or fight.

He pushed the boxes away and reached down to grab Maria's shoulders. She flinched as his gray weathered hands touched her with clammy lust.

The stench of cheap wine mixed with stolen cough syrup stained his horrid breath, and a ratty beard and putrid clothes testified to his life of homeless decay. Maria tried to get away, but the man deftly pinned her against the concrete blocks of the supermarket.

"Leave me alone!" she screamed. "What do you want?"

"I'm just being friendly, little miss, that's all. Now, just calm down there, calm down." He pressed hard against her shoulders. "Now, what's your name?"

"It's none of your business!"

"Not much respect for your elders, little girl," he said. "What are you doing out here in the dark all by yourself?"

"I want to be left alone."

"A pretty thing like you shouldn't be all by herself. Why, someone bad might come along," he grinned. "Why don't I just sit down here by you and keep you warm."

The old lecher put his arm around Maria's shoulders and forced her up next to him. Once seated, he did not let go. Maria struggled against his surprisingly strong hold.

"Let go of me!" Maria screamed into his ear. "Just leave me alone!"

"Now, little girl, I'm just trying to help you survive out here by yourself. When you're on your own, you learn how to get along in order to stay alive."

"I was just fine before you came along." She struggled harder, pushing the old man away, but his grip was incredibly tight. She kicked her legs and yelled louder, hoping she could scare him away. He pressed his scraggly face next to hers and let out a high-pitched laugh that made Maria shudder.

With suprising quickness, the old man rolled Maria over on her back, causing her to scream as loud as her tired lungs could muster. She thrust her head side-to-side and scratched at the old man's arms. She hit him hard on the side of his face with her closed fist. He blurted his gross laugh again and scooted farther up her body, pinning her arms to the cardboard with his knees.

Now, rage replaced fear.

No tears came from her eyes, only a fierce look of determination. She brought one foot up behind the wino's head and kicked him hard in the ear. He yelled out, but the blow barely slowed his assault. He tore at the collar of Maria's tee shirt. The girl twisted her body violently, trying to throw the man off, but his weight was too great to overcome. He bent his foul face next to hers and licked across her mouth.

Maria bit his nose, but he kept coming. She kicked with her knees against the man's back as his scaly hands pawed under her ripped tee shirt.

Suddenly, the old man slumped motionless on top of the girl, pressing the full weight of his body against the thin child. Maria screamed louder than ever. Struggling furiously, she realized the man was not moving and pushed with all her strength to move him off of her.

A hand grabbed the shoulder of the man's filthy shirt and tugged him to the side.

"Come on, Honey. Let's get the hell outta here!" A woman stretched her hand toward Maria.

"Just leave that son of a bitch there. Maybe he'll rot before morning. You come with me, Sweetcakes."

Maria had trouble standing to her feet, the fight taking more out of her than she realized.

"There, there", the woman said. "Take your time. That old codger won't be bothering you anymore tonight. Here, take my hand. What are you doing out here all alone?"

Exhausted and confused, Maria did not answer.

"Well, you just come home with Mona. We're going to clean you up and get you something warm inside."

FIVE

Maria reached over and lifted the pink-and-white striped shade, squinting hard to protect her eyes against the blast of warm sunlight. People walked past on the sidewalk outside, along a busy street that seemed somewhat familiar.

She pulled back the patchwork quilt and tried to remember where she was. Images of the night before blurred in her mind. She remembered the putrid smell and the high-pitched laugh of the disgusting old man and her struggle to get away from him. The thought of his hands on her body made the hair on the back of her neck stand on end.

She stretched her arms above her head and yawned, surprised to find her muscles sore from the fight. Trying to balance herself on unstable legs, the room began to spin and she stumbled against the nightstand, knocking over the alarm clock and several framed photographs. She crashed to the floor and was sitting looking dazed, her legs spread wide apart, when Mona rushed through the door.

"So Sleeping Beauty finally wakes up," she said, hands on hips. "I figured you hadn't slept much lately, but you sure made up for some of the lost time."

"What time is it?" asked Maria. She vaguely remembered the woman.

"Little after two or thereabouts. You all right? Looks like you took a tumble." Mona put her arm around the girl's shoulders and helped her to the bed and then sat down beside her.

"Where am I?" Maria asked.

"My place. I'm Mona." She reached over and shook Maria's hand. "We never really got introduced. I found you last night behind the Publix trying to get away from some horny old fart. I coldcocked him with a piece of concrete on the back of his puny skull. Hope the rats got a few bites before he came to."

"Yeah, I remember . . . kinda. I'm sure glad you came along. That guy was strong."

"Ah, Sweetcakes, you could've handled him. You looked like you were holding your own pretty well. I just helped a little." Mona had fought off more than one bum herself, beginning when she was even younger than Maria. "What were you doing out there alone at night? It's pretty easy to see you're not used to being on the streets."

"Maybe not before," Maria said.

"Want to talk about it? Did you have trouble at home? Fight with the folks?"

"I don't feel so well, Mona," Maria said, not ready yet to go into the details with a complete stranger, even though she felt a true warmth coming from Mona.

"That's okay, Honey. You just rest here and I'll get you something to eat. Once you get some food inside you'll feel like a million bucks. Now go ahead, put those toes under the covers."

Maria happily complied, causing Mona to give her a wink before heading to the kitchen. Maria was glad to be in a warm bed and away from the old man, away from Father

Morton, away from the horrible scene at her home. As she rested between cozy flannel sheets, Maria gazed at the collage of posters and pictures on the wall. Most were rock groups foreign to the teenager: The Doobie Brothers, CCR, Cream.

Then she remembered the photographs she'd knocked over. She quickly got out of bed to replace them before Mona returned. Putting them back on the nightstand, she saw that a few of the photographs were snapshots of Mona horsing around with a couple of cute young guys, but several showed Mona with some older man with silver hair and a tanned face.

One picture was taken on a Hawaiian beach, the man's arm wrapped proudly around Mona's voluptuous figure, prodigiously displayed in a bright green-and-pink string bikini. Another photo showed the couple on a snow-covered Italian mountain wearing matching ski attire. Another found Mona and the older man in bathing suits again, this time on the deck of a cruise ship, hoisting tropical-looking umbrella drinks, with a turquoise ocean in the background. Finally, there was one of the silver-haired man alone, dressed in safari garb with one foot propped on the head of a dead rhinoceros. On one corner he had written: "This one's for you, Hot Stuff. Love, Flemming." Maria thought the dead animal with bulging eyes and bloodied mouth looked repulsive.

After replacing the photos, she wandered over to the shelves. They held hundreds of paperback romance novels, multicolored souvenir ashtrays, stacks of lavender-and-yellow stationery, and a small crucifix on a stand with a rosary hanging around its base. The crucifix was a welcome sight, even though Maria had fled the sanctuary of the church.

"So, ya feeling any better, Sweetcakes?" Mona carried waffles and orange juice on a breakfast tray like Maria had seen Ricky Ricardo bring Lucy on an old rerun. There was a paper flower by the fork.

"Yeah, I think so, a little," Maria said, returning to the bed.

"Made the flower myself," Mona said proudly. "I know it ain't much, just something my mom taught me when I was a kid. Go ahead, eat."

Maria took a bite and, not realizing the depth of her hunger, devoured the meal like one of the new kids at church after first coming to live at the dorms.

"Hey there, Sweetcakes, slow down. Take your time, no one's going to bother you here."

Maria stopped to take a long sip of orange juice.

Just as she started attacking the waffles again, there was a loud knock on the front door. "You finish that up, Honey," Mona said, jumping up as if shocked by a live wire. "I'll be right back."

Maria took another bite. She hated to ask, but wondered if there were any more waffles. She could hear Mona talking with a man in the other room. They sounded as if they knew one another, but weren't all that happy about it. Maria moved to the doorway to see if she could hear what they were saying. The man told Mona times and addresses for meetings over the next four or five days.

Maria went over to the bookshelves and pulled out one of the romance novels. None of the titles were familiar, so she reached for the one with the brightest cover. She propped a life-sized, stuffed pink pig up against the end of the bed as a backrest and started reading.

Halfway through the first chapter, Mona rushed into the room and quickly sat on the bed. "Follow my lead, Honey," she whispered. "You're my sister's kid from Jacksonville. Got it?"

Maria looked bewildered. "What?"

"Please, Sweetcakes. Just do what I say."

"But —"

"Mona, introduce me to your guest," a dark-complected man said with a deep Spanish accent. He leaned against the doorjamb with his arms folded across his chest. His smile revealed a gold front tooth, and his black eyes were suspicious, an aura compounded by black hair slicked back into a long greasy ponytail. A scar extended from his left nostril across his cheek, ending in a shortened left ear with barely enough lobe remaining to anchor three small gold loops.

"Oh, sure Miguel. This is Maria. She's my sister's kid," Mona said.

"I didn't know your sister had kids."

"Yeah," Mona said. "We haven't seen each other since Christmas two years ago. And now, she's so grown up!"

"So I see," Miguel said with a grin. "So I see."

"Yeah, we're just going to bum around for a week before she has to get back to school. I'm gonna take her down to the beach tomorrow. We've been looking forward to this for a long time, haven't we Maria?"

"Yes, we have," said Maria quietly.

"You don't look so good, Maria," Miguel said. "You been sick?"

"She's just getting over the, uh, flu," Mona interjected. "That's why her mother sent her down here . . . to relax. And she can't do that too good with us in here yacking like a bunch of women at a laundromat. Come on, we gotta scoot and let Maria chill."

"Yeah. Sure, Mona dear. Whatever you say." Miguel stepped back toward the door to the hallway. He turned to Maria again. "Nice to meet you, Maria. I'll check in on you later to be sure you're feeling better. Mona and me, we go back a long way. I wouldn't want her favorite niece to have a bad visit in my town."

He smoothed the top of his hair with the palm of his right hand, a red gemstone reflecting the sunbeams coming through the window. "You know, the more I think about it, I *personally* need to make sure you have a good time here in my neighborhood. I think I'd better come by tomorrow and go to the beach with you, just to be sure you are taken care of. I will be your *personal* tour guide. Yeah, that's it. How does that sound, Maria?"

"Oh that's okay, Miguel . . . We—" Mona argued.

"How does that sound to *you*, Maria?" Miguel repeated.

"Fine . . . I suppose," Maria said, looking for a hint in Mona's eyes.

"Good, good," said Miguel. "It's all settled. I'll come by around two. Mona, why don't you fix us a picnic lunch?"

"A what?" Mona asked.

"A picnic lunch. You know, some sandwiches and chips and stuff like that. We'll have a family picnic on the beach. Doesn't that sound good?"

Neither girl answered.

"What d'ya think, Maria? Doesn't that sound nice?" Miguel asked.

"Sure, fine," Maria said. She could tell Mona didn't like the idea, but she wasn't sure if she should refuse.

"Good. I'm already looking forward to spending more time with you, Maria. I hope you come to like my neighborhood very much. You will see, I can be a very good friend to have." Miguel turned again to go. Just before leaving the room, he turned one last time toward Maria and smiled, again showing his gold tooth.

"MRS. MILTON, thanks so much for your time. I've been looking forward to meeting with you about the foundation." Andrew Janis extended his hand as Victoria stood behind the chrome and glass desk in her penthouse office on West Peachtree Street.

Fifty stories below, a thick manicured carpet of winter fescue covered a small park at the foot of the IBM Tower, where the Bradford pear trees and dogwoods hung onto a few remaining dark red autumn leaves. The top of the towering Peachtree Plaza, a few blocks further downtown, disappeared into a front of dark clouds. The heavy cumulous layer sealed the city tight like a cast-iron lid, trapping it inside an eerie simmering caldron.

"My pleasure, Mr. Janis." Victoria was her customary business self: pleasant, but to the point. "I'm anxious to hear your report. It's no secret my intentions of bringing the Olympics to Atlanta focused on the plight of poor children. The establishment of the foundation is as important to me as the athletic events themselves."

"Yes, ma'am," Janis replied. "I'm very much aware of your intentions and have thoroughly researched our options. My recommendations are based on findings after meeting with our legal consultants at Dix, Hartford & Dyer, the executive director of the MetroAtlanta United Way, Senator Hawkins, Speaker Dibbs, the governor, and the presidents of Bell South and Coca-Cola."

Janis tried to gage reaction in Victoria's expression. He needed to appear thorough, but not overdone, in order to establish a critical comfort zone between himself and the CEO. But Victoria's poker face gave nothing away.

"We have agreed," Janis continued, "on the format outlined in this presentation and the strategy for amassing contributions. We forecast this program will net two hundred million dollars by the end of 1997."

He placed a packet on the desk and pulled out a summary outline of the portfolio he planned to discuss. Janis did not intend to review all the details of each foundation with Victoria, or with anyone else for that matter.

"I see you've put a good deal of time into this plan, Mr. Janis," Victoria said, as she leafed through the papers. "Who are your targets for contributions?"

"Of course, Mrs. Milton, the primary source of revenue will be our mandatory contributions from official sponsors of the Olympic Games, as outlined on page twenty-three. Part of the responsibility of all major sponsors of the games will be a contribution to the foundation in proportion to their contract with AOC. These funds will be paid over a two-year interval and account for about seventy percent of the net income. We also will target individual contributors, but their funds will be partitioned from the main foundation according to smaller specific projects."

As Janis stopped for a minute to let Victoria catch up, he admired the abstract watercolor of a southwestern landscape on the wall behind her desk. A Larson, Janis thought to himself. He had grown to appreciate the artist himself. Many corporate bigwigs had begun collecting Hal Larson's peaceful depictions of earthen monuments rising from the desert floor. More suggestion than realism. Truly brilliant. He must collect several of the artist's works . . . after this was over.

"As you can see, my data show our target individuals and corporations give fundamentally to programs with which they have an emotional tie," Janis continued. "Contractors tend to give to building projects, doctors to health programs, the grocery industry to food projects, and so on. We will establish categories within our foundations, sub-foundations, if you will, to elicit these kinds of contributions from valuable independent resources."

Victoria continued paging through the documents, nodding as Janis talked. As she had expected, the report was impeccable. Janis was very well educated and garnered a wealth of experience in banking commerce under the tutelage of J. Caldwell, Victoria's dear friend.

"Well Mr. Janis, it looks to me as though you have compiled an excellent package, the culmination of years of education and experience." She closed the portfolio and turned to look out at the rain that had begun to fall on midtown. She spoke slowly, in a sedate, dreamy tone. "You are to be commended for the job you have done and I am confident you will be successful in your valiant endeavor to raise the social status of thousands of children in the state of Georgia."

Janis clenched his fists in silent exultation.

Victoria rose to her feet, stepped from behind her desk, and faced the wall of glass. She held her arms outstretched like an evangelist, speaking more to the buildings before her than to the man in her office.

"Multitudes will realize for the first time the opportunity of a bright and jubilant tomorrow. They will look to the heavens and see *radiance.*" Beams of sunlight broke through the dark sky, silhouetting Victoria's visage in an angelic glow against the backdrop of Atlanta skyscrapers.

"Indeed, this one hundredth anniversary of the modern Olympic Games will be revered as one of the greatest philanthropic achievements in the annuls of American history."

Victoria turned from the window, and extended her trembling, age-spotted hand. "I am proud to shake your hand, sir."

Janis followed her lead cautiously, stunned by the words he had just heard. The two shook hands, and Janis turned to leave. As he opened the heavy mahogany paneled door, he smiled to himself.

It had been easy. He was quite sure now, his plan would work.

Heavy clouds once again extinguished the light, and a frightening Georgia downfall commenced.

MARK LAY ON THE COUCH in the den of his modest brick house in Toco Hills. It had been a long day, and sleep came easily.

At 7:30, he'd had a four-hour marathon with Hank on athlete security in preparation for hiring the squadron of officers needed to ensure the safety of all participants in the games. From there, he rushed immediately to the airport for a one o'clock meeting with the head of security. While the airport staff was well versed in standard security operations, Mark found them to be neophytes when it came to the myriad of potential confrontations that could arise during the transport of major forces of people from hot spots around the globe.

It took all afternoon just to begin the basics of special force operations for security. Another meeting was scheduled for next week to assign groups of airport staff to task forces to function in the network of airport security during the months preceding the games and on up through the closing ceremonies.

Mark rolled over on his side, unaware that the object poking him in the side was the missing fork from his every-day, stainless steal set making its way from a hiding place underneath the back cushion.

Last night he had been at his office computer until af-ter midnight running background checks and assembling the personal and professional histories on all cabinet mem-bers and their executive assistants.

Everything had gone well until he started looking into the background of Caldwell's assistant, Andrew Janis.

Six

It was p-a-r-t-y time, and on his way home, Darryl celebrated the best day of his life with the Motown review on Fox 97 cranked to full throttle. He could hardly drive for playing bongos on the steering wheel, his thighs, the seat next to him, and the vinyl lining of the inside of the door. Insulation being scarce inside '83 Honda Accords, the dashboard made the best sound, and when rapped by rhythmic fingertips, it resonated a medium-pitched boom.

He was a new man. Life was good.

He popped into the parking lot of Claudia's Flowers on Memorial Drive, causing the front end of the car to temporarily leave the ground. Jumping out, Darryl bebopped to the door, his feet never touching the smooth asphalt.

His dream of working for AOC had actually become reality. Who would've believed a no-name black kid from a dirt-poor Southern family could become responsible for insuring one of the biggest events in the history of the human race?

"That's right, I'm bad!" he said, opening the door for a young girl coming out of the store with a basket of daises.

"Believe it if you can, it's Mr. Olympic Man!" He spun around and crouched down like a member of the Four Tops. The girl's face momentarily showed horror before she scampered off to the safety of her mother's car. Darryl just laughed and went inside.

"Looking sharp today, my man," he said, breezing by the teenager sweeping up near the front counter.

"Oooooh yeah, love them Heels!" he said, high-fiving a kid wearing a UNC basketball tee shirt. "The *only* college basketball team! Mark my words: 24-3 by March. I smell *another* national championship!"

Darryl could find no wrong with the world. He looked around for the biggest, the best, the most obnoxious arrangement of roses he could find to take home to surprise Esther. He purposely hadn't called her from the office about the meeting with Simpson. Although she deserved much more than roses, they'd have to serve for now. The forty dollars in his pocket could only buy flowers—diamonds would have to wait.

"Can you put these in one of those long, skinny white boxes like they do in the movies?" he asked the lady behind the counter.

"I'd have to take them apart, sir," she replied.

"That's okay, darling. I've always wanted to give my wife flowers in one of those boxes. You know, with a big bow. Got any of them bows?"

"Sure do. Be back in a minute."

True to her word, she returned in a flash and presented him with a glossy white box of giant golden blossoms wrapped with a bright yellow bow. "I sure hope she likes them, sir," she said with a smile.

"You can bet your sweet buttons," sang Darryl, holding out a single rose to her—he had picked one out of the refrigerator while she was in the back. "I sure appreciate your help ma'am."

She blushed.

Back in the car, Aretha boomed "R-E-S-P-E-C-T," and Darryl sang right along full bore. With the windows down, he received scornful looks from nearby drivers stopped at red lights, but he didn't notice. They wouldn't have bothered him if he had.

NO FILE FOUND flashed again from Mark's computer screen. He remained undaunted, though he'd been at it now for nearly three hours. It was a little curious he'd struck out with all the conventional national data banks. Just who was this guy, Janis, anyway?

Maybe this job was his first real shot at the bigtime. Perhaps there was no reason for the state or feds to have the lowdown on him. Strange, though, the paltry information on his past. Typically bank officials dealing with state accounts, municipal bonds, and funds from local county and city governments face background clearances for FDIC, which then, of course, become the dominion of the federal government, accessible by all cleared agents thereof.

To the uninformed, such overview by Big Brother amounted to blatant invasion of the private sector, but in truth, keeping tabs on those handling public money constituted public protection. When the voters in a school district approve a bond referendum for capital improvements and the school board hires a financial consultant to compile the proper documents for the sale of the bonds, the consultant is often the local banker.

Mark bushwhacked his way through the access codes of the personnel records at the Midland Bank, Chicago. The cursor flashed for several seconds before scrolling out the info.

Andrew B. Janis, born February 16, 1956, Miami, Florida.
Father: Bruce S. Janis, owner Southland General Contractors, Miami, Florida. Died: May 1, 1964.

Mother: Evelyn Hoover Janis.
Siblings: none.
Spouse: none.
Children: none.
North Miami High School Honor Graduate, 1974.
Attended the Governor's Honors program for gifted
students in math.
Graduated, summa cum laude, Yale University, BA
in business administration, 1978.
Employed by First Bank of Florida, 1978-84,
promoted to vice president of corporate financing.
Employed by Midland Bank of Chicago, 1984-
1993.
Current address: Atlanta Olympic Committee,
P.O. Box 100, Atlanta, Georgia 30202-100.
Hobbies: Deep-sea fishing, tennis.
Speaks French.

Mark thumbed through the modem directory from his
secret service logs and dialed up the alumni directory of
Yale University. Janis' name was listed in the class of '78,
but no notes were elaborated. Under class highlights, Janis
was included on the roster for intramural tennis, nothing
else.

Mark accessed the alumni mailing list. No Janis appeared under the "J's."

"That's strange," Mark said out loud. "Not a member
of his own alumni association."

He typed another command, this time looking into tax
returns. Two more commands took him through the IRS
channels, by the corporate returns, and into the individual
accounts. Mark's first attempt to pull up Janis' information
took about ten minutes and produced zilch.

Now he was worried. Who didn't file a tax return?
There was no way possible without some pretty spectacular

tricks. Mark checked the social security number again. It was right.

"You idiot," he blurted at the screen. He had meandered into the listing of sole proprietors by mistake.

Back to the second sub menu, Mark found the employees with maximum social security withholding. Five minutes later, he had found Janis' return, about fifteen pages with extensions and amendments. Janis was doing very well, netting about six hundred thousand dollars in taxable income last year.

Mark rubbed his eyes. A little more than expected for an assistant banking executive. Maybe he learned well from watching others invest their money.

Mark tabbed through the return.

A fifteen percent interest in Global Construction, Inc., a general contracting company in Miami, showed a loss of fifty thousand dollars.

A fifty-five percent interest in the Piedmont Bank, a small one-building bank in Miami, showed an income from salary and stocks of two hundred fifteen thousand dollars.

On an extended return, amended schedule C showed an annual income from a trust of one hundred seventy-five thousand dollars. The trust was in his name and had been established in 1964. Total assets: $1.8 million.

Mark looked back through the bio he printed out from his search. 1964, the year his dad died—probably life insurance.

Mark printed out a copy of the tax return, then escaped back to the submenu for individual returns. He typed in, EVELYN HOOVER JANIS, and waited. Several minutes later, he located her return. An annual income of dividends and interest form an assortment of stocks and bonds was listed at about sixty thousand dollars, with the assets of the trust in her name established in 1964 of six hundred seventy thousand dollars.

"Momma was greedy," Mark said to the screen. Looked like she had pulled out most of the cash up front. In her defense, he thought, she spent money raising the kid.

Mark escaped back to the submenu. He did not print a copy of Evelyn's return, didn't think it was important. He typed BRUCE S. JANIS, and waited. In seconds, the message came across the screen, RETURNS PRIOR TO 1984 ON DISC. REFER TO SECTION RT.12.34D. Mark had no idea what section RT.12.34D was.

He sipped his lukewarm coffee and leaned back with his fingers interlocked behind his head.

Snooping through financial records punched a surefire hole into the soul of his target, yet why Janis' two other business interests did not appear on any other cross-references was puzzling. Another twenty minutes of typing codes, dialing numbers, and staring at the monitor revealed neither Piedmont Bank nor Global Contractors, Inc. were represented in the Miami Chamber of Commerce, the Better Business Bureau, or any of the six Rotary Clubs in the Miami area.

Mark was not sure what this all meant.

"MARIA!" Miguel called out from the living room. "Honey, how 'bout bringing your old *amigo* a cool one."

Maria looked over the ice chest at Mona. For the life of her, she couldn't understand why Mona was friends with such a sleazeball. He was watching *Let's Make a Deal,* while the girls finished the preparations for their picnic.

"I'll be right in, Miguel," Mona answered, arching her eyebrows at Maria.

"No. Let Maria bring it to me."

Maria heard the thud of his repulsive boots against the top of the coffee table.

"Don't let him scare you, Sweetcakes," Mona whispered. "Just give him the beer and come back and help me finish packing."

Maria carried the Corona by its long neck and handed it to Miguel at arm's length.

"*Muchas gracias*, Maria," he said, snatching the beer. She turned quickly to leave, but before she could escape, Miguel leaned over the arm of the chair and grabbed the squealing girl around the waist, pulling her onto his lap and holding her tight with his left arm. He gulped half the beer and then belched loudly. The smell seeping from his mouth made Maria feel sick to her stomach.

"So, Maria. How do you like it here? Pretty nice, eh?"

"I like Mona very much," she said cautiously.

"And how 'bout me? Eh, Maria? How do you like me?"

She wedged the point of her elbow into his chest. "I don't know you."

"I want to change all that, Maria. I think you would like me very much. It takes time to get to know a person, just ask Mona. I know it's hard to believe, but Mona didn't like me much at first. And look at us now. *Samos familia.* You know: family."

"Can I go help Mona now, please?"

"*Si*, sure. Help her get our picnic ready. You like picnics, Maria?"

"Yes, I like picnics," she said, shivers racing across her back just from the sound of him saying her name over and over. "And if I don't help Mona, we won't get to have one today."

"*I* say if we have a picnic, Maria." His arm tightened its grip around the girl's thin waist and his face grew stern. "*You* need to learn who your friends are in this world."

Setting the bottle down on the floor beside the armchair, he grasped Maria under her jaw with his right hand. She refused to show her fear, but with the suffocating force around her waist and the pressure against her face, she could not move. Miguel smiled, showing his gold tooth. He kissed Maria's mouth hard, his open lips engulfing hers.

"I think we understand each other," he said, relaxing his strong hold.

Maria vaulted from of his lap and raced to the refuge of the kitchen, hearing Miguel's vile laughter mixed in with the cheering on TV.

"Are you okay, Sweetcakes?" Mona asked.

"Yeah, fine."

"You sure?"

"Yeah," she said, fighting back tears. "No problem."

THEY FINISHED PREPARING THE FOOD, and the three descended the stairs outside the apartment building and loaded into Miguel's convertible 1984 Cadillac. Maria had never been in a convertible, and when they roared off, the open airy feeling of freedom made the bright blue expanse overhead seem even bigger.

She rested her head against the back of the seat and closed her eyes, enjoying the breeze through her hair—the ends whipping her face like the wings of a thousand butterflies beating in unison. The warmth of the sun on her bronze eyelids, along with the noise of the wind and passing traffic, soothed her into another world. As the staccato of the tires thumped over the joints in the pavement, a vision of her family eating dinner together formed in her mind. Salty tears squeezed between her resting lids, and the damp drops, cooled by the rushing air, pinched Maria back to reality.

The drive to the beach took less than thirty minutes, and they pulled into a public parking lot facing the crashing waves. The temperature was a balmy ninety degrees, and everywhere colorful umbrellas sprouted from the white sand, protecting couples and families from the autumn sun.

Maria wore a pair of old blue-jeaned cutoffs and a pink tank top Mona found buried in a drawer. Both fit like a sack. Mona picked up the basket of food from the trunk and walked behind Maria, who carried towels and one of Mona's romance novels. Miguel followed, too closely for Maria's comfort, with the ice chest and a newspaper.

Mona picked a spot near a couple with two infant sons and began spreading out the towels. One of the little boys wasted no time coming up to Maria and describing in five-year-old broken speech every detail of his sand structure under construction. In minutes, she was on her knees helping the young boy, who incessantly directed the precise location of each new bridge and spire of the sand castle.

Mona smiled, watching Maria with the boy. That's what she should be doing, baby-sitting instead of running away on the streets by herself. Mona hoped to return Maria to her family, to the normal life of a kid in junior high school.

"She is a very pretty girl," Miguel said.

"Yeah, she's a sweetie," Mona said. "I'm going to miss her when she has to go back to Jacksonville."

"When does she have to go back?" Miguel asked, easing back on his elbows, still wearing his silver-toed boots and black pants.

"I hope she can stay for a week, but I'm not sure what my sister will say. You know, with her missing school and all."

"This sister of yours, she is older?"

"Yeah, she's about five years older than me. We used to get along real good, too. I miss her." Mona rolled over on her stomach, trying to encourage Miguel to leave her alone.

"You got a picture of this sister, Mona?" He unbuttoned the black shirt down to his navel.

"She never much liked pictures of herself," Mona mumbled, feigning a semiconscious stupor. "Maybe I've got one of when we were kids."

"I want to see it when we get back."

"What's all the sudden interest in my family, Miguel?"

"Everything concerning Maria interests me. She is so young, so fragile. She needs someone watching out for her, someone to take care of her. You remember, Mona, you were about her age when I found you."

Mona sat up quickly. "Look, Miguel, Maria's nothing like me. Got it? She's got a family back home waiting on her. She's only going to be here a couple of days, a week at the most. You just stay away from her, hear me? Just stay away."

"No! You look, bitch." Miguel grabbed Mona's face, bunching her cheeks into a painful mass. "Don't forget who you're talking to. Don't forget who made you. I own you, see, and I can cut you off like that." He snapped his fingers so close to her face that his thumb gouged her eye.

"Knock it off you bastard," she said, trying to get away.

"Don't think you're fooling me with this shit about a sister in Jacksonville. I'll know the truth before the sun goes down today. If you got a sister, I know people who will find her. You don't, and Maria's mine. YOU GOT IT?"

He shoved her face hard against the sand, holding his grip against the back of her head. When he finally released her, Mona rolled away, gasping for air and coughing sand out of her lungs.

Miguel got up from the towel and walked off toward the boardwalk. Kicking the sand off his boots, he headed toward the sidewalk snack bar with a neon sign in the shape of a hamburger. He was unconcerned how the bruises on Mona's face would effect business—clients would understand, they always had before.

MIGUEL LEANED AGAINST THE COUNTER and ordered a box of Moletti thins. He was admiring the approach of a bikini-topped rollerblader and didn't notice the two men walk up behind him.

"Nice day, eh Miguel?"

Surprised to hear his name, he turned around quickly and saw two men. His face flashed in instant recognition and fear of the bigger, burly man, but he quickly was all smiles. "*Amigos*, long time no see. How you doin', man?" His lower lip quivered.

"If you have the time, Miguel, we'd like to speak with you a moment," said the smaller one. Both wore black, the smaller one a tropical wool, double-breasted suit and a black Panama Jack hat to make him appear taller.

"Hey man, I got my lady over there on the beach, man."
Miguel pointed to the place he wished he were at the moment. "I need to get back to her. Hey, but it's good to see
you guys. Maybe we talk later this afternoon, okay?"

"I'm afraid our schedule is full later. Let's talk now."

The big one landed his gorilla paw on Miguel's shoulder, tacitly encouraging him to the back of the snack bar.
When Miguel resisted, the ape slammed Miguel's back
against the concrete block wall. Miguel lost his breath and
bent over at the waist, experiencing a hint of the discomfort he had inflicted only minutes ago. Staring at the sidewalk, Miguel watched an enormous black-sheathed knee rise
quickly toward his face, striking him in the nose and abruptly
standing him at attention.

"Adrianne wants her money," the small one said coolly.
"She's been very understanding up till now. She asked me
to collect your debt. Immediately."

"You broke my fuckin' nose!" Miguel cried, blood raining from around his fingers, obscuring the tattooed snakes
and skulls on his arms.

The larger one took Miguel's right arm and pinned it
against the concrete wall, interlacing the four fingers of
Miguel's right hand.

"The money, Miguel," the small one said again.

"I don't have it just now, but I can . . . "

Miguel's fingers made a sound like snapping twigs. A
scared, pitiful scream exploded from his throat, partly out
of pain, but mostly with terror of what the gorilla planned
next. His fingers hung contorted from his hand, sickly perpendicular to their normal alignment.

"I believe we understand each other?" The expression
on the face of the small one never changed.

The gorilla moved to Miguel's left arm, holding it parallel to the ground. Miguel's heart now threatened to break
out of its cage, as the massive hairy arms made their way
toward the four still-functional fingers awaiting their discipline.

"Wait, wait," Miguel pleaded. "Look, I got something Adrianne will like better than the money!"

The small one cocked his head. "Better than money?"

"*Si, si.* I guarantee it. I got just what Adrianne wants. It's a goldmine, man, worth ten times what I owe her. You gotta give me a chance to make good. Come on, man, what good am I crippled for life? Give me a chance!"

The small one took off his hat and pulled a silk handkerchief from the inside breast pocket of his coat. He blotted his forehead and smoothed back his greased hair.

"You see, I don't trust you, Miguel," he said soothingly, like a grandfather parlaying life's truths to his grandson. "I don't think you have anything of interest to Adrianne. No, Miguel. What I think is you're lying through your miserable gold tooth just to save your worthless ass from my collection agent here. I think if I let you go now, you'll run all the way back to West Havana. I think it would be prudent to end your zero life now and take your car and whatever else I can find back at your shithole of an apartment."

"No, no, *amigo.* I ain't got nothing back at my place. And my car, she ain't running so good. The transmission, I think. It's about to quit. Wouldn't do Adrianne no good. No, man, what I got for her is *cherry*, man. It's top of the line, first class. I mean, she's gonna thank me for this. I mean it, man."

The small one turned away from Miguel to look at the beach. The breeze did little to cool his face. He rubbed his forehead for a minute in silence.

He stepped close to Miguel until the brim of his hat brushed against Miguel's realigned nose. He spoke in a quiet voice. "What you say better be true, Miguel, because you are betting your life on it, what measly worthless life it is. If you don't deliver by noon tomorrow, my friend and I will be here by three to feed you to the sharks, piece by piece, starting with those juicy fingers. *Comprendé, amigo?* Noon, tomorrow."

"*Si, si.* Noon tomorrow. No problem, man."

The big one looked disappointed at having to drop his grip on Miguel's arm. He stepped back, straightened the knot of his tie, and followed the small one down the board-walk.

THE ROOM WAS DARK except for the psychedelic kaleido-scope of pink, yellow, aqua, and lavender spots cast against the walls and ceiling from the slowly rotating carousel night-light on Mona's dresser. The intruder silently crept through the familiar surroundings, the socks on his feet choking off each step like a silencer on the end of a hot muzzle.

Mona flinched slightly when the fourteen gauge needle slipped under the pale unblemished skin covering the in-side of her right elbow. Maria lay asleep upon a bed of com-forters on the floor next to Mona's single bed, her thin arms naked to the assailant. He knelt beside her, unaware that his right foot pinned several strands of the girl's long hair between his sock and the shag carpet covering the floor. As he reached for the second syringe in his back pocket, the intruder turned on the ball of his foot, pulling the strands of Maria's hair away from their roots.

She opened her eyes and reached up to brush away what-ever it was that had tugged her hair, her hand hitting the intruder's leg.

"Who's there?" she asked, trying to focus her eyes. She tried to sit up, but a strong hand slapped her in the face, knocking her back against the floor. She was awake when the sharp stick punctured her forearm, but the effects of the drug took hold before she could scream.

With considerable effort, the intruder folded the young limp body over his shoulder, the smashed fingers on his right hand throbbing under the load, then headed out the front door and down the stairs to his awaiting car. Reaching the parking lot, he dumped the girl into the trunk and, after stopping at a McDonald's drivethrough for a large cup of coffee, sped north on Interstate 95.

SEVEN

Dawn snuck into the hushed city shrouded in pale pink clouds pierced here and there by fulgent rays of sunlight blazoning the majesty of another day. Bending through the exfoliative woods, the first thin light created an iridescent autumn glow in the front yards of the elite Buckhead neighborhood.

Not far from the white-columned grandeur of the Governor's Mansion nestled the home of Colonel Hank Powell. Its high-pitched roof, twelve-foot ceilings, baronial windows, and deep rolling acres of lush, winter fescue lawn were the fruits of an exhaustive tour of Fulton County with an attractive and thorough ReMax realtor. The family had been pleased at the culmination of the search, as was the realtor, who received a handsome seven percent commission from the sale, and, in turn, paid off the balance on her 1995 Jaguar XJR.

The captain of the Peachtree Battle Atlanta Lawn Tennis Association team wasted no time sleuthing the tennis prowess of the newest arrival to the neighborhood. Along with a group of engrossed fellow teammates, he interrogated the prospect and listened intently as Hank described his brief, but impressive, tennis history.

While stationed in Australia one summer, Hank had played a daily match with the CO on the camp's manicured chalk-lined grass courts. During the months down under, his finely honed forehand became accurate to within a ball's width of any three-inch line, and even more intriguing to those now almost sitting in his lap, Hank's backhand had become nearly flawless.

Although Hank had not played much since the pastoral stint, his wide-eyed neighbors delighted in his stories of post-match Elephant beers under the shade of broad green-and-white striped umbrellas. Like Scrooge wringing his hands over newfound treasure, Hank's soon-to-be captain placidly invited him to join the team, careful not to appear anxious, ever cautious not to reveal the kill-or-be-killed attitude of the war in which he was about to enlist.

Hank's gregarious side couldn't resist signing up with the gang.

As would any new neighbor, he wanted to join in and become a part of the group. He signed his name to the ALTA registration card while his teammates nodded approvingly with arms folded across their chests—another comrade in arms.

And so began the adventure that would take him to the farthest corners of the city, over the hard-packed clay battlefields of Bitsy Grant, beyond cracked and splitting asphalt grounds of Decatur city, across the red and green Laykold of South Gwinett High School, and into the abyss and lightning-fast recesses of glazed concrete at Washington Park—ever searching for the hallowed stone tablets of tennis achievement, the precious Holy Grail of weekend wannabe professionals, the gold medal of Herculean racket stardom. . . the ever cherished ultimate symbol of tennis glory—a cheap white plastic bag tag with the words, "Division Champion" emblazoned across its face.

THE SIMULATED-OAK BLINDS splintered the morning light into a distorted geometric design of light and dark lines. Mark lay in bed reviewing cascades of lists in his head. Although the eerie circumstances surrounding Janis' personal history should have bothered Mark more, this morning he was more concerned over the frustrating delays in obtaining the electronic surveillance devices planned for outside the athletic dormitories.

The small private firm under contract to deliver the system piddled five days behind schedule, with the welcoming day for athletes rapidly approaching. In less than two weeks, the first wave of competitors would exit the debarking corridors of Hartsfield International Airport for their on-site preliminary training sessions.

Common sense dictated the average lunatic terrorist would prefer striking during the televised glory of the games themselves, but Mark knew his team and his facilities must be prepared for the unexpected. And Mark did not like betting. And he hated Las Vegas.

Mark was ready to play hardball. He wanted an emergency meeting with Hank and the board of directors of AOC at noon today. Already, he had planted a seed of doubt with Hank and Victoria early in the week, suspecting incompetence among the small firm.

His stainless steal Timex read 7:15. He hesitated waking Hank up early on a Saturday, so he ambled into the kitchen to brew a pot of coffee.

He reached into the back of the kitchen cabinet next to the sink to find his favorite Swiss-mocha blend of instant coffee. The white paint chipping off the cabinet door bothered him, chafing his one obsessive character trait—organization.

"I will paint you this winter," Mark promised out loud, adding another item to his mental personal "to-do" list.

The small three-bedroom house he had bought in Decatur near the Emory University campus shared the traditional design in the neighborhood of red brick on all four sides, a porch spanning the front of the house supported by six columns made of the same red brick halfway up, and traditional, white Doric columns continuing to the roof, a mahogany stained front door framed with side lights and a half-circle transom above, and two five-by-seven paned windows through which the living room could be seen on one side of the Georgian granite entry hall and the dining room on the other. In spite of his security background, no curtains hung over any of the front windows.

Although extremely careful with the lives of others, Mark was often inconsistently careless with his own.

Beneath the gray slate roofing tiles, the floors of the house were made of two-and-three-quarter-inch white oak planks that had been painted a light yellow-green by a previous owner. Before moving all of his furniture in, Mark had devoted his first week in Atlanta to stripping the floors bare in the front rooms, exposing the rich beauty of the natural grain. He then spent three days eating out while applying three coats of matte finish varnish.

A faint hint of the distinctive polyurethane aroma still lingered in the kitchen where he sat at the table sipping his coffee and perusing the Weekend Edition of *The Atlanta Journal.*

Chimes from the grandfather clock in the living room bonged the arrival of eight o'clock. Mark decided he'd given Hank long enough to get up.

"Good morning, this is the Powell residence," answered the friendly Jamaican voice. Hank had met his wife in France, and while she had lived in Paris for five years, her calypso alliteration concealed her European influence.

"Good morning, Samya, this is Mark."

"Well hello, good friend, a happy morning to ya. And how are you this beautiful day?"

"Fine thanks," Mark said. He loved listening to her talk. The easy-flowing melody calmed his anxiety. He understood why so many people visited the islands. "I hate to bother you so early, but is the boss available?"

"Oh, I'm sorry, Mark, he left about ten minutes ago. Has the big tennis match today, ya know."

"Tennis match? At eight o'clock . . .on *Saturday?*"

"Yes. Quite an event, I'm told. Hank had to leave with his gear for the courts a wee bit early, ya see, for practice before the competition."

"I see. And where exactly is he playing this morning?"

"Oh my," she replied. "The matches are at different sites each week. Just a minute, please Mark, and I'll consult the printed schedule in the kitchen. I am almost sure he pinned the roster on the bulletin board. Yes, here it is. They are playing at Druid Hills at nine o'clock. As I recall, his partner and he are playing number two this week, a prestigious designation I'm told."

"Gee, I'm surprised you aren't going to be there cheering him on," Mark said.

"Oh I want to be there, for sure, but I'm helping Miss Felicia with a school project on Brazil. We began early this morning scanning photographs onto the hard drive for her animated show. It's really quite fascinating."

"Sounds like it. School projects are certainly different than when I was in school," Mark said.

"Oh, indeed. The entire production is narrated by a little cartoon coffee bean."

"Maybe we could put her on the Olympic staff for PR," Mark joked. "I sure hope I can see her project when she's finished."

"I will be glad to print you a CD copy this morning," Samya offered.

"Thanks so much, Samya, I'll look forward to it. Thanks for the scoop on Hank. I'm going to run over to the club and talk to him there when he's off the court. It's always a pleasure talking with you. Give my best to the kids."

"I will, Mark. Thanks for calling."

IT WAS NOW A LITTLE after 8:30. Hank played at nine and the match would last about an hour or so. That left Mark about two hours to patronize his favorite place for breakfast.

He saved the Waffle House for special occasions, rare unhurried times like a lazy Saturday morning when he could actually relax, read a novel, and break every low-fat health-conscious rule ever written.

It was not the food that drew Mark to the trucker's haven. Heaven forbid he regularly poison his lean, trained body with cholesterol and shocks of sodium chloride. Food had little to do with the allure of the one-room rectangular eatery constructed of concrete block and trimmed in yellow plastic.

The attraction was ambiance, an open-armed welcoming come-as-you-are feeling so characteristic of each one of the more than one thousand Waffle Houses in the southeastern United States.

This morning was no exception. Pushing back the door, he had barely stepped across the threshold before the inundation began. "Mark, where you been?" and "Mark, my man!" and the ever traditional, "Mornin' Mark!"

Ah, there's no place like home, there's no place like home.

He settled at his favorite booth clearly marked, "Please reserve for two or more guests," but the waitress did not mind a bit. She hurried up to the booth carrying a cup of steaming coffee and a knife, fork, and spoon tightly cocooned inside a white paper napkin with "Waffle House, Always Good Food, Always Open" printed in yellow across the top. She was a pleasant-looking woman, in a bowling alley sort of way, with blonde hair that would be pretty had it not been teased into a nest on top of her head. Her clear smooth skin was well hidden beneath rouge and blue eyeshadow, and her broad red-lipsticked smile hinted one or two missing teeth on the sides.

"Sugar, I was 'bout to call the cops on you. Where you been hiding?" It was Dorothy. Mark knew it would be, and why he so eagerly laid claim to this particular booth.

"Oh, I've been here and there," Mark said. "My job keeps me busy." He couldn't help smiling, he felt so good.

"Yeah, you big shots at the Olympics. Hoppin' cross-country at the drop of a hat. Leaving us poor working stiffs here to clean up after you."

She chewed her gum hard as she talked, trying to act tough, but Mark loved her just for being so damned down-to-earth real. He had half a mind to ask her to marry him right on the spot, amour notwithstanding.

"Now, Dot, you know only my boss has all the glamour," Mark said, stirring the non dairy creamer into the dishwater-spotted mug holding his coffee. "Not me. They keep me busting butt on the little stuff."

"I know what you mean, Sugar. You do all the work and somebody else gets all the glory. That's the story of my life." She pulled out the pad of yellow tickets and began checking boxes and making notes to the side. "The usual?" she asked, but turned away to go back behind the counter before he could say yes.

A Dale Earnhardt look-alike put quarters in the juke box, and Garth Brooks sang about his friends in low places. Mark turned to where he had left off in *The Door to December,* by Dean Koontz, and began reading about the dark supernatural hiding in all of us, knocking to come out. The story was easy for Mark to believe, having seen the dark side of a lot of otherwise normal-looking people. Satan often lurked behind innocent eyes.

In the background, over the sound of banging pots and pans and clean dishes being stacked for the next round of grease, Mark heard Dorothy yelling orders to the cook. "One hash brown, scattered, covered, and smothered. Two over-easy on wheat, hold the butter. Waffle, light, bacon on the side. Three sunny-side up, grits, toast, sausage."

The cook's head remained still, as though he were performing surgery on a patient lying flat across his griddle rather than scrambling eggs and frying meat. Never interrupting his culinary mission for a moment, his big hands reached for and found baskets of eggs, slabs of pork, stacks of bacon, and the necessary accouterments for cooking them, while the orders from the six or seven waitresses on duty reverberated in his ears.

Dot wheeled around the corner of the countertop carrying Mark's breakfast. "Hot and sassy, just like me," she sparked. "Need more coffee, Sugar?"

"Yes, please, and a glass of grapefruit juice, too."

"For you, honey, I'll squeeze it myself," Dot said, eyes twinkling behind the fourteen or fifteen coats of mascara clogging her lashes. "Anything else?"

"Just your hot buns on a plate," Mark teased, surprising himself with his brashness.

"My place or yours, wild man," she said, disappearing behind the counter again.

A young boy, probably in kindergarten, eating with his dad in the adjacent booth, stood on his knees so he could continue battling his Power Rangers atop the small shelf separating the two booths. He was a terrific-looking kid, with a red Georgia Bull*dawg* sweatshirt and a baseball cap with "MATTHEW" stitched across the front.

"Matthew, who's winning?"

The young boy smiled and tipped his head down, hiding his eyes from the stranger speaking to him. The boy punctuated his *pows, ah-ha's,* and *eh-yeah's* louder than before, as the two plastic combatants landed blows across one another's chest.

"I'm betting on Jason, the Red Ranger," Mark continued, trying to raise a response from the boy. "Is he your favorite Ranger?"

The boy shook his head, no, punching the bad guy in the stomach three more times.

"I thought Jason was everyone's hero. Now who could be better than the Red Ranger? Surely not Kimberly."

Matthew looked up with a frown. "Oooh yuck! Not Kimberly. She's a girl. She can't beat Jason. The White Ranger's best. He's Tommy. He used to be the Green

Ranger. But he turned bad. Then he was good again. The White Ranger is the best. Toys-R-Us is out of White Rangers. Jason's pretty good, too. He used to be my favorite."

With that explanation, Matthew returned to his battle between good and evil.

Mark hoped that for Matthew, good would always win as easily as it did this morning.

HANK WIPED THE SWEAT from his forehead with the blue Fila wristband around his left forearm.

30-15.

Just two more points and the match was theirs. His partner met him again at the baseline for the pre-serve conference.

"Now, Hank, let's go down the middle with this one," his partner advised. "A good flat serve about three-quarter pace would be great. Remember on a first serve to his backhand, he sometimes lobs it over me, so you be ready to retreat on my word."

Hank nodded obediently to his partner, who was, after all, a *veteran* of ALTA.

"Okay, buddy, I know you can do it." The partner slapped Hank on his rear end and returned to his battle station, hopping ready on the balls of his feet, precisely one racket's length from the net.

Hank let out a deep breath, tossed the ball above his head, a little higher than his captain's critique at the last practice, bent his knees in proper stance waiting for the ball to reach its apex, then with all his might accelerated the head of his glossy new 6.2 Wilson, oversize Hammer racket, reaching out for the pinnacle of maximum leverage and crashing his all important first serve into the net.

"Shit," he muttered.

Partner turned around and said quietly, "No problem. Hang in there." He clenched his right hand into a fist.

Hank bounced the ball five times, gently rocking back and forth on his front foot.

The toss.
The crouch.
The hit.

A slicing motion imparted sidespin to the ball just like Andre, Pete, or Martina.

The ball followed an elliptical path over the net, then with the spin creating a vacuum in the air ahead of its path, dipped quickly into the court just inside the service line.

A perfect second serve.

Their opponent, a cagey older player with a symphony of bag tags dangling from his wares, returned the serve with an even better backhand slice, barely clearing the net and whirling toward the virgin white shoestrings of Hank's just-out-of-the-box Air Nikes.

With a grunt, Hank managed to scoop under the pinning accuracy of his elder opponent and wiggle the ball back over the net, floating it in like a lame duck.

In the tennis world, Hank's shot was a "sitter."

The older opponent dripped saliva onto the court as his tongue hung from his mouth in anticipation of smashing an overhead winner.

Drawing his weapon over his head, his eyes grew as large as tennis balls and his delicate temporal veins engorged to the size of racket strings as he attacked the net.

Facing him only a couple of feet away feeling the fury of the older man's hot breath, Hank reacted as any normal middle-aged, red-blooded man would under the circumstance—he wheeled on his feet, turning his back to the incoming shrapnel, praying the blow would not leave a scar.

With eyes reflexively closed, Hank received the good news of his opponent's misfortune—a distinctive *smack* of a tennis ball being stopped by the tape along the top of the net.

"Yes!" Hank's partner yelled. "Great get, Hank!" High-fives all around under grim scowls from the other side.

Hank wiped the sweat again from his forehead on his way back to the baseline, a trip that seemed longer than the last.

"Hank, that was major league!" his partner said following on his heels. "Okay, now on this serve, we need to go wide, you know, stretch him out on the backhand side. Look for the lob again, buddy. Hey, great shot on that last one." Another smack on the rear.

Gee, doesn't this guy ever slow down?

Hank finally began to comprehend league tennis.

He glanced over at the court-side picnic tables covered with red-and-white checked tablecloths, plates full of brownies, fresh-baked cookies and cakes, bowls of fruit, and ice chests brimming with cokes and beer. This was not a match, this was a way of life.

More bounces of the ball, six maybe seven times. A pesky yellow jacket attacked his face, breaking his concentration. Hank stopped to swat it away.

"Sorry, guys," he said stepping back to the line. The opponent held up his left hand courteously acknowledging the interruption.

More bounces. The toss. The crouch. The hit . . . a pounding first serve, at least 100 mph, clearing the net by fractions of a millimeter and landing directly where the horizontal line delineating the back of the service square joins the vertical line along its widest boundary.

ACE!

Hank's partner vaulted into the air, dropping his racket and raising his hands to the heavens. He turned screaming, "Way to go, Hank!" reaching for a double high-five.

After minutes of on-court celebration, with teammates outside the chain-link fence playing backup to their lead like the Pips to Gladys Knight, Hank and his partner met their two combatants at the net for the traditional handshake and the obligatory exchange of "Good match."

Hank's captain met him at the gate to the courts with tears in his eyes. "By George, I believe we have a ringer!"

He patted Hank on the back a little too enthusiastically, as the victorious warrior scanned the horizon for the closest bench on which to collapse.

HANK HAD NOT MOVED an inch from the concrete hospital bed supporting him when Mark arrived, glowering over him.

"Tough match?"

"You have no idea." Hank slowly raised his right leg to cross it over his left. "I thought this would be fun, a way to stay in shape and get to know the folks in the neighborhood. Hell, these guys are out for blood. At least I won."

"You get paid for this, Hank?" Mark asked with a grin.

"You kidding?" Hank said, toweling off for the hundredth time. "We pay to play. So what's up? No, hold on, don't tell me. You wanted to take me to brunch at the Ritz?"

"Anything for you, champ," Mark said. "No, seriously, I'm having trouble with DEP Electronics. They were supposed to install the electronic sensors for the security system for athletic housing yesterday, and. . ."

"Site 111?" Hank interrupted.

"Well, really both 111 and 112, but I would have been satisfied with 111. I can't get these guys in gear. I called yesterday morning to confirm they'd be on site—you know damn well they're a week late already—and the operation manager gave me his word the system would be installed by the end of day. I even talked to the president of the company. We agreed to an inspection at 5:30 and no one was there. The crew never showed up, and I haven't heard from them. I want to recommend to Victoria and the board we trash these guys and start over."

Hank looked at the empty Coke bottles on the ground. "No time for that, my friend. Those systems have to be operational next week, minimum. I bet you and I working as a team can get their butts moving."

Hank chugged the remaining Diet Coke and belted out a bass-pitched belch. "Let me get my stuff," he said. "We'll make a house call right now. These guys can't be any tougher than the Iranians . . . and I had those egomaniacs eating Cracker Jack crumbs out of my hand."

IN VALDOSTA, Miguel stopped at another McDonald's for breakfast. Back on the interstate he took the next exit into a rest area and pulled the Cadillac to the end of the row of parking spaces. When he opened the trunk, the girl squinted her brown eyes, drawing a hand up to block the sudden brightness.

"Good morning, Maria," Miguel said in a loud voice, his gold tooth reflecting sunlight in her face. "How are you feeling this beautiful day?"

"Where am I?" the girl asked, collapsing her head against the spare tire wedged behind her back.

"Why, you are with me, *amiga*," Miguel said, trying to be pleasant. "I decided to take you on a little trip, just the two of us. You know, kind of a adventure. I'm Indiana Jones and you're my assistant."

"Where's Mona?"

"Mona couldn't come," Miguel said. "She had work to do today, but she said to have a real good time. She was sorry she couldn't come with us, but you know how it is, gotta make dollars to pay those bills." His hair seemed greasier than usual from the hours spent driving the night before.

"Where are we going?"

"We're gonna visit some friends of mine. You'll like them, just wait and see. They're Mona's friends, too. That's why she felt so bad about not coming with us."

"Why do I feel so funny?" She sat up in the trunk, steadying herself against the sides of the trunk.

"Last night while you were asleep, some bad guys broke into Mona's place. You two were real lucky I was downstairs when they busted the door. I heard the guys and came up just in time to sneak you out. Man, I thought there was going to be real trouble. Look where they hit my nose. Look what happened to my hand. Man, I took a beating trying to get you out. You owe me a lot, man. If I hadn't took those guys on, no telling what they would've done to you. I guess I'm your hero, huh?"

Maria didn't answer. She climbed out of the trunk, aiming to stay away from Miguel. When her feet hit the asphalt, her knees buckled, and Miguel caught her around her waist.

"Hold on there, little *señorita*. Let me help you."

She hated his arm touching her, but the mysterious paralysis in her legs persisted and just putting one foot ahead of the other seemed to require extraordinary effort. She stumbled to the front seat of the car where Miguel helped her sit down.

"I bet you're hungry, little girl," Miguel said, leaning down beside her. "And look, your hero comes through again. A nice hot Egg McMuffin from Mickey D's. Plus we got cold orange juice and a warm Danish roll. That sound good, babe?"

Though she despised having to rely on the mangy rodent for anything, at the moment, her options were limited.

"That sounds really good," she said. "Thanks, Miguel."

He reached into the back seat and pulled out her breakfast. Forgoing manners, the weak girl shoveled the food in her mouth.

Miguel stroked Maria's hair with his good hand. "You know, I'm gonna to miss you, little *señorita*. We would've been tight."

Maria did not pay any attention to his mumbling.

This time, though, she should have listened.

EIGHT

Victoria Milton arrived at her office earlier than usual. Though the games were months away, the list of details needing her attention grew longer and more complex each day, and on this morning she parked her white Coup de Ville in her reserved space at the IBM Tower an hour before dawn's light painted the autumn horizon.

Preparations for the 1996 Summer Games were unprecedented, and with more countries represented than ever before, more athletes housed, and more tickets sold than the Los Angeles and Seoul Games combined, the accomplishment would be nothing short of phenomenal.

When Stefanie Gaulding, Victoria's executive assistant, arrived at the office, she heard Victoria already on the phone with Hank Powell discussing the week's most immediate crisis, glitches in the athlete housing security system. The contractor for the system could not ship the necessary computer chips out of South Korea. Apparently, a fishing boat had meandered across a sensitive meridian, and in response, the North Korean officials had ordered military blockades of the waters.

Stefanie immediately began researching possible routes of exporting the exotic silicon chip needed for the Facial Contour Identity system, the backbone of the ID LOK program. Without the chips, the entire system proved no better than an honor code for keeping undesirables out of housing areas.

Victoria appeared at the office door. "Hank's done it again," she said. "If we can find a way to get the chips, they've promised to have the FCI units on-line by the deadline."

"That's great," Stefanie said.

"Here's several numbers in Korea to call," Victoria said, handing Stephanie the recently faxed information from Hank. "If they don't work, try the ones in Japan."

The FCI system constituted the electronic barricade between the athletes staying in the dorms and fanatics in the outside world. Using the technology employed at supermarket checkout counters, the camera of the FCI units at every dormitory entrance would strobe across an athlete's face to register a digital map of the contours. Then a microcomputer would instantly compare the digital data, the code on his or her badge, and the central system clearance list before unlocking the door to the building.

FCI units would not provide the precision of retinal scans or fingerprint matches, but Mark and his staff were confident they were adequate for screening the majority of traffic entering the housing facilities. Besides, FCI was much cheaper. The ubiquity of the technology in everyday life had driven down the cost of units to the point that Radio Shack would probably introduce a similar version for homeowners within a couple of years.

Stefanie dialed another number in Japan, hoping to find passage out of Inchon, South Korea and into Qingdao on the Shandong Peninsula of China.

"I found it!" she said.

Victoria hurried from her office.

"I've lined up a freighter sailing from Shanghai to Taipei in two days," Stefanie said excitedly. "But I still need to get them from Qingdao to the south docks."

"That's great work, Stef," Victoria said, with some tension passing from her face.

"I think with a couple more calls, we'll have it licked." Stefanie quickly resumed her search for the missing Chinese connection, and Victoria returned to her desk for a conference call with the assistant director for Awards and Ceremonies at AOC and a professor in musicology at Emory University. She dialed the number for the Emory University professor and received his voice mail box. She looked at her watch. Seven o'clock, an hour before the predetermined phone appointment.

"Age is catching up with me," she said to herself, replacing the receiver on the desk set.

Victoria rubbed her eyes and propped her head in her hands, her elbows resting against the glass top of her handcrafted desk.

If anyone had asked, Stefanie could have testified that her boss was showing the effects of stress. Uncharacteristic flaws had crept into Victoria's customarily unblemished veneer. It was the manner in which she assembled pieces that caught Stefanie's attention: robust thrown with serene, subtle with bold. Perhaps the CEO's forthright and businesslike demeanor had been nothing more than a well-rehearsed facade, increasingly difficult to maintain under the burden of Olympic magnitude.

The bell on Victoria's intercom sounded its gentle feminine chimes. Victoria pressed the button on the desk set and spoke into the speaker.

"Yes, Stefanie."

"Mrs. Milton, Mr. Rose and Dr. Spellman are on the line for your conference call."

Had an hour passed already? Victoria glanced at her watch.

"Thank you, Stefanie." She connected her line with theirs and thanked the men for their time.

"I'll only keep you for a few minutes, gentlemen. I know Mr. Rose and his associates have this issue well in hand, I simply wanted you both to know my feelings."

"Yes ma'am," the two men said in unison.

"Please understand, it is not my intent to micromanage . . ." Victoria paused briefly, subconsciously realizing her guilt, "but, I am very concerned about the status of our obtaining appropriate orchestrations for the national anthems of all participating countries."

"I assure you, Mrs. Milton, we are working diligently on the problem and will have the necessary tapes catalogued well before the opening ceremonies," Mr. Rose said.

"And you, Dr. Spellman? Do you feel confident regarding our progress?"

"To be frank, Mrs. Milton, our challenge is significant," Dr. Spellman answered. "Most of the former Soviet states' anthems are available, but some of the recordings are quite poor. I am analyzing them as they arrive to determine which I can make presentable electronically and which are beyond hope. Depending upon your budget, Mr. Rose, I will recommend several be rerecorded with a new orchestra. The additional problem we are facing is the ongoing struggles in the former Yugoslavia and the recent thrust of democracy in places like Thailand. There may not be usable orchestrations available at all. There is some indication the anthem in Thailand may change with the influx of elected officials, but the final decision has not been made. It puts us in the precarious position of trying to predict the outcome of an unstable political situation."

"I see," said Victoria. "And if we obtain tapes, even at the last minute, how will that effect Mr. Rose's organization?"

Without hesitation, Dr. Spellman answered, "If I have at least two or three days, I can improve even the worst recording considerably, using computer-assisted wave analysis techniques. Of course, I can only assure authenticity if I can obtain the score. Also, I must mention, you would be restricted to my interpretation of the music." He chuckled smugly.

"I'm sure we could count on your talent," Victoria said. "It's important to maintain consistency among the anthems."

"I agree, Mrs. Milton, but then again, I am limited by what I receive," Dr. Spellman spoke quickly, obviously well versed in his field. Neither Victoria nor Mr. Rose knew, but Dr. Spellman's doctorate in music was on computer-assisted compositions and the reconfiguration of sound waves, precisely the expertise this Olympic task demanded.

Spellman continued, "Should the recordings be substandard, I can subtract background noise easily. However, adding additional violins to the string section, making the sound of two bassoons instead of one, or creating a strong brass section where none exists is possible, but time-consuming. You see, I would have to produce the sound waves I wish to add using composition software and then edit the track to match the original. Indeed, quite an exciting piece of work, taking five or six days in the lab.

"Would it be simpler to rerecord a work, if it required such involved manipulation?" Mr. Rose asked.

"Probably," Dr. Spellman answered. "But, you would have to consider the availability of the score, the time necessary to hire musicians, locate a conductor, and book a recording studio with a mixer, an editor, and all the people behind the scenes for a masterful recording. Quite probably, arranging a quality recording at the last minute would be beyond the scope of reality. In straight terms, I may be your last hope."

No one said anything for a minute. The other four lights flashed on Victoria's phone, and nothing would be decided today on this issue. How could anyone predict what might happen in Bosnia or Croatia or Thailand months from now?

"Gentlemen," Victoria said, breaking the silence, "I appreciate your time. Dr. Spellman, I know we will be talking again soon. Mr. Rose, if you would please keep me informed on your progress in your weekly notes. How we manage these anthems must be one of our fundamental convictions to respecting and honoring every participant in these games. I know you agree, this matter requires our serious attention."

A duet, "Yes, ma'am."

As she replaced the receiver on the desk set, the Austrian-accented chimes sounded her intercom again.

The *Atlanta Journal* reporters had arrived for their conference regarding the fifty thousand dollar block ticket plan AOC recently announced. Many editorialists saw the newly adopted promotion that presold two tickets to every Olympic event to a few wealthy people for a fifty thousand dollar "donation" as a conflict with the premise of the games and as AOC turning its back on its commitment to guarantee equal access by all people of the world.

Victoria checked the mirror on her desk, then intercomed to Stefanie. "Send them in."

SODIUM LIGHTS suspended from the cement ceiling of the parking garage cast a dense yellow-orange glow that hung like an eerie San Franciscan fog in the stale basement air of the IBM Tower on West Peachtree Street. It was never advisable to walk alone in downtown Atlanta, a city that in some years recorded a higher per capita crime rate than New York, but even the boldest city-life lover would have felt uneasy crossing these ominous gray tiers of concrete unaccompanied.

In the far corner of the lowest level, parked next to a forest green Q45, Andrew Janis sat cloaked by dark-tinted glass of his black Acura NSX, staring at the revolver on the dashboard a foot-and-a-half away.

The calm of the parking deck was perfect. The conditions ideal.

Alone at three o'clock in the afternoon, no secretaries or businessmen entered or exited their cars. Lunches at the Hard Rock Cafe and Planet Hollywood had ended over an hour ago, and the tenants of the gothic marble building were busy empowering one another, facing problems head-on in strategic teams, employing hands-on management, decentralizing decision making, and maximizing profits.

There it lay, the key to his escape.

He stared for minutes at a time, hardly blinking, his eyes focused on a dream of precious freedom. Sitting just inches away was a life void of betrayal and rejection, full of peace and harmony and goodness.

He picked up the gun again.

Turning it in his hands, he caressed it as though it were a bottle of newly discovered medicine, a miraculous cure against the HIV virus, or cancer, and he were a poor soul slowly wasting away.

So many times in the same situation, consumed by the urge for calm, the need to press a soothing steel barrel against his temple and twitch his right index finger in a tender, sweet finale.

He turned the gun slowly side to side, rubbing it against his thigh, pressing it against his cheek, clenching his eyes as he passed the trigger guard, warm and moist with his sweat, across his lips.

He relived the day again in his mind, the day his life ended, nearly thirty years before . . . the images remaining clear, as if they had happened only week ago. Walking down the aisle of the funeral home, he saw uncles and aunts sitting on either side, some cried, some clung to their spouse or to their children. His cousins looked up at him with stares of wonder, most of them sobbing relentlessly as he slowly advanced along the navy blue carpet in his black dress shoes and dark gray suit, which had poorly fitted his thin nine-year-old frame only once before. His eyes were dry and his face blank. Only his left hand showed the effects of the day's gravity, fingertips blanched from his mother's tight grip as she paced him toward the casket in the front of the room. Arriving at the gilded box, he looked into the open lid. His father did not look real, sort of waxy, pale, stiff, not like he remembered him at breakfast two days before.

"Let it be now."

Janis' response to the tragic loss of his father had failed to progress through the normal stages of emotion leading to recovery and the restoration of mental health. Hearing his mother's explanation of the accident—his father fell ten stories from a steel girder at a construction site—Janis spent scant hours in denial, but proceeded quickly to anger where he remained abeyantly scarred, never advancing onto depression and acceptance.

In adolescence, he became increasingly removed from his peers who regarded him as odd and aloof. He realized he hated his life, hated his mother, and yearned only for an escape from his existence.

While his mother found solace in the two million dollar life insurance benefit, Janis loathed his father for having lived secure and justified in a plan that might someday replace himself with a large sum of cash. His attitude toward the insurance money never matured beyond a nine year-old's reasoning. Obviously, his father had been a selfish, irresponsible son of a bitch who never really cared for him, but who instead treasured a feckless life, neglecting the needs of a son he should have loved, nurtured, and guided through the strife of growing up.

By his death, his father robbed him of the infrequent, but revered attention Janis esteemed as a child. Exaggerating the premise of *work ethic,* his father often left the house for a job site an hour before Janis rose from bed, and did not return home until hours after the boy's witching hour. Still, Janis cherished any show of love from his father, no matter how sporadic or how paltry.

As a young man, his anger had been an ally, the fuel for his achievement, the energy behind nocturnal marathons at Yale, the motivation for a conniving and defrauding advancement at the bank, the stimulus for his business scheme in Florida.

Working fiendishly, Janis intended to amass his own wealth and forget his father's. Years of his unrelenting savage pace, though, beget greater conflict against the haunting memory he could not forget, but refused to confront.

His hands shook, clutching the butt of the revolver. He closed his eyes, trying to clear his few remaining thoughts in a transcendent meditation.

His breathing slowed, and he felt a slight chill of the sweat covering his body and evaporating into the air.

He let go with his left hand, his right hand raising the gun to his temple. His finger squeezed the blue steel trigger, rotating the chamber a little, a little more, a little more . . .

Crash!

The sound of smashing metal was unmistakably fender against fender.

"Why in the hell don't you watch where you're going!"

"*Me* watch? I was just backing out nice and slow. You must have been going forty miles an hour in a parking deck, asshole!"

The startling sound jolted Janis from his trance. He opened his eyes and sadly watched the two young men argue. Every muscle in his body became limp, and the gun slipped from his fingers and bounced off the padded leather of the passenger seat.

As he continued to watch the furious waving of hands nearby, a tear of regret eked out of his right eye, so very close to where the glorious seed of relief could have been planted.

HEADING NORTH on a section of Interstates 75 and 85 known as the downtown connector, the red Cadillac cruised with the top up and the windows down.

The Atlanta air was cooler than it had been in Miami the day before. The wind rushing around the chrome sideposts of the windshield invigorated the girl sitting in the passenger seat, as close to the door and away from the driver as possible.

The lingering effects of the drugs had dissipated, and she was almost enjoying the trip to the new city, if it weren't for the sleazeball steering the car through the midmorning traffic. She cherished the moment, though, thoughts free from horrific visions of her family twisted and bleeding on the floors of her home.

"That's where the Braves play," Miguel said pointing across the car to the enormous round structure on the right. "And that's where they'll play next year, after the Olympics." He pointed to the state-of-the-art Olympic Stadium under construction immediately adjacent to the old Atlanta-Fulton County Stadium.

The new showplace rose gigantically above the freeway. Cranes and scaffolding surrounded walls of block and steel, and workers hung precariously from thin planks at the top of the construction.

"You like baseball, Maria?" Miguel asked.

"I never watch it, but my dad did," Maria said. A chill ran down her spine, realizing what she had just said.

"Your dad *did?*" Miguel asked slyly, cocking his head to the side. "He doesn't live with you anymore?"

Maria sat silently, mad with herself for foiling Mona's story. Since breakfast in the roadside rest area, she had become relaxed, and now the frustration with her circumstances began boiling inside her.

"Where are we going, anyway!" she snapped. "I want to stop and call Mona!"

"*Si, si*, little *señorita*. We will call Mona, after we get to where we're going. We're almost there now. You will like my *amigos*. They will come to be your *amigos*, your very good *amigos*."

She watched out the window as they drove under huge expanses of concrete supporting Interstate 20 above. Billboards displaying Olympic sponsors' goods and services lined the downtown expressway as if the young girl were not riding in a car at all, but in an air-filled raft tumbling over tortuous churning white water bordered on both sides by canyon walls of glitzy enameled graphics and surreal photographs of athletes in action.

The car exited a short tunnel and Maria could see the blazing gold-leaf dome of the capitol building reflecting sunlight against the adjacent buildings. The glass cylindrical Peachtree Plaza Hotel complex towered high above the other skyscrapers of the city. Had she known they were there, Maria would have loved the horse-drawn carriages assembled along International Boulevard next to the Peachtree Plaza. She would have been thrilled to tour the downtown avenues snuggled under a wool blanket in the back of a polished turn-of-the-century mode of transportation, with muscle provided by gentle, old gray mares wearing diapers.

The interstate turned west before heading north again, passing under an enclosed MARTA track, the Atlanta rapid rail system, where an electronic sign digitally counted down the number of days until the opening ceremonies of the 1996 Games.

Facing the interstate on the west were attractive brick dormitories for the Olympic athletes, where workers applied finishing touches to the buildings that later would become the property of Georgia State University.

Miguel pulled off the interstate and turned onto Tenth Street, near the gothic architecture of the IBM Tower and its gilded pyramid crown.

They crossed Peachtree Street and turned left onto Piedmont, stopping at a well-preserved old home with white siding, four chimneys, and a front porch that wrapped around one corner and extended the full length of one side of the house as well. The corner lot at Ninth Street had three huge oak trees in front of the house and a yard ten inches deep in leaves. Behind the house, the driveway widened into a small gravel parking lot large enough for about two dozen cars.

Miguel parked next to a white 740i BMW. The only other car in the lot was a sky-blue VW bug with the license plate, LUVDROP, and a rainbow of Deadhead bear decals dancing across the rear window.

"We're here," Miguel announced opening the car door. "Man, it feels good to stretch. C'mon, Maria, I want you to meet Adrianne."

Maria reluctantly got out of the car and stepped into the bony shadows cutting across the yard. Almost instantly, clouds converged over the sun and suddenly dropped the temperature ten degrees. Maria held her hands tightly around her arms as she walked behind Miguel up the sidewalk toward the front door.

Miguel pulled back the screen door, and used the brass knocker in the middle of two stained-glass front-door windows to inquire within.

A girl about nineteen, wearing a red World Cup warm-up suit, answered the door. Her straight blonde hair was pulled back in a ponytail, and her stunning Swedish features beguiled her southern heritage only until she opened her mouth.

"Glad to see ya, good lookin'," she twanged in a slow, syrupy drawl. "But I'm afraid we ain't open for another six hours."

The girl could only see Miguel. Maria stood behind him out of view.

"I'm here to see Adrianne, *señorita*," Miguel said. "She's expecting me."

"Well then, if that's the case, come on in and set your handsome self down right over there and I'll let Miss Adrianne know you're here." She pointed in the direction of a small red velvetized room located to the right of the pink-marbled entry. "Oh, and who do we have here," she said, seeing Maria for the first time. "What a lovely young lady. She your daughter?"

"This is Maria," Miguel explained. "She's here to see Adrianne, too."

"Oh . . . I see," the blonde girl said slowly, smiling broadly again. "Miss Adrianne will be delighted to make your acquaintance, Miss Maria. Please make yourself comfortable and I'll collect her straightaway."

She accompanied them to the parlor, where the carpet was red, the upholstery was red, and even the ceiling was covered in red velvet, billowing from above like the inside of an Arabian tent. The girl paused to offer the guests lemonade before gliding up the stairs in search of Adrianne.

Maria sat on a red velvet footstool in front of a red velvet armchair with red velvet throw pillows. If obnoxious monotony won awards in *Architectural Digest,* this room would be cover material. Mercifully, the seams of the chair and the borders of the curtains were sewn in thick gold roping that appeared to be added as an afterthought, perhaps to introduce a second color to the decor.

Maria desperately wanted to talk to Mona. She sat impatiently, wondering who this Adrianne person was. Over the velvet-covered speakers, Frank Sinatra sang about New York, New York.

At the sound of creaking from the staircase, Miguel quickly stood up straight and buttoned his shirt in a futile attempt to improve his appearance. He smoothed his hair back with his hands and turned to give a short tense glance back at Maria.

Adrianne descended the stairs elegantly, wrapped in light green chiffon that spilled off her shoulders, exposing most of her chest, then tightly molding around her thin waist before falling loosely to the floor. Her bleached auburn hair had been straightened and cut to brush against her naked shoulders. She moved with the sophistication of royalty and with an air of arrogance and power that frightened Maria.

"So, Miguel," Adrianne began. "You decided to show after all. Obviously, you value your meager life. And you brought a friend along, I see."

"*Sí*, Adrianne, just as I swore I would," Miguel stammered. "You can always count on me to keep my . . ."

"Don't talk, Miguel," Adrianne interrupted, patting his cheek with the back of her right hand. "It only makes things worse."

Miguel quickly became silent, hanging his head and sulking like a wounded pet.

Adrianne crossed the room toward Maria. She peered down and delicately placed her hand under the wide-eyed girl's chin, lifting her head.

"Stand up girl, and tell me your name."

Miguel said, "She's Maria, a kid from . . ."

"Shut up, Miguel," Adrianne shouted without looking at him.

"Tell me where you're from, Maria," Adrianne said, her features softening.

"Miami, ma'am," she said with her knees starting to shake, her mind searching and confused, not knowing whether to lie or tell the truth.

"And where do you live in Miami, Maria?" Adrianne continued in a slow, direct tone.

Maria wondered again who this woman was. It scarred her to see Miguel kowtow so readily. Sweat broke out across her body and her heart raced.

"Tell me the truth, girl!" Adrianne demanded, clenching Maria's chin tighter.

"I live with Mona," Maria said quickly.

"Ah, yes, Mona," Adrianne nodded again. "Dear, sweet Mona. I haven't seen dear Mona in years, and we were once such good friends."

Adrianne stared blankly toward the ceiling as if remembering something special in her past. Maria felt an instant of relief, but then the woman's focus returned to the quivering girl.

"And who else, Maria, just Mona?"

"Yes, just Mona."

"Good, good," Adrianne said.

103

"You said your family was in Jacksonville," Miguel started before another glare from Adrianne returned him to his cage near the doorway.

"Don't let him upset you, Maria," Adrianne continued. "You don't have to worry about Miguel anymore. Now Maria, is Mona family, dear?"

Maria wished the woman would let go of her chin. She wished she could leave now, run out the door, somewhere, anywhere, just away from here.

"Well, not exactly," Maria said. "We're not related or anything, but she's my family now."

Adrianne's face came closer. "Where are your parents, Maria?"

Maria's eyes opened wider. She could smell the expensive fragrance coming from behind the diamonds and emeralds dangling from Adrianne's earlobes. She did not know whether to make up a tale about a family waiting for her back in Jacksonville, or say her parents were feuding in divorce and sent her to live with her mother's friend in Miami. Her skin was wet beneath Adrianne's hand.

"Answer me, girl!" Adrianne shouted an inch from Maria's nose. "Where are your parents?" She pounded each word separately with emphasis.

The longer she hesitated, the more fiercely Adrianne scowled, her gaze bored through the young girl with a supernatural strength, like a laser melting through steel. Adrianne raised her free hand, about to strike Maria, as her grip on the girl's face bruised even harder.

"DEAD!" Tears exploded in rivers from the dam bursting inside. "They're dead, all right?"

Adrianne let the frail body collapse back to the foot stool, and the distraught child covered her face with her hands.

"I see," Adrianne said, one side of her mouth rising in an evil asymmetrical grin.

Majestically, she turned away from Maria and approached the cowering Miguel, who had retreated to the safety of the marbled entry. Adrianne showed no emotion for Maria. She spoke to Miguel with her eyes not fully open, in a perpetual cast down appearance of contempt.

"I assume she's clean," Adrianne said.

"As driven snow," Miguel answered, showing his gold tooth.

Adrianne turned her back to Miguel. "Your debt is paid. Do not return or I'll have you killed."

"I knew you'd like her," Miguel said. "I tried to tell —"

"Leave now, Miguel," Adrianne said, pointing to the door without turning around.

Obediently, he opened the front door silently with his good hand. Looking back, he could only see Maria's feet, the rest of her hidden by the wall between the parlor and the entry.

The sounds of her weeping had not softened, and he almost felt sorry for her.

NINE

Honey, you want ranch or peppercorn dressing?"
Esther called to her husband in the other room.
"Which is the good stuff?" Darryl yelled back, shift-
ing through his CD collection.

Esther smiled. "Neither one's got any fat, mister. If
that's what you're asking," she said, another perfect ribbon
of tomato peel falling into the sink.

Damn that woman, Darryl thought as he slipped the
disc into one of the slots of the six-disc holder. "Peppercorn, I guess. Could you melt a little butter and pour it on
top of mine?"

Esther laughed at loud. "Hot butter on salad? You crazy,
man?"

"Hell, it was just a thought," Darryl muttered to himself. He loaded up the discs. Al Green was the headliner,
followed by Aretha Franklin, Whitney Houston, The Four
Tops, James Taylor, and, only because his wife insisted,
Michael Bolton.

Darryl started the system, even though the guests
wouldn't arrive for another thirty minutes. He grabbed a

Wilson tennis racket propped against the entertainment center and used the handle as a microphone, lip-synching to Al's old recording of the Beatles' "I Want to Hold Your Hand."

He tiptoed into the kitchen, singing into the red "W" like he was on stage in the Omni in front of thirty thousand screaming fans. He grimaced on the high notes, just as he imagined Al would do. He took Esther's hand and danced on stage with the lucky girl he had plucked randomly from the front row.

Esther was not impressed. She slapped at his hand. "Let me be if you wanna eat tonight." But the star kept right on singing and spinning his partner in one-handed shag maneuvers.

The song ended, and Al kissed the lucky fan tenderly on her lips, slowly breaking his embrace so she could treasure the magic moment forever in her hope chest of most precious memories.

Then, with a bow, the king of soul was ready to set the table.

Basting brush in hand, Esther opened the oven door, releasing a scrumptious cloud of peppers, onions, and pork. Arranging the knives, forks, and spoons on the white tablecloth, Darryl grinned sheepishly and called to his wife in the kitchen. "Can't we just use the paper plates left over from the cookout?"

Esther's eyes opened widely and she dropped the brush. Running toward the dining room she screamed, "No we can't use paper plates! This is going to be a formal dinner. Get the china from the cabinet and set the table right."

Shaking her head, she returned to the sizzling meat on the oven rack.

He waited a few minutes before calling out to her. "Honey, you want cloth or paper napkins?"

"Paper napkins!" Esther said, charging out of the kitchen again. "What's wrong with you. You don't use paper napkins with your good china."

She crossed right past her husband to a large drawer in their heavy dark cherry hutch and fetched white linen squares with roses embroidered in one corner.

"And you'd better fold 'em nice 'n neat," she ordered, returning to her culinary haven.

After a few minutes, Darryl came in the kitchen and retrieved a Georgia Tech tumbler and three mason jars and placed them appropriately by spoons and knives.

Esther hoofed to the dining room. "Darryl," she puffed. "Don't even think about usin' those crummy glasses!"

She collected them all in a flash with the four fingers of her right hand and waved them above her head. "I oughta knock some sense into your fool head! Now get the crystal from the hutch, and don't make me come in here again!"

Darryl couldn't help it, he loved to tease his wife, a habit perfected growing up in a house with three sisters and only one bathroom. On one occasion, he'd dabbed drops of pine sap onto his oldest sister's curlers, the ones she slept in every night to relax the texture of her hair. She'd just about killed him the next morning when the curlers were glued to her scalp. Then there was the time he recovered an old siren from a dilapidated engine at the volunteer fire department and wired it so that it sent a nerve-shattering blast at precisely the moment his littlest sister kissed her first boyfriend on the front porch.

Darryl waited until he heard Esther plopping homemade biscuit dough onto a greased cookie sheet. Yeah, he thought, her fingers oughta be good and messy about now.

"Honey, do we gotta have these candles on the table? You know the smoke bothers me and all. How 'bout a couple of them nice plastic apples from the bowl in the den?"

He had gone too far.

"Mister!" she screamed, charging the dining room a third time. "You mess with them candles, son, and you eat Kibbles and Bits for dinner with Alfie. Now quit your horsin' around and get in here and open the wine. They'll be here any minute and I don't got no time for your shenanigans."

She stomped the hardwood floor hard with her right foot in disgust.

Darryl completed his duty in the dining room in quiet obedience, careful to allow an appropriate time for cooling off, and then snuck into the kitchen behind Esther, who was breaking the French bread she had toasted and seasoned the night before into croutons. He reached around and grabbed a breast with each hand in a reverse cross-your-heart bra hold.

"Boy oh boy!" he said. "Major-league yabbos! I like what pregnancy does to these babies."

Esther could not fight back the smile inching across her face.

"I'll just have one of these for dinner," he said. "Hmmm, 1995, good year."

They both giggled like teenagers.

"Would you *pul-eaze* cut it out," Esther pleaded. "And open that bottle. What if Linda and Malcolm caught us."

Darryl relaxed his grip and walked to the counter next to his wife. He rummaged through their miscellaneous drawer, so vital to every kitchen, and found the old corkscrew his daddy used on holidays and family reunions. The reminder of his father elicited warm memories. But they mixed bitterly with his thoughts of tonight's guests.

"Why do we have to have dinner with them anyway," Darryl groaned. "I'm surprised Malcolm will even come in the house, me being a traitor to the race and all."

"Now don't you two get to arguing tonight," Esther said. "I've worked hard on this dinner and I don't want you to ruin it over some high and mighty political talk. I'm not gonna stand for it tonight, you hear me?"

"It's not my fault, Esther. You know how Malcolm is. He's the one always bringing stuff up, not me."

"Well, just don't pay him no mind, Honey, at least not tonight. Just ignore him. Okay? Please?"

"All right, Esther," Darryl sighed. "When he starts in, I'll just look at your radiant face and smile."

"Thanks," she said, kissing him. "It's like the good book says: 'A soft answer turneth away wrath.'"

WHILE ESTHER tended to the last few details in the kitchen, Darryl went into the den and prepared for Malcolm. He promised not to argue, but he would be damned not to at least hold his ground.

Darryl pulled a pictorial biography of Martin Luther King, Jr. and a collection of essays by conservative editorialist Jeff Dickerson from a shelf at the end of the room and placed them prominently on the coffee table in front of the couch. In the center of the table, he placed William Bennet's *The Book of Virtues*.

On one end table, next to a coaster for Malcolm, he opened Thomas Sowell's book on the damaging effects of favoritism shown blacks in colleges and universities. On the other end table, he stationed a dog-eared copy of James Schlesinger's *The Disuniting of America*, each strategically angled so the evening's dinner guests were certain to notice.

The trenches were dug.

Just as Darryl spotlighted the last revered text, the doorbell rang.

With the home field advantage set, Darryl called out to his wife, "I'll get it, Honey," and proudly gaited to the door to welcome the guests.

"Howdy, howdy, ya'll! Linda, it's so good to see you," Darryl said, accepting her hug and extending his hand to her husband. "Malcolm, you look well."

"As do you, Darryl," Malcolm said stately, returning the handshake. "I see wealth and status agree with you."

Darryl burst into a hearty laugh. "They sure do . . . if I knew 'em!" he blurted boisterously, slapping Malcolm on the shoulder. "Come on in and sit down. Can I get you some wine or a beer?"

"A glass of wine would be nice," Linda said.

"Beer for me, old man," Malcolm followed, pausing near the couch, not far away from the opened scriptures on the side tables. "So how does it feel to be an Olympic high roller, hobnobbing with CEOs and corporate capitalists?"

"Good so far," Darryl called from the kitchen. "I'm hoping something will rub off." He poured the Zinfandel into one of his aunt's good crystal glasses, but served the Michelob Light in the bottle.

Esther turned down the heat on all the food and hurried to the den to see her dear friend. "Hey, girl, come here and give me a hug."

"Look at you, little momma," Linda answered, placing a hand on Esther's belly. "Starting to show some." They both squealed in delight and retreated arm in arm to the kitchen, anxious to gossip about everyone they knew.

Darryl sat on the hearth across from Malcolm, leaving the couch vacant for the ladies, should they join them. Disappointed his trap had been foiled, Darryl hoped for another chance during dessert back here in the den.

"So how is it going with AOC?" Malcolm started amicably. "Does the greed and bigotry ever become unnerving as you write million dollar policies for a bunch of white companies?"

What an asshole, Darryl thought. But he kept his anger in check.

"Up to this point, I've found the Olympic committee to be very businesslike and extremely efficient."

"Oh, I'm sure they are," Malcolm said. "After all, they're earning two and three hundred thousand dollar salaries. Except for Victoria Milton. What's she paid? The figure seems to have slipped my mind . . . what is it, uh, five hundred thousand dollars?"

He knew damn well what she was paid. Everyone did. The *Atlanta Journal* had printed the salaries of all the executive directors on the front page. Nearly all of AOC's financial dealings were public record, and Darryl knew Malcolm kept close track of the data as ammunition in his bitter war on corporate America.

Malcolm was the president of the Atlanta chapter of the NAACP, as his father had been over a decade before, and as his grandfather had been years before that. His bloodline had long distrusted whites, especially those in corporate or management positions.

Both men, though, had experienced prejudice at the same high school and, later, in the same marketplace. Both had fathers who could not attend any school or church they pleased, and whose families had suffered the cruelty of prejudice and hate.

The argument between them was philosophical. One saw government involvement in society's economics, education, and domestic interactions as the hope for his race, and fervently lobbied to expand the government's role in insuring opportunity. The other regarded his people individually, each charged with the personal responsibility for his or her own actions and each representing the best sole guarantee of a prosperous future. In his mind, Dr. King's dream of equal opportunity and the lawful protection against racial discrimination had been misrepresented by some intending to *guarantee* advancement under the law *because* of race.

"What could she possibly do to earn a half-a-million dollars?" Malcolm continued. "They never would've paid a black woman that kind of money for the job."

"Maybe if it was a black woman that got the Olympics for this town, they would," Darryl retorted. "And you know Colonel Powell, director of security, is black."

"Oh, they have to have tokens, Darryl. Remember, the world is watching."

Darryl knew this discussion led to trouble, and thinking of his wife, he changed the subject.

"Boy, doesn't that pork roast smell good! She's made those homemade biscuits like she used to make for breakfast, too. Malcolm, ain't it funny how the longer we're married, the fewer mornings I see biscuits for breakfast."

"You know, Linda's the same way," Malcolm chuckled. "When we first got married, I woke up to the smell of bacon and eggs and pancakes every morning, and every night it was a ham or chops or spaghetti with homemade meatballs. Oooh-eee, those were the days."

"Don't you know it," Darryl agreed, slapping Malcolm on the knee. "What happened? Did we just get old and fat so they don't love us any more?"

"Don't know, brother. Guess it's just not the same fire."

"Well, it ain't because there's no log burning inside on cold winter nights!"

They both roared.

"Ya'll come on, the food's on the table," Esther called from the kitchen.

The two men rose to join their wives in the dining room. Linda commented on the beautiful table, and Darryl's eyes cut to Esther, who did not say a word.

Darryl sat at one end of the mahogany table and Esther at the other, closest to the kitchen. Malcolm and Linda sat across from each other along the shorter diameter. All four friends talked jovially about their adventures in high school and about work and their family plans. Esther beamed as she gave a progress report on the baby growing inside her, amidst Darryl's jokes that it better look like him.

"I've noticed the mailman hanging 'round a lot lately," he teased.

"That's because he knows how to treat a lady," she shot back.

On several occasions, Malcolm made comments about the new Republican Congress, prodding Darryl for a reaction. Each time, Esther looked at her husband intensely, and he would just grin widely, shake his head once or twice, and rave again about the roast or the vegetables or the wine. Malcolm's quip about a balanced budget amendment being coldhearted toward the poor made Darryl squirm but not respond, other than complimenting Esther on her sensational casserole.

Over key lime pie and cinnamon coffee sweetened with Kahlúa, conversation turned to plans for the coming weekend, and the trouble started.

"So, what are you two doing this weekend?" Linda asked, taking another bite of pie.

"Darryl and I are working on where this child's gonna sleep," Esther said. "We've just about finished painting the walls. Next is the wallpaper trim along the ceiling, little bears holding hands. They're so cute."

"I'll be glad to get it done," Darryl said. "And get this little precious snoring away in her crib!"

"You mean, *his* crib," Esther corrected her husband.

He just smiled back.

"Well, if you need a break, my friend, come join us downtown for a march," Malcolm said. "It'd do you good to get out with some *real* working folks doing something for a *real* cause."

Esther looked nervously at Darryl who tried to grin again, but he had already expounded the virtues of her pie, its crust, the coffee, the cinnamon, the napkins, and the candles on the table.

Darryl shifted in his chair. "And, what cause might that be," he said, feeling in complete control of his emotions, but neglecting the influence of the wine and the Kahlúa.

"I'm sure it's something great," Esther interjected. "Has anyone heard what the weather's supposed to do Saturday?"

"The disgrace of our state flag," Malcolm said, seeming to have not heard Esther.

"Our state flag?" Darryl repeated, incredulously.

"Yes. I am leading a march to the Coca-Cola Building where the Georgia flag flies every day, protesting the company's humiliating endorsement of the memory of slavery."

"You can't be serious," Darryl said. "You think Coca-Cola wants to endorse the memory of slavery?"

"They certainly do, every time they fly the Georgia flag."

Darryl thought he had heard it all, but as much as he might have liked to let this one go for his wife's sake, he just couldn't help himself.

Malcolm continued. "We plan to put pressure on Coca-Cola to discontinue flying the flag and to convince the state legislature to purge the Confederate symbol from our state's emblem. The stars and crossbars of the Confederacy are a hideous reminder of a dark ruthless time, and everyone repulsed by the inhumanity of slavery should join us in our mission to erase this blot."

"Sounds like a lot of hoopla for a flag," Darryl said, trying not to sound patronizing. "I mean, I wish our flag didn't have the stars and crossbars, but, Malcolm, there are so many issues that are a lot more important than some flag, crossbars or no crossbars."

"I know you're outta touch, Darryl. But, the stance your taking here is unbelievable," Malcolm said. "African-Americans throughout the state are in an uproar over the status of our flag. You'd have to be living in a cave not to know that."

"I'm ashamed to say you may be right." Darryl looked down at the few graham cracker crumbs remaining on his plate.

"Ashamed!" Malcolm said. "What the hell do you mean by that?"

Esther tried to signal her husband to stop before things got out of hand. "Linda, have you been to Phipps since they put all that marble on the floor?" she asked.

"I sure have," Linda said, playing along. "Can you believe it? And the brass railings, it's just fabulous. Malcolm's favorite is NikeTown with all the Michael Jordan stuff."

"Oh, Darryl's too," Esther agreed. "He goes nuts over the Carolina section." The two friends laughed, hoping to restore congeniality to the room.

The men disregarded their wives' appeal for civility.

"That's right," Darryl continued. "I'm ashamed. I'm ashamed that people of my race would get so worked up over a damn flag when we've got fourteen-year-old black girls thinking it's no big deal to get pregnant. I'm ashamed my young brothers and sisters aren't finishing school, but dropping out to sell drugs and mug folks and steal cars. I'm ashamed of all the fathers that ditch their wives and kids and don't pay a red cent in support, just leaving their own flesh and blood to fend for themselves. Now that's bad, brother! And it's our own fault, too!

"Our fault!" Malcolm screamed. "Our fault for what?" He crept to the edge of his seat.

"For blaming it on being poor!" Darryl yelled back. "Or for not having a daddy or not going to this school or that school! Hell, in my neighborhood, everybody was poor and lots of kids didn't have a dad or a mom, but we damn well knew right from wrong."

Darryl rubbed his forehead, his tongue feeling the lubrication of the evening's alcohol.

"I'm sorry Malcolm, but you're wrong. I think it is wrong for the leadership of a great organization like the NAACP to keep on promoting marches for things like a flag when kids are killing kids in the streets over gangs and drugs and nobody's fussing at the parents, telling 'em to get off their butts and take responsibility for their families."

"You know damn well, Darryl," Malcolm wailed, getting up from his chair. "The NAACP works every day to get Washington to give us the money we need to fight these urban problems. With the new Congress, we'll be lucky to pay the power bill at the headquarters."

"That's my point," Darryl fumed right back. "It's not Washington's job to keep girls from getting pregnant. It's our job, right here in the neighborhood." He also stood now, pounding his fist against the table with each word. "If we'd do our job as adults and quit looking to someone else for a handout, things could change. Real change!"

116

Malcolm's face flooded dark red. The veins under his skin bulged from dangerously high pressure, and his shirt turned wet with perspiration. He held his right hand out in front of Darryl's face, almost hitting his nose as he waved it frantically under protest.

"I knew you were no better than a damned overcooked white man from the first time I met you. A no-good traitor to your own people, just a damn dipped cone from the Dairy Queen, that's what you are. A high-flighting capitalist loaf of Wonder Bread masquerading as black. The problem with you, Darryl, is you ain't got no heart for *real* people, with *real* suffering."

"Don't pull that shit on me, Malcolm," Darryl shrieked, pounding against the white tablecloth. "I grew up just as poor as anybody. You cheating thugs are the ones keeping our people in chains, not white people. It's your programs that make the patients of a good black doctor wonder if he's really any good, or just a nigger that some school gave a diploma so's they could meet the federal quota. And you expect us to listen when you preach what's good for us! Well, your message that we're downtrodden and pitiful and en-titled to this job and this program just don't hold water any more. The Declaration of Independence says 'All men are created equal,' and it's time we act like it. Our problems are *our* problems and it's not somebody else's fault. It's time to stand up and do something for ourselves. *Your* heyday is over, my friend . . . done, killed, and buried! Praise the Lord for that!"

The two men glared at one another, leaning over the table, nose to nose. The sudden quiet in the room had the two women still seated at the table quivering with fears of what might come next.

The only sound was heavy breathing coming from the two boxers standing toe to toe in the center of the ring.

After several minutes of silence, Malcolm growled through clenched teeth. "Esther, thank you for the good food. Linda, get your coat, we're going home."

The two men still did not move for another minute or two, seemingly paralyzed with fury, cursing one another with each exhalation, daring the other to blink first.

Finally, after Linda returned with the coats, Malcolm turned away from Darryl and stormed out the front door.

WITH THE ADDITIONAL POLICIES pouring in, Sylvia found keeping her corner of the office tidy next to impossible. Still, she sought to maintain the decorum suitable for a man of her uncle's growing esteem.

She checked her watch again. Since coming to work for her uncle, she had never seen him arrive at the office past eight o'clock.

It was now nine.

After a lot of internal debate, she decided to go ahead and call, to see if everything was all right. But just as she was picking up the phone, a well-dressed gentleman waltzed in carrying a bouquet of flowers.

"I'm looking for Sylvia," Janis said, clean and polished and in an upbeat mood. He turned his head slightly to one side and grinned down at the pretty girl behind the desk. "That wouldn't be you, now, would it?"

She blushed a bit. "Why, yes it is."

Janis swiftly thrust out the bunch of exotic flowers. "For you, my lady, with my most sincere appreciation. You have single-handedly ensured the success of the 1996 Olympic Games." He even bowed at the waist.

"Why, I . . . I don't know what to say," Sylvia stuttered.

"My card, miss," Janis said regally, as if presenting himself to a member of the royal family. "I am assistant director of finance for AOC, and you, my dear, have been indispensable in arranging the liability policies for our immense construction projects underway. I don't know if you realize it, but we are in the midst of the greatest renovation Atlanta has ever seen. And, I am taking it upon myself to recognize a few of the heroes behind the scenes of the Olympic Games."

"Why, Mr. Janis, I just don't know what to say. I never expected to have someone award me with, with anything. Especially not a beautiful arrangement."

"My dear," he continued. "These in no way approach your eloquence. On the contrary, they are only a small token of our esteem for the mastery you've displayed in building our monuments of global peace and prosperity."

"Really, Mr. Janis, I'm overwhelmed," Sylvia said.

"No, my dear girl, it is I who is overwhelmed by your accomplishments. You see, my duties also encompass the 1996 Olympic Foundation funds for the needy and underprivileged children in the metro-Atlanta area. You may not be aware, but the underwriters of the policies you have arranged will donate a portion of their proceeds to the Olympic Foundation, of which I am in charge. Sylvia, not only are you insuring construction, you are touching the tender lives of thousands of children."

"Oh my, I had no idea." Sylvia touched her hand to her lips. She felt a rush of pride swell within her chest. "Well, Mr. Janis, I can't thank you enough for the lovely gift. But, I'm especially glad you came by and told me about the wonderful things the foundation will be doing. If there's ever anything I can do to help, I hope you'll call me."

Bingo!

Switch from mock pompous grandeur to seemingly off-the-cuff. "Well, Sylvia, if you have a few minutes I'd be most interested to see just how you've managed such an array of information. The electronic network must be a real bear."

"Oh no, Mr. Janis," Sylvia said. "Not at all. Really, it's all quite simple. Here, let me show you. Come around and sit here so you can see."

She turned the screen around, and after inquiring about Janis' comfort, his desire for coffee, and if there were glare from his vantage, she proceeded through the menus for client information, policy outlines, benefit schedules, liability limitations, and insured-worker data forms. It was there, the screen displaying information entered about the personal history of individual construction workers, that Janis focused.

"I didn't realize the enormous amount of information you maintain on each insured worker," Janis said. "Did you enter all this information yourself?"

"Quite a bit," Sylvia replied. "Not all of it. We've expanded the staff after winning the AOC bid, and they did most of the work on data entry." She got up from her chair. "Would you like to see where they all work?"

"Oh no," Janis said quickly. "I wouldn't dream of interrupting them. Really, I've taken too much of your time already."

"No bother. I've enjoyed your visit."

The phone rang. Janis looked at his watch.

He listened to Sylvia answer a call from a foreman at the aquatic venue construction site where a worker had been slightly injured by a falling pipe wrench. She handled the questions professionally and connected the man with the claims manager.

"One last question," Janis implored.

"Yes?"

"I see you've proceeded through several submenus . . ." Janis said. *Each protected by an access code.* ". . . to retrieve the different information here. It must be cumbersome to research a specific claim, for instance, like for the gentleman who just called. You must be an expert at tabbing through menus."

"I'm sure it appears that way, Mr. Janis. But actually each main category has an access code that takes me directly to the screen I need." Sylvia typed in a series of numbers and a policy appeared for the aquatic center, a curved modern-looking facility seating almost fifteen thousand people and costing seventeen and a half million dollars to construct.

"Wow!" Janis proclaimed. "What if you needed to access a particular construction worker's data sheet, say the poor guy injured at the aquatic site."

He glued his attention to the number pad on the right of the keyboard.

"No problem," she said, typing 24 27 35 44 55 . . .

". . . *twenty-four, twenty-seven, thirty-five, good they're in ascending order, then two fours and two fives . . . twenty-four, twenty-seven, thirty-five, two fours and fives, got it . . .*"

"That's truly fascinating," Janis said, as the information on the worker appeared on the screen. "Gosh, I've taken up too much of your time. I've really got to be running. If I could just see your boss for a second."

"He should be here any minute," Sylvia said. "If you'd like to wait."

"Yeah, sure," Janis said, wanting to write the numbers down quickly before he forgot.

"You can take a seat over in the alcove," Sylvia said, as Janis worked his way around the desk. "Thanks so much for the flowers."

"The what?" Janis replied, truly stunned.

Leaving Sylvia to her routine, Janis looked up from the *U.S. News and World Report* he was pretending to read when he heard Darryl Clements' voice coming down the hall. Not wanting to appear anxious, he did not get up from his chair immediately. Instead, he maintained acting as an executive who normally hurried through a hectic schedule, but had a welcome open morning to make important "thank-you" calls and tie up a few loose ends.

He stretched and sported a casual yawn, contagious enough to make him yawn again.

He pretended not to hear Darryl's conversation with Sylvia.

"Sorry I'm late," Darryl apologized. "Bad night last night. Esther almost left me." Seeing the look of despair on his niece's face, he quickly added, "It's okay now. I convinced her again I'm still the man of her dreams. I just promised not to talk to anyone in her presence ever again without her permission."

Sylvia looked confused.

"It's a long story," he said, shifting through the mail she just handed him. "Just take my word for it, you don't want to know,"

"Okay. Oh, a Mr. Janis is here from AOC to see you," Sylvia said. "He says he'll only need a minute."

Darryl frowned at his watch.

"He's a really nice man. Look at the flowers he brought me."

Darryl raised his eyebrows suspiciously.

Sylvia read his mind. "Would you quit being an uncle! He was just saying thanks to the whole office for our work on the construction insurance policies, that's all."

It was 9:30 and Darryl was supposed to be at the IBM Tower in half an hour. He walked over to the man engrossed in the magazine and extended his hand.

"Mr. Janis, I'm Darryl Clements. Sylvia said you needed to see me?"

Janis acted startled and looked up from the page in front of him, that could have been upside down for all he knew, and clasped Darryl's hand eagerly and firmly.

"Yes, sir, Mr. Clements," he said. "Thanks for agreeing to meet me."

"I have to be at the IBM Tower at ten, I could see you then if it's more convenient."

"Oh that's quite all right, Mr. Clements," Janis said. "If you could, sir, I just need your signature on a couple papers for the Olympic Foundation account."

"Yeah, okay," Darryl replied. "How 'bout following me into my office. I need to collect a few things for the meeting."

Janis followed, obediently.

"Now what's this account about, and how can I help?" Darryl asked, quickly scanning his office for the needed materials.

"Well, actually, sir, this is just a bookkeeping matter we may never really need," Janis explained.

"Come again?"

"You see, the life insurance policies your company has written for unmarried construction workers with no immediate family have included an option for these individuals to assign their benefits to the charitable trust of the 1996 Olympic Foundation, should they meet with the tragedy of an untimely death. I'm sure the chances of anything so disastrous happening are few and far between, but just in case, we are delighted that, out of the kindness of their hearts, some workers wish their insurance benefits to help needy children in the Atlanta area—quite an admirable act of humanitarianism, wouldn't you say, sir?"

"Yeah, sure," Darryl mumbled, searching through stacks of paper for this week's report for Mrs. Milton.

"Since you have distributed, with remarkable skill I might add, the life insurance policies for the construction workers across nearly seventy-five different underwriting companies, as prescribed by the AOC specs, we in the financial department have set up a single account into which all benefits would be deposited should an unlucky and family-less soul meet his Maker while under our employ."

"Sounds good to me, where do I sign?"

"I've marked the documents with yellow arrow labels."

Darryl quickly penned his signature five times, thanked Janis for coming to his office and for bringing the generous gift to his secretary, then hurried down the hall, hoping he would not be late for the meeting.

JANIS RETURNED to his NSX parked in the sun. He removed the T-tops and put them in the trunk, wanting to enjoy the unseasonably mild wind.

The morning had been profitable.

He headed west toward town on Ponce de Leon Avenue, stopping at a BP station for gas and to make the call to Miami.

He pumped the handle a few more times until the digital readout stopped on a multiple of five; he hated loose ends and odd cents on gasoline charges. Besides, it made checking his monthly statement a snap, never having to look twice as long as the total bill ended in a multiple of five.

He pulled his car around to the phone booth on the side of the gas station and dialed the Miami number, inserting the necessary number of quarters into the slot. The phone rang twice.

"Hello?" It was a female voice with an Hispanic accent.

"Mr. Miras, please," Janis said blandly.

"*Si, un momento, por favor.*"

A few seconds later a suave voice, smooth and sultry, came on the line. "*Si*, this is *señor* Miras."

"I'm ready for you," Janis said. "Now."

"I understand," Miras replied. "How urgent are your plans? My daughter is having a few friends over this evening and I'd like to be here with her." His monotone Latino sentences were slow and concise.

"It would be best for you to see her tonight, because you will not be home for several weeks."

"Good. Then I will leave tomorrow morning," Miras said, sophistication belying his profession. "When should we meet?"

"I'll have a packet at the front desk when you check in," Janis said. "You did receive the information?"

"Yes, last week. I have a few suggestions, but basically it will be similar to our work here," Miras said.

"Only you will *personally* see to all of this business."

"Yes, as agreed," his calm manner rising from years of stoneheartedness. Perhaps he showed no emotion because his vocation had drained his last drop of sentiment like the scores of morticians who siphoned the blood from his countless victims.

"Until tomorrow, then," Janis said.

"*Si, manana.*"

Miras hung up the phone and returned to the deck overlooking a turquoise and emerald bay, and his awaiting ten-year-old son and twelve-year-old daughter. Under the shade

of a tan canvas umbrella, the three resumed an engrossed
battle to monopolize real estate, and it was Papa's turn.

TEN

Afternoons like this one, temperatures in the mid-sixties with fresh crisp breezes, giant oak trees heavy with bright orange leaves, sent Mark daydreaming. As he sat at the stoplight at the corner of Ponce de Leon and Piedmont Avenues, Mark turned up the volume to one of his favorite Eagles songs, "Wasted Time." He sang along with Don Henley's rugged tenor and saw images of a jubilant closing ceremony marking the end of a safe and peaceful Olympic competition. There'd been not so much as a frown from anyone, save maybe athletes finishing fourth in their events.

With the Korean impasse creatively navigated, the FCI units were busy scanning cheekbones and gonial angles, and Mark's attitude had vastly improved in contrast to the previous week.

He zigzagged to Techwood Drive and turned south, heading toward the Olympic dorm complex. Out his right window was Grant Field, home of the Georgia Tech 1990 national champion Yellow Jacket football team, and where not long ago workers pulled up the Astroturf field and

planted genetically engineered grass sod. Two blocks to
the west, cool gusts whipping through the midtown canyon
of buildings batted a Georgia state flag in front of the Coca-
Cola complex.

Mark pulled into the parking lot of the athletic dormitory village construction site just as Glen Frey's voice took
over the *Hell Freezes Over* compact disc. Mark loved most
everything done by the Eagles. He turned off the engine,
tilted his head back against the headrest, and took a sixty-
second vacation, humming along with closed eyes.

Midway through the second verse, Mark's AOC-issue car
phone blurted its irritating ring that had frazzled his nerves
many times before; there was no getting used to the obnoxious signal.

"Damn, that thing!"

Mark shut Glen off, and quickly punched the green send
button before the confounded alarm could scream a second time.

"Mark Townsend," he said.

"Mark, Jerry. How's it going?"

Amazing, these car phones. A call from D.C. sounded
like it came from across the street. "Careful, Jair, this line is
open."

"Wish it mattered. I'm afraid you're going to be disappointed, I found zilch. Nothing, not a damn thing. This
guy isn't in any file with FBI, CIA, secret services, the Penta-
gon, or any state penal system. Only the usual financial stuff,
but that's it." The voice paused a few seconds, waiting for a
response. "If he asks for a loan, my bet he's good for up to
a half a mil."

Mark's mind raced for other options.

"Well I guess I should be glad he doesn't have a record,"
Mark finally said.

"You sound disappointed."

"It's not that, Jerry, it's just bizarre he doesn't show up
on somebody's data. Can you imagine going all through
school at Yale, working at all the Yaley-type summer jobs—

you know, banks, law firms, financial consulting groups, the government—and never having had a background check run? It's just damn strange."

"Or, damn careful," Jerry interjected. "Sounds to me like someone hiding his past. Then again, maybe you're just making a big deal over nothing. Hell, if you don't have a reason to be worried, don't make one up."

"It's my job to be curious. If he gets blackmailed and ends up embarrassing AOC, it's my ass on the line. I hate surprises, and something tells me we're in for one with this guy."

"Anything else you need me to look into?"

"Can't say now, bud," Mark said. Above the roof of the athletic dorms, opposite the parking lot from Mark's car, was a worker suspended ten stories high from what appeared to be a string threaded over a steal pulley at the end of a crane.

"Well if I know you," Jerry said, "and I do, better than I'd like, you'll get this guy's number before it's all said and done."

"I hope so," Mark replied, slumping over the steering wheel so he could get a better view of the worker, who now leaned over the short wall of the bucket holding him so he could grab a reddish-brown girder running along the crest of the roof. Mark thought, that is one crazy son of a bitch.

"Just don't lose any sleep over it," Jerry said. "By the way, how much you getting these days, anyway?"

"'Bout four hours a night," Mark answered, concentrating on the scant details he had uncovered about Janis' past.

"Not sleep, you dickhead!" Jerry said, laughing gregariously.

The insinuation did not register. Mark's attention stayed keyed on the worker perched over the roof. The man slipped trying to stabilize his swaying bucket against the girder, flailing violently with his free hand until it found one of the three chains triangulating off the main cable down to the sides of the bucket. The brief panic disappeared as instantly as it rose, and the worker resumed his precarious stance, this time one leg secured inside the bucket and one dangling over the outside.

"All in a day's work," Mark figured.

"Huh?" Jerry said.

"Nothing, bud. Thanks."

Mark hung up the phone and opened the notebook sitting on the seat next to him and logged in the time and the essence of the conversation with Jerry from Justice. He was careful with the details of his personal notes, another habit ingrained from the secret service.

Peculiarly enough, the potential powder kegs of other directors did not bother Mark nearly as much as the mystery surrounding Janis, the secrets of his unknown past exceedingly more dangerous than the mountains of personal filth already uncovered among the AOC executive council. In what was becoming the *Peyton Place* of the AOC, Mark discovered one of the directors was recently divorced after an eighteen-year history of wife abuse—a prime target for extortion. The brother-in-law of another leading official was in jail for opening fire on customers in a Pizza Hut in Greenville, South Carolina, in 1988, killing two and wounding seven for no apparent reason other than his bill was overcharged by three dollars and thirty-two cents. Then there was the assistant director who was sleeping with his daughter's boyfriend of four years, a tangy twist that prompted Hank to cover his face with both hands and fume, "Now I *have* heard it all!"

None of these details bothered Mark. He had dealt with worse, or at least variations on the same theme, during his tenure as a secret service agent in the Sodom and Gomorrah of the United States. Affairs, abuses, extortions, thefts, lies, even suspiciously timed suicides were all part of the routine decay in Washington, D.C.

Mark valued information. Like a speculative investor risking millions in the market, he reveled in discovering nuances and undetected subtleties of character that provided him the edge in performing his job. And, Mark's investigatory acumen was keen, for in Washington, where the rules were played according to Darwin's book of social hierarchy, he had survived fanatical schemes both inside and outside the White House.

Walking along the sidewalk encircling the nearly complete dormitory on the southern most edge of the complex, Mark gazed up at the first of four buildings that would house four thousand visiting athletes. He considered the sixty-two million dollars going into this one project, a mere pittance compared to the 1.7 billion dollar budget of the games. Not far away on Hemphill Avenue, over eleven million dollars was spent to house six hundred fifty athletes; on Eighth Street, twenty-three million dollars for thirteen hundred athletes; on Turner Place, twelve million dollars for eight hundred athletes; and on Center Street, eleven and a half million dollars for seven hundred athletes.

The enormous responsibility for these competitors, many traveling to the United States for the first time in their young lives, bore down on Mark like the tons of concrete being hoisted into the air on its way to becoming another piece in the architecturally impermeable barrier against the outside world.

Thousands of athletes.

Millions of visitors.

Mark felt lightheaded for a moment, squatting near the sidewalk for a few seconds in order to keep from falling down.

No, he thought, the mystery surrounding Janis was unacceptable.

There in the shadow of the twelve-story redbrick structure, Mark recommitted himself to revealing the truth behind *every* director, no matter how clandestine, no matter how inexplicable. Every detail had to be investigated, every lead followed. Any possible tie to a radical group or lunatic terrorists had to be avowed.

The possibility for disaster was simply too terrific.

MARIA SAT ON THE BED while Misty finished drying her pixie-cut red hair.

About an hour before, Adrianne had consoled her with a promise to put her on a bus back to Mona the next day. Adrianne would talk to Mona in the evening and arrange the trip. Maria felt at ease knowing she would be back in Miami by tomorrow. Adrianne had even gone as far as giving the girl a hug before plopping her in Misty's room to pass leisurely the afternoon hours.

After a little small talk, Misty resumed her sundry preparations for the imminent night shift. The eighteen-year-old girl bent over at the waist brushing her hair back over her forehead.

"It took me a while to fit in, too," Misty screamed at Maria over the din of the hair dryer. "I ran away twice before realizing it wasn't so bad. You'll see. Adrianne is good to us."

"Well, I'm going home," Maria said softly, her eyes scanning the room.

Clearly, the same decorator responsible for the red room on the first floor had trod up the stairs and down the hall to the fourth door on the right.

Apparently exhausted by red, he became reinvigorated with lavender, painting it on the walls, carpeting it on the floors, quilting it over the bed, pillows, and dust ruffle, and draping it over the two floor-to-ceiling windows facing the oaks in the front yard. The room looked as if an army of California raisins, ill from the arduous march deep in the South, had thrown up everywhere.

"There," Misty said with a heavy sigh. She replaced the hair dryer on the shelf, then collapsed in a backward swan-dive onto the bed. "I don't think I slept a wink last night. Of course, I *did* have Alex."

She bounced back up on her feet, standing naked in front of the mirror on the wall above her dresser and fluffing her hair with her fingertips.

"I'm always restless after Alex. He's *sooo fine*, I'd almost be willing to see him for free." She laughed out loud. "But Adrianne won't have none of that. 'Got to pay them bills!' she always says. Good ole Adrianne. Always looking out for us!"

"Who's Alex?" Maria asked. "Your boyfriend?"

"Are you kidding?" Misty laughed even harder than before. "He's not my boyfriend, but I make him think he is. He's a regular, Honey. You'll see, regulars are the best kind. They treat you right. You want to take real good care of regulars, to keep 'em coming back for more."

"You're a prostitute?" Maria asked.

"Honey, don't say it like that. I'm in the therapy business, personal entertainment for troubled hearts." Misty sounded almost convincing. "I caress my clients warmly, tenderly, and give them something they need, something they can't find anywhere else . . . well, not like me anyway. I take pride in what I do, after all, *I am the best!*"

"But, what do your parents think?" Maria asked.

"My parents?" she said, flexing her legs. "Babydoll, my so-called father started having his way with me when I was ten and he didn't stop to take a breath till I left at thirteen. My mother was so drunk she didn't know the difference. I don't think she would've cared had she known . . . she just lived for the next shot of booze, no matter where it came from."

"I could never sleep with a stranger," Maria said slowly, looking at the floor.

"Honey, didn't you ever hug someone you hardly knew? Didn't your folks ever have over friends, you didn't really know them or care anything about them, but you gave them a hug anyway? Now didn't you?"

Maria thought for a minute. She could not remember hugging anyone outside her immediate family. She shook her head 'no.'

"Well, that's all it is, Honey," Misty explained, not paying any attention to Maria's response. "Just like giving someone a big hug. Only these guys really need us. You know, it's like we're the only happiness they have in the whole wide world."

She jumped back up on the bed with a nail file and sculpted her long perfect nails. "I don't know about you, little girl, but I feel it's real important to help other people. Like, if we would all just help each other a little more, this world would be a lot more happier place."

Misty opened the drawer in the nightstand next to the bed and pulled out two bottles of nail polish, one almost blood red and one crystal clear.

"Here," she said handing the red bottle to her visitor. "Use this one first and let it dry good, then paint on the clear to make the color deeper."

"Oh, I don't want to take your polish . . ." Maria started.

"Just go on. Lord knows you could use some sprucing up, girl."

Maria shifted herself on the bed and sat cross-legged while she methodically applied the red polish to her left index fingernail.

"Maria, you got to shake it good first," Misty instructed.

"Oh yeah," Maria said, blushing. "Guess its been a while since I painted my nails."

Maria remembered once when she was about seven or eight, sitting on her mother's bed, trying on necklaces and clip-on earrings while her mother dressed for a fund-raiser at the church. She could hear her mother's voice telling her the silver-and-turquoise set looked fashionable, but the oversized green pearls made her look like an Egyptian princess. Pain from the loss swelled inside again, but not as bad as before.

Misty turned back to face the mirror and unscrewed the cap off a tube of mascara. She leaned forward, close to the mirror, and brushed the blue tinted liquid onto her upper eyelashes. She held her mouth opened wide as she applied the thick makeup as if her lips were tethered to her eyelids.

"Don't you think it's good to help people out, Maria?" Misty continued. "You know, people in need, I mean in *real* need. You wouldn't just turn your back on someone who really needed you, someone who lives a whole week just to be with you, someone yearning just to hear your voice, to feel your touch." She swayed back and forth like she was rocking in a swing. Then, she opened her eyes suddenly and stared riveted at Maria. "You wouldn't just say, 'Sorry, bud. See ya later,' would you Maria?"

"Well, I guess not," she hesitated. "Not when you put it like that. But, I would just . . . just . . . *talk* or something . . . I mean, try to make them feel important."

Misty turned away from the mirror and laughed at the naive girl seated on the edge of the bed.

"Honey, there are times when *talk* just won't cut it. Haven't you ever heard of *body language*? Believe me, these guys have heard enough talk. That's all they've got all their life . . . talk from their mothers, talk from their wives, talk from their boss. They're sick of talk. Talk ain't gonna help them one bit. They need to *touch* somebody. Somebody warm and caring. Somebody sweet and gentle, who understands what they need . . . and likes giving it to them!"

There was a knock on the door, and the pretty blonde who Maria had met with Miguel at the front door stuck her head into the room.

"Miss Maria," she drawled. "Adrianne wants you downstairs in her office, jack-quick. She has Mona on the phone from Miami."

"She does?" Maria said, jumping up.

"Come on, Sugar" the blonde said, "I'll show you where her office is at."

Maria bolted toward the door, completely forgetting about the polish drying on her fingers. She skipped every other step, bounding down the stairs and through two or three rooms before coming to Adrianne's office near the back of the house.

ADRIANNE FAKED a look of pity as she handed the phone to Maria.

"It's Mona, dear," she said sadly. "She wants to talk to you."

Maria eagerly took the phone. "Mona, is that you?"

"Hey there, Sweetcakes. How you doin'?"

"Oh Mona, it's so good to hear your voice. I've been wanting to call you ever since Miguel brought me here. He had to leave and I'm here talking with Misty in her room . . . it's all purple! You wouldn't believe it, Mona! You just gotta see it! I can't wait to see you tomorrow. Adrianne said she'd put me on a bus early in the morning so I could be there before dinner time. Okay?"

"Maria . . ."

"I could just walk from the bus station if you already have plans, I don't mind."

"Maria," Mona said, trying to break in.

"Just where is the bus station, anyway? Is it far? 'Cause I can walk a long way, no problem."

"Maria," Mona said again. "Sweetcakes, listen to me. You know I'd take you if I could . . ."

Slowly, the words began to sink in.

". . . but, I'm just so busy here, with my job and Miguel. And, my place is so small. Besides, I wouldn't be no good at raising a kid . . ."

"Oh, please, Mona, please let me come live with you!"

"Maria, I just can't have someone else here with me, you know . . ."

"I promise to be good," Maria pleaded, tears rolling down her bronze cheeks. "I won't be any trouble, really. And I'm a good cook, too. My mother taught me all kinds of stuff. And sew! You name it, mister, I can sew circles around the best of them. Please, Mona. Please! You gotta let me come back. You're my home, Mona. You're all I got!"

"Now, Maria. You'll be just fine there with Adrianne. She's an old friend of mine, and I know she's going to treat you right. And you'll have all the other girls there to help take care of you, too."

"I don't want anybody else, Mona. I just want you. Can't I come live with you, please? I'm real small, I don't eat much, and I'll work . . .yeah, I'll pay rent, you know, pay my own way. Please, I promise not to be a burden. I just gotta come home . . ."

The pleas crescendoed into uncontrollable sobs.

For a few seconds, there was not a sound from the other end.

"Sweetcakes," Mona said, her voice cracking for the first time. "I'm just no good for you. It was sure good getting to know you, though. Take care of yourself, Maria."

The next thing Maria heard was the dial tone.

Her eyes suddenly became dry. She felt as though she had fallen from the sky into an infinite desert, hot, vacant, desolate, burning. She stood motionless against Adrianne's desk, continuing to hold the phone to her ear.

After several minutes, the dial tone faded into an empty hum, as did her hope.

ELEVEN

Colonel Powell shifted uneasily in the audience, swiping away emotion with the back of an index finger as he watched his daughter return to her seat amidst a thunder of rousing ovation in the middle school commons area for what had become a monthly routine—student exhibition night.

Hearing the thrilling applause ricochet off the mauve-painted walls, Hank found it hard to remember why he had been so hesitant to enroll Felicia in the three-year-old charter school, the first of its kind in the state of Georgia, now that he had witnessed his fourth student exhibition program of the fall semester and his daughter's best performance yet.

Felicia's multimedia program on Brazil, using the school's newly acquired computerized projection system to cast her slide sequence and video series onto a billboard-sized screen, had been a huge hit. Her animated coffee bean character created in CorelDRAW software was especially engaging, and her editing of the Copland pieces and PBS clips to convey points on the economic and social challenges facing the emerging South American power showed exceptional insight, not to mention countless hours in the computer lab and in front of the screen at home.

Felicia stood and bowed a second time, the applause continuing long after most hands in the audience began to sting.

Peculiar, how innovation had never intimidated the colonel before. Indeed, he welcomed, even sought out technical advances in his field of surveillance, security, and international negotiation, but when it came to public education, he looked askance at the inventive teaching approach at Hertwig Middle School.

Hank was a little ashamed of himself for having jumped to so many outrageous conclusions. Looking back, he realized his response was quite illogical, given the dismal ranking of the state's primary and secondary academic performance compared with the rest of the nation. Now, with pride radiating from his face, he was thankful he had given the Hertwig faculty their chance.

While Felicia finished answering questions from the panel of four community members designated to review her work, Hank prepared himself for taking his seat on the panel for the following six students.

At Hertwig Middle School, not only were the students graded by their teachers, but also by a panel of professionals from other schools and select lay members from the community, who had been briefed on the expectations of the assignment.

Members of the Hertwig community were expected to do a lot more than join the PTA and contribute to the football boosters.

Several parents and businessmen stopped Hank on his way to the front of the room to express their amazement at his daughter's presentation.

Beaming, Hank accepted their praise.

As he took his place at the rectangular table, he was surprised to find his palms wet with sweat. But, then again, the emotion was genuine. He considered participating in his daughter's education his most important role.

As THE SUN crept closer to the tops of the pines in the western horizon, Bubba Maxwell, Dan "The Man" Humphrey, and Phil Jenner collected their tools along the concrete slab high above Sanford Stadium. From their roost, the view of downtown Athens, Georgia, located an hour or so northeast of Atlanta, was unlike that anywhere else around the small college town. The three crewmen stood near the edge harassing one another about their chances of scoring big with one of the many coeds browsing the storefront windows.

"They'd want me for my worldly experience," boasted Dan, leaning against one of the cement pillars supporting the massive addition to the Bulldog's football stadium, site of the semifinals and finals of Olympic soccer.

"Get outta here, man," argued Bubba. "If they'd want anyone, it'd be me. A *real* man." He beat his fists against his chest. At six feet eight inches, two hundred seventy-three pounds, Bubba towered over his two coworkers. Though his physique was more flab than muscle, he exploited every opportunity to remind them of the fact. Although he had not yet mentioned it again today, Bubba had played one season of college football at the University of South Carolina, before flunking out his freshman year.

"Both you eat shit," Phil said, never being known for his scopic vocabulary. In fact, many of the field men on the construction site would not work with him because they thought he was way beyond stupid, approaching complete mental incompetence.

"All they want to do is ride a horse like me," Phil said, whinnying like a stallion.

"Shut up, bonehead," Bubba shouted. "You're gonna get us all laid off."

"I ain't getting laid off," Phil said, concocting his best comeback. "I'm gettin' laid!" And he spit another brown stream of tobacco juice over the edge, letting the excess dribble down his chin without caring to wipe it off.

Bubba laughed to himself. "You dipwad. If you think any of those babes would look at your skinny ass, you're as crazy as you look."

All three laughed together, and Phil shot another stream onto unsuspecting laborers on their way home.

They had been on the same crew for the same construction company for nearly six months now, almost a world's record for concrete finishers, and certainly the longest time for any of these three drifters. Their unlikely friendship grew from the first day they were together on a job at Duke University in Durham, North Carolina, and had survived countless arguments that raged everyday over domestic political issues about which none of the three had an inkling of knowledge.

Facing west and gazing at the coeds coming to and from the downtown area, the three men continued fantasizing about how much females adored each of them for impossibly outrageous reasons.

So intent was their interest, none of the three noticed they were not alone on their perch.

A fourth man, dressed in blue jeans, a green plaid flannel shirt, and a yellow hard hat, kept to the shadows as he approached the workers from behind. Mirrored Ray Bans hid his black eyes from view as he ceaselessly combed the area for a worker he might have missed.

He carried a pick handle close to his side in his right hand, pausing for a second behind a pillar five feet from the three men, and then, with two quiet steps, moving directly behind the largest one.

Bubba was between his two friends listening to Phil lie about his luck with women when the solid oak handle hit the biggest man precisely at the base of his skull, sending him over the edge of the structure and onto the densely packed soil below.

Phil was speechless, bewildered by his friend's urge to jump.

Dan The Man was still peering over the edge when the pick handle cracked his skull in three pieces, an instant before the ground multiplied that number several fold.

"What the . . .?" Phil started, turning around just as the wooden weapon met him squarely across the bridge of his nose.

The blow buckled his knees, collapsing him into a limp pile on the slab.

The fourth man removed the bandanna from Phil's head, then used the pick handle to shove the dead body off the precipice and rejoin his mangled mass of friends.

The impersonated worker then used the bandanna to wipe the small traces of blood from the slab and tossed the rag onto the melding minds below.

As the sun set out of view, blood trickled from Phil's ears and nose, pooling with fetid puddles of saliva and stale tobacco juice.

IN THE FRONT OF THE ATLANTA CIVIC CENTER, masses of people milled about following a performance by the Atlanta Ballet Company. Maria crossed Pine Street and entered the warmth of the civic center under the safeguard of large numbers of ballet lovers. She was not sure if Adrianne had noticed her absence, but she wanted to become invisible as quickly as possible.

She headed to the ladies' room where she slid into the end stall and balled up to stay warm. She watched the parade of feet pass below the door and overheard ladies chatter excitingly about the performance.

"Bernard looked flat to me," one lady said, wearing brown lace ups and white stockings with embossed stripes. "I bet he's sleeping with the stage crew again. I swear, Elizabeth's greatest challenge is keeping the company from hopping from bed to bed . . ."

"Or dropping to their knees. . ." a voice blurted from the stall next to Maria's.

The woman facing the mirrors laughed. "If all we had to do was direct productions, this business would be simple."

Another set of dress shoes entered Maria's view.

"It's such a waste of beefcake, too! A pity, he's determined to chase after crotches with balls!"

"Almost makes you want to sprout a couple!"

The two women howled, rushing out the door.

Maria inched her way into the bustling crowd in the atrium. She joined a group walking briskly out the front glass doors, keeping pace with them across Piedmont Street and right onto Ralph McGill Boulevard. At Courtland Street, Maria left the others and headed toward the tall buildings of downtown. Alone on the street, she began running to keep warm and to ease her fears of empty dark alleys she passed. Since her stay in the civic center, the temperature seemed to have plummeted another ten or fifteen degrees. With the wind chill whipping through the canyon of buildings, the effect was well below freezing.

Maria ran two long blocks to the Marriot Marquis hotel where she darted through a door held open by a red-and-gray uniformed doorman for a lady in a full-length mink coat and a man in a tuxedo.

She turned up the escalator and hid in a darkly lighted corner on the conference room level of the high-rise structure. Warm air poured from a vent in the floor next to the yellow-and-orange plaid cushioned sofa where she huddled, thawing her frozen toes and fingers. Her ears felt like they would crack off if someone thumped them with a feather.

"What cha doin' there?" an older man called out to Maria from down the hall. He was dressed in a dark gray suit with a name tag over his chest pocket, and he wore white gloves. "You ain't supposed to be here, girlie."

Maria just stared at him, frozen in fear and in fact.

The man kept coming toward her with a stern expression.

"What cha doin' here, I axed ya? Say." Doubt wrinkled his black face.

Maria just stared.

"Come on with me. You ain't staying here." He reached out to grab her arm and Maria jumped up from the sofa, but she was trapped in a corner with no good route of escape.

"Don't be givin' me no trouble, girlie. We have security here. Now come with me." The man held out his hand, indicating he wanted her to take it.

"I was just cold and wanted to warm up a little," Maria stuttered.

"My gosh, girl, you're freezing." The man could feel through his dress gloves the girl's arms were like ice. "What cha doin' here? Where's your parents, Honey?"

"Really, mister, I was about to be on my way when you came. I'll be going now. I didn't mean to bother anyone."

"That's okay, that's okay," the man said. "Here, you set yourself back down here, and I'll be right back. I got a pot of hot water right around the corner. Let me get some hot chocolate. You wait here now." And the man disappeared.

Maria did not know whether to stay near the warmth of the vent or bolt down the escalator before the man returned.

A couple of minutes passed, and all Maria could picture was the man coming back with the police, ready to put her in jail. She was about to run down the escalator when the man appeared, alone, and carrying two steaming Styrofoam cups. His face had changed to a smile, showing large gaps between dark teeth.

"Here ya go, girlie. Drink this."

Maria took one of the cups and sipped the boiling tan liquid. The chill faded.

"What you doing all by yourself? Awful cold night to be out, ain't it?" The black man kneeled several feet away from the sofa, drinking from the second cup.

Maria did not answer. She kept huddled to herself, drinking the hot chocolate.

The man gazed out the huge plateglass windows over-looking the Hilton Hotel across the city. Cars hurled down the one-way street toward the city.

"I can remember being off by myself sometimes, too, when I was about your age. Sometimes just wanting to be alone. I didn't talk much back then either." He spoke quietly, his voice rugged by time.

Maria nodded.

"One thing I learned, though, from my momma. Always stuck with me, through thick and thin. Even when I was by my lonesome, down and out. When I didn't think nobody cared about me no how. She used to tell me no matter where I went, no matter how far away, the Man Up-stairs always was looking down on me. He was there to watch o'er me, comfort me." He paused as limousines stopped below in front of the hotel to let off ladies in jewels and men in patent leather. "Momma said that, she did. She was a wise woman."

"Thanks for the hot chocolate," Maria said getting up and heading toward the escalator.

"Ain't there no one I can call for ya?" the man asked. "Ain't there no one gonna be worried 'bout cha?"

Maria stood still. Finally she shook her head, 'no.'

"Well, you just remember what I told ya. Don't be think-ing you gotta face the world by your lonesome." The old man stood by the window, his eyes twinkling with wisdom.

In a flash, Maria crossed the plush carpet back toward the man and standing on her tiptoes kissed him on the cheek, then ran to the escalator.

Tears flooded his eyes.

"You take care o' yourself now," the man yelled as he watched the young girl go down the conveying staircase. "You just come back here if ya need help. Ya hear me?"

He shook his head and sighed, "Damn world."

IN SECONDS, Maria was back on Courtland Street. The commotion of the city had not subsided. She passed several couples and groups on the sidewalks, bundled in fur, leather, and cashmere. None of them noticed the single young girl in a torn warm-up suit jacket, rushing by with her hands thrust deep into the pockets.

She was still running as she passed by Mick's and a seafood restaurant nestled in the basement of a shopping center. At the top of the hill, International Boulevard intersected with Peachtree Street where the heart of the city beat feverishly well into the morning hours.

Astonished by all the lights, Maria forgot the cold for a second. She stared up at the skyscrapers, her eyes becoming fixed on a black convertible Cadillac thrust sideways into the second-story side of a corner building at the intersection. She had heard of Hard Rock Cafes, but had never seen one. Above the eccentric ornament was a spinning globe with the words, "Save the World."

She lingered in front of the cafe until her eyes caught sight of several horse-drawn carriages lined along the side of the Peachtree Plaza Hotel. She carefully approached a black mare eating oats out of a muzzle-looking sack. The horse was predictably unflappable by the girl, his nerves frazzled dead by ages of traffic and pedestrian noise.

"Hey, Pretty Boy," Maria said, stroking his forehead. He seemed oblivious to her caress, concentrating only on the mush in his mouth.

"His name is Nelson," a young man called to her. He wore a thick leather jacket, and pulled his scarf tighter around his neck. "He's always been a lady killer. He'll stand there for hours without moving and let you pet him. 'Course if I tried it, he'd kick me in the butt, less I had a handful of sugar cubes."

"Is he yours?" Maria asked.

"Sure 'nough. We've been riding together for, uh, let's see now, about ten years." The young man again tightened the scarf around his neck. "Man, time flies by."

He added more oats to the sack.

"Sure is cold out tonight. Puts a damper on my business, too. Not many folks out on the streets on a night like this. It's a good time for a ride, though. Snuggle up under those wool blankets in the back and mosey 'round the city streets—really a lot of fun. How 'bout it, Miss, want a ride?"

"Sure!" Maria said. "That'd be great." She paused and the excitement faded. "How much is it?"

"Twenty-five for the downtown tour. Thirty-five if you're wanting to go out the Buckhead way."

Maria looked down at her feet and was silent.

"No money, huh?" the young man said.

Maria shook her head, no.

"Well, you're in luck, little Miss. I'm having a special tonight, seeings how there's no line out here. A quick tour for you, free of charge."

"Really? You mean it?" She bounced on the ice cubes masquerading as toes.

"You bet. Climb aboard."

As she stepped toward the carriage, a viselike grip on her shoulder choked her momentum in midstep.

"I'm afraid she won't have time this evening, friend," growled the giant Maria had seen outside Adrianne's. "We're running a little late, and need to be getting back home, don't we Maria?"

Maria's face bleached white with terror.

The young man felt suspicious. "Hey, this your dad, or something? Maybe he can go along too."

The brute tightened his grasp even more, threatening to snap Maria's back like a toothpick. "Your offer is mighty nice, boy, but we have to go. Come along, Maria."

He threw the girl into the front seat of the late model Mercedes. She had yet to breathe. He slammed the door shut, hammered the car into drive, and skidded the tires a half a block down International.

TWELVE

Stefanie Gaulding looked up from the keyboard and admired the flowers on her desk, their fragrance just as sweet as it had been the day before, when the gentleman from the finance department stopped by to introduce himself.

His memory prompted her to open the thin drawer in the middle of her desk and check her hair in the compact mirror she always left open next to a box of paper clips and rubber bands. Making him a copy of the names, addresses, and phone numbers of all the construction contractors working for the AOC had been her pleasure.

Stefanie faced her keyboard and began typing the news release for the week, summarizing new employees, progress on construction, updates on international visitors, and lists and lists of new sponsors recruited in the never-ending effort to amass the 1.7 billion dollars budgeted for the Olympic Games. About a third of the funds would come from corporate sponsors of the games, some willing to pay forty million dollars for VIP status, while others would ante up only a fraction of that amount for the simple right to include the word "Olympic" in their advertisements.

This week's report included an official pet food of the games and an official brassiere manufacturer. Apparently there were corporate executives willing to bet their entire advertising budget for the next several years that the global community of consumers would choose a bra or a brand of puppy chow because of a trumped-up Olympic tradition.

Sending the twenty-four page document to the LaserJet printer, Stefanie reached for the ringing phone.

"Victoria Milton's office, may I help you?"

"Stefanie, this is Hank Powell. Is the chief in?"

"No, I'm sorry, Colonel. She's meeting with the network this afternoon." Stefanie was already writing 'Colonel Powell' on a phone message pad. "I can reach her through her mobile phone if it's an emergency, or . . ."

"No, I don't think that will be necessary. I've got to get to a meeting myself. Connect me with her voice mail if you would and I'll activate her pager."

After a brief pause, Victoria's voice said, "Go ahead, please."

"Victoria, this is Hank Powell. I have just learned of the deaths of three construction workers at the soccer venue in Athens. Apparently, three concrete finishers fell from a multistory project. OSHA officials are present, and there have been no citations thus far. Fortunately, all three were single and without dependents. I'm on my way to the airport for a meeting with the security force there, but I'll keep you informed on any developments. Hope all is well."

IN THE LOBBY of the IBM Tower, Mark talked animatedly with an attractive staff member from the telecommunications department who had sat next to him during the morning's seminar. The two met for the first time during the briefing with executives and technicians from NBC who, for a paltry four hundred fifty-six million dollars, had won the bid to broadcast the Olympic Games in the United States.

Also mingling within the carpeted walls of the upscale conference room were representatives from the European Broadcasting Union, which paid two hundred fifty million dollars for European rights, a Japanese consortium of networks, paying nearly one hundred million dollars for the Japan market, and executives from smaller markets in Africa, the Middle East, and the Far East, who together would contribute toward the five hundred fifty million dollars AOC budgeted for the television rights alone.

Michelle Britton attended the miniconference to glean insight for prospective advertisers, while Mark had been there because his staff would piggyback some of the network's hardware for the integrated security system.

During the half-day seminar, the two had whispered comments, asked one another questions, and made wisecracks.

Standing close to each other in the hectic lobby, the two maneuvered towards plans for the weekend, exchanging hints and innuendoes. Approaching a conversational climax, Mark spotted Janis crossing the lobby, heading toward the elevators.

Mark became distracted by the stone-faced enigma that had stymied him for weeks. Janis stopped midway in his trek to shake hands with another assistant director in the finance department, a heavyset silver-haired man with gray skin and a cigarette dangling from his lower lip. As the two colleagues spoke, a newspaper wedged under Janis' arm slipped to the granite floor, spilling open full view of the front page.

Mark's eyes flashed to the masthead of the paper Janis had dropped—*The Athens Banner Herald.*

Strange paper to be reading, Mark thought.

"Mark . . . Mark, what do you say, sound good to you?" Michelle asked.

Mark watched Janis pick the paper up and continue on his way to the elevator doors.

"Hell-*low*," Michelle implored, snapping her fingers in front of his face. "Hey Mark, you still here?"

"Oh, yeah . . . Sorry, Michelle. I thought I saw someone I knew. Forgive me, what were you saying?"

Her face sank, obviously embarrassed by the fact that her offer for a potentially intimate weekend had gone unnoticed.

"Never mind, I need to go now, anyway," she said, abruptly moving toward the front doors. She turned back and gave a quick wave, but then paused to say, "Call me later?"

Mark nodded and shouted back, "Sure!" but he was already thinking about Janis and the newspaper. Mark headed quickly to the elevators and the eleventh floor. When the doors opened, he saw all the members of the AOC finance department listed in gold letters. A six-inch stuffed *Izzy* doll, the official mascot of the 1996 Summer Olympic Games, sat on top of the sign with one padded cartoon hand raised in a wave.

"That fool thing *does* look like a blue slug with rings," Mark said out loud, recalling an uncomplimentary letter to the editor he had read in *Atlanta* magazine.

As he approached Janis' office, Mark slowed his pace and listened for conversation coming from the suite. There was none. The hallway was deserted, and Mark stopped to listen near the glass partition behind which Janis' secretary sat.

Not a word.

Mark moved back to the middle of the hall and marched on by Janis' office, straining his peripheral vision for any hints of activity. The secretary seated at her desk had dictation phones over her ears, but instead of typing, she wrote notes on a pad.

Mark nonchalantly continued on to an office two cubicles farther down the hall and introduced himself to a lady whose nameplate at the edge of her desk read, Virginia Hardin. She was the secretary of Gene Buchanon, a new name to Mark and apparently some kind of staff member in the department.

"Good afternoon, Virginia," Mark said with a smile. "I'm Mark Townsend with AOC security." He set his card on her desk in front of her.

"I'm afraid Mr. Buchanon is not in at the moment, would you like to leave a message?"

"Oh, that's okay, Virginia. I'll check back with him tomorrow. There's no hurry." Mark pretended to start to leave and then said, "Hey, Virginia, you know anybody who takes *The Athens Banner Herald* around here?"

"Sure don't. Why do you ask?"

"I saw someone in finance carrying a copy of the paper, but I'm not sure who it was." Mark loosened his tie and tried to look casual. "Say, do you have a subscription list for the department, you know, regular mailers that the members receive?"

"Well, I'm not exactly sure what periodicals the department subscribes to. Maybe Mr. Lockhart's secretary might know." Disappointed she could not finish repairing her broken nail, Virginia hoped for a quick end to this interruption.

"Would you do me a huge favor, Virginia, and call Mr. Lockhart's secretary for me and see if she knows anything about department subscriptions?" Mark shoveled charm with the biggest front-end loader he could simulate.

"I guess I could do that," Virginia said, frowning.

"You're an angel!"

She punched three numbers. "Joan, this is Virginia. I got a guy here from security asking about subscriptions the department receives."

She put her hand over the phone. "Monthly or weekly?"

Mark thought a second. "Weekly or daily."

"Weekly or daily," Virginia relayed.

Both were quiet.

"She says there's only two periodicals taken daily, *The Atlanta Journal* and *The Wall Street Journal*."

151

"How 'bout weekly?" Mark was not sure if the paper he had seen might be printed only once a week.

"No newspapers weekly, only magazines," Virginia said. "You want a list of *them?*"

"No," Mark said. "That won't be necessary. Can she tell me if an Athens newspaper is available through your periodical service?"

Virginia looked at Mark like he was crazy, but asked about Athens newspapers in hopes the strange man would finally go away.

"No Athens newspapers on the selections available form. Anything else?" she quipped smartly.

"No, thanks," Mark answered, barely noticing her attitude. "You've been very helpful."

"Sorry I had to bother you, Joan", Virginia said. She listened for a minute, then burst into laughter, undoubtedly at Mark's expense.

Virginia hung up the phone and looked at Mark. "Now what?"

"Could you tell me what time everyone checks out of here in the evening. I'd like to meet with Mr. Buchanon later, but I have an appointment this afternoon that might run late."

"Mr. Townsend," Virginia said, as if with her last bit of patience. "We make it a point to close shop by 4:30. If you want to see Mr. Buchanon, please be here by four."

"You bet. I understand. Hey, Virginia, thanks so much for all your generous assistance."

RETREATING DOWN THE HALL, Mark wondered what could be Janis' interest in Athens. Perhaps he's a Bulldog fan, keeping up with sports news. No, that can't be it, Janis would take the campus paper for the best sports coverage, not the city paper.

But, what then?

At the elevators he heard Janis telling his secretary he'd be back at two o'clock. Mark spotted a drinking fountain and hid his face as Janis stood tapping his foot in front of the elevators.

When the doors opened, Janis went in. Mark waited a split second, then darted into the back of the car, keeping his back to Janis as he nudged by him.

Mark studied the back of Janis' neck. His hair had recently been cut, ending in a razor-shaved contour curving up at the sides toward the back of his ears. Mark thought he smelled Old Spice cologne.

The elevator doors parted at the lobby, and Mark hesitated to let Janis walk several feet ahead before following. Exiting the front doors, Janis whipped out a pair of black-framed Wayfarers and punched the button on his Acura remote control, unlocking his car doors.

Mark hurried to his Taurus, keeping his eye on the direction the NSX took. He dialed the number for his office and left a message for Marvelyn that he had gone out for lunch and should be back by two.

Mark followed several car lengths behind Janis, as they both drove north on West Peachtree Street. Janis then veered onto Peachtree Street where the two roads merged.

Peachtree Street at West Peachtree Street.

Mark smiled. It reminded him of a time during his boyhood when his Uncle Joe had been frustrated by Atlanta road planners. During a visit for a family reunion, Uncle Joe, the older brother of Mark's father and the unequivocal example of the family's stubbornness, had taken it upon himself to hunt for an antique chest of drawers Mark's mother wanted to convert into a vanity for the powder-room sink. Uncle Joe planned his excursion carefully, interrogating a dozen or more antique shops over the phone before embarking on his mission.

"This won't take long," he said with confidence as he left the house. "Almost all of the shops are on Peachtree Street. I'll be back in a jiffy."

Hours later, Mark's father was about to call the MP's at Fort McPherson to launch a reconnaissance battery for his lost brother when Uncle Joe traipsed through the entry hall, fuming and exhausted from a day lost on Atlanta roads.

Red faced, he exclaimed with his jaws locked in anger he was damn glad he didn't live in some backward blankety-blank city where every other blankety-blank road was named blankety-Peachtree-something.

Mark chuckled at the memory of his family. Of course, Uncle Joe had been right. Over forty streets in the metro area started with the word, "Peachtree."

Mark thrust his foot on the accelerator to pass a MARTA Bus stopped near the intersection with Peachtree Circle.

Ahead, just after crossing north over Interstate 85, the black NSX turned left into Huey's and disappeared down the steep hill behind the small building that served as the restaurant's parking lot.

Mark slowed to let Janis exit his car and go into the open-air cafe before steering his own car into the parking lot.

Mark waited in his car for several minutes to see if he would recognize anyone coming to meet Janis. Only groups of two or more poured into the cafe, and eventually Mark got out of his car to have a look inside.

The front door was on the side of the cafe and led to a tiny entry, about the size of a bathroom at a gas station. The walls were covered with posters and paraphernalia from Mardi Gras, complete with hordes of plastic beads of all colors and shapes, party hats, and masks. On one wall was a panoramic photograph of runners passing the cafe taken during the annual Fourth of July Peachtree Roadrace.

Mark stood in the cramped quarters with ten or eleven other people waiting for a table, but he could still see all of the seating inside the cafe and most of the tables outside, situated under an off-white awning facing Peachtree Street.

At an outside corner table, Janis sat alone, reading a newspaper and eating an omelet and a half-dozen order of Beingets.

Mark surveyed the setting and grudgingly decided to abandon his quest for the day, concerned the only seat available might not be hidden very well from the object of his interest. He hated leaving the tantalizing aroma of cinnamon coffee and red velvet cake.

THE SOUND OF A KEY being thrust into the bathroom lock startled the young girl. She quickly jumped down from the side of the tub, where she'd been trying to peer out the window. From where she'd stood, she could barely see the top row of the bricks and the heavy, black, wrought iron bars on the building next door.

She had not seen or spoken to anyone since the Great One ushered her into this sanctuary, and hunger pangs began overcoming her fear of what might come later in the day.

The dim light from the hallway did not accompany the intimidating beast as he interrupted Maria's solitary confinement. His massive frame silhouetted against the baroque wallpaper on the far wall.

"Miss Adrianne wants to see you," he said.

Maria's slight delay caused his huge arm to grab her by the neck of the tattered warm-up jacket and dangle her down the hall, the balls of her feet hardly brushing the floor.

His clutch relaxed at the entrance to Adrianne's office, and the young girl fell to her knees before the heavy door, cracked a quarter open. Inside, a dim glow rose from the coals in the fireplace at the opposite end of the room, and a solitary Tiffany lamp cast thick shadows over most of the room.

The dark red carpet on the floor seemed thicker to Maria than before, and the desk seemed to have doubled in size since she had stood next to it last evening, devastated by Mona's words.

"Sit down, Maria." Adrianne's voice reverberated through the dark.

Maria slid her way to a leather armchair in front of the desk and sat down.

"Good to see you, Maria," said the woman, hidden from view. "Did you have a pleasant night on the town?"

Maria could not locate the voice. Panicked, her eyes jolted around the room, but she dared not move her head.

"I've had runaways before, Maria. Young girls seduced by the mystery of the city."

Maria could hear Adrianne move in the room, but still could not see her. She stared straight ahead, feeling her heart pound violently. She took short, racing breaths, and her hands and feet felt numb.

"I grew up in Atlanta, Maria," Adrianne continued. "My father was a respected banker in downtown during the days when a few powerful men governed most of the state. He was a state senator and a former city council member who did a great deal to make Atlanta the economic force that it is today."

Maria could feel Adrianne come closer.

"He was a large man, Maria, and preferred expensive custom-tailored three-piece suits, and he walked with a black cane with a gold-plated knob on the end. His sideburns were long and almost met with a long bushy mustache that curled up on the sides."

Closer still.

Cold terror radiated through her bones. The girl fought to control trembling arms.

"I studied him well, Maria. Although he never knew me until the end, I knew almost everything about *him*, about his business, about his associates."

The invisible woman's voice became harsh and bitter, her words spitting as she hovered nearer the shaking child.

"He was a very wise man, Maria, but also a very *stupid* man. He was obese and insensitive and incredibly selfish."

Although there was a fire smoldering in the fireplace at the other end of the room, Maria was freezing.

"He brutally visited my mother at his whim, one or two nights a week, sometimes more. She was only fifteen, but he beat her and raped her, and never showed her anything but contempt."

Adrianne's face appeared in the glow behind her desk.

"He never realized that I knew who he was until the night he met me face to face."

The woman's voice became quietly monotone.

Maria could not blink her eyes, fixed on the spectral apocalypse a few feet away. The girl's eyes watered, but her lids would still not move, held steadfast by phantom fingers.

"Then he realized the error of his ways, he understood the meaning of the word *consequences.*"

A pause. Maria's blood stopped moving.

"The police found his head in an alley where I left it to be gnawed by a mutt German Shepherd."

Maria felt as if she were hundreds of feet under water, suffocating from the unwieldy pressure and starved for air.

Adrianne's demonic eyes turned red as they bore into the horrified face paling across from her. The formerly gentle contours of the matron's face vanished and were inexplicably replaced by sunken hollow cheeks and occult orbits.

"I extract revenge upon those who cross me, girl," she hissed with squinting eyes and terse lips. "Make no mistake about it, I own you, Maria. You belong to me."

Maria felt her head spin. She knew she was about to pass out. She braced her arms to the chair, trying to keep from sliding to the floor.

"Go behind me, girl, and take the jar from the bookshelf."

Maria could not move.

Adrianne's eyes grew suddenly large. "*Do what I say!*"

Maria faltered toward the bookshelf, wobbling on feeble legs, not discerning where she stepped within the cavernous room. She groped for the jar until her fingers found a six-inch-tall mason glass in the center of the second shelf.

"Bring it here, girl," Adrianne said. "Set it on the desk, in the light."

Another pause.

"I want you to see inside."

Maria felt liquid sloshing around within the jar as she jerked her way to the desk. She moved the container close to the desk, but the jar slipped from her sweaty hands, dropping freely the last three or four inches to the top of the desk and landing with a loud *thud.*

The noise fractured the room's density, slamming Maria's heart to a standstill. Recognizing the grotesque contents floating in the murky jar, Maria shrieked with aching fierceness.

Under the blood-colored light, suspended in stained formaldehyde, were three young human toes mutilated at one end from a smashing impact.

Maria swayed dizzily side to side as Adrianne continued.

"The next time you leave here without my permission, girl, you will pay for your sins . . . with *FLESH!*"

Maria fell against the desk.

"Leave me now!" Adrianne glared up at the girl and panted hotly in her face.

Maria revived her senses and ran to the door.

Her drenched hands fumbled with the knob deliriously. Madly, she gripped at the latch and threw the door open and fled up the stairs.

THIRTEEN

"Did you have a pleasant lunch, Mr. Townsend," Marvelyn asked as Mark ambled around the corner toward his office.

"I can't get used to you calling me 'Mr. Townsend,'" Mark said, sucking up the last swallow of Diet Coke from a Hardee's paper cup. The mushroom-swiss burger in his stomach was not nearly as satisfying as a Cajun omelet and an order of Beingets would have been.

She smiled up at him, looking over half-lensed reading glasses. "Rather I call you little Marky-Mark like I used to do in Germany?"

"Gosh no, Marvelyn! I think that's a rap band or something." Mark leaned against the doorjamb leading to the colonel's office. "Then again, maybe it would help me with the babes."

They both laughed.

Marvelyn passed Mark the stacks of paper she had bound in turquoise plastic covers.

"They're all set, dear. I believe the Colonel will be a tad late to the meeting. Mrs. Milton called and asked to join you two, and the Colonel obliged. That woman wants in on everything!"

"Every chief has his own style," Mark agreed diplomatically. "I mean *her* own style."

Mark went to his desk to check his voice mail and fax messages. An airport security liaison droned on about the progress on the new three hundred million dollar international concourse under construction. Another faceless official reported on the progress at Agnes Scott College in Decatur, where security officials would reside during the two weeks of the games.

He flipped through one of the documents with SECU-RITY printed boldly in red across the cover. Marvelyn had done a superb job with the background searches, her work saving Mark hours at a word processor.

Still, the Athens newspaper would not leave his mind.

He looked through the yellow pages for newsstands and bookstores in the midtown area and called the six closest to the IBM Tower. None of them carried the *Banner Herald*, and the clerks working the front desks could not suggest a local source for the paper.

Mark unfolded *The Atlanta Journal* on the corner of his desk, looking for a hint of notable Athens news. There was nothing in the front two sections about Athens. The local section did not encompass areas farther north than Gainsville, so Mark turned to sports to see if anything remarkable jumped out at him. There were two stories about UGA football, one about basketball, and one about the new women's soccer team, a first at UGA. On the back page was a piece about an indoor facility under construction for Olympic rhythmic gymnastics.

His eyes focused on the Olympic story, reading the six paragraphs curiously. The writer reported AOC approved a three hundred fifty thousand dollar contribution to the University of Georgia for constructing a one million dollar indoor arena for the gymnastic event. Vince Dooley, the athletic director for the Bulldogs, was quoted as saying he

160

was pleased by the opportunity to build the facility that would become an indoor training center for the football team after the Olympics.

Mark shook his head at the end of the concise composition, frustrated by the arcane clue.

"No bolt of lightning there," he said out loud. "The football team gets a practice field for two-thirds the cost."

He groaned heavily and threw the paper across the room, causing pages to unfold and settle randomly into a carpet of fresh newsprint.

"Mr. Townsend," Marvelyn said over the intercom. "The Colonel and Mrs. Milton have arrived."

"Thanks, Marvelyn. I'm on my way."

"Would you like coffee, dear?"

"You know, that sounds great," he replied.

"Meet you in the conference room."

MARK GATHERED THE DOCUMENTS on the directors and their closest assistants and headed down the hall to the conference room. Hank and Victoria were both seated at the rectangular table talking seriously about her concerns with athletic housing. Hank was calmly reassuring his boss everything was on track when Mark entered the room with the turquoise reports.

Mark had not seen Victoria in two weeks, and at first glance he was startled by her appearance. The CEO showed pronounced signs of stress.

Her face had deep furrows, making it look as if she had weathered a sailing expedition around the Cape of Hope.

"I'll start in personnel," Mark said. "Binder marked one-zero-zero-three." His words never wavered from the executives at hand, but his mind remained riveted on an Athens periodical.

"DAMN IT, JACK, I told those birdbrains to quit riding the cable!" Harold Dixon was beside himself, yelling across the Ocoee River gorge in the Tennessee mountains to the foreman. The beleaguered man on the other side waved back to his boss and pointed to his ears, indicating he couldn't hear over the roar of the crane a few feet away.

Dixon's face turned red, and he pointed angrily at the two men suspended high in the air atop a gargantuan granite boulder hoisted by the screaming crane.

Slowly, the crane operator swiveled the eighty-foot steel scaffold sixty degrees west toward the center of the dry riverbed, careful not to sway the rock or its two daredevil hitchhikers.

"Those assholes are gonna kill themselves," Dixon grumbled.

As owner and president of Dixon and Associates, he'd threatened to fire any crew member who rode with cargo being transported by crane. Such carelessness broke about a hundred OSHA regulations, not to mention being as stupid as playing Russian roulette with a double-barrel shotgun. He stomped out the door of the mobile home that served as the on-site contractor's office and headed down the thirty-foot bank toward the riverbed. Sure, they may be six weeks behind, but that's no reason to risk lives.

"Some heads are gonna roll!" he shouted as he slipped on a patch of loose dirt near the top of the bank causing him to slide most of the way on his butt. He stumbled to his feet and continued down the riverbank with his laced leather boots nearly half-full of sand and rocks.

Two hundred feet upriver, a temporary dam designed and patented by Dixon and his younger brother, Dave, detoured the rushing water east around the construction site for the Olympic kayaking venue, keeping the work site clear and dry while crews strategically positioned rocks according to the kayak architect's drawings. The creative blockade had a functioning gate allowing planners to release a small flow of water to pass over a course for testing various positions of the artificially located obstacles. The system accelerated construction by months and was a celebrated milestone among water course contractors.

The foreman waved an orange flag at the crane operator, signaling the precise position indicated on the gridded blueprint he held on a clipboard.

On the opposite bank, a Latino man dressed in blue-jean overalls and a yellow hard hat knelt on one knee, chewing on a dry reed and watching the progress of the crew.

"Hey, Billy!" Dixon screamed at the foreman again, hobbling near the bottom of the bank. "Billy!" he shouted again, to no avail.

When he finally reached the riverbed, Dixon stopped to unlace his left boot and dump a pound of rock. He continued yelling at the man guiding the boulder, now hanging more than fifty feet in the air. The whining crane engine stifled his hollers before they reached the foreman's ears.

THE TWO WORKERS high in the air sat on the rock and held onto the cable with one hand while taking turns spitting at targets down in the kayak course.

They laughed and swatted one another on the back, congratulating their sly accuracy, while their foreman standing yards below piloted the rock into place.

"Lousy derelicts," Dixon fumed. "Nobody can possibly be that lazy."

The workers had acquired the habit of riding along with the biggest boulders from the trucks to the riverbed just so they would not have to climb the rocks a second time to release the chained straps from the crane cable.

"A little farther west," the foreman yelled, thrusting the orange flag toward the target.

The crane operator focused on the foreman's hands, oblivious to the boulder or the two men on top and hidden from view at ground level.

"I can piss farther than you from here," one of the workers wagered.

"No way, dude. I can hit that big rock there near the bank on the fly."

"Not with that twig in your pants, you can't."

"You're on!"

The taller of the two with thick wiry, blond hair stood up, letting his left hand slide up the cable as he rose to his feet. Fumbling with his zipper, he reached his right hand up to his mouth and pulled off his worn leather glove by biting the end of the middle finger between his teeth. He still could not manage to pry the zipper open with one hand.

"The damn thing is rusted closed, son!" his partner howled, doubled over in laughter. "Guess you don't let him out for air much, huh?"

"Ah, shut up!" the skinny one said exasperated, releasing his left hand from the cable and grabbing his fly with both hands.

"Oooh, Evel Knievel," the fat one said, lying on his side, laughing outrageously.

Fighting the front of his jeans, the skinny one lost his footing on the granite, the eroded soles of his ankle-high workboots sliding over the face of the rock, and he swaggered near the edge of the boulder, losing his dark green hard hat over the side before saving himself by the cable.

His drunken jig made the seated worker laugh even harder than before.

"Hell, we'll be on the ground before you pull that worm free!" he said.

Cursing his seated friend, the skinny worker unbuckled his belt and released the snap at the front of his waist, exposing white boxer shorts with red hearts.

"Get a load," the fat worker bellowed. "Your momma give you those?"

"Shut up, Butch. These were a Valentine gift. Something you wouldn't know anything about." His embarrassed face darkened as he readied himself for the launch.

A sudden jolt from the cable smashed the skinny worker to his knees, slipping him slowly toward the edge of the rock.

"Butch! Butch!" he yelled violently, stretching his hand out toward the fat worker who had wrapped both of his legs about the base of the cable.

"Hang on, man!" Butch screamed back.

On the ground below, the foreman shouted, "What the hell was that?" He waved his arms furiously at the crane operator to stop the rock where it was.

High above, the skinny worker's hands frantically searched for holds in the smooth granite. His fingers split and bled as he gouged them into tiny cracks and sharp crevices in the irregular surface. For a moment, his fingertips would find a cleft, only to have the rock crumble, his fingers slip free, and his fall continue.

"Grab the chain, grab the chain," Butch screamed, as his coworker slipped farther and farther over the edge of the big rock.

On his knees, Butch leaned as far as he could with an outstretched arm, but still several feet from his falling buddy.

The skinny worker reached for the chain encircling the rock, but there was no clearance for his fingers between the chain and the granite.

He jammed three fingers inside links of the chain just as he dropped off the side of the boulder. The weight of his body hung in space by the fragile bones of three fingers. He screamed wildly from the cutting pain.

The foreman turned to see one of his crewmen dangling from the giant rock still more than fifty feet in the air. "Just hold it there!" he shouted at the crane operator. "Hold it still!"

Other workers ran into the riverbank and peered up at their friend. The foreman racked his brain for a solution to the crisis. He finally instructed the crane operator to lower the rock as slowly as he could without swinging it.

With the first turn of the crane's pulley, another terrifying jolt in the cable suddenly dropped the stone about a foot.

The skinny worker shrieked in pain as the force of the abrupt shock sliced his smallest finger from his hand.

Blood from the wound flowed down his arm, splattering drops onto his face and stinging his eyes. His legs swung back and forth as he struggled to avoid plummeting to his death.

Butch clutched the cable like a baby with both arms and legs.

The skinny worker repeatedly yelled for help, his hoarse cries contrasting with the serene chirps of the forest. The pressure on his two fingers increased, threatening to severe his last thin tie to life.

More and more blood gushed from his hand and onto his face.

"Lower it down! Damn it, lower it down!" His vain yells bounced off long green needles covering the pines that bordered the riverbed.

On the ground, workers congregated near the hanging boulder.

Butch hugged the cable tighter, afraid to look down, chanting an incoherent refrain from numb lips.

Without warning, the cable suddenly snapped completely in half several feet above its couple, plunging both workers and their enormous cargo to the riverbed.

On impact, the massive granite split into two fragments against the earth, crushing the skinny worker into an unrecognizable mush of bright red flesh.

As the dust settled, workers rushed to the accident hoping to recover an injured—but alive—Butch.

The foreman arrived first and found his crewman dead, face first against the smooth surface of cut stone, his blood trickling down the glittering rock and puddling in the trough created by the two giant pieces of granite.

On the far bank above the riverbed, the unknown observer removed his hard hat, wiped his forehead, and disappeared into the woods.

THE MEETING HAD GONE WELL, even though it lasted an hour longer than planned. Victoria insisted on asking pointed questions about every executive Mark reviewed, testing everyone's patience with her excessive thoroughness.

But Mark was perplexed by his bosses' dismissal of the Janis mystery. Neither seemed at all surprised Mark was unable to unravel greater detail of his past. As Mark became more insistent that a potential powder keg existed among them, Victoria grew insulted that anyone would question the judgment of her longtime friend and confidant, Caldwell Lockhart. As the meeting approached four hours, Mark retreated from his position, surrendering to the CEO's assessment and deciding for himself that further investigation would have to continue on his own.

After the two officials left the conference room, Mark remained in his office alone to think about his next move. Searching for a distraction from the riddle plaguing his mind, he switched on the walkman sitting next to his computer.

Billy Joel sang the last few phrases of "Uptown Girl," one of Mark's favorite songs. He leaned back in his swivel chair, remembering Christy Brinkley strutting across the screen in the song's video.

"What a hot babe," Mark said to the empty room.

Watching the scene in his mind made him remember he was supposed to have called Michelle that afternoon. He wrote himself a note to call her when he arrived home.

The news came on the radio, fading in and out of tune as Mark fought with himself over the strange man in the finance department.

"Today in Washington, Congressional leaders blasted the White House for . . ."

Mark rubbed his tired eyes as he thought of ways to pry into Janis' history.

He considered hopping a plane to Miami, but could not figure a way to miss days from his responsibilities at AOC. He could fly down on the weekend, but businesses would be closed and his ability to interview people diminished. Perhaps the trip was important enough to take off days during the week. But, then again, Victoria had expressed reservations about his hunch and probably wouldn't give her blessings to his continuing research.

". . .and in the State Capitol, lawmakers began meeting in preparation for a debate over . . ."

The words from the radio hit him like a fist.

"That's it! The capitol building!" he blurted excitedly. He quickly grabbed his coat and ran to the elevators, hoping he wasn't too late.

When the doors opened to the garage, he bolted across the concrete floor to his car. He thrust the key into the ignition and roared up the exit ramp. He committed himself to a Peachtree Street route, expecting lighter traffic than the late afternoon jam on the downtown connector.

Several spots were opening up on Mitchell Street as state employees fled the downtown hub after work, and Mark skidded into a slot a block away from the capitol. He dashed up the capitol steps to the newsstand just inside the front doors.

An elderly black man was locking down the bars as Mark sprinted to the counter.

"Excuse me, sir," he stammered. "Could I bother you for just a second before you close shop?"

"Too late," the man said. "Gotta go now."

"Please, sir, this will only take a second."

"Sorry, son. Got Hawks tickets tonight. If I'm gonna eat before tip off, gotta go now." He padlocked the second window and moved to the door.

Mark racked his brain for a way to make this man listen to him.

"A walkin' dog and FO (Frosted Orange) at the Varsity would taste a lot better with a fifty dollar bill next to it," Mark said, holding the bill in front of him.

The old man stopped what he was doing and looked back over his shoulder.

"Now I suppose it would, at that, mister," he said, taking the bill from Mark. "Now what can I do for ya."

"I'd like a copy of today's *Athens Banner Herald*, please," Mark said anxiously.

"Damn, boy. You're wanting to pay fifty bucks for that measly fold?" the old man asked. "I almost feel bad taking your money for that."

The old man reached under the counter of his stand and extracted a crumpled copy of the Athens paper. He handed it to Mark and said smiling. "Well, almost."

"Thanks, buddy," Mark called over his shoulder, rushing out of the deserted lobby. "Hope they win tonight."

"Me too," the old man said, shaking his head. "Lenny's got his work cut out for him, though. Playing the Hornets, boy, I'll tell you. . ."

The rest of the impromptu sports commentary echoed unheard through the stately halls.

FOURTEEN

B ack in the car, Mark rocketed through the pages. He only glanced at the front-page headlines, not that different from the Atlanta paper he had read earlier in the afternoon and now lay haphazardly across his office floor.

He quickly scanned articles on pollution in the Chattahoochee River, a scandal in the mayor's office, UGA news, and other small-town and regional reporting, looking for anything which might stand out linking the periodical and Janis.

In the sports section, he inadvertently ripped several pages while savagely scouring for a breakthrough. With hands dry and cracked from the fall winds, he licked his fingers repeatedly in order to grab the page corners. He went through the whole paper again.

Nothing.

He furiously slung the paper into the passenger seat after finishing the back page of the last section, and he hammered the steering wheel hard with both hands.

"This is driving me insane!" he screamed inside the car, exhausted from chasing a criminal he was not certain existed.

"You're really losing it, man," Mark said to himself.

Maybe they're right, he thought. Maybe there's just nothing here. Maybe the guy's just an average Joe trying to do the best he can in a demanding job, with a world of responsibility, fighting like the rest of us to keep his head above water. Maybe he's as squeaky clean as the Pope . . . maybe I need a vacation.

Mark sighed deeply, closed his red eyes, and rested his head against the steering wheel. After several minutes of stillness, Mark sat upright in the seat again and casually reached for the disheveled paper on the vinyl seat next to him. He peacefully returned to the front page with a renewed interest in the day's news.

Uncluttered and chipper, his mind absorbed the nuances of local, national, and world events while he rested undisturbed on an empty street on a Friday night in downtown Atlanta.

On the eighth page of the front section, two short paragraphs appeared: Workers Fall To Their Death.

At first, Mark passed over the brief report and concentrated instead on the editorial on the opposite page praising AOC for awarding the rhythmic gymnastic venue to the University of Georgia. When he was about to turn the page, his eyes caught the word "Olympic" in the steady prose about three unlucky concrete finishers.

According to the article, three single white men in their late twenties or early thirties fell from several stories while working on a high-rise structure at the Sanford Stadium. The fatal accident occurred late the day before, after all other crews had left the site. The men were apparently preparing to leave their job, the site for the Summer Olympic soccer competition, when they slipped from the edge of the structure. None of the three men had families.

"That's peculiar," Mark said, rubbing his chin. "All three fell at the same time."

Could it be Janis knew one of the men, was at war with the contractor, had a vested interest in the construction?

Maybe I *will* keep looking, he thought.

"I JUST CAN'T DO IT," Maria said again.

The three girls sitting on the bed were joined by two more, ambling into the purple room still wearing their night-clothes, even though it was after two o'clock in the afternoon.

"Sure you can," Misty said, popping up off the lavender bedspread and grabbing a hairbrush. "It just takes a little time to get used to. I kept my eyes closed for at least a month or so, but then I learned it ain't so bad."

Betty Jo, the blonde who looked Swedish but talked Texan, rolled on her back squealing, "Yeah, Honeychild, 'specially if it's A-L-E-X!"

"Hey, I haven't known Alex but a year," Misty argued. "I'm talking about before him, right after I first started. I learned it ain't so bad. Like I told you before, Maria, we're just helping a bunch of sweet ole guys get through their dead-end lives. You'll see. Besides, you got *us* to help you through the beginning. After the first time, it's all down-hill."

"I just can't," Maria countered. "Not with someone I don't even know. I just gotta get out of here."

"And go where?" one of the girls in pajamas sneered.

She was a tall thin black girl named Stacey, older than the others, probably twenty-five or so, with short, straight hair cut just below her ears. She was pretty in her own lanky way, with intense eyes that were a spectacular natural, light gray color with hints of blue, giving her dark face a mesmer-izing sensuality.

"Just where do you think you can go?" she asked again. "If you run, the cops will eventually get you. Then it's jail or a kid's home, depending on what state you're in when they snatch you."

She walked away from the wall and sat on the bed next to Maria.

"Or you could and end up in a foster home. That's what happened to me. I ran away from my home when I was your age. I remember thinking I could make it on my own too. Lasted about two months before I got caught. I spent four nights in the local jailhouse with drunks and muggers gropin' all over me, then five months at the farm with a bunch of hoodlums, before they trucked me off to a foster home—supposed to be real good for me—supposedly I was *real lucky.*"

She rolled over on her side and propped her head on one hand with her elbow buried deep in a bold purple and white striped pillow cover.

"Let me tell you, sister, it was no picnic. The family they sent me to had no kids. My foster mom wanted me for the state money they got every month for taking care of me. Think I ever saw any of it? Huh! She bought herself dresses and things, that's all. Nothing for me. And, the old man? He thought I was a toy. His wife never said a word. Believe me, girl, it's a helluva lot better here with Adrianne. She watches out good for us."

"Don't ya know it," Betty Jo agreed, slowly. "I got paid eight hundred bucks last week!"

The other girls in the room all chimed their congratulations together.

Misty joked, "Girl, I'm surprised you can still walk!"

"Honey, it was nothing! I'm the product of a good Texas upbringing. That's what's done it," Betty Jo drawled. "Sugar, I got enough spark in these thighs to light up the whole city!"

"You tell 'em, child!" Stacey yelled, reaching over the bed to slap a high five with Betty Jo.

All the girls in the room hugged on each other or smacked another's rear end or affectionately threw an arm around a sister's neck while yelping and hooting like a band of cowpokes sitting around a fire.

They truly were family.

Still sitting on the bed, Maria brought her knees up to her chin and wrapped her arms around her legs, drawing further within herself and away from the jovial gang of girls in the room. Maria liked the girls fine, they were kind to her and seemed genuinely interested in her.

But she knew she was not one of them, and never could be.

SATURDAY NIGHT IN SAVANNAH and the River Walk whirled with sightseers and shoppers bundled up and strolling along the sidewalk. The Savannah River flowed lazily by on one side and scores of novelty stores, pubs, and restaurants housed in historic renovated buildings buzzed with energy on the other.

Among the crowds, Mr. Miras stopped at a large window in front of a candle shop to watch a lady dressed in colonial garb raise a wooden paddle from a vat of melted wax. As she lifted her hand, thin red candles, each about a foot long, dangled from the plank, as wax coalesced to rows of wicks draped over wooden pegs above. She smiled to the man on the other side of the window, and he, in turn, graciously smiled back.

The clerk motioned for him to come inside the shop, and he returned a look of surprise and pointed to his own chest asking, "Me?"

Pleased with the attention, the woman nodded repeatedly and waved to him again. Miras acquiesced and stepped up two cobblestone stairs at the front door to the shop.

"Good evening, sir," she said in a friendly southern voice. "You seem interested in what I am doing."

"Why yes," Miras said. "I don't believe I've ever witnessed candles being made."

Spiced fragrances permeated the little shop, a throwback to a time when Oglethorpe colonized the area as a buffer between the Spanish and English territories. Scents hung in the air as if the candles being manufactured there were already afire and emitting invisible clouds of ambrosial smoke.

The pleasing aromatic mix reminded Miras of a time or a place in his past that he could not pinpoint exactly, perhaps a celebration or a holiday. He breathed in deeply and the rich bouquets serpentined through his mind, teasing his memory with some forgotten experience. It smells like incense, he thought, with hazy reminisces fading in and out of focus . . . hmmm, incense . . . yes, that's it! The Buddhist funeral. The scene from nearly twenty years before became clear to him. Once, through an ironic twist of fate, he was forced to attend the funeral of one of his victims, a Chinese owner of a dry cleaning chain who had found himself on the wrong side of a group of ruthless businessmen. A peaceful ceremony; how serenely perfumed it was!

"And this is how it was done when the British came to Georgia in 1733," the chubby clerk said, interrupting his psychic interlude. "There were only about a hundred and twenty-five settlers on the first boat across the Atlantic with Edward Oglethorpe and Colonel William Bull. They stopped briefly in South Carolina and then came here to Savannah."

She slid the wooden paddle into a rack already holding five or six identical pieces of wood with their virgin candles dangling below. Then she stirred the wax with a large wooden spoon, as she continued her story.

"The land here was ceded by the chief of the Yamacraw Indians, Tomo-Chi-Chi, whom Oglethorpe befriended and later took back for a visit to England."

She turned to the wall behind her and adjusted the fixtures controlling the temperature of the molten mass.

"Could you imagine being an Indian in England for the first time?" she asked, blotting her damp forehead with the back of her embroidered sleeve.

"Must have been a spectacle," Miras said blandly.

"I can't imagine!" she exclaimed, never doubting for a minute the man across the counter was anything less than engrossed in her historical soliloquy. "The settlement was established primarily as a philanthropic measure by a group of English clergymen bent on rescuing unfortunate souls from poverty. In other words, we're all descendants of vagabonds!"

"I see," Miras said.

"Contrary to popular belief, though, they weren't all prisoners, just folks down on their luck."

"Well, that's a relief," Miras responded, quite satiated with eighteenth-century Georgia.

"I'll say!" the woman smiled.

"What an array of unusual color," Miras said, picking up two candles and closely examining them. One was a deep indigo, the other a bright goldenrod.

An expression of self-complacency radiated from the clerk's face. "The pigments used in those candles were handed down from the Indian natives in this area—the Creeks, Cherokees, Choctaws, and Chickasaws. Lovely aren't they?"

"Extraordinary. These are natural occurring pigments?"

"Yes, sir," she said. "I made most of those myself the very same way our ancestors did over two hundred years ago."

Miras' fascination with the candles even surprised himself. "I'd like a box of the assorted colors."

MOMENTS LATER, Miras returned to the brisk evening air with a white cardboard box containing two dozen handmade candles tucked securely under his right arm. He headed toward his planned destination, the Salzburg Tavern, about fifty yards down the walk. With each step, the small, steel heel protectors on his dark, brown, Ralph Lauren alligator shoes made tinny clicking sounds against the cobblestone sidewalk.

He smiled at the passing ladies, as strangers do in the South, and he tipped his head toward any man who first did the same.

At the door to the tavern, several college students, apparently without I.D.s, tried to gain entrance past a rotund doorman. The conversation seemed congenial, and Miras guessed they would eventually succeed.

Inside, he found an empty stool at the bar where he set his box of candles. He loosened his coat and shouted an order for a Coors Light to the bearded bartender. The tremendous volume from the small band on stage was uncomfortable, and, although not conducive to conversation, was ideal for his intention.

The pub was already busy on the weekend night, and after one sip of beer, he was surprised to see the young people from outside already crowding around a table next to a five-foot wooden replica of a giant German stein.

Miras drew a slender black cigar from his breast pocket and lighted it, casually spotting the group of men he knew would be there.

When the cigar was a third shorter, he balanced it on the side of an ashtray next to the white cardboard box and retired to the mens' room. Once behind the stall door, he removed a clear plastic bag from his coat pocket and squeezed a small dab of the black grease inside onto his hands. He smeared the sticky paste across his knuckles, then returned to the pounding sounds of the band.

He messed up his hair with his dirty fingers as he approached the table where the construction workers congregated. Miras was surprised to see five men at the table instead of four.

He loathed surprises.

The packet from Janis had contained only four pictures, and instantly the idea of aborting the mission crossed his mind, but the rush of the job was too powerful to resist.

"Excuse me, my man, I wonder if I could ask a favor?" he shouted into the ear of one of the workers whose face he recognized.

"Yeah?" the man said, staring at the fashionably dressed foreigner.

"Well, I've run into a bit of a fix," Miras said, skillfully disguising his Hispanic accent with a refined impersonation of a Massachusetts native. "I picked up a nail with my tire. I'm in the alley out back, but in trying to raise the car, I bent the jack and now it won't budge."

Dumb-ass Yankee, the man thought. The town was full of 'em, snooping around where he and his buddies worked on the site for the Olympic yachting venue.

"I wonder if you and your friends would help me change the tire," he continued, anxiously checking his watch. "I'm already late, and I can't wait for a wrecker."

The man did not reply. He ignored the request, enjoying the jokes of his friends at the table.

Miras then drew three, crisp, one hundred dollar bills from his breast pocket.

"Really, sir," Miras pleaded, showing the bills in his hand, "I'll make it worth your while. It would cost me this much for a tow, anyway, and I really can't take the time."

The man stared at the money, then looked up at the stranger and smiled, crumpling the bills into the pocket of his flannel shirt. He held out his hands across the table, interrupting wisecracks in midsentence.

"Hey, guys," he yelled. "Come on, follow me, we gotta help this dude out."

The other four yelled back obscenities to their friend and made crude comments about his mother's habits. They certainly won't be missed, Miras thought to himself.

"No guys, really, listen up," the worker screamed, rising to his feet. "It'll only take a minute. Look, the stupid Yankee can't jack up his own car out back, it'll be a snap."

"Oh man, I already done enough work for one day."

"Yeah, me too."

"Hey, come on. Afterwards the drinks are on me!"

Hearing the reward, the other four eagerly stood and stumbled from the table toward the back door.

Entering the stillness of the alley, Miras walked several feet ahead of the entourage.

The blackness of the night and the faint sounds from cars coursing the boulevard on the other side of the high bank bordering the alley were in stark contrast to the blasting sounds they had just left behind in the tavern.

"It's here, just around the corner, gentlemen, by this dumpster." He pointed ahead to nothing in particular. "I sure do appreciate your help with this matter. I don't know what I would have done if you hadn't . . ."

Miras disappeared around a corner in the alley a split second before the gang of men reached the same turn, but just long enough to don leather gloves and draw his two concealed pistols.

As the men came into view, they were met by an empty alley and a barrage of gunfire.

Emptying one gun at a time, Miras slowly circled the men as he fired, making the attack appear as though more than one mugger were involved. He strategically pelted each man with at least two bullets, careful to ensure one fatal shot per victim.

Seeing their buddies slump to the ground, two of the construction workers in the rear tried to turn and run, but Miras expertly landed shots into their temples before they could cover more than a few feet.

The men did not scream during the attack, the gunman's accuracy silencing them with each first bullet. The small caliber pistols popped liked a string of fireworks, but no geometric designs burned in the heavens; only faint wisps of hot blue smoke rose in the chilly air, completely disappearing before leaving the confines of the backstreet tomb.

The professional ambush was complete in seconds.

Five bodies lay contorted in the alley with pools of their blood mingling along ruts in the asphalt. The dead eyes of the victims were open, wearing terminal casts of rage and fear and remorse.

Miras knelt by the corpse and recovered the driver's license of the one man he didn't know. He studied the photograph and personal information. Thomas Foster of Panama City, Florida.

"I'm sorry, my friend. This was not intended for you."

Tenderly, he reached down and closed the man's lids.

A blast of night wind rolled down the corridor, blowing a warm fetid smell of raw flesh, causing Miras to quickly turn his head away from the havoc he had induced.

He then lifted the wallets of the other four, removed the money and tossed the billfolds into a trash can next to the attack, certain to be found by the most inept investigator.

Scanning every direction for the unlikely sign of a witness, Miras stooped by one of the victims and recovered his crumpled hundred dollar bills before vanishing into the shadows.

Minutes later, with the mission complete, the hired killer reappeared at his bar stool and enjoyed a second beer along with the last third of his cigar; he thought of his children and looked forward to showing them the handmade candles he had bought for them less than an hour ago.

FIFTEEN

For the second time, Darryl smacked the drowse button on the alarm clock, this time knocking it on the floor. "Vickie will be here any minute, Darryl, and I won't be here to make sure your carcass is outta the sack, so you'd better get up now," Esther yelled from the bathroom vanity.

She tied the bow on the back of the only Sunday dress that would still accommodate her growing abdomen. Before leaving the front of the mirror, she patted the sides of her hair for the twentieth time.

Her baby somersaulted inside.

"Darryl, he just kicked a whopper!"

There was no response from the heap beneath the wadded sheets.

"Darryl, I said our boy's kicking again."

Still nothing.

Exasperated, she punched her snoozing husband in the leg on her way out of the bedroom.

"Ouch, woman! What're ya doing that for?"

"You know if you're late for church, *I'll* be the least of your worries." Esther's voice trailed down the hall as she hurried to the kitchen to grab the plate of brownies out of the refrigerator that she had made the night before for choir practice.

"Yeah, yeah, yeah," Darryl moaned, rolling onto his back and stretching his arms above his head, smashing his hands against the walnut headboard.

"Shit!"

"I heard that," Esther scolded in a faint voice from the other end of the house. "She's here, Darryl, I gotta go!"

He sat up on the edge of the mattress, rubbing his face and groaning.

A devout Baptist, Darryl had missed church fewer than ten times in ten years, but on more Sunday mornings than he cared to admit, mustering the energy to get up was a struggle.

But he finally made it out of bed, showered, and picked out a freshly pressed, pinstriped navy suit and slipped on the slacks. He opened the top drawer of the worn-out chest and grinned to himself, picking out a pair of red-and-white striped socks. He pushed the drawer shut, subconsciously shifting it to the left a little as it closed so that it would slide around the metal reinforcements his daddy had added decades ago. When Darryl was little, he used to hang on the front of the drawer to see inside, before he was tall enough to peer down into it on his own. After years of strain, the maple dovetails finally gave way, and when the boy was six, the front panel broke off.

He loaded up Mr. Coffee and dumped all other sections of the paper onto the floor, except the sports. Skipping over prolific NFL reports, he dove headfirst into an article about the upcoming ACC basketball season. He read voraciously about his beloved Tar Heels and the predictions for their finishing the season atop the ACC.

The aroma of coffee brewing on the kitchen counter broke Darryl's concentration. He looked up at the daisy-shaped clock on the wall and jumped to his feet, trembling in fear of his life.

"Damn it all!" he screamed, leaping to the counter and jerking the coffee-maker plug from the wall outlet.

"*COME ON, DARRYL!*" he could hear the woman scream out to him as he ran up the grassy hill toward the sanctuary. "Hurry up, boy, you're late!"

At eighty-three, Miss Hepzabah still had a set of lungs like a blacksmith's bellows, and the temper of an Irish schoolmarm.

She stood with one foot ahead of the other, jutting her lower jaw forward with a stern face frenzied by Darryl's tardiness. Darryl thought of his mother's childhood friend like a great-aunt, calling her Aunt Virgiline as did the rest of the family.

"Hurry up!" she yelled again. The platinum-blue hairs of her Sunday wig were stiff against the wind blowing up the hill, and her silver cat-eye glasses and black wool coat were all a part of the comforting weekly heritage upon which Darryl depended.

"I'm sorry I'm late, Aunt Virgiline," Darryl apologized, out of breath.

The old lady grabbed his arm and walked him quickly into the church. "And, what kind of tie is *that* to wear to church," she said scornfully. "Not too respectful of the Lord's house, if you ask me! Looks like something you'd see on a vagrant downtown."

"I'm sorry, Aunt Virgiline, I was just looking forward to the next season and . . ."

"And those socks, Darryl. I could see you across the road, flashing like a barber pole! What's got into you, son?"

"Nothing, ma'am. I just thought they matched with the . . ."

"Your momma's probably turning in her grave about now, boy. No respect, I say. You youngsters just don't have your values straight at all." She shook her head side to side in disgust. "Come on now, stand up straight. Quit that slumping over. Boy o' boy, are you ever a needing to hear what Reverend Whitaker's got to say."

She looked straight ahead as the two marched down the aisle and assumed their customary spot, fourth row near the aisle on the far right-hand side of the church.

"Hope your ears are cleaned out," she finished just as the music director came to the pulpit.

Every voice lifted the strains of "What a Friend We Have In Jesus," especially the young people in the back, where four male ushers, about Darryl's age, stood guard at the ends of the last pew, keeping careful watch over their younger sisters and brothers sitting in the very seats they had occupied only a short decade ago.

After several hymns and announcements about youth activities and a church luncheon next Sunday, the minister of music introduced a small thin lady about Aunt Virgiline's age who stepped up to the pulpit and disappeared behind the ornate white wooden podium.

The voice, wavering with age, rose seemingly bodiless from behind the microphone as the grandmother of twelve began her appeal to the congregation. She was a proud woman, proud of her heritage and of becoming the first and only female deacon of the church.

A hush of respect fell over the church as she spoke.

"My friends, you know why I'm here. I have been here many times before, speaking to you from this old heart that has endured years of strife but has only sung never endin' praises of glory."

Faint sounds of "Yes" and "That's right, sister" rose from the people in the pews.

"From this old mouth that stayed empty many a time in the past when my daddy was out of work and my momma was left a cryin' at supper time with no food on the table, but we never hungered for the Word of God nor ever ceased praisin' His name." Her voice became stronger as she spoke, driven with emotion and power.

"Yes, sister," came from a man in front, and a multitude of "Amens," bounced off the walls from members seated throughout the sanctuary.

The old woman continued, "And I know you have heard me speak here before, with this old brain that is gettin' weak with age and can't remember yesterday very well, but can envision the streets high above paved of gold, where a chorus of angels sings 'Glory to God' and where there is true peace and happiness *for all of God's believers!*"

She raised her hands in the air as her amplified voice quivered passionately, consuming the many friends seated below with fervor and causing them to raise their hands and bow their heads in worship.

"This mind may be old," she roared, "but it knows well *where this soul is a goin' on that day of reckonin'.*"

"Hallelujah, sister!" "Amen!" "Praise God!"

The congregation rocked in the sentiments of their elder loved one. Aunt Virgiline fell to her knees at her seat holding her hands high over her head, joining the concert of "Amens."

Darryl rested his hand gently on her back. "Amen," he said.

Mr. Miras stood in the phone booth outside the motel and waited for Janis to answer the phone. He used his long retractable blade to scrape away some of the grease still under his fingernails from the night before.

"Hello."

"There were five instead of four," Miras monotoned.

"What? That can't be," Janis answered. "Who was it?"

"A Thomas Foster. He had a Florida driver's license. Panama City address."

"Was he hit?"

Miras uttered a low chuckle. "No choice."

"I'll check it out," Janis said, hanging up the phone.

Miras left the phone booth and walked across the parking lot to a rental car shop next door. The fake Massachusetts drivers license he used to register the rental was a professional masterpiece, virtually undetectable from an authentic original.

He walked to the new Chrysler Cirrus he had chosen from the wide selection of cars at the rental company and threw his Boston Celtics duffel bag in the back seat and settled behind the wheel.

Nice, he thought, quickly becoming accustomed to the new car.

He turned the key in the ignition, found an AM talk radio station, and headed west on I-16 toward Macon on the way to Columbus, about four and a half hours away.

The scenery on the interstate was unexcitedly pine trees, scrub brush, and brown open fields, and the only thing keeping him awake was a lunatic fascist on the radio ranting about all the foreigners President Clinton was letting into the country. People actually listen to this, he thought.

Late that afternoon just outside Columbus, Miras pulled off the highway into a rest stop where several tractor trailer rigs were parked for an early dinner or rendezvous with other members of the 'road club.' He circled the parking lot once then parked behind a group of pine trees at one end of the rest stop.

He approached the nearest rig, sitting silently next to two other idling trucks. It was a bright green tractor pulling a dull gray trailer filled with the latest rock and roll compact discs.

Miras stepped up on the passenger side and peered through the window. He tried the door, but it was locked. Cautiously, he hopped down from the step and crept toward the cab parked in the adjacent space, a magnificent shiny dark blue truck with a matching tanker trailer with large yellow CAUTION-FLAMMABLE signs painted every six feet.

The falling sun cast long shadows over the quiet parking lot, wrapping the eighteen-wheelers with dark cellophane fingers. The still, dry air awaited a peaceful twilight.

He reached up to the door on the passenger side, and again found it locked. He climbed the short chrome ladder and looked through the tinted window; the curtain separating the cab from the sleeping quarters was drawn, but he noticed it move now and then from a rumbling encounter on the other side.

He pulled a six-inch retractable knife from his pants' pocket and used the metal butt to tap against the closed window, careful to keep himself out of the view of those inside.

No response.

He waited a minute then rapped again, louder and longer.

Over the idling engine, he heard swearing inside from gruff male voices.

He stood on the top rung, leaning to one side of the door in anticipation of it swinging open.

Miras had hardly flipped the knife over into a working position before the door flung open and a bare-chested black man in boxer shorts angrily stuck his head through the opening, spitting obscenities at whomever interrupted his treasured afternoon intermission.

In a fluid expert swoosh, Miras lacerated the man's neck just above the larynx, spewing cartoid blood across the vinyl interior of the cab.

Reflexively, the man clutched his neck with both hands and fell back, weakly coughing a gurgling drowning sound.

Suddenly, unexpected dread grabbed Miras, never before having considered an occupational hazard of AIDS.

"Sam, who is it?" the other gruff voice asked from behind the curtain.

Miras shoved the black corpse across the cab and into the driver's seat, careful not to touch the blood pouring from the cut arteries.

He wished he had worn gloves.

"Sam, what the hell's going on?"

A husky white man in his midforties with two days growth over his sagging jowls thrust his bald reddish head through the curtain. The bewildered wrinkles on his face quickly blanched to horror as his myopic eyes focused on the bleeding lover slumped over in the front seat.

The trained assassin stretched his arm over the back of the passenger seat and carved a matching semicircle under the trucker's chin, once again, ushering his victim silently into the next life.

Ironically, the killer was struck with uncharacteristic fear.

The bald man's blood gushed downward onto Miras' right hand and arm. Immediately, the attacker grabbed a piece of the curtain and worked violently to wipe the blood from his skin. He rubbed over and over with his free hand, finding little success with the ineffective, nonabsorbent material.

"No doubt fireproof," he seethed at the dark cloth, his emotions boiling at the possibility of a terminal virus—a fateful quirk Edgar Allen Poe would have enjoyed.

For an instant, Miras debated running to the restroom and scrubbing his hand, but he opted instead to continue on schedule to his appointed round with four men in the next town.

Miras climbed into the sleeping compartment. Folded on the small shelf above the single-sized mattress were a pair of worn Levis. He grabbed the jeans and shook them upside down until they relinquished a set of keys on a chain with a white rabbit's foot.

"Not too lucky today, my friend," he mused.

At the far end of the shelf, Miras found a bottle of Listerine and dumped the gold liquid over his left hand and arm. Though the thought of smelling like mouthwash the rest of the day was not appealing, he hoped the alcohol would kill any unwelcome viruses swimming among his pores.

He unlocked the green tractor, set the engine idling, then returned to his rental car, which he pulled around next to the polished chrome wheels of the blue tanker trailer. Recovering his duffel bag out of the back, Miras hurried over and tossed his belongings into the bright green cab. He climbed behind the wheel and steered the rig loaded with CDs down the return ramp, parking it alongside the pavement a few hundred yards from the state highway.

He left the engine running, and hopped down from the cab.

On the driver's side of his truck, Miras pried the toolbox and found a couple of greasy rags in the lower compartment among a set of box wrenches and several adjustable diesel engine tools.

With the rags in hand, he jogged back to the tanker rig with the two dead men inside and proceeded to destroy evidence of a murder.

None of the drivers in the other three rigs ever rolled down a window or opened a door for air, apparently enthralled in rapture and oblivious to their outside surroundings.

When he reached the blue tanker, he hurried to the far side, hidden from the other trucks. There, he knotted the two rags together and immersed them into the fuel tank. He used the dripping rags to slosh a stream of fuel onto the asphalt leading about ten feet from the truck.

With the fuse in place on the pavement, he struck a match and watched the familiar sight of the chasing fire. He watched the oily liquid until it began throwing a line of black smoke, then darted back to the bright green rig already in position toward the state highway.

About ten yards from his getaway rig, Miras heard the first explosion. Intent on his escape, he did not turn to see the blaze licking the limbs of nearby pine trees and billowing a column of dense black smoke into the air.

The second blast, exponentially more powerful than the first, shot a mushroom of fire into the heavens, rocking the arsonist's truck as it merged with traffic on the highway over a hundred yards away from the point of impact. The intense heat exploded the rental car into the air and crashed it upside-down onto the pavement, where its charred remnants turned slowly against the friction of the asphalt like a switched-off propeller.

Glowing scraps of metal and fiery chunks of rubber flew from the colossal inferno, pelting the other trucks that had served as convenient afternoon one-room motels.

Four naked truckers ran on trembling legs from their cabs, never blushing as they scampered for the safety of the forest on the northern border of the rest stop.

AFTER TEN MINUTES of bouncing in the rig at fifty miles per hour, Miras exited the highway at Columbus. He turned down a road lined with honky-tonks and tattoo parlors advertising specials for the college students from Auburn University that flooded the streets on the weekends. He checked his watch and shifted down as the rig approached the intersection leading to Golden Park.

As the bottom half of the sun disappeared behind the horizon, Miras brought the truck around to a side street opposite where construction was underway for the Olympic softball venue.

The diesel rumbled in neutral.

Miras unzipped his NBA duffel bag and retrieved a pair of high resolution binoculars, focusing on a group of workers collecting their tools and materials at the end of a day of blasting granite. One worker, wearing protective lead-lined gear, returned boxes of explosives into a red armored-car-looking truck with Hayes Demolition signs painted in white on the side. The others tossed equipment into the back of a red GMC pickup.

Miras put the binoculars on the dashboard and reached into the duffel bag again to find the apparatus of straps and buckles he had fashioned from military-issue paratrooping gear left over from his mercenary days.

He turned around in his seat and slipped the straps over the back of the driver seat, snapping fasteners securely along the sides. He pulled the harness over his shoulders and between his legs, firmed up the tension, and buckled the straps tightly around his torso.

After zipping up the duffel bag, he tossed it out the door.

On this Sunday evening, there were no other cars on the streets around the construction, giving the killer free passage to the road ahead. He revved the engine and proceeded slowly toward a stop sign where his side road dead ended into another street curving toward the work location.

Periodically, Miras glanced through the binoculars at his targets.

Two of the men playfully tossed clods of dirt at each other, spraying clouds of dust into the filtered sunlight each time a chunk landed on mark. The older of the two was clearly the better marksman, staying clean while his younger coworker repeatedly shook loose dirt from beneath his shirt.

The big armored vehicle pulled out of the dirt lot and headed in the opposite direction from the bright green rig. At the stop sign, Miras slipped the gearshift lever to N and watched a magnified view of the last four workers climb into the pickup and head for the road home. He waited for the four doors to slam before turning left onto the intersecting road.

The tractor trailer rig started picking up speed along the sweeping curved runway on a course toward the dusty vehicle that lay only a short distance ahead, but out of view.

The demolition worker behind the wheel of the red pickup impatiently whipped his small truck onto the road toward downtown Columbus, flooring the throttle all the way.

Just as the pickup's dual tires bounced onto the pavement, the right rear quarter panel suddenly collapsed like wadded paper under the massive impact of the hurling rig.

Instantly, the rear of the truck became airborne and the gasoline tanks in both sides of the bed exploded into flames.

The men riding unbelted in the truck tumbled unrestrained over one another, the crumpling steel fracturing their bones and the broken glass flying from the windshield and side windows gashing their faces, arms, and legs as if they rolled within a barrel pierced by an armory of knives. Flesh and blood mingled inside the cab like a crazed beast had been unleashed.

The pickup rolled onto its roof, squashed like an empty can of Bud, and wedged under the front bumper of the stolen rig, spraying a barrage of sparks as it slid along the pavement.

Miras unbuckled his straps and continued accelerating his truck, aiming the thundering mass toward the trees lining the edge of the road. He opened the door and stepped down onto the small landing on the side of the cab, still holding onto the steering wheel with his right hand.

As the flaming pickup and raging tractor trailer crossed onto the dirt shoulder, the assassin leapt from the cab and rolled clear from the hurling train an instant before it slammed into a host of pines, throwing fiery chutes in every direction from a central ball of flames.

Miras grinned, watching the glorious finale of a long day's work that had begun on the coast of Georgia. His black eyes glistened with pride, basking in picture perfect timing.

He rolled onto his back and gazed at the orange and purple above. The warmth of the blaze on the side of his face reminded him of camping as a youth and the serenity and oneness it engendered.

There, facing heaven, blanketed by autumn air made warm by distant billowing flames, Miras relished satisfaction.

JANIS HOPPED UP THE STAIRS of the IBM Tower and waved at the security guard in the lobby.

"Working late again tonight, Mr. Janis?" the uniformed man asked.

"Harvey, I'll only be an hour or so. I brought you some coffee cake from Entenmann's bakery. Didn't want you to get too bored around here."

"Gee, thanks, Mr. Janis." The security man held the box up to his nose. "Smells great! Want to join me for some before going upstairs?"

Janis barely slowed down, heading for the elevators. "Can't tonight, buddy. Gotta make sure we have all the funds we need to pull off the games, you know."

"Sure, Mr. Janis." The young black man smiled and waved as Janis disappeared behind the elevator doors.

He did not exit on the floor for the finance department. Instead, he stopped at the personnel offices, resting dormant under the red glow of exit signs and security lights.

Using a master key, he unlocked the secretary's office he had used seven or eight times before, sat in her familiar plaid chair, and clicked on the brass gooseneck lamp atop her desk.

Janis chuckled to himself.

The lamp had been a present from him, a feigned show of appreciation. For Victoria Milton and Darryl Clements' secretaries, bouquets of flowers were the gifts of choice to reward their altruistic dedication on behalf of his fictitious foundation, but, in all three cases, his true intention was the same.

In the after-hours' dark, the lamp cast just the right amount of light needed to illuminate the computer keyboard. Over the modem, Janis dialed into the insurance data bank and opened the personnel file menu, selecting the subcontractor title. He instructed the machine to search for Thomas Foster, and within seconds a screen appeared listing him as an employee of the steel subcontractor for the Wassaw Sound venue in Savannah.

Janis selected the insurance directory, and the computer demanded an access code. Janis typed in the number he'd sweetly extorted from Darryl's secretary and was rewarded with the life insurance screen for Thomas Foster.

Janis immediately tabbed to the worker classification line. Class Seven.

"What luck," Janis said in the dark.

He paged down to the beneficiary line.

"Son of a bitch!" he yelled, angrily shoving himself back from the desk and slamming the back of the ergonomic chair into metal filing cabinets behind him.

Typed on the beneficiary line was the name LaRouge, R., with an address listed in Panama City, Florida.

Janis leaned over in the chair and rested his elbows on his knees. He ran his fingers over and over through his hair.

Thus far, every worker had been targeted for their lack of family. No loose ends, no one around to scream for a lost loved one or, more importantly, to demand his insurance benefits.

Everything had proceeded as planned, the account amassed millions every week.

Janis felt cocky. He could not resist the temptation for another juicy sum.

After several minutes in silence, he rolled back to the desk and moved the cursor to the beginning letter of the name. He pressed the delete key eleven times, then typed, "none."

He tabbed down to the second-to-the-last question on the insurance form that asked, "Do you wish to assign your benefits to the 1996 Olympic Foundation?" He deleted the "x" in the no box and marked the yes box instead.

"A half a million here, a half a million there, and pretty soon you're talking real money."

Sixteen

The critter darted like a miniature fighter pilot about the antique-looking light fixtures suspended high from the yellowed plaster ceiling, creating a pandemonium sideshow to the endless verbosity and offering Mark a welcome distraction to the oral handball being played across the table.

For the third time, the naughty fly lighted on the bulbous nose of the state senate majority leader, as his red complexion deepened with frustration and embarrassment.

Mark's chuckles grew, watching the man's stubby arms wave in front of his face and over his glowing dome in cumbersome attempts to ward off the relentless assault. Mark's composure melted before the comedy playing in the room.

An outspoken councilwoman from south Atlanta ducked the soaring bug as it curiously explored the shiny rhinestones stuck haphazardly to her silk hat.

Mark searched desperately for a distraction, fearing the status quo jeopardized his job. He looked past the long line of heads cocked in attention to the laborious discourse of yet another AOC meeting. A few feet away he found

Michelle wearing a blank gaze, attesting her mind, too, was someplace other than inside the paneled room.

Mark studied her form in detail.

She sat with her legs crossed, showing her deliciously nylon-covered thighs. Her voluptuous right foot played with a black patent-leather, high-heel pump she had kicked off during one of the congressmen's orations, her thin toes sensuously chasing the shoe in a circle, rubbing playfully through the mustard-colored carpet that reminded Mark of the paint on his first grade classroom walls.

His eyes finally attracted her attention, surprising her by his salacious expression amidst the quibbling that had been running on for over two hours.

Squirming in his chair next to other assistant directors, Mark watched the august group of legislators, city councilmen, the governor, and the AOC executive board fight for their own special interests in the Olympic Games. When the governor stood up, everyone else rose accordingly, finding their feet tingling with blood for the first time in hours.

Mark broke away from the other security staff members attending the meeting and scooted around the table to where Michelle collected her papers into an attaché case.

"I thought they'd never shut up," he said, surprising her from behind.

"Oh, Mark," she said, startled. "Yeah, I know. Can you believe it?"

"Want some lunch?"

"Sure, that'd be nice. I gotta call the office, though, before I go." The two walked closely together, rubbing their shoulders as they exited the conference room and headed down a hall toward the atrium of the capitol building. "Let me go make a call over there at the pay phones and I'll meet you in the lobby in a couple of minutes."

"That's a big ten-four, Rubber Duck."

She crossed her eyes at his lame attempt to be funny.

Mark crossed his arms across his chest and leaned against the marble wall enjoying a fresh breeze blowing in through the propped-open front doors. Another heavenly fall day in the South.

With the atrium crowded with state employees on their way to lunch, Mark caught sight of Janis at the old man's newsstand.

Mark watched keenly as Janis paid the old man then slid two small newspapers under his arm and hurried out the doors.

Mark quickly crossed the lobby and approached the newsstand.

"Excuse me, sir," he said anxiously to the attendant, unaware of the large woman who had arrived at the newsstand just ahead of him.

"No, excuse me!" she announced haughtily, pressing a *Glamour* magazine and a ten dollar bill at the older black man. "I believe I was here first."

She was enormous.

"Pardon me, ma'am. I didn't realize you were . . ."

"I should say not!" she fumed. "You obviously were centered on yourself, content in your own little world and your own little concerns, oblivious to any and everyone around you who might be doing business here."

Mark half expected the marble floor might crack under the stress as she walked off.

"Help you, sir?" the older man asked from behind the counter.

"Yes, please. I'm interested in the papers the gentleman just purchased a minute ago."

The old man's face furrowed. He paused for what seemed like days to Mark. "Oh, yeah. That fella who just left. Wanted a copy of the *Savannah News* and the *Columbus Ledger Inquirer.*"

"I'd like copies too, please," Mark said.

"Strange papers to be reading, if you ask me," the old man said, pushing the brim of his hat up above his receded gray hairline. "What's all the interest in Savannah and Columbus? Nothin' happenin' there, mister. Nothin' ever

197

happens in Columbus, 'cept maybe a cow dyin'." He chuckled at his own joke.

"Yeah, well, thanks a bunch," Mark said, taking the two papers and hurrying back to where he had left Michelle.

Unaware of the noise and confusion in the capitol lobby, Mark stuck the Columbus paper under his arm and ripped through the Savannah news. His first survey found an entire section devoted to Wassaw Sound and the Olympic venue construction. His eyes scoured the pages for information, but came up empty.

He dropped the first paper at his feet and hurried into the Columbus paper, glancing up quickly to see if Michelle were approaching.

Mark was amazed the paper had little news about anything worthwhile. How do they stay in business?

On the fourth page was a large black-and-white photo of charred trees and the skeleton remains of a pickup truck. An accident with a tractor trailer rig early Sunday evening had left four men dead in the pickup truck, but there was no sign of the driver of the eighteen-wheeler.

Mark almost turned the page, but caught glimpse of the word, "Olympic," near the end of the article.

The four men in the burned pickup truck had worked for Hayes Demolition, Inc., a subcontractor for the Olympic softball venue at Golden Park.

Construction workers killed, same as in Athens.

Mark stooped down and grabbed the Savannah paper again. He rushed through the articles, then stopped abruptly.

There it was.

On the fifth page of the front section was an article about five men shot in an alley behind the River Walk. All five worked for a steel grid subcontractor for the Olympic yachting venue.

Mark felt drops roll down his spine. He stared at the article long after he had finished reading the words for the third time. His mind raced trying to piece together some theory connecting the three accidents.

"You ready?"

He flinched and nearly dropped the paper.

"Mark. Are you all right?" Michelle asked. "Your face is white as a ghost."

He closed the paper hastily as if he had been caught enjoying a *Playboy* in middle school. "Yeah, sure. Let's go, I'm starving."

"Why are you reading a Savannah newspaper?" Michelle's voice was a pleasant improvement over the exchanges in the conference room earlier that morning.

"Oh, I guess someone left it here where I was standing, and I, uh, just picked it up to pass the time . . . while I *anxiously anticipated your return*," he charmed.

JANIS CAREFULLY CLIPPED the picture of the burned truck and the lengthy article below it and painstakingly glued the newsprint to a cardboard page in the blue binder. Next, he drew out the Savannah paper and excised the article about the alley mugging, artfully positioning it on another piece of cardboard.

So many weeks of planning. So much attention to detail. The anticipation had been exhilarating, but the completed plan was disappointing. Nothing else to do. Nothing else to live for. No climax awaits.

He did not focus on anything in the room, searching instead for the soul of his lost father, wandering through the afterlife, screaming his father's name. Begging him to explain why he had died constructing a skyscraper, why he had left his only son, why he thought money could replace love.

Janis yearned for a gun, or a knife, or a rope—anything to take his life and to stop the pain.

SEVENTEEN

There's a Miss Ruby LaRouge here to see you," Sylvia said over the intercom.

"Who's that?" Darryl asked, looking up from his keyboard. "Does she have an appointment?"

"Well, not exactly," Sylvia whispered. "But she seems very distraught. Says she's been passed around by all the managers of our venue subcontractors, the general contractors, the Savannah police, and now AOC."

"Sounds like a nutcase," Darryl quipped.

"Please. I think you ought to talk to her."

Darryl looked at his watch. He was behind schedule again.

"Okay, Sylvia," he sighed. "Send her in."

Darryl swiveled around to face an attractive but unkempt young lady in her late twenties enter his office.

"Miss LaRouge, I'm Darryl Clements. How can I help you?" He extended his hand in greeting the young woman wearing a wrinkled yellow sundress and a discolored white cardigan sweater. Her beige lace-up shoes had red mud stains on the sides.

"You in charge of insurance, sir?" she asked in an unmistakable Cajun accent. "That's who I need to see, the man in charge of insurance."

"Well, ma'am, I'm the director of insurance for venue construction. There are other offices handlin' policies for other aspects of the Olympics. What exactly are your concerns?"

"My concerns?" Her swollen eyes filled with tears. "My concern is Thomas Foster, or I guess I mean *was* my concern, sir. See, me and him were gonna get married after this job, see, and now . . ." She burst into violent sobs. "Now he's done got shot in an alley in Savannah."

Darryl felt uncomfortable having the crying girl in his office. He pushed the intercom button.

"Sylvia, would you please bring Miss LaRouge a Coke and some Kleenex?"

"Yes, sir," Sylvia answered, and in less than a minute, entered and offered the distraught girl something to drink.

"Sylvia, maybe you'd pull up a chair and set a while," Darryl pleaded, dreading to face tears alone.

"Sure," Sylvia replied.

"There, there, now miss. Just take it easy," Darryl said. "Take your time and tell us the whole story."

Sylvia inched her chair closer to the crying girl, looking on with genuine sympathy.

"Well, like I said," the girl continued. "Me and Thomas had it all planned out. We were getting married as soon as he was through working in Savannah on the shipyard. I didn't like him being there much anyhow. He does real dangerous work, you know, climbing up beams and bolting 'em together. I don't like it, but there was no changing the man."

Darryl sat patiently on the edge of his desk, rejoicing the sobbing had subsided.

"Last weekend, Thomas was out with some of his buddies from work and they were all gunned down and robbed in an alley out behind where they were drinking. I couldn't believe it when I heard—couldn't believe Thomas was gone and I would never see him again."

The crying started up again, but the girl was able to compose herself and continue her story.

"Later when I talked to the police department and to Thomas' boss down there in Savannah, they told me Thomas had left his insurance money to a charity here in Atlanta. It was a lot of money, sir. I don't know the exact amount, but it was a heap."

She blotted her eyes with the tissues Sylvia provided. "Sir, my Thomas was a good man, a caring man, but I don't believe he would've gave all that money away and left me with nothing. I think something's wrong here, but nobody seems to be able to help me. They told me you would know the answer. That's why I come here now, to find the answer. You tell me Thomas gave all that money away, and I'll leave and never bother you again. But, sir, please look in your books and see if Thomas did what they say."

Darryl sat with his mouth open. He was aware of accidents at the construction sites and had been involved with the investigations regarding safety precautions and OSHA regulations for the underwriters, but the transfer of funds bypassed his office completely.

"Miss LaRouge, I'm so sorry to hear of your loss," Darryl said. "But Miss, my office only contracted with the insurance companies who were the underwriters for the construction crews at the various venues around the southeast. We followed the specifications handed down from AOC and arranged the policies accordingly. There must be sixty or seventy underwriting companies for our part of the Olympic venture alone. About all I can tell you is which company wrote Mr. Foster's policy and how much the benefits were."

Ruby LaRouge nodded silently, tears dropping from her eyes.

Darryl's heart melted, desperately wanting to help.

"Look here," he said. "Let me show you the information we have. Maybe it'll make you feel better looking over this with me."

Darryl went back to the chair behind his desk and turned the computer screen on his desk.

"See, Miss, in here we have all the files for the employees of every contractor working on the venues." Darryl punched a few keys and showed the list of general contractors and their subs as of last week.

"Now we can call up any individual worker by going through this menu," Darryl explained, clinking on the appropriate window and opening another colored screen. The computer demanded the access code for employee information.

Darryl turned to Sylvia and asked, "What's the code for employee information?"

Sylvia did not hesitate; she worked in the files almost on a daily basis. "Don't you remember, you made up the access codes."

Darryl grinned. "I know it's something to do with the Heels, but I can't remember which one."

"It's 'Chapel Hill.'"

"Oh yeah," he said, typing in the code. The submenu for individual worker data flashed onto the screen.

Darryl tapped in 'Foster, Thomas' and his data sheet appeared.

"See here, Miss," Darryl pointed to the screen at the line reading 'beneficiary.' "This is where he indicated no beneficiary on his term life insurance policy, and here," he paged down to the bottom of the form, "is where he marked his intention to donate any benefits upon his demise to the 1996 Olympic Foundation."

Ruby LaRouge stood up and leaned over the desk to peer closer at the screen. "But, that ain't Thomas' writing. That's just a computer saying he done it. Thomas didn't talk to no computer, did he?"

"Well, that's true, Miss," Darryl conceded. "He filled out a form through his foreman and they forwarded it to us and we fed the information into this program."

"I wanna see the form Thomas filled out," the young woman said. "Then I'll be satisfied and I'll leave you alone."

Sylvia came closer to the desk. "We do have those forms in storage, Miss LaRouge. It may take me a few minutes to locate Mr. Foster's form, but I can sure try."

"I'd sure appreciate it if you would," Miss LaRouge said.

"Really, it's no problem. Let me just write down his form number from the screen here and I'll be back as soon as I can. Mr. Clements, would you read me the code number for Mr. Foster?"

Darryl returned to the top of the page. "It's H-12007."

"Thanks," Sylvia replied. "I'll be back in a flash. Miss LaRouge, why don't you come out here in our reception area and flip through a magazine. I'll try to hurry."

The two women left Darryl alone in his office.

SYLVIA UNLOCKED THE HEAVY METAL door and slapped the wall in search of the light switch. Going to the storeroom was considered scum duty by Darryl's employees; the huge room contained thousands of cardboard file boxes stacked on metal shelves. The dust was typically an inch thick in the room, and Sylvia had to blow away a dense layer from the card catalogue before opening the "H" drawer.

She thumbed through the index cards in the oak chest of drawers Darryl had bought from a school auction. He'd picked up the antique when he first started his business. Although elaborate software was available for warehouse storage, Darryl felt the card catalogue worked just fine for him.

Sylvia found the card for the H-12000s; it read 47-5, directing her to the fifth shelf in the forty-seventh row.

She paced down the aisle of gray metal shelves, pulling behind her a stepladder on wheels. At the forty-seventh row, she wheeled the ladder next to the shelves and climbed up the six steps to view the top platform.

Rolling the staircase to the far end of the shelves, she scaled the elevator a second time. She found boxes H-11000 and H-13000, but box H-12000 was nowhere to be seen.

She looked across the shelf below. She backed the stairs up and looked at the top shelf, about midway down the line. No sign of H-12000.

Frustrated, Sylvia ran back to her desk and told Darryl what she had found.

"All the other boxes were in order," she said, exasperated. "The only box missing was the one I needed."

"It'll turn up," Darryl reassured her. "Did you see if anyone in the back was using it? Maybe somebody's on a case outta that same box."

"I didn't ask anyone. Maybe I'll go see now if anyone has it."

"Honey, don't spend anymore time on it now. The information on the computer is gonna be the same as the data sheet. Go tell Miss LaRouge that you'll locate the sheet this week and you'll give her a call once you find it."

Darryl spread his arms over his desk covered with stacks of files and paper-clipped reports.

"I got plenty of work to keep you busy for the next several days," he said, looking down at his cluttered desk. "And to put it quite frankly, Miss LaRouge's concern just isn't gonna pan out. Besides, we can all think it's crazy, but for whatever reason, it looks like Mr. Foster wanted his money to go to the children's fund."

BACK IN HIS OFFICE after lunch, Mark took out the Athens newspaper and folded back the other pages so only the article about the construction accident showed. He arranged the Savannah and Columbus papers the same way and put them all in a row on his desk.

He dialed directory assistance for the Cleveland, Tennessee, sheriffs department.

Once connected, Mark discovered all the officers assigned to the construction accident at the Ocoee River were in a meeting and would not be available until tomorrow morning, at the earliest.

He met a similar obstacle in the Savannah police department.

Mark tried the Columbus sheriff. Another female voice answered and directed his call to the first officer to arrive on the scene of the tractor trailer accident.

"Deputy Clark at your service."

Geez, sounds like he's eighteen, Mark thought.

"What can I do you for?" Deputy Clark asked.

"First of all, thanks for taking the time to talk with me this afternoon," Mark said, employing all his diplomatic skills acquired from the master, Hank Powell. "I know you must be swamped with work and I'll only take about five minutes."

Mark could hear the young man on the other end chewing something as he spoke.

"Hey, buddy, think nothing of it. Shit, nothing happening 'round here this afternoon anyhoo. What's on your mind?"

"I'm interested in the accident involving the tractor trailer rig last weekend. Can you tell me what happened?" Mark sat ready with a pen and yellow legal pad.

"Ooooo-weee, it was a mess!" Deputy Clark snorted. "When I got there, the boys inside that pickup was already toast." Mark could hear chewing between every two or three words. "First thing I did was get on the horn for the fire trucks before the whole damn town burned down. Took out seven acres, ya know, and nearly reached old man Blanchard's place."

"Could you tell what happened, deputy, *what caused the accident?*"

"Couldn't say for sure, good buddy," the deputy continued. "No sign of the truck driver no where. The truck was registered to a single operator out of Wilmington, North

Carolina, but his wife filed a missing persons report on him a couple days after it happened. No one seen hide nor hair of him since he left home last Wednesday on a run to Mobile."

"I see," Mark said, listening as Deputy Clark paused to spit.

"Got to talk to some fancy insurance fella outta Hollywood, California, though, 'bout them compact discs he was hauling. Guess Madonna's gonna lose a few sales this week, huh?" The deputy laughed heartily at his remarkable induction.

"You may be right there," Mark agreed. "So there's been no progress in locating the driver?"

"Nope."

"Any fingerprints or other identifying pieces of evidence, like blood or hair?"

The deputy laughed uproariously, ending in a siege of glottic hacking that sounded like he might choke to death while holding the phone.

"Son, there weren't nothing left from that there fire but charred bits of dirt and steel. Even them CDs in the back was melted in a blob, kinda like that robot bad guy did in *Terminator 2*. You know, when they got him in that steel factory and the heat was so bad he split up into them little wiggly blobs."

"Yeah, okay, I see," Mark said disappointedly. "So the entire accident remains a mystery."

"You got that right, good buddy, lest you know something I don't."

"'Fraid not."

Mark frowned. He was beginning to sound like the deputy.

"If you locate the driver," Mark said, clearly enunciating every syllable, "would you be so kind as to call me?"

"You got a big ten-four on that, Rubber Duck," the deputy said.

Geez, Mark thought.

Eighteen

According to Mark's experience, motives for perpetrating crimes fell into one of three categories: sex, greed, or power. And while he had not eliminated any of the possibilities in the Janis case, greed or power seemed the most logical.

Engrossed in his self-appointed mission, Mark slighted any private life. Over the past three months his friends, neighbors, and hobbies became a hodgepodge of background noise and motion, like unedited film clips awaiting a director's sense of order.

For lack of attention, his kitchen cabinets continued exfoliating their paint, and every morning before filling the automatic coffee maker Mark brushed away curved peels of enamel that had dropped like dead leaves during the night onto the ceramic tile countertops. Old sheets still draped his bathroom windows, and the luster of his unfettered hardwood floors now seemed out of place beside cracked fixtures and broken appliances, including the cantankerous old garbage disposal that hung beneath his chipped porcelain kitchen sink, behaving obstinately as a daily reminder of the lord's domestic neglect.

Nevertheless, when he left his office again late in the day, Mark did not venture straight home to mend his ways, but instead he chose a quick dinner at Chick-Fil-A.

Mark knew he should discuss with Hank what he had found, or more accurately, suspected, but he hesitated involving his boss in an affair the CEO, out of blind loyalty, had clearly instructed him to leave alone.

He needed *hard* evidence.

Salting his waffle fries, Mark watched puzzled as the white crystals completely missed his unseasoned potatoes and danced away from him across the table. With his mind hopelessly preoccupied, he had shaken the paper packet backwards, aiming the falling stream toward the center of the table.

Which am I now: Larry, Moe, or Curly?

He quickly brushed the salt off the table, deciding it was time to take action. The mystery surrounding the assistant director of finance had grown too great to sit back and watch from the sideline—the struggle was beginning to control him instead of the other way around.

After eating, Mark resolved to go back to the IBM Tower and snoop through Janis' office. Perhaps there would be a clue on his desk or in a drawer; Janis may have become careless and overlooked a piece of damning evidence amongst his notes or calendars. Perhaps Mark could finally put this issue to rest.

"WORKING LATE TONIGHT, SIR?" The guard greeted all after-hours executives with the same stock salutation.

"Just a few lose ends to tie up," Mark replied, signing in his office number. "Have a good evening."

He rode up to his floor, just in case the security agent happened to notice where the car stopped. Then he descended the stairs one floor to the finance department. Mark had to use his passkey to unlock the stairway door.

The floor was dark and silent. Brushing his hands along the grass-papered walls, he stepped toward the elevators where an emergency light cast a golden glow, making the mauve carpet look plum colored in the incandescent haze.

Mark continued down the hallway to Janis' office. Suddenly, he heard a loud slam of a door, and with his heart in his throat he fell to his knees, crouching below the large glass window in the wall, hidden in the shadow of the hallway.

He did not move for several minutes, staying crouched and listening.

After a minute, the sound of a man whistling came from far down the hall, followed by a second loud slam of the heavy metal door leading to the service area of the building—a member of the night janitorial crew ambling through another boring shift.

Mark rose slowly to his feet and used his key to unlock the door to Janis' office.

In the dark, he crossed the room and flicked on a small brass desk lamp with an unusual gooseneck shape, showering the top of the desk in a pale yellow light that barely reached to the edge of the desk. The orderliness of the desk spoke shrewdly of its owner; no loose papers, only neatly typed documents organized in color coded files banked in four tidy piles.

Mark replaced the files exactly as found and flipped on the computer. He scrolled through the daily calendar, jotting down a few of the corporate presidents and wealthy dignitaries Janis had met over the last month. Then he turned off the computer.

Mark searched the desk drawers, all unlocked except the large bottom drawer to the right. Mark fought the urge to pry it open.

A light rain began falling outside. Mark hastened his pace, reviewing the bookshelves opposite the desk, eyeing the plaques and photos on the walls and canvassing every possible connection between the office and unlawful conduct.

He went to a door behind the desk and tried the knob. Locked. Mark inserted his passkey, but the tumblers inside the bolt did not budge. He pulled out the key and turned it over and tried again. Nothing.

Why would Janis change the lock?

Mark returned to the desk to hunt a key to the door, but there was none. He had to find a way inside.

He was about to leave when the door to the office creaked open.

A shot of adrenaline instantly surged through his veins as he lunged at the desk to extinguish the lamp just as a narrow beam of a flashlight shone from the door.

Mark scuttled under the desk and inched the leather-back chair toward him, panicking at the likelihood of being found out. Hank would be pressured to fire him, irreparably disgracing Mark's career. Visions of seeking employment at a local police department shot through his mind.

The security guard from the downstairs lobby flashed his beam throughout the room. Then, just as suddenly as he came, the guard closed the door and locked it.

Mark sat motionless, listening.

After a few minutes, he heard the loud slam of the heavy metal door at the end of the hall, the security guard apparently using the service elevator to return to his post.

Mark rose and checked the desk in the dark for any misplaced folders. He crept out the door and locked it behind him.

Determined not to leave empty-handed, Mark entered the office adjacent to Janis' in hopes of better understanding the closet arrangement. This office was much smaller. Behind the desk was an identical door, and when Mark tried the passkey, the door opened easily. Inside was a rather large walk-in closet containing file cabinets and boxes of personal items. Mark felt sure the room behind Janis' desk was similar.

Mark found a light switch, but before flipping it on, he drew the door closed and stuffed crumpled paper under the door. Janis' closet had to be on the other side of the wall.

Mark stacked a few of the boxes in the corner and climbed up the cardboard ladder. Near the top, he reached up to dislodge the rectangular ceiling tile separating the room from the crawl space above.

As he dislodged the tile, his fingers scratched against a sharp barb on the metal framework, drawing blood.

"Damn it!" he cursed, licking the gash.

As he examined the cut, his left foot slipped off the edge of the box and tumbled five feet to the carpeted floor. The contents of the boxes spewed across the room.

"Son of a bitch," he grumbled, getting to his feet and replacing the boxes against the wall.

He climbed a second time and managed to pull himself up into the crawl space. Using his ring of keys, he pried up a ceiling tile from the adjacent closet and excitedly peered down into the room.

Mark reached down in the pitch black, extending his arm as far as he could. His fingertips barely brushed against the top of a metal shelf, but he could not tell how large the shelves were.

He turned around into a sitting position and dropped onto the metal shelves. His eyes still could not gather enough light to make out where he was.

Carefully trying not to turn the shelves over, he scaled down the front of the shelves and successfully jumped the last two feet without pulling the metal shelves over with himself. The room felt colder than the rest of the building—an icy breeze seemed to blow through the closed door. He blindly found the door and inched his way in the immense darkness in search of a light switch. Finding it, he flicked the plastic toggle up, but no light shown from above.

"Give me a break," Mark fussed in the dark.

He flipped the switch up and down several times and groaned.

Stumbling sightlessly around the floor, Mark found a small card table near the door with a folding chair pushed up under it. His hands passed over the table and found a lamp with the familiar gooseneck contour. Switching it on revealed a room filled with metal shelves with boxes and boxes of files.

He pulled the chair out from the table and collapsed against the metal backrest. He pulled a dusty file from the front of the nearest box, an inch-thick folder of pages from some sort of worker's compensation insurance report. Mark leafed through hundreds of actuarial tables and forecasts for various occupational hazards facing employees. The document contained thousands of facts and figures for jobs ranging from hair dressers to dental hygienists, liability attorneys to social workers—page after page tabulated the risk of losing a finger or straining a back or being blinded on the job for a countless array of businesses.

Mark closed the file and reached for another folder from the same box, sending a cloud of dark dust particles floating into the blonde fog filling the room.

He studied the second file and to his astonishment it continued with more tables begun in the first. Mark pulled the third and fourth file from the box, more of the same.

Insurance tables. What's with the insurance tables?

Mark replaced the folders and stood up to open another box off a higher shelf. He pulled out another file, this one comparing the life insurance policies purchased by various employers. Bar graphs showed the average amount of coverage sought by a typical restaurant owner, a shoe salesman, or a bank employee, depicting two standard deviations on either side of the mean. Near the back, more graphs reported that on the average, city councils purchased two hundred thousand dollar term life insurance policies for their police employees and fifty thousand dollar policies for sanitation workers, the latter as riders on mandatory disability policies.

Mark opened more boxes and found more files on insurance-related data: premiums, benefits, limitations, exemptions, exclusions, and so on, customary information in a Blue Cross & Blue Shield office, but in an assistant director of finance?

Mark was certain he had uncovered a clue, but for what?

He leaned back in the chair and stared at the ceiling, juggling pieces of evidence over and over in his mind. As he reclined, his leg bumped the table and scattered several sheets onto the floor.

Afraid of shuffling the pages out of order, Mark quickly leaned down to pick them up.

Beneath the table, Mark's eye noticed a dark brown plastic trash can with discarded newspapers extending above the rim.

His heart skipped a beat. He recognized the print.

Maintaining his methodical approach, Mark first finished replacing the insurance sheets in their original order.

His hand shook in anticipation as he reached for the trash can under the table. He pulled the can into the light and retrieved the paper, which was actually two newspapers: *The Savannah News* and *The Columbus Ledger Inquirer.*

Mark spread the papers out on the table. Large sections had been cut out. Forgetting caution, he folded up the sliced pieces and stuffed them under his shirt. "What's he going to do, have me arrested for stealing newspapers out of a trash can?"

Mark's energy rose to a level he had not enjoyed since leaving the governor's office on the way to joining the White House staff. He felt like whistling or singing while tidying up the secret annex.

With everything in order, Mark turned to survey the metal shelf behind him and his route to the ceiling passage. In the light of the brass lamp, Mark practiced his footholds on the two lower shelves, making sure he could find secure footing before he turned out the light. He felt comfortable where his right foot fit, but the second step was a little tight.

Grabbing the frame of the shelf, Mark's right hand clutched next to a blue three-ring binder.

He froze in his sprawled position.

He could not move, his eyes fixed on the binder.

At the front cover, a tiny wisp of yellowed newspaper shown above the edge of the notebook.

He stepped down from the shelf and untucked his shirt to use the tail as a hotpad around the spine of the blue binder. He drew it slowly from its place, like a chef removing a prized soufflé from the oven. Again, he took a seat at the small card table and opened the notebook with the eraser end of a pencil.

Mesmerized by the stories, Mark turned the pages deliberately, scrutinizing the sheets of stiff paper with glued newspaper articles attached, each from different newspapers but describing similar news: an accident or shooting or stabbing involving construction workers from an Olympic venue.

Finding one empty page at the end of the notebook, Mark was engulfed in a sense of urgency.

Could there be plans for more?

He would have to work fast. There was no way of knowing when Janis would notice the missing book. He pulled the newspapers from his shirt and squashed them in the back of the blue binder, careful not to touch the book with his bare fingers. He ripped his shirttail off and tied the cloth around the spine of the book so he could carry it without disturbing latent fingerprints.

Mark cut the light and climbed the metal cliff to the awaiting crawl space. He repositioned the ceiling tile and dropped down into the closet next door.

NINETEEN

Mark was relieved when the elevator bell finally
sounded; impatience was now his worst enemy.
Standing next to a bush silk tree in front of the
closed elevator doors, he played out different scenarios in
his mind for the coming hours, trying to keep his fear in
check. He was not afraid of Janis, but he worried about
overlooking a law of evidence or forgetting a critical procedure.

He had to remain focused.

Entering the elevator, he rehearsed the exact words he
would say to Hank over the phone. He had to reveal the
essence of the evidence, but at the same time remain cautiously vague over an unprotected cellular line.

Seconds after beginning the descent, the elevator slowed
to a stop just one floor below.

Mark's heart raced. Realizing other execs were working late did not make the delay any less unnerving.

The doors parted and Mark reflexively gasped.

Janis briskly stepped into the car. "So, I see someone
else is burning the midnight oil, too, eh?"

Mark clenched his jaws tight in response to the friendliness of his voice. As nonchalantly as he could, Mark switched the blue binder from his left hand into his right, away from Janis.

"Yeah," Mark finally answered as calmly as possible. "Seems like there's always a deadline to meet."

He pretended to scratch his nose while mopping the moisture forming above his mouth.

"These late nights are becoming much too frequent, I find," Janis complained. "And we still have months to go. This summer I might as well set up a tent in my office."

Or your closet, Mark thought.

"Well, it keeps the old Olympic torch lit," Mark said. "I made a promise to the council. I look at it as my duty to mankind."

"Yes, yes. You're quite right, my friend," Janis agreed, noticing a bare ring finger on Mark's left hand. "But, I still look forward to a couple of hours of recreation after a long day. Don't you?"

Mark did not reply.

Janis moved closer. "I've found this remarkable enterprise located just off Piedmont, uniquely qualified to relieve the stress of a night like this. A magnanimous hostess named Miss Adrianne has concocted the most favorable of remedies to cure ills such as ours."

Mark swallowed hard, his prey just inches from his face.

"And I hear she has a new arrival," Janis winked. "Fresh as spring."

Mark managed a curt smile. "I have an urgent appointment."

"*C'est dommage*," Janis quipped in diminishing arrogance.

With a jolt, the doors slid open and Mark pretended to fiddle with his notebook in order to let Janis exit first. Mark kept a distance of several yards, waiting for him to leave the lobby before signing out at the guard's counter.

Hurrying to his car, Mark saw Janis' NSX pull out onto West Peachtree, peeling rubber across the asphalt. He could not resist the temptation to follow the speeding maniac, telling himself it would only be for thirty minutes or so, an hour at the most, before continuing on to Hank's house.

Mark kept three cars between his front bumper and the black Acura, but he had no difficulty spotting the two-seater turning east onto Ninth Street, not far from rolling hills and massive oaks in Piedmont Park.

Janis pulled into the gravel parking lot behind Adrianne's, and Mark turned into the alley next to the brick manufacturing building just down the hill.

In spite of the changing season, hot rock and roll bellowed from several unglazed windows in the aging house. Frigid bursts of impending winter were impotent against the passion raging beneath the weathered slate tiles of Adrianne's place. The parking lot was full of Cadillacs, Mercedes, and rusted Ford pickups as men from all walks of life mingled in lust with the family of girls inside.

Mark crept up the hill to the parking lot in time to see Janis spring from his car and pounce on the front stairs like a wild animal. He watched Janis go through the front door, then checking his watch, determined he would stand his post for fifteen minutes before keeping his rendezvous with Hank.

INSIDE, COUPLES ARM IN ARM crossed in front of Janis, who removed his coat while waiting in the entry. Unlike with the other customers, none of the girls eagerly welcomed Janis and showed him to the lounge. His reputation for heavy-handedness already scarred the faces of three of the girls. His hundred dollar tips were the only reason Adrianne did not refuse his business.

"Ah, Mr. Janis, a pleasure to see you, sir," Adrianne greeted slyly, extending her hand palm down. "It's been such a long time since we've been graced with your presence."

He received her hand with a kiss. "And what a glorious vision you are this evening," Janis returned. "I'm finding my schedule more and more demanding, leaving me little time for life's more, let's say, *gratifying* distractions."

One of the bar staff brought Janis a scotch and water in a Waterford tumbler. He sipped the drink and held it up to the light, turning the glass slowly. "But, you know, it keeps the old Olympic torch lit. Just doing my duty for mankind." He burst out into a huge laugh.

Adrianne grinned superficially. "Which I'm sure you do. Let me show you to your room, Mr. Janis. I have a special surprise for you this evening. Someone who has just recently joined our family and who will be most excited to meet you. She is untamed and may require your singular talent for management."

"I have every confidence in your selection, Miss Adrianne." Janis downed the drink in two swallows as the two slowly climbed the stairs to the second floor.

She guided her client down the hallway to the end room on the right. "Here we are, sir," she said, opening the door to the small room decorated in brown and brass. "I have chosen this last room for your privacy, and," Adrianne leaned close to Janis, her lips almost brushing his ear as she whispered, "just in case things get noisy."

Adrianne crossed to the window overlooking the rear of the house. "I'm afraid this room is directly above the furnace and becomes frightfully warm. I'm going to open this window now so that you won't have to interrupt your appetite later to do so."

Janis stood beside Adrianne looking out over the parking lot below. "Sounds like I'm in for quite a match," he mused.

Adrianne glided toward the door. "Given our past relationship, Mr. Janis, I'm quite sure you'll come out on top." Then she left him alone reclining on the bronze quilted bedspread surrounded by gaudy felt wallpaper and gold tassels.

MARK NOTICED THE LIGHT turn on in the upstairs window. He felt sure he saw Janis' face behind the woman who had just opened the window. Mark had no urge to wait while the two engaged in some twisted evening entertainment.

OUTSIDE THE DOOR to Janis' room, Adrianne tightened her grip around Maria's neck as she spoke her final warning to the trembling child.

"This is the time, Maria," she hissed. "I will not accept any trouble from you. If you want to walk tomorrow the same way you do today, girl, I will receive a superlative review of your behavior." The woman panted like a beast. "Otherwise, there will be new additions to the jar in my office. Do you understand me?"

Maria stood ready to collapse, the pressure at her neck causing her head to pound and her face to turn red. She said nothing.

Adrianne shook the girl in rage, repeating, "Do you understand me, Maria?"

"Yes!" Maria managed to yell.

"Good. Now go inside."

Adrianne opened the door in front of them and shoved Maria into the room with Janis.

"Well now," Janis said in a low chilling voice. "Quite an attractive addition to the family, indeed. And what might your name be, dear angel?"

Maria kept her eyes bolted to the floor. "Maria," she quivered.

"My, my: Maria, what a lovely name," he said, rising from the bed and walking behind the frozen girl. He scooped a handful of her hair between his fingers as he stood gazing over her shoulder. "Adrianne didn't tell me you were so . . . untouched."

"Please, sir, don't hurt me," Maria pleaded. "Please, sir, just let me go. I don't want to do this. I don't want to cause you any trouble, sir. I just want to leave this place."

Drops fell from her eyes and pooled on her bare toes.
She never raised her head from its downcast position. She
did not want to see the man's face.

"Now Maria," Janis comforted. "We both know that can't
happen, dear." He felt relaxed in the room, her fear ener-
gized him. "We all have our plights in life, our roles to play,
we can't escape fate. Destiny has put us together here, tonight, in this room, for a reason. Neither of us may understand fully the purpose, but it is clearly inevitable what is to
occur."

He tugged at the bow behind Maria's neck, and the lace
gown she wore slipped to the floor.

She raised her hands to her face and sobbed into her
thin palms.

Janis viewed her crying as weakness. Anger overwhelmed him.

"Stop that wailing!"

Maria's sobs grew deeper and louder.

Janis raised his hand high above the young girl and
struck her hard from behind, smacking the side of her face
with such force she sailed across the floor crashing into the
outer wall of the room just below the open window.

Instinctively, Maria screamed out wildly in pain, holding the throbbing side of her face.

"Please, mister," she wailed, "please don't hit me!"

Janis grabbed the thin girl's long hair and tugged her
to her feet. She yelped like a wounded pup before being
smacked again with an open hand across her face.

Her shrill screams carried clearly on the cold wind,
reaching Mark's intent ears. Unsure if the sounds were pain
or pleasure, he rose from his crouch beside the fender of a
Mercedes and maneuvered through the shadows to reach
the back of the house. He was careful to keep out of sight
of the dark man standing at the corner of the front porch.

Maria continued crying uncontrollably as Janis flung
her limp body onto the bed. Hitting the mattress, the girl
immediately rolled over and tried to run for the door. With

the back of his hand, Janis whipped the child's face a third time, slicing her cheek with the diamonds of his Yale class ring.

This time, Mark distinctly understood the frail shouts of agony, and with no regard for his own position, bolted up a short flight of stairs and busted through a back door into a short hallway outside the kitchen. He was momentarily stunned by the sight of scantily clad girls busy at the counters preparing finger sandwiches and snacks, but he took no time to enjoy the view, and with the music blaring, they did not notice the intruder.

From around the corner, however, a giant man in a black suit charged at him. "Who the hell are you?" he shouted, reaching into his suit coat in search of his gun.

Without hesitation, Mark ran straight at the ape and tackled him to the ground. With all his might, he slammed his fist into the man's nose, then darted up a back staircase near the kitchen.

Another scream came from behind a door in front of him.

Again, without thought, Mark aimed his aching shoulder at the door and blasted through. Before him stood Janis with his hand raised, about to strike the prostitute he held pinned against the bed.

Mark caught the raised arm and deftly yanked it behind Janis' back. He then threw him hard against a small lamp table, shattering it into a million pieces of glass. He mercilessly pounded Janis' face and then with a sweeping fury of ecstasy, Mark jammed his knee into the criminal's groin.

Mark stood triumphantly, forgetting for a moment the gorilla downstairs on his way to seek revenge. When he turned to see if the girl on the bed were all right, his jaw dropped in astonishment.

"You're just a kid!" he gasped.

The young girl still cried hysterically, protecting her face against what she thought might be another man about to beat her.

Mark hurriedly took off his jacket and wrapped it around the shaking girl.

"Come on," he said. "Let's get the hell outta here!"

He held his arm tightly around the girl's shoulders and kicked Janis in the side one last time as the two stumbled to the door. Mark was almost carrying the distraught girl, weak and bleeding from the brutal beating.

Two men approached them from the far end of the hall. Both dressed in black, one was the mammoth Mark had already been introduced to downstairs, the other a short man, wearing a hat.

"Stop there!" the short one commanded, pointing his gun at the couple.

Mark pushed Maria down the stairs and jumped after her just as gunfire rang out behind them. Glass from the back window crashed and shattered.

Helping the terrified girl to her feet, Mark could hear the thudding footsteps of the men running down the upstairs hall after them.

"Sweetheart, we have to hurry," Mark said.

The two hurried down the back stairway and darted into the kitchen. One of Adrianne's girls jumped from behind the counter and smashed Mark in the back of his head with a cast-iron pan.

Dark spots danced in front of his eyes as he struggled to remain conscious.

Maria screamed, "Stop it! Stop it, Betty Jo. Leave him alone!"

"Ah, shut up, kid!" the blonde yelled back. "You ain't going nowhere girl!"

Regaining his senses, Mark spun around on the heel of his shoe and drove his clenched fist into her pretty sculptured nose, knocking her off her feet and sending her spread-eagle into pots and pans stacked near the sink.

At that instant, a second girl lashed at Mark with a meat cleaver swinging above her head. The beautiful black girl let out a high-pitched primordial cry as she attacked the intruder.

Mark adroitly ducked the sharp blade and kicked the side of his shoe into the attacker's svelte belly.

She landed hard against packages of flour sitting on a far counter, exploding clouds of white flour across the floor, counters, and ceiling.

"Come on!" Mark yelled. As Maria scampered to him, he grabbed her arm and hurried to the hall toward the broken, open back door. A few feet from the door, a bullet whizzed by Mark's ear, missing his head by inches before smashing into the doorjamb.

With stern determination, Mark snatched Maria around the waist with his hands and hurled her headfirst through the open door. She landed on her side and tumbled down the few stairs into a heap on the ground. Mark fell on his chest against the hardwood floor of the hallway as more gunfire pounded from behind.

Mark dug his elbows against the white oak floor and crawled through the open door, rolling down the stairs and landing on top of the terrorized girl.

"Stay low!" he said, pushing her ahead of him and away from the house.

Bullets sailed from the back door and hit the dirt around the unlikely couple.

At the edge of the parking lot, Mark jumped to his feet and slung his arm around Maria's waist, carrying her through the dark under the enormous oak trees outside the house.

Mark could hear the two men screaming to one another as gunfire continued storming around him. He darted behind trees, racing down the bank toward his car.

At the fence, he tossed Maria over the rail, sending her rolling down the hill on her side. He crossed behind her and skidded against a carpet of dead leaves. He caught up to the girl at the bottom of the bank.

For the first time in that instant, their faces met.

"Come on!" Mark screamed. "Don't stop now. My car is just down this alley. We can make it!"

He scooped up her limp body in his arms and ran down the alley toward his car. As he set her on the hood to open the front door, a pair of headlights cut through the black night, blinding Mark as he squinted down the alley at the oncoming car.

He threw the girl across the front seat, then turned the ignition, praying out loud the car would start quickly.

The engine turned over, and immediately Mark jammed the gearshift lever into reverse, nearly ripping the handle from the steering column in the process.

Blue smoke flew from the screeching tires as he sped the car backwards away from the bright oncoming headlights. At the end of the alley, Mark slammed the car into drive.

Just as the chase car sped into the cul-de-sac in front of Mark's Taurus, he floored the accelerator and rammed the black sedan directly at the driver's side door crashing the car into the brick wall lining the alley below the bank up to the old house.

Mark could see the faces of the two fierce men who had been firing at him moments before. Pinned between his grill and the brick wall, they looked defenseless until the massive ape behind the wheel pulled a gun and began shooting into the windshield of the Taurus.

"Get down!" Mark screamed, shoving Maria onto the floorboard.

Without rising, Mark shifted the car into reverse and backed up, smashing his rear bumper into the loading dock behind him. Glass shattered and fell from the windshield onto his face and arms. The sound was deafening, and the hot smell of blood seemed to accompany every bullet.

Mark pulled the lever down into drive, and stomped on the gas, hurling his car into the black sedan for a second time. The shooting stopped, and slowly Mark sat up and peered over the dashboard of the car.

Silence fell upon the alley.

Quickly, Mark shifted the car into reverse and backed away from the gunmen. Leaving even more rubber behind, he sped his car out of the alley and onto Piedmont Street, straining to see through the wind barreling through the huge gaps in his shattered windshield.

Maria maintained her fetal position on the floorboard of the car. Mark could not hear her whimpers, he was fixed on saving her life.

TWENTY

Constantly checking the rearview mirror for signs of Adrianne's gunmen, Mark skidded around the corner of Ponce de Leon Avenue, speeding east toward his Decatur neighborhood. He dialed Hank's home number.

Maria still had not moved from her balled-up hiding place.

With his face numb from the icy wind careening through the broken windshield, Mark held the phone to his frozen ear waiting for someone to answer.

"Mark, what the hell is going on? You were supposed to be here by now." Hank's voice was a mixture of concern and irritation.

"Can't talk now. There's been a change in plans."

"Change, hell!" Hank screamed. "You get your ass up here right now and tell me what exactly is going on or your butt is in a sling that I'm gonna tie to the top of the IBM Tower, boy!"

"No can do, boss," Mark returned. "Ran into an emergency that I have to handle, pronto."

"Does it involve Janis?" Hank asked.

"In a way, but not directly with AOC."

"Where are you now?" Hank said. "Sounds like you're in a wind tunnel."

Under the tense circumstances, Hank's description hit Mark funny. Laughing he said, "You ever see *Ace Ventura: Pet Detective?*"

"What!"

"Never mind," Mark chuckled. "Look, I'll be at your house within one hour, guaranteed. Everything will make sense when I see you."

"It better." The harshness in Hank's voice then subsided. "Listen buddy boy, you be careful out there. I want to see you in one piece. Whatever is going on, it's not worth risking your life over, you got that?"

"Roger that one, chief," Mark replied. "All will be clear in an hour. I'll see you then."

Mark hit the red button on the handset and dropped it on the seat next to him. With all that had happened during the evening, his muscles stayed flexed and tight. His foot rammed the accelerator against the floor, and he hardly noticed his Taurus racing at over seventy miles per hour passed every car on the city street.

He checked the rearview mirror for the thousandth time and eased off the throttle.

Turning left onto Clairmont, he finally felt safe from the thugs left behind in the alley, and his interest turned to the shivering girl. Even at full force, the Delco heater could not keep up with the wind storm blowing through the broken glass, the steady gusts threatening to scar both passengers with frostbite. Until now, panic had fueled a sweltering fire, warming them from the inside out. Only now did the two notice their painfully blue extremities.

"How you doing, Hot Shot?" Mark called to the kid.

"Cold!" Maria answered.

"I know, me too." Mark's nose felt like it would crack off his face from the slightest bump. "We'll be at my house in a second and get thawed out. Then I'll make a couple of calls and see where you can stay for a while."

Maria abruptly uncoiled from her cocoon and sprang onto the seat next to Mark.

"Please mister, please don't send me away!"

Surprised by her sudden outburst, Mark slowed the car and pulled into a Majik Market parking lot.

"Now, Honey, just settle down a minute," Mark said. "Everything's okay now. Nobody's going to hurt you, I'll see to that. You see, I live alone, you can't stay at my place. I know a church that can take care of you . . . ."

Maria quickly opened the door on her side of the car and started to bolt.

"Hold on there, little lady," Mark said, grabbing her arm. "What's the matter?"

"You don't understand." The little face was stern and determined. *"I've already been to a church and I'm not going back! I'd rather take my chances on my own."*

"With those hit men after you? How long do you think you'd last on the streets by yourself?"

Tears swelled in Maria's dark eyes again. "I don't care! I know I can't trust anyone anymore!" Sobs flooded from within. "I'd rather just be left alone!"

She buried her face in the too-long coat sleeves covering her hands and cried hard.

Mark put his arm around the girl's shoulder and pulled her next to him.

"Listen . . . listen, uh . . . hey, I don't even know your name." He reached under her chin with his right hand and tipped her face up into view; the girl kept her eyes cast down, continuing to spill tears across the front seat.

"Come on, Sweetheart, tell me your name."

Too distraught to say anything, her wailing crescendoed until finally breaking into coughs.

"Hey, hey, Little One, take it easy," Mark said softly. "Now listen to me." He put his hands on her shoulders and turned so the two faced each other. "We are going to get through this together, you understand? I'm not going to leave you, and I'm not going to let anyone hurt you . . . not ever again. Do you hear me?"

The girl nodded silently.

"But, you're going to have to trust me, okay?" He brushed back strands of her brown hair from her cold face.

"And a good way to start is by telling me your name."

"M-M-Maria," she quivered.

Mark smiled, and brushed the back of his fingers against her smudged cheek. "There now, that wasn't so bad, was it?"

He tipped her face up again. "Nice to meet you, Maria, I'm your friend, Mark."

TWENTY-ONE

Mark propped the phone on his shoulder and cut the bottoms off a pair of old maroon sweatpants left over from his early days in Washington when the vice president attended every Redskin home game. Everyone on the secret service team got a pair from the owner of the club after an end-of-the-season party.

He had already sliced away about ten inches off the sleeves of a Gold's Gym sweatshirt; years ago, it too had been a favorite. Now he was just relieved it had been in the *clean* laundry basket.

"Hello?" the woman answered, a little piqued to have been bothered after ten o'clock at night.

"Miss Marvelyn, this is Mark."

"My heavens, son. What makes you call me so late? Are you all right?"

"Yes, I'm fine," Mark said. "I'm sorry to bother you this late, but I need a favor. It's kinda an emergency."

"Sure, dear. What's the matter?"

"I need you to come over and stay the night tonight."

"You need me to do what?" The phone had awoken the older woman dosing on the couch in front of a black-and-white *Perry Mason* rerun. She was not sure she heard Mark correctly.

"Really, Marvelyn, I need you to come over tonight if at all possible. It's a long story, but I've got a little girl staying at my house, and I can't be here alone with her all night."

"I'll be there in fifteen minutes." Having known Mark all of his life, Marvelyn did not unleash a flurry of questions.

Mark spread the home-tailored sweatpants and shirt out on the bed in his bedroom adjacent to where Maria enjoyed a hot shower. Then he closed the bedroom door and returned to the den to wait.

He checked the clock to be sure he had time to arrive at the appointed meeting with Hank, then collapsed in a soft leather reclining chair in front of the TV.

He fell asleep on the second breath.

"IT'S ABOUT DAMN TIME!" Janis fumed, closing the glass door against the Arctic wind. "I've been here almost an hour freezing my ass off!"

Mr. Miras replied in his customary suave demeanor. "I did not receive the message until minutes ago."

Janis' teeth chattered as he spoke. "I had the front desk page you immediately after I called." He wiped his dripping nose with the back of his sleeve, grimacing in pain from the swelling brought on by the madman's fist back at Adrianne's. He raised the lapels of his suit coat in a vain effort to warm his neck. The noise from the traffic passing by the BP station on Peachtree made it hard for him to hear the cursive expressions on the other end of the line.

"I was in another room," Miras explained, "being *entertained.*"

"Well you're damn lucky you called when you did. I was about to storm the hotel myself."

"Might that have exposed us?" Miras said, rather enjoying irritating his high-rolling friend.

"Listen to me," Janis ordered. "We've got a problem. I was followed earlier this evening by someone working at AOC. I've seen him before at executive council meetings, I think he works in security. I'm worried he knows something."

Miras was unaffected. "How could he know?"

"I don't know," Janis said with growing agitation. "But I want to make sure."

"What would you have me do?" Miras asked.

"Tomorrow there will be a packet at the front desk for you, it'll have his bio from the AOC bulletin. Check him out."

Miras paused for a moment, then said, "And the final job?"

Janis quickly answered, "It's still on, of course."

Miras nodded at the other end. After a few seconds of neither man speaking, Janis offered, "Who knows, maybe there will be an AOC executive who just happens to be involved in the accident, too."

THE DOORBELL SHOOK MARK back to the real world. He rose from his recliner, surprised by how easily he had fallen asleep.

"Thanks so much for coming, Marvelyn."

"Mark, are you okay?" she asked. She carried an overnight bag, a liter of Coke, and a box of mint Girl Scout cookies.

"Yeah, everything's all right," Mark said, taking the bag and treats from her arms and leading her to the kitchen. "It's a long story, Marvelyn. I'm not sure how it will all turn out. Have a seat in the den. I'm going to look in on our houseguest."

Mark hurried down the hall to his room. He had not heard a sound from that end of the house since passing out in the recliner. The anxiety he felt as his feet pounded the polished hardwood floors amazed him; he had only known this kid for an hour or so, she had only uttered a dozen words. And yet, he felt gripped with a devotion that was foreign to him, almost uncomfortable.

He reached the door to his room and hurriedly turned the knob.

There she was, fast asleep, swallowed up by his Gold's Gym sweatshirt and Redskins' pants. He quietly crossed the room and turned out the light in the bathroom and the two lamps on his nightstands. Gently pulling the bedspread from the bottom of the bed, he covered the child and pushed back the wet long hair away from her shoulders.

In the hall, he whispered and gestured for Marvelyn to come to his room.

Seeing the child, she gasped and put her hand over her open mouth. Marvelyn looked at Mark then looked at the girl again.

"Who is she?" Marvelyn whispered.

Mark motioned for them to go back to the den. He pulled the door closed and slowly released the knob.

"Who is she?" Marvelyn said, sitting down on the crowded sofa.

"I don't know," Mark answered.

"What do you mean, you don't know," Marvelyn said sternly. "How did she get here."

Mark crossed the den to the kitchen and picked up the binder still wrapped in his torn shirt. He opened the book on the coffee table and sat down on the couch beside her.

"There's an assistant director of finance at AOC named Janis," Mark began, using his shirttail to turn the pages of the notebook. "He's killing construction workers."

"He's what!" Marvelyn shouted.

"I know it sounds crazy. Just give me a minute to explain."

Mark got up from the couch and walked to the mantle over the fireplace. He looked at the photos of his father and himself taken on a French beach when Mark was a toddler.

"It all started when I was compiling personal histories on the AOC directors and ADs for internal security." Mark ran his fingers through his hair as he spoke. He never turned away from the picture of him and the general. "You know those reports, because you typed them for me. Well, I don't know if you remember, Marvelyn, but one of those reports was a fraction of the size of all of the other ones."

Mark faced Marvelyn and sat on the hearth, holding his head in his hands. "I searched every database I could find: secret service, CIA, FBI, Justice, the IRS, federal penitentiary files, state prison records, class records at Yale, personnel files at the Midland Bank, national and state chamber of commerce registries, civic clubs, real estate records, state patrol files both in Illinois and Florida . . . everything! But, nothing came up on this guy, I mean nothing!"

Mark looked up at Marvelyn. "No big deal, right? Maybe he's just young, maybe he's never had a speeding ticket, maybe he's just squeaky clean . . . maybe I was making a mountain out of a molehill."

He leaned back and looked at the ceiling. "You remember that meeting I had with Hank and Victoria in our department conference room? Remember how long it lasted?"

Marvelyn nodded.

"At that meeting I reported my suspicions about Janis. You know what Victoria said? She blasted me, and I mean hard! In so many words she said that Janis had been handpicked by her dear lifelong friend, Caldwell Lockhart, and that I'd be out on my ass before Janis would!"

Mark rose to his feet again, upset by the memory of the meeting. He paced fiercely back and forth in front of the fireplace as he continued his story.

"Well, I figured it was time to drop the whole thing. After all, I couldn't afford to get cut off from AOC over a hunch. So I cooled it. Left it alone. Chalked it up to experience and went back to focusing on our security network."

Mark stopped abruptly, and with a faraway look on his face, he held up his hand and pointed a finger in the air like a prosecutor in front of a jury.

"Then I saw Janis in the lobby of the IBM building. There he stood, casually talking to another man in finance, and under his arm was an *Athens Herald*. An *Athens Herald!* Now what in the hell would he be doing reading an *Athens Herald?*"

"Mark!" Marvelyn scolded. She used to do the same thing when his dad would slip and used profanity in front of her. The general cursed like a sailor, but out of respect, never formed an off-color remark in Marvelyn's presence, at least not without her calling his attention to the fact.

"Sorry, Marvelyn," Mark apologized. "Anyway, I tracked down an Athens paper and stowed it in my desk at the office. It didn't mean anything at the time, but later when I noticed Janis at the state capitol newsstand buying a Savannah and Columbus paper, I knew something was up. Look here at this book. This was in a closet in Janis' office."

Marvelyn read the first few articles about construction accidents, then looked blankly back at Mark.

"Don't you see? He's behind these accidents, Marvelyn. In his closet where I found this book were boxes and boxes of insurance actuarial tables and reports on life insurance coverage. He is somehow directing these insurance benefits to himself."

Marvelyn remained skeptical. "Mark, how could he steal benefits? They're paid to these poor men's families. Surely their wives would be screaming if they didn't receive any insurance money from their husbands' deaths."

The older woman looked back down at the open blue binder. "Dear, couldn't it be you've overreacted?"

Mark was dumbfounded by Marvelyn's response.

"What does this all have to do with the girl in your bedroom?"

Mark had almost forgotten. "Tonight, as I was leaving the office, Janis boarded the elevator. I followed him from

the IBM building to this whor—I mean, this house of ill re-
pute on Piedmont Avenue. I waited in the parking lot to
see where he would go, and I heard Maria screaming her
lungs out from a room upstairs. I couldn't just stand by and
let someone beat her to death. So I busted in the back and
went upstairs to help. Low and behold, it was this scumball
Janis in the room with her, slapping her face until she bled."

"My heavens," Marvelyn gasped.

"Damn straight," Mark slipped, feeling a surge of emotion as he recalled seeing Janis standing over the bleeding
girl. "Well I drove him into the wall and grabbed the girl
and ran out of the place."

"How did you know she wanted to go," Marvelyn interrupted. "Maybe she works there, Mark."

"Believe me, Marvelyn, this girl didn't belong there. It
was easy to tell. Janis was beating her up 'cause she wasn't
cooperating!"

His heart began to pound as the memories clearly came
to mind. "Two of the so-called guards of the place shot at us
as we ran away to my car."

"Oh my heavens! You could have been killed!"

"I know," Mark continued. "But we weren't. We made
it safe and sound, and I'm not sending that kid back to that
dungeon no matter what!"

He rubbed his hand across his forehead as moisture began to bead along his brow. Just thinking about what he
had been through made him shake. "And what's more,
Marvelyn, I'm going to bring that piece of crap down. He's
behind a lot worse than what happened tonight. First thing
tomorrow morning I'm going to the insurance director's
office and get to the bottom of this. I want you to stay here
and take care of Maria. She's going to be pretty shaken
after tonight."

"I'll stay as long as you need me to. I know you'll find
out what all this means, and I'll be behind you every step of
the way."

Sweet Marvelyn, Mark thought. There are so few saints like you.

He collected the blue binder and the newspaper scraps from Janis' closet and put them on the antique vanity by the front door. Then he went back down the hall and tiptoed into his bedroom to check on Maria, before heading toward a midtown meeting with his boss.

TWENTY-TWO

After only about four hours sleep, Mark sat awake at his kitchen table sipping a cupful from his second pot of coffee. The meeting with Hank had gone better than expected. The colonel shared his suspicions and had agreed to present Mark's findings to Victoria in a meeting at eight.

The hallway light flipped on.

Marvelyn came into the kitchen wearing a flannel bathrobe and pink fluffy slippers.

Mark smiled to himself thinking she looked like she had just stepped out of an episode of *The Honeymooners*.

"Good morning, dear," she said. "Did you get any sleep?"

"Not much," Mark answered. "So much to think about. Pretty important day coming up. I've been thinking about the next steps to take. I want to be sure not to miss anything. The last thing I want to happen is for this guy get off 'cause I missed something."

Marvelyn poured herself a cup of coffee and joined him at the table.

"What *is* next?" she asked.

"I'm not sure," he said, rubbing the day-old growth on his chin.

The tension rising from him was so strong it seemed to dim the kitchen lights.

The sky outside was predawn black. Frost hung on dead leaves and formed a crusty layer of sleep over Mother Nature's eyes as winter's first freeze ushered in a day overcast in gloom.

Marvelyn sat quietly and let Mark take his time.

"I'm supposed to meet Hank in Victoria's office at eight o'clock," he said. "But I'm not going to show."

Marvelyn remained calm. "Why not? Didn't it go well with the colonel last night?"

"Yeah, it went fine," Mark said. "That's not it. Quite frankly I'm scared to take the time."

"What?"

"I mean it, Marvelyn. I'm scared to waste time trying to convince Victoria we have a problem while this maniac is still loose plotting another kill. What if she doesn't buy it?"

Marvelyn cupped both hands around her mug. "What do you mean?"

"Well, she could hold her ground and call all this just a bunch of speculation." Mark rose from his chair and looked out the back window.

"She could put everything on hold and insist on consulting with her beloved Mr. Lockhart before continuing with the investigation."

"Maybe that would be a good idea," Marvelyn offered. "Maybe you and Hank ought to talk to Mr. Lockhart and show him what you've uncovered."

"Yeah, and then what?" Mark snapped, turning away from the window. "He'd want to meet with Janis, right? And Janis is no idiot. I'm sure he's got a whole story cooked up to cover himself. And in the meantime, someone else gets killed and more money is mysteriously transferred to this asshole!"

"Mark!"

"I'm sorry, Marvelyn, but I'm not standing still anymore. I'm going to do everything in my power to nail this guy *before* someone else gets killed."

"So, what are you going to do?"

"I'll be sitting outside the insurance director's office when it opens this morning. I'm banking on the two of us unraveling the money transfer."

"And, what if you can't?"

Mark did not respond. His mind was already down the road, solving another dilemma.

"Mark," Marvelyn said again. "What if you can't find out how he's been transferring the money?"

He touched her face gently with his fingers. The muscles in his shoulders and those running up his back relaxed.

"What would I do without you, Marvelyn?" he said softly. "Don't worry about me."

"Oh, but I do . . ." the woman started.

"Don't. I'll be fine. I just need you to stay here and take care of Maria. Feed her a good breakfast and let her watch TV. The kid probably hasn't watched a cartoon in ages."

SYLVIA WAS THE FIRST TO ARRIVE AT THE OFFICE.

Mark sat in the parking lot, waiting for the lights to switch on inside. He wiggled his toes over and over to keep frostbite at bay.

The instant he saw activity, he left his car and ran up to the office doors, shaking them on their hinges.

"We're not open yet!" Sylvia yelled.

"I'm with AOC security." Mark's breath froze on the panes as he spoke. "I need to see Mr. Clements right away."

"Mr. Clements has not arrived yet," she screamed. "Come back a little later or call me and I'll be glad to make you an appointment."

Mark pulled his ID from his wallet and plastered it to the window. "This is an emergency!" he yelled. "I must see Mr. Clements first thing!"

Sylvia stared at the plastic coated card pressed against the glass.

Mark glared back. "I'm not leaving, Miss. You might as well let me in."

Grudgingly, she unlocked the door, unleashing the cold air from outside.

"Thanks," he said. "I'm Mark Townsend, assistant director of AOC security. I need to see Mr. Clements right now."

Sylvia was a little put off by the man's abruptness.

"Like I told you, sir, Mr. Clements has not arrived yet, and when he does, he has a full schedule for the day. I'm afraid I'm going to have to make you an appointment to see him."

Mark followed her down the hall toward her desk.

"Listen, this is an emergency," he said calmly. "I cannot wait till tomorrow. I can't wait an hour, I have to see Mr. Clements first thing."

"I understand you feel you must see him, but . . ."

Mark leaned closer. "This is a matter of life and death, Miss," he said sternly. "If I don't see Mr. Clements now someone may die!"

Sylvia was silent.

Mark did not move and did not blink.

"Please sit down right over there," she finally instructed. "I'll tell Mr. Clements you're here when he arrives."

"Thank you," Mark said. "You have been most helpful."

At ten minutes after eight, Darryl came down the hall from the rear parking lot.

Mark bolted from his chair to meet him before he reached Sylvia's desk.

"Mr. Clements, I'm Mark Townsend with AOC security." Mark extended his hand.

Surprised, Darryl looked at Sylvia for a clue.

"I'm sorry, Mr. Clements, he was here when I arrived. I told him you have a full schedule today, but . . ."

Mark interrupted, "What she's trying to say, sir, is I'm very persistent."

Darryl set down his briefcase.

"I see you are at that," he said, shaking Mark's hand. "How come you're here so early in the morning? Security got different hours from the rest of us?"

"I'm afraid this is an emergency, sir. Could we step into your office?"

Darryl's smile slipped off his face. "Come on inside and tell me how I can help."

The two men left a frustrated Sylvia alone in the reception area and entered Darryl's office. Mark closed the door behind them.

"What's on your mind?" Darryl asked.

Mark unwrapped the blue binder and opened it on Darryl's desk. "I think we have a problem. I wish I had more time to fill you in on all the details, but this was found in an office of an AOC official."

Darryl reached to page through the book, but Mark grabbed his arm. "I'd appreciate you turning the pages with one of these."

Mark handed him a pencil with the eraser down.

Darryl gazed back at him. The puzzled expression was mixed with a dash of suspicion.

"Just what exactly does this mean?" Darryl asked.

"This official has gone to great effort to chronicle the unfortunate deaths of the construction workers working on Olympic venues." Mark paused a moment to let what he had just said sink in. Then added, "Don't you find that strange?"

Darryl continued turning the pages of the notebook. "Why, this has stuff I haven't heard of."

Mark looked surprised. "What do you mean? Wouldn't you have records of all accidents involving the workers?"

Darryl could not lift his eyes from the book. He paged through the articles for a second time. He acted as though he had not heard Mark's last question.

"Mr. Clements, wouldn't you . . ."

"Call me Darryl," he said, looking up from the book with a grave expression. "I heard what you asked. Look here, man." Darryl pointed at the article from the Savannah paper. "This was no accident, this was a street murder, so my office was never notified of these deaths. And, look here."

Darryl turned to the Columbus cutout.

"See, this one was a car accident. These didn't happen at the venues."

"But the workers still had life insurance through AOC," Mark prodded.

"Probably," Darryl agreed. "But we keep careful records of venue accidents for OSHA and local officials. The investigations are real thorough. I've got all the coroner's reports and police documents for venue accidents. But, if someone walks out of their house and gets struck by lightning or something, I probably wouldn't get a call."

Darryl looked down at the pages in the blue binder again. "That's what's real strange about this. How would someone know about this car accident or the mugging in Savannah?"

The two men looked at each other.

Darryl asked again, "How would he know about these guys getting shot or the guys killed in the tractor-trailer accident?"

Mark raised his eyebrows. "Unless he knew they were going to happen."

Darryl stared in Mark's eyes.

"Now hold on here. Your telling me somebody had these guys killed? That's a little far-fetched wouldn't you say?"

"You tell me," Mark said. "How much money are we talking about? Looks like he could have planned this for the life insurance benefits."

Darryl looked back down at the articles in the blue binder. He turned the pages slowly, assessing where the accidents had occurred. He rubbed his chin and shook his head slowly side to side.

"Looks like a lot of Class Seven workers," he said slowly to himself.

"What?"

"Class Seven workers," Darryl repeated. "Looks like these accidents involved a lot of Class Seven workers."

Mark was confused. "Class Seven, what's that?"

"The AOC specs break down the more than fifteen thousand construction workers into categories for insurance purposes," Darryl explained. "AOC called for higher benefits for riskier jobs. The guys running a crane don't get as much benefit as the guys walking the steel a hundred feet in the air. The greater the risk, the higher the benefit. Seems like all the guys talked about in this book you brought are all Class Sevens."

"And, Class Seven workers. Do they get high benefits?" Mark knew the answer before he asked the question.

"The highest."

It was falling into place. Mark's concentration deepened as Darryl continued.

"See here, these guys in Tennessee were moving giant rocks weighing several tons. Over here . . ." Darryl flipped the page in the binder, ". . . these guys worked for a demolition company, you know, blowing up rock with dynamite."

Without pausing, Mark asked, "So how much money we talking about?"

Darryl shook his head again, turning forward a few pages, then flipping back to the front of the book. "Can't tell you exactly. See, the specs call for a *range* for Class Seven workers."

Mark felt a surge of excitement. He could feel he was getting close. "What kind of range?"

"AOC gives the underwriters some leeway in the term life and disability benefits." Darryl said. "Even within each category."

"Okay, so what about Class Sevens?"

Darryl swiveled in his chair to face the two black notebooks. He turned through a couple of chapters in the first book, then slammed it shut and opened the second. After shuffling several pages, he pointed to the bottom third of a sheet and said, "Here it is."

Printed in the "CLASS VII" column headed "LIFE BEN-EFITS" were the numbers "$500,000-1,000,000."

Mark reflexively sunk into the armchair behind him.

"Hey, you okay?" Darryl asked. "Buddy, you don't look so good."

Mark forced the shock to pass quickly from him. He moved his chair up to the desk facing Darryl. He grabbed a pencil and flipped the pages in the binder back to the beginning.

"Look here," he said. "Let's count up the number dead."

He sounded morbid, but at the moment he could not care less.

Mark found a notepad. "Call them out to me, and give me your best guess if they're Class Seven or not."

Darryl shook his head. "I can't guarantee I know the class of worker just from looking at these articles."

"That's okay," Mark said. "Just give it your best shot. I want to get some handle on the money involved. It'll give us both an idea if we're on the right track."

Darryl shrugged in agreement and with his pencil in hand, looked at the first page. "Three in the first article, I'm guessing all Class Seven."

He turned the page. "Let's see here . . ." he mumbled the words to himself as he quickly scanned through the newsprint, ". . . four in the second, definitely all Class Seven."

"Three here, looks like they were Class Sevens."

The newspaper articles bounced around all over the southeast. Workers met their untimely demise on buses home, in restaurants, and on the freeway. The carnage entailed a house fire, an apparent suicide, a Mafia hit, and a trio of drug overdoses. The vast majority of deaths occurred elsewhere than at a venue construction site.

". . . Four, Class Sevens . . . uh, four more. Damn, all Class Sevens again!"

Darryl felt nauseated. The grotesque pieces of a revolting mural were beginning to meld together. Sweat broke out over his brow, and he punched the intercom and asked Sylvia to bring him a Coke.

Darryl fought to clear his throat.

"Excuse me. Two more here—uh um!—both Class Sevens."

Mark, on the other hand, was feeling better with each article. He eagerly continued tallying the dead as Darryl called them out.

"Two . . . no, make that three, uh, hold on a minute. Yep, all Class Sevens."

"Four more, Class Sevens."

After several minutes, they finished the thirty pages. Mark looked up from his notepad, startled by Darryl's ashen face.

"Eighty-seven total," he said without expression.

TWENTY-THREE

Darryl leaned way back in his chair holding a wet cloth over his forehead. "Hey look," Mark said. "There's no way you could have known."

"You seem to be taking it pretty good," Darryl groaned, his voice quivering like he'd been up all night drinking.

"It's not that I'm glad about this," Mark replied. "But you got to understand, I've been hunting for some kind of clue for weeks. I knew this guy was dirty. I *knew* it. But, I couldn't prove a thing."

Darryl took the rag off his head. "So, what can you prove now, Sherlock?"

Mark stopped.

"Well, nothing exactly," he admitted. "But, we're not done."

"Oh yeah?"

"Come on, you got to help me unravel this." Mark stood up and started pacing around the office. "How could someone steal the insurance benefits."

"Maybe he went to the homes with a gun and said 'Give me your check or I'll blow you away,'" Darryl chided.

Mark glared back at Darryl.

"Okay, okay. I want to ream this guy just as much as you." He slammed his elbows onto his desktop and grabbed his temples. "It's just that my stomach ain't cut out for chasing no murderer."

Mark grinned. "Hey man, you're doing just fine. I had zilch till you started helping."

"So who is this guy, anyway?" Darryl asked.

Mark hesitated, unsure if it were prudent to reveal his suspect. After all, Darryl was right, he could not prove a thing. All his evidence was conjecture.

Darryl silently watched Mark wrestle with his request to know. It was a hurdle of trust that in his mind he had earned.

Mark turned away from the desk and faced the door to the office. He took two steps in thought, then spoke to the wall.

"His name is Janis. He's the assistant director of finance under Caldwell Lockhart."

"I'll be damned," Darryl swore to himself. The idea that their man could be so high up in the AOC was dumbfounding.

Mark turned back around. The two men looked hard at each other, internalizing the bond just created by the shared suspicion.

"Okay then," Mark started. "How could he get the benefits from the families?"

DARRYL AND MARK moved behind the desk and watched over Sylvia's shoulder.

Darryl pointed to an article on the desk.

"Okay," Mark said. "First thing is a list of the workers killed in Savannah."

Sylvia flew through the contractor's file, found the list of workers, and identified those who were terminated from payroll on the day after the mugging.

One name stood out to her.

"Look," she said, pointing to the names on the screen. "That's the Thomas Foster that Miss LaRouge was asking about."

Mark looked at Darryl, who stared to the heavens as if he had just seen a ghost.

"What?" Mark queried.

"My gosh, why didn't I remember!"

"What? what?" Mark prodded anxiously.

"There *was* someone asking about life benefits," Darryl explained.

"Who?"

"This lady named LaRouge came to our office all upset 'cause she'd been told her fiancé hadn't left her his insurance."

"Yeah, yeah," Mark said. "So what did you do?"

"Well, we called up his file on the computer and it said he had left his benefits to the Olympic charity for kids."

"To *what?*"

Darryl nodded his head. "Yeah, it all checked out. AOC set up the 1996 Olympic Foundation for helping poor kids in Georgia, see, and on our forms is an option for a worker to assign his benefits to the charity fund. This lady felt sure it was wrong, but his file said he had directed the funds to go to the charity and not to her."

While the two men talked, Sylvia located Thomas Foster's file and his data showed on the screen.

Darryl pointed to the line where the benefits were directed to the charitable fund.

"But I never found the form," Sylvia interjected.

"What?" Mark felt out of the loop.

"The form Mr. Foster would have filled out at the job. The one we key into the data bank here at our office. I never found the original."

"That's right," Darryl said. "I remember now. Miss LaRouge said she wouldn't believe the computer until she saw the form Thomas filled out himself. Then she'd be satisfied."

"But, I never could find it," Sylvia added.

"So, where is it?" Mark asked.

Sylvia answered first, "It should be in our warehouse room, but I couldn't find the file box. The box preceding this one and the one after were both right where they should be, but this one was missing."

"Show me," Mark said.

THE THREE OF THEM STOOD looking up at the rows of file boxes on the gray metal shelves.

What Sylvia had told them was true, the box for H-12000s was not where it belonged.

"What could have happened to it?" Mark asked.

"Beats the heck out of me," Darryl complained.

Mark walked to the end of the row of shelves.

"Who else has access to this room?"

"Only our staff here at the office," Sylvia answered. "Most of our group doesn't ever want to come in here. They send a secretary if they can get away with it."

"But who at AOC could come in here?"

Darryl piped up, "Nobody at AOC. They got no reason to want to get in here."

"Then it's got to be here," Mark said. "Let's split up and look around."

The three went separate directions in the twelve thousand square-foot room. On one wall near the back of the room, Mark found a pile of old boxes split with age. They looked like a collection waiting for the dumpster outside once the mound grew large enough. He shifted through the dusty heap wondering if the box had found its way there by mistake. Throwing lids to one side, he checked the numbers on the outside of each discarded piece of cardboard.

Nothing.

Across the room at the other corner of the back wall were stacks of new boxes unfolded and lying flat next to a stack of unfolded lids. Mark poked around for a clue. A few of the boxes had been folded along their scored lines and assembled into working form. About ten were stacked ready to hold more insurance forms arriving from the field.

Mark quickly grabbed each one and looked inside, hoping to find a few of the H-12000s.

Frustrated, he kicked one of the empty boxes and sent it flying around the corner of a row of shelves. He punched a couple more boxes with his fists, releasing the tension brewing inside. He sat on the cold concrete, staring at the boxes. The fatigue from a sleepless night suddenly hit him.

It's got to be here, he thought.

In the distance he heard Darryl and Sylvia shouting to each other about places to look for possible scenarios that would account for its disappearance.

Mark restacked the boxes he had attacked and walked over to retrieve the one he had kicked. Turning the corner, he saw several hundred sheets of paper scattered across the floor next to a box with the bottom ripped out.

"Hey guys, over here!"

The other two joined him quickly. They each excitedly rustled through the stack in search of H-12007. Sheets flew in every direction behind the circle of three as they flung discarded forms from their area of focus.

"This is it, this is it!" Sylvia screamed, holding up the form.

The other two dropped their forms and hurried behind her. Six eyes scanned down the form to the beneficiary line.

Next to the "Assignment of Benefits" question, in poor half-cursive-half-printed penmanship, was the name, Ruby LaRouge.

Darryl exhaled slowly. "Son of a bitch!"

THE THREE HURRIED DOWN the hall back to Darryl's office like a medical emergency team on their way to a code red.

"What's next?" Darryl asked, as they arrived.

"We've got to figure out who changed the data in the computer." Mark's step quickened as he thought out loud. "We need to know who had access to the file from the time

252

it was created." He was almost running wind sprints between the office walls. "Somehow, we've got to find out every time this file was opened. I don't think this was an error in the original data entry. Someone changed it on purpose."

Mark crossed quickly to the phone and dialed the number for the Justice Department in Washington.

"So what's up?" Darryl asked.

"I've got a friend in Washington who can give me the name of someone here in Atlanta who can help."

A female voice answered on the other end of the line. "United States Justice Department, may I help you?"

"Jerry Ackworth, please."

"WHICH ONE OF YOU IS MARK TOWNSEND?"

The man standing at the door to Darryl's office looked like he'd been wandering in a daze since about 1969. His faded tie-dyed tee shirt had holes worn through the shoulder seams, and his pale blue jeans were almost white.

Mark was not surprised.

"I'm Mark Townsend," he said holding out his right hand.

The bearded fellow waved nonchalantly and walked passed Mark. "I'm Fanny," he said, slamming a leather satchel right on top of the blue three-ring binder opened on Darryl's desk. He didn't wait to be introduced to Darryl or Sylvia.

Mark darted to the desk.

"Careful! This book's damned important." He picked up the dirty bag and closed the book with a cloth, moving it to the protection of a bookshelf on the far side of the room.

"Who the hell are . . ." Darryl began, but was cut off by Mark holding a finger up to his mouth.

"Sorry, man," the hacker said. "Didn't see it." He slid behind the desk and plopped into Darryl's chair. "This the file, man?"

"Yes," Mark said, forming a row with Darryl and Sylvia behind Darryl's chair and noticing the widening bald spot on Fanny's crown. "Jerry said you could help us find out when this file was opened."

"No problem." The hacker eagerly typed several commands, paused, then typed another stream of codes. Mark's first impression was that Fanny was still high from the night before.

In minutes, the hippie pushed away from the desk. "Created 0942, October nineteenth at the mother station, I assumed that's here?"

"Well, here in our office," Sylvia answered. "There's a room across the hall with several . . ."

Fanny interrupted, acting like her words were not worth his attention. "Opened a second time 1322, October twentieth, again at mother station."

Sylvia started again, "Probably the backup processor double checking the entry. Mr. Clements insisted that we review all entries a second time for accuracy to ensure . . ."

"Then it was opened at 0940, November eighteenth."

Sylvia hesitated to be sure he was through talking. "That would've been when Miss LaRouge was here and we showed her Mr. Foster's records." She spoke quickly, trying to get all the words in before being cut off.

The hacker eased back up to the desk and typed a few more commands. "No more entries from the mother station till today."

He pushed back the chair like he was going to leave, carelessly running one of the wheels over Darryl's foot.

"Hold on there," Mark blurted. "How about other entries? *No one* else could have opened this file?"

Fanny grabbed the handles of his tool bag. "That's all I see, man," he said coming out from behind the desk.

Mark hurried closely behind him. "How about access from sources other than here in this insurance office. Couldn't someone get into the file over a modem?"

Fanny turned around to face Mark. "Yeah, someone could get in over the phone. You didn't ask me to check that." The disgusted hacker shook his gaunt pale face back and forth, implying Mark's understanding of computer software was, at best, feeble.

"Well, we need you to research that for us. Let me be clear, we need to know of *anyone* opening this file between the time it was created until today."

The hippie slammed his bag back on the desk and settled into the desk chair again.

"All you had to do was say so, man."

He folded his legs in a yoga position and pulled the keyboard into his lap, leaning back in Darryl's chair and typing on the keys like he were playing a musical instrument for his own relaxation. His long dirty toenails hung over the edge of the well-worn leather and hemp sandals loosely hanging from his bony feet, which were either numb from the cold morning or made unaware of the freezing temperature by pharmaceutical insulation.

He looked up from the screen. "It's gonna take a minute, if you guys want to chill out a while," he said, barely waiting for phrases to blimp onto the screen before his fingers raced across the keyboard canted on one thigh.

"We're okay," Mark assured him. "We'll wait here."

"Whatever," the computer whiz slurred back.

Darryl and Sylvia sat in the armchairs opposite the desk while Mark resumed his aerobic traipsing.

All three were startled by the shrill sound of the printer jetting ink onto a continuous feed sheet.

They huddled around the desk.

Aware of the audience, Fanny ripped the page and a half off the serrated chrome teeth and tossed it onto the desk. "It's all there on the printout."

Mark was first to pick up the sheet.

Between lines of technical jargon was a date and time the file had been opened from a source outside the insurance office. On that occasion, the file had been opened at night, at 2011 hours. The phone number printed beside the entry had a local prefix.

Mark grabbed the phone and started dialing.

"It may be a computer, man," Fanny quipped with eyes half closed.

Mark looked up, intent on the ringing coming over the line.

"Mr. Proctor's office, Mable speaking. How can I help you?" The voice sounded grandmotherly.

Mark shrugged at the others in the room. Darryl moved close so he could hear over the receiver, too.

"Is Mr. Proctor in, please?" Mark asked.

"No, I'm sorry, he's in a meeting and will not be back to his desk until after one o'clock. Is there anything I can help you with?"

Mark paused, thinking of an angle to get the woman to tell him who Mr. Proctor was.

"I'm Mark Townsend with the IRS." Everyone's afraid of the IRS. "I have a document I need to get to Mr. Proctor this afternoon. Could you give me directions to your office?"

"Yes, sir, I'd be happy to," the secretary answered. "Are you familiar with Atlanta, sir?"

"Yes, I am."

"We're located in the IBM Tower on the fourth floor. When you exit the elevators, turn right and our office is the fourth on the left."

Mark's heart quickened. He fought to keep his voice from quivering.

"Will you be there over lunch, Mable? Someone has to sign for this parcel."

"I leave at 12:15, sir, but there is always someone here who could sign if I am not around."

"That won't be necessary," Mark said. "I'll be there within thirty minutes."

Fanny still would not shake hands. With his bag slung over his shoulder, he held up two fingers in an antiquated peace sign and left the office without a word.

TWENTY-FOUR

Mark pulled into his usual spot in the basement parking deck and glanced at his watch, remembering that he told Marvelyn he would call to check on Maria around ten o'clock. He decided to wait until after meeting Mable and finding out who this Mr. Proctor was.

Wild visions formed in his mind of an underground criminal network within AOC reaching as high as the CEO. *Maybe that's why she objected so strenuously to my suggestions about Janis.*

The elevator doors opened and Mark stepped aboard the empty car, dismissing his last thought as absurd and cursing his own unbridled imagination.

Arriving at the specified door, Mark found a woman in her late sixties sitting behind a desk with a nameplate, Mable Stevens, near the front edge between a brass desk lamp and her computer terminal. She nodded to Mark as she spoke, writing a message for her boss on a steno pad.

"How do you do, I'm Mark Townsend from the IRS. I believe we spoke not long ago."

"Why yes, I'm Mable Stevens. I hope you didn't have any trouble finding us here."

"None at all," Mark replied. "Your directions were perfect."

"Well that's good," Mable said, removing her reading glasses and letting them dangle from the gold chain around her neck. "As I recall you had something for Mr. Proctor?"

"Yes Ma'am, that's correct, but I'm afraid I can't leave the package with you. On my way up the elevator, I received the message on my pager to only deliver the papers to Mr. Proctor in person."

"Oh?"

Mark held his hands palm up out to his sides and shrugged. "I've been instructed to deliver the document only to Mr. Proctor, so I'll have to come back later."

"I see. Well I'm sorry you made the trip for nothing." Mable's hands trembled slightly as her eyes left Mark and darted over her desk as if she were searching for something. "Here, couldn't you sit down for a moment and have a cup of coffee? We have a fresh pot just around the corner."

"Well, I guess I could stay just for a few minutes," Mark stammered, pretending to acquiesce. "After all, it is pretty cold outside today."

"Oh indeed. I still haven't got the chill off from this morning." She pushed her chair back from her desk and invited Mark to sit in an armchair while she served the coffee.

"Cream or sugar?"

"No ma'am, just black."

With the secretary gone, Mark rapidly searched through the papers on her desk, scavenged through two of her drawers, and peeked into Mr. Proctor's empty office.

"Here we are, Mr. Townsend. Steaming hot!" Mable handed him the Styrofoam cup with a white napkin. "That should melt the frost from your bones!"

"Thank you, ma'am." Mark hastily took his seat. "Hits the spot."

Mable pulled her sweater tighter around her shoulders. "Are you a family man, Mr. Townsend?"

"No," Mark replied. "Not much time for that in the IRS."

"I guess not."

They exhausted the subjects of the weather and the Olympics as Mark finished about half his coffee. Finally, he felt he could move in to the real matter at hand.

"What exactly does Mr. Proctor do for AOC, Mable?" he asked.

"Oh my, he does so much, it's a little hard to describe everything." Mable patted the sides of her teased white hair. "He spends most of his time organizing volunteers for the games. There'll be a need for tens of thousands, you know."

"Does he deal with anyone in finance that you know?"

"To be honest, I can't think of anyone in the finance department that has ever called Mr. Proctor. No. I think the answer to that would be definitely no."

"Does the name 'Mr. Janis' ring a bell?"

Visibly distraught by the question, Mable tipped her head down and stared at her desk, tapping a finger to her lips. The soft wrinkles in her forehead deepened over the several seconds of silence. She shook her head deliberately side to side.

"No. I'm sorry. I can't recall anyone by that name."

Mark continued on his search. The woman seemed willing to help.

"Mable, does Mr. Proctor ever need to access insurance files from the computer for any reason?"

This question brought a hearty laugh from the secretary, surprising Mark by her unexpected reaction.

"I'm sorry, Mr. Townsend, for laughing at you," she said, covering her mouth. "You see, Mr. Proctor despises computers. If you look in his office you'd see there is not one on his desk nor anywhere nearby. I have to enter the lists of volunteers for the personnel department records. Mr. Proctor can't find any records on our computer without me."

Her soft creased cheeks blossomed with pride. "I honestly think his greatest fear is coming to the office and finding out I'm sick at home," Mable laughed. "But, I'll have you know I haven't missed a day yet."

"I'm sure that's true," Mark said. "So the only computer in the office is the one here on your desk?"

"That's right, Mr. Townsend. At the ripe old age of sixty-three, I'm pretty indispensable around here."

The two chuckled together.

Mark sipped the last swallow of lukewarm coffee.

"Well, Mable, how about you then. Do you ever have a need to access any insurance records?"

"Never. I can't think of any reason to access an insurance file. None of the volunteers have any sort of benefits. We don't keep that kind of record on anybody."

Mark pretended to be surprised by the time on his watch.

"My heavens! I can't believe I've wasted so much of your time." He rose from the chair and buttoned his coat.

"I want to thank you for your kind hospitality," he said, trying to hurry back to Darryl.

Mable extended her hand cordially. "It's been a pleasure visiting with you. You've changed my opinion of the IRS."

Mark grinned genuinely. "Well, thank you, Mable. We're not all bad guys."

As HE WALKED by the secretaries' desks next door, he played the facts over in his mind about Thomas Foster's insurance data. Surely someone had altered the file from Mable's desk after hours. But, it did not appear to have been Proctor, and Mark could not bring himself to believe Mable was involved.

He glanced at each secretary down the hallway. There must be something he was missing, a clue of some sort.

A few feet away from the elevators he stopped.

Mark turned around and slowly walked by the three secretaries again between the elevators and Mable's desk. All three setups were identical. A walnut-colored desk, a computer terminal, a phone, stacks of papers, an Olympic pencil holder, and a desk cover with the Olympic rings stenciled across the white vinyl sheath.

But, there was something different on Mable's desk . . . something the others did not have. What was it?

He continued on to Mable's office with a picture of the other desks freshly etched in memory.

He stood silently in the doorway. Mable did not notice him at first, reviewing documents on her desk through the correction of her half glasses.

"Excuse me again Mable."

"Oh yes, Mr. Townsend." She smiled widely.

"I couldn't help notice the lovely brass lamp on your desk, such an unusual design with the long curved neck. Do you recall where you bought it."

The woman looked flustered and with a violent jerk touched her forehead with the tips of her fingers.

"Oh my! Mr. Townsend, now I remember that name!"

The woman's face flushed.

"When you asked me about Mr. Janis, I felt sure I recognized that name but for the life of me I couldn't put a finger on it. Why, he was the nice young man who showed up one day with this lamp . . . for *me*! He went on and on about how he wanted to show his appreciation for all I was doing for the poor children in Atlanta. I was truly overwhelmed, but he seemed very sincere. He gave me this lamp, he said, to save my weary eyes from strain. It really is very lovely, isn't it?"

"Yes it is," Mark said excitedly. "Simply magnificent!"

Twenty-Five

D id you sleep well, dear?" Marvelyn smiled at the odd-looking girl consumed in a sweatshirt and pants ten times her size.

Maria stood in the hallway rubbing winter's breath from her skinny arms.

"Is Mark here?"

"No, Honey. He had to go to work. I'm Marvelyn. Mark called me last night and asked me to stay with you two for a while."

Maria came into the kitchen and pulled up a chair at the Formica table top. "Are you his mother?"

Marvelyn chuckled, "No, Honey, just a close friend. I've known Mark since he was a baby. I worked for his father in Europe years ago."

"Are his parents dead?"

"Yes, dear. The general passed away about six years ago and Mark's mother died a few months later. She really found life difficult after the general passed on."

"I know that feeling," Maria lamented.

Marvelyn sensed the pain in the girl's words. She gently brushed her hand over the back of Maria's head and poured her a glass of orange juice.

"Now how about a nice hot waffle?" Marvelyn offered, setting the juice on the table in front of her. "That sound good to you this morning?"

A wide grin crept across the young girl's face.

"Good," Marvelyn said. "It'll just take a minute."

Sitting in the cozy kitchen beneath the pale yellow glow of a milk-glass fixture, with a friendly chaperon busily preparing her a wholesome breakfast, Maria felt reborn. The golden beams cast from the ceiling were like from heaven, unfiltered and radiant. The horror of Adrianne's threats still remained very much alive in her mind. When she awoke a few minutes before, she instinctively canvassed the front yard through Mark's bedroom window, fearing she might see a black sedan parked at the curb with two thugs inside.

Maria took a deep breath, thankful she was alive. Freedom felt so good, she swore to herself she would never again take it for granted. In spite of the clouds and cold blustery weather, this was a glorious day.

Maria noticed a small framed picture on the wall of Mark dressed in a suit standing next to an older man wearing wild golf pants and a white beret. He's *so* handsome, she thought. I wonder if he's married.

"Who's that with Mark in that picture?"

Marvelyn closed the door to the toaster oven and came closer to the table.

"Why that's the vice president, dear."

"*He knows the vice president?*" Her brown eyes grew wide.

Marvelyn smiled at the child. Now she was glad Mark had brought her home. He was right to have rescued this innocent girl. She felt ashamed for having questioned his judgment.

"Yes, Honey," she said. "Mark used to work for the vice president. Mark is a very important man. He was in charge of the vice president's secret service team in Washington, D.C."

"Wow!" Maria gushed. "So he's been in the White House and met the president and everything?"

"Yes, that's right. His office was in the White House."

"Gosh!"

The bell sounded on the toaster oven and Marvelyn returned to the kitchen counter. She scooted the hot waffles onto a plate and plopped two slabs of butter on the steaming pastry, tapped a fine sprinkling of cinnamon over them, and doused both in an ocean of maple syrup.

The aroma of cinnamon and maple seasoned the midmorning with a Christmaslike joy and excitement.

Marvelyn sat the plate down in front of the girl, then took a seat at the table across from her. Maria bowed her head and gave thanks for the food and for Mark's heroics. The faint whispers of faith rising from the girl's lips evoked tears within the caring eyes of her guardian.

Maria tore into the waffles as she had back at Mona's. The contrast of last night's encounter made the breakfast in the security of Mark's home that much more precious.

"My heavens! You have quite an appetite for a little girl," Marvelyn said carrying the plate back to the kitchen.

"Waffles are my favorite. Will Mark come home soon?"

"No, Honey, he will be working all day," Marvelyn said, returning with two more steaming waffles. "He's on a very important project at the moment. But, he did say he'd call this morning to check in on you."

"Gee, I hope so. Can I talk to him when he calls?"

"I don't see why not," Marvelyn said.

"Is he married?"

"No, he's not."

"Does he have a girlfriend?"

Reading between the lines, Marvelyn laughed at the girl. "No, dear, he doesn't have a girlfriend. He stays very busy at his job. He works for the Olympics, you know."

"The Olympics? What does he do?"

"He's one of the directors for security for the Summer Games in 1996. It's an incredible amount of responsibility."

With only two bites left on her plate, Maria jumped from the table when she heard the phone ring.

"Now, just hold on there a minute, Honey," Marvelyn instructed. "I'd better answer that."

"If it's Mark, please let me say 'Hello!'"

Marvelyn picked up the receiver.

"Hey there!" Mark boomed. "How are my two favorite girls in the whole world!"

Marvelyn smiled. "Well, you certainly sound chipper. Things must be going better."

"The best, Marvelyn. We've got the noose over his neck and all I gotta do is pull up the slack."

The crackling over the line told Marvelyn that Mark was calling from his car.

"Where are you headed now?" Marvelyn asked.

"Back to Darryl's office."

"Who?"

"Darryl Clements. The insurance contractor. Remember I went to his office this morning. Great guy! And a big help. You wouldn't believe what we've found. Looks like our suspect knocked off eighty-seven workers for the insurance money."

"Oh dear me, Mark. Are you sure?"

"Looks like it," he said. "I'm on my way back to finish running down the exact means of transfer. We'll have him by this afternoon. I'm sure of it."

"Well, please be careful," Marvelyn pleaded. "If he's done what you suspect, he won't hesitate to do the same to you."

Mark loved to hear her concern.

"I'll be okay, Marvelyn. He doesn't know we're onto him."

"Well, watch your back just the same."

Mark smiled to himself. I'm gonna bring her a dozen roses tonight when this is over.

"How's our little guest?" Mark asked.

"She's about to wrench this phone out of my hand to speak to you," Marvelyn joked.

"Good! Put her on."

Marvelyn handed the phone to the shaking girl.

"Hello?" she quivered.

"Hey there, Hot Shot! How're you doing?"

Maria had trouble catching her breath. "Great!" she said dizzily. "I've never felt better! I just love it here. Marvelyn cooked me some waffles and they were the best ever!" Maria wanted desperately to say the right words, but talked so fast, she could not remember what she had said the instant it left her lips.

"That's just super."

A flurry of sentiments stirred as he spoke to the spirited girl—happiness, concern, fear, devotion, love—the re-kindled emotions choking him as he drove through midtown with thoughts he actually might have saved this girl's life. The rush greatly exceeded that which he had felt during his security days when the governor and vice president had stood so many times relaxed and smiling in front of thousands of people, lightheartedly waving to eager constituents while, because of Mark, the razor edge of death's cold sickle had swung harmlessly by.

"I can't wait to see you," Maria said. "When are you coming home?"

"I've still got a lot to do today. But, I'll get home just as soon as I can. You just relax and watch some TV. I'll get us some Chinese takeout for dinner. You like Chinese food, Maria?"

"Oh yes, that would be great. Can't you come home for lunch?"

Mark laughed. "Sorry, Hot Shot, I got a full load this afternoon. You have fun with Marvelyn. She's like family to me, you know."

"She has been so nice to me."

"Well, I gotta go now. You have a good day and I'll see you this evening, okay?"

"Okay, Mark. It was sure good to talk to you!"

"Thanks, Sweetie. You too."

Twenty-Six

Mark anticipated hanging Janis with the zeal of a missionary out to save the world. He slammed the door of his faithful Taurus sedan and sailed up the walk leading to Darryl's office building, unaware of the Latino man sitting in his parked rental car in the street opposite the parking lot.

Miras had been behind Mark the entire morning, listening quietly outside the door to Darryl's office to the conversation inside. Pretending to wait for an appointment, he had waved to Fanny from behind a magazine as the hippie meandered into the building.

He returned to the cover of his rental car before the hacker left.

Miras pushed "Mem 01" on the mobile phone and waited for Janis to answer.

"Yeah?"

"He's back at the insurance office."

"What did he do at AOC?"

Miras shifted the phone to his other hand so he could read from a notepad from his chest pocket. "He talked to some secretary named Mable Stevens in . . ."

"Shit!"

"What?"

"He knows."

"How?"

"I don't know *how*, but he knows," Janis said again. "That's the computer where I accessed the files of the workers."

"So, what now?" Miras asked.

Janis answered without hesitation. "Hit him at the stadium job."

"Today?"

"Yes, today!" Janis yelled, irritated by the question.

Miras waited for the tension to pass.

"How do you suggest I get him to the stadium? I don't suppose it's on his schedule for this afternoon."

"I don't care how you do it," he screamed at the phone. "Just be sure he's in the accident with the other three!"

"What about the insurance man?"

"Hold off on him," Janis ordered. "I can see how much he knows later. He's just a contractor himself, not an AOC official. He can wait, but Townsend's got to go. Today!"

"LOOK AT THIS," Darryl said, jutting the legal-sized file at Mark when he came in the door.

Mark threw his coat over the back of an armchair and opened the file.

Darryl talked while Mark read.

"Sylvia dug this out of our files on the 1996 Olympic Foundation after you left. They're documents directing benefits from the workers leaving their money to the charity to go straight to that bank in Florida."

Mark listened and flipped through the papers simultaneously.

"See, the dead workers were all Class Sevens, right?" Darryl continued. "And Class Sevens don't have no one at home. They're drifters mostly. Loners. That's the type attracted to dangerous construction jobs. Shoot, what woman in her right mind would marry a man who walks four-inch beams thirty stories up for a living?"

Mark looked up at Darryl.

"Anyhow, see, if the worker doesn't have a wife and no dependents, it would be easy to change his beneficiary to the charity fund without anybody noticing. The only one who'd know is the worker . . . and he's pushing up flowers."

Mark nodded in agreement. "Sounds like a foolproof plan."

"Yeah, it does," Darryl said. "Then there's the kicker— Class Seven's have the highest benefits, between a half a million and a million bucks each."

Mark joined in, "So if you're gonna kill workers and steal their benefits, might as well go after the ones with the most benefits . . ."

". . .and the least chance of having any family to ask questions," Darryl said, finishing the thought.

"You got it!"

Darryl put both hands on his hips and grinned ear to ear.

"Not feeling too bad, now, eh?" Mark asked.

"Never felt better," Darryl quipped. "Matter of fact, I'm getting downright hungry!" He slapped his belly and sloshed it up and down. "Maybe I'll have an executive for lunch."

Mark laughed with Darryl.

Mark returned to the file Sylvia had found. Near the bottom of the fourth page was the name of the bank to which benefits were to be sent: The Piedmont Bank, Miami, Florida.

"Eureka!" Mark blurted. "This is it, Darryl! I know this bank. It's Janis'." Mark pointed to a paragraph on page three. "Look here, what he did, was set up an AOC edict directing the underwriters to send the charitable benefits of dead workers to an account in the Piedmont Bank. He's probably siphoning the money off as fast as it comes in."

"What about audits, though?" Darryl asked. "He can't get around audits."

"Hell, this account is for charity! It's probably scheduled to be audited once a year! By that time, Janis would be long gone. Besides, I bet Janis was on the committee who decided when and who audits the accounts!"

"Probably owns that company, too," Darryl said.

"Exactly."

BACK IN HIS CAR, Mark dialed Hank's number. He knew he would be hot, but wanted to talk with him before arriving back at the IBM Tower with his latest information on the traitor.

A strange female's voice answered the phone. "AOC security."

"This is Mark Townsend calling for Colonel Powell. Who is this?"

"Oh, Mr. Townsend. This is Phyllis from down the hall. Marvelyn called in and said she'd be out all day so I'm covering the phone. It's been wild around here. The Colonel has been looking all over for you. He's in a meeting right now, but he left specific instructions to interrupt it if anyone found you. The whole staff has been out looking for you, sir."

"Well, Phyllis, I guess you win the blue ribbon. Go ahead and tell the Colonel."

Mark waited anxiously for the explosion that would surely erupt over the phone in a few seconds. To his astonishment, the deep voice was calm and concerned.

"Missed you this morning in Victoria's office," Hank said. "S'pose you had something more important than meeting with the CEO about *your* accusations concerning a murder conspirator within the executive council?"

Mark got the message.

"Sorry, boss. But, really, I had no choice. I've got a pretty good idea that Janis has plans for another hit soon, and I needed help uncovering the details of the money transfer."

Hank responded with a few remarkably even-tempered uh huh's. Mark almost wished Hank would yell and scream. For all the time they had spent together, only now did Hank's expertise become real to his protégé.

Finally, Hank asked smoothly, "What did you find out this morning?"

"We've got the whole ball of wax," Mark reported excitedly. "We know how he targeted the workers, set up their insurance classification, how he altered their beneficiary data to funnel funds into a charitable front that only he controlled, and how all the money went through a Florida bank that Janis owns. We got him, boss."

"Sounds like you've been busy."

"Just trying to make you proud," Mark said, only half joking.

"I think it's time for you to come on in, Mark." Hank's tone became serious. "This is not one for you to handle on your own. You get in here and I'll have the Atlanta chief of police waiting in your office. Capish?"

"Roger that, boss. I'm on my way right now. The printouts of the workers insurance records and the originals they filled out on site are in a file sitting next to me along with the blue binder. I believe the police will be very interested in meeting our friend."

"Okay, then, see ya in a few minutes," Hank said, and hung up the phone.

Mark replaced the phone on the pedestal, but before the locks clicked the handset in place, the obnoxious ring nearly jolted him from behind the wheel.

Hank had probably forgotten something.

"Hello, Hank?"

The only sound over the line was the crackling of mobile interference.

"Hank?" Mark repeated.

"Mr. Townsend," the voice was dry and foreign.

"Who is this?" Mark asked.

"Sir, I believe your kitchen cabinets are in need of attention."

The accent was definitely Hispanic, but completely unrecognizable to Mark. What was he talking about? Something about his kitchen cabinets?

"What did you say?" Mark asked. "Who is this?"

Reflexively his foot eased off the accelerator and his car slowed to a crawl in the slow lane on Peachtree Street near Peachtree Battle.

"Otherwise," the man continued, "it is a very nice house."

He rolled his "r's" and his "i's" sounded more like long "e's."

Miras enjoyed the advantage. "I'm afraid, though, I made a minor mess in the entry way. I hope she was not a relative."

The words were like being hit in the face with a shovel. Mark pinched his eyes shut hard, trying to squeeze from his mind the sentence he had just heard.

His heart slammed into his stomach.

"If you touched as much as a hair —"

Miras chuckled into the phone. "I don't believe it touched her hair at all."

Mark fought the urge to break down and plead not to cause any more harm. Without looking in any direction, he smashed the throttle to the floor, the Ford engine revving as he swerved madly around traffic and sped through intersections at fanatic speed.

"What do you want?" Mark said.

Miras did not answer at first.

"Answer me!"

"She is a lovely young girl, Mr. Townsend. Is she your daughter?"

Mark's voice remained firm. "No."

He cranked the steering wheel hard at Ponce de Leon and jammed the pedal down, straining every ligament in his right leg.

"I like her very much, Mr. Townsend, but . . ."

Veering into Scotts Boulevard, Mark slammed into a Chrysler, broadsiding the car and sending it into a spin across four lanes of traffic. Mark failed to regain control and flooded gas into the V-8 at maximum thrust, hurling toward his house in Decatur.

"But, what!" Mark screamed into the phone, his emotions splintering his trained facade.

"But, you leave me no choice."

Mark's face flushed from enormous pressure swelling in his veins. "I will do anything, you hear me! Anything! Tell me what you want, JUST DON'T HURT THE GIRL!"

The words he waited to hear. Miras smiled smugly.

"I do not," he started, then paused dramatically, caressing the tension. "I do not want to hurt the child, Mr. Townsend. There is already so much pain in the world, and she is so young . . . so tender . . ."

The Taurus spun its back tires around the turn at Clairmont Street, and a Federal Express truck collided with a VW at the intersection in order to avoid the crazed man in the crumpled sedan running yet another red light.

Mark listened intently, trying to memorize every nuance of the voice for the future manhunt—his mind was in shock and reverted to the instincts ingrained by his professors at the academy and by years of secret service.

"You will meet me this afternoon at the construction site for the Olympic Stadium," Miras instructed.

"I'll be there," Mark shot back. "There better not be a scratch on the girl, you miserable scum, or . . ."

"Save your threats, Mr. Townsend," Miras interrupted fluidly. "I have no desire to harm the girl. Her participation in this matter is only necessary to secure your own."

The dial tone returned.

Mark threw the phone at the passenger door and sped the Taurus down North Decatur Street, two blocks from his house.

The speedometer flew over the century mark in Mark's quiet neighborhood as he barreled toward his two loved ones held hostage by the ruthless wretch.

He leaned down, reaching under the front seat, and found his 9mm Beretta holstered against the floorboard.

Clutching the steering wheel with white knuckles, he prayed Marvelyn would be all right as the car missed the driveway and ramped over the curb, plowing parallel trenches across his hibernating lawn and coming to halt near the living-room window.

Mark bound from the car with his Beretta in hand and jumped the front steps leading up to the porch, bursting through the open front door screaming, "Marvelyn! Maria!" before freezing in the entry at the sight of blood pooling around the corner from the living room.

The lifeless house creaked.

Mark listed toward the wall, his feet unwilling to move.

He peered around the natural hardwood molding he had refinished the previous summer while awaiting his first day on the job at AOC—a day to which he had anticipated with excitement, joining forces for the greatest humanitarian event in the history of mankind, an occasion for peace and celebration . . . and harmony . . .

His eyes deliberately followed the warm red gloss, the pool narrowing to a stream just around the far edge of the oak doorway, coursing a random path to the small puncture just above her left eyebrow.

Mark slumped to the floor.

"Oh God. Marvelyn."

He gently placed his right fingers at the side of her neck out of procedure, not of any hope of feeling a blessed throb of life.

Mark rested one hand on the woman's head and brushed her eyelids closed with the other.

So infinitely unfair.

He roared at the painted walls as if they were to blame.

TWENTY-SEVEN

The sky darkened and a bitter wind froze the precipitation into a flurry of icy tacks, sharp against his face. Mark returned to his car and slammed into reverse, grinding the rear tires against his yard and trenching more clumps of sod along the way. He drove deliberately, under control, figuring through the traffic cautiously, subconsciously obeying each sign and light. He punched in the number for Darryl's office on the handset.

"Mark? Is everything okay?" Sylvia was shocked by his gruff, whispery voice.

"Let me speak to Darryl."

"Sure," she said quickly. "Hold on a minute."

A click was followed by the sounds of Bach's *Christmas Oratorio,* then another click. "Mark, what's up, buddy?"

"Darryl, I need you to call Colonel Hank Powell at AOC security and tell him Janis has planned an accident at the Olympic Stadium construction site. Tell him Marvelyn was murdered at my house and . . ."

"What?" Darryl shouted. "What happened at your house?"

Mark allowed a brief pause. He focused all his effort on channeling his emotions into concentration.

"Darryl," he continued calmly. "Just listen. Call Hank and tell him Marvelyn's been murdered and that there are more planned at the stadium. I have not called the police yet about Marvelyn, so ask him to do that, too."

"Where are you now, Mark? Is there anything I can be doing to help?"

"I'm on my way to the stadium now. The bastard that killed Marvelyn has a kid that was staying at my place."

"Mark, No! They've kidnapped your kid?"

"Darryl, it's a long story," Mark said. "She's not my kid, but . . ." emotion broke him for a second. "Just give Hank the message."

"Hey, man. You just hang in there, ya hear?"

"IS EVERYTHING OKAY WITH MARK?" Sylvia asked. "He sounded real strange on the phone. I didn't recognize his voice at first."

"It's bad, Sylvia. Real bad."

The expression on Darryl's face made her uneasy.

"Tell me. What's going on?"

Darryl grabbed his coat off the rack in the corner of his office and hurried toward the door.

"I'm going to the stadium. Call Esther and tell her I might be late tonight."

"Darryl!" Sylvia screamed. "You'd better tell me what's going on!"

Darryl stopped at the door and turned around. He crossed the room back over to where Sylvia stood.

"Honey, there's been another killing. This time it was a friend of Mark's. Somehow the killer kidnapped a kid staying at Mark's place and is planning some more trouble at the stadium. I'm gonna head there now to see if I can help."

"Help! You're just gonna end up dead like these other poor souls, Darryl! Don't go!"

"Honey, don't you worry your pretty head," Darryl said, touching her cheek. "I'm gonna be okay. I ain't stupid. I ain't gonna get in front of no bullet. But, Honey, I gotta go. I gotta help Mark if I can, he's in big trouble."

She dropped her chin to her chest and nodded her head in agreement.

Darryl rushed out the door. "Hey now, don't forget to call Esther, ya hear?"

MARK TOOK THE PERIMETER FREEWAY SOUTH, planning his route to the stadium over the interstate instead of the surface roads where noon congestion often reached a standstill. He followed the exit ramp onto I-20 west, about twenty minutes from the construction site.

Even the interstate became unusually sluggish, causing Mark to fly into the restricted multiple-passenger lane and race unsafely by the slower traffic.

He wondered how Maria was holding up. Poor kid. Geez, even though it had only been a day since he rescued her, he was beginning to think it was *she* who had rescued him. His work hadn't filled him with this urgency in so long. Maybe he'd been pushing too hard since his father died. Maybe he'd forgotten how to care.

And maybe a young thirteen-year-old Cuban kid had given that back to him.

Cars started honking at him, seeing he was a single passenger in the diamond lane. A few gave him the one-finger salute.

Mark didn't notice. Or care. He floored it.

His Beretta lay next to him on the seat.

STEEL-GRAY CLOUDS ushered in the afternoon in Atlanta, the second half of the matched-set morning. Gagged and bound inside a burlap sack, Maria flopped limply, exhausted from struggling against the ties around her wrists and ankles. Scenes from the fresh nightmare replayed in her mind, seeing Marvelyn bleeding on the floor in the living room. She assumed the man driving the car was one of Adrienne's thugs charged with recovering her lost merchandise. The terror of returning to the madam's control and the certain loss of toes made Maria wretch.

She coughed blood onto the rag restricting her mouth, searching for wisps of oxygen. Her thin legs uncontrollably kicked the sidewalls of the killer's car.

The car jolted to a sudden stop, crashing Maria's head into the trunk's front wall. Next, Maria heard the metal clanking of keys unlocking the trunk lid.

DARRYL WHEELED THE DECADE-OLD ACCORD wildly in and out of the midday traffic on Peachtree Street, trying to avoid businessmen, delivery trucks, and shoppers.

He punched the numbers for Colonel Powell's office into his mobile phone.

"AOC Security," Phyllis answered for the umpteenth time this morning.

"I need to talk to Colonel Powell," Darryl said loudly. "This is an emergency."

"May I ask who's calling?" Phyllis asked, woefully unprepared for the events of the day.

"Listen!" Darryl shouted. "This is an emergency. Get him now!"

Silence at the other end.

"Hank Powell."

"Colonel, this is Darryl Clements. I'm an insurance contractor . . ."

"Yes," Hank interrupted, "I know who you are, Mr. Clements. What's the trouble?"

"Mark told me to call you with two messages." Darryl paused, thinking of words to use. "Ain't good news, mister."

"I understand, Mr. Clements." The worst images of tragedy immediately shot into Hank's mind.

"Marvelyn's been killed at Mark's house," Darryl reported. "And he says there will be another murder at the Olympic Stadium today."

Hank felt all strength flow, as if the breath had been knocked out of him.

Darryl continued, "I don't have details, just the message."

"Where's Mark now?"

Darryl dropped the phone, careening his car onto the sidewalk in front of the Fox Theatre to avoid a line of vehicles stopped at a red light at Ponce de Leon Avenue. A police car rammed the rear fender of Darryl's Accord just before he managed to escape the intersection unscathed. The impact fishtailed his rear tires into the oncoming traffic parked at the red light, bouncing him side to side like a pinball.

He managed to keep the car headed downtown without raising his foot off the throttle, leaving a snake's trail of rubber behind. In his rearview mirror, seven or eight cars plowed into one another.

Darryl recovered the lost phone.

"Sorry, had an interruption back there," Darryl yelled over the screeching of his engine.

"Do you know where Mark is?" Hank repeated.

"He's on his way to the stadium. Whoever killed Marvelyn took his kid to the stadium. Sounds to me like a setup to kill Mark."

Hank felt fear for the first time since an Islamic terrorist had held a gun to his head.

"Listen," he told Darryl. "You get back to your office and let us handle this. No need for something happening to you."

Veering onto the sidewalk again, the Accord plowed over a flower stand near Underground Atlanta. Hank could hear the skidding tires and the grinding roar of the four cylinder compact.

Darryl tugged the steering wheel hard to the left, then quickly to the right, throwing his weight against the car door. He tried to grab the car phone again, but finally gave up and focused on the last remaining quarter-mile to the stadium construction site.

TWENTY-EIGHT

Rising before him, the arched facade of the Olympic Stadium cast diffuse shadows across the enormous expanse of red soil, unearthed to support the one hundred sixty-eight million dollar memorial to the Centennial Summer Games.

Gazing toward his skyrise destination, Miras shielded his eyes from the sun cracking through the dense overcast.

Hundreds of feet above where he stood, steel workers busily strapped girders to one another along an overhang engineered to cover the uppermost sections of seating.

Crane engines whined as operators reared beams into the waiting hands of construction men laxly straddling the unsupported structure as if they were only inches off the ground instead of twenty stories.

The smooth Latino lifted the trunk lid and found his yellow hard hat on top of the spare tire bolted beneath the rear window.

Faint moans permeated the rough sack sprawled across the trunk.

Miras threw the burlap satchel over his shoulder, picked up a clipboard out of the trunk's side compartment, then headed to the farthest of two construction elevators leading to temporary foreman's platforms high above the field.

Maria's neck kinked at the bottom of the sack, pressing her chin against her chest and further constricting her gasps for air. Slowly, she regained consciousness as the cutting Arctic wind dissipated the exhaust fumes.

Miras waved to several workers he passed on the way to the elevator. He received no questioning gazes as he pulled the metal cage closed and punched the button to ride to the top. The site was a clamor of pounding, hammering, and banging. No one noticed the nonchalant foreign man, nor the wriggling burlap bag.

At the top level, Miras slid open the cage door and drug the sack onto the small platform.

The wind swirled constantly in the mammoth fortress. Several pages of architectural plans clipped to the foreman's stand hung down the platform's side, fluttering like a white flag.

Miras gathered a bright yellow nylon rope from a corner of the platform and looped it around one of the four giant girders running underneath the plywood on which he stood. By no accident, the beam he selected extended to a second foreman's platform about a hundred feet away at the pinnacle of the other construction elevator.

"Please, please . . . let me out . . ." The frail murmur had barely enough thrust to be heard by an ear pressed firmly against the burlap.

Miras retrieved a three-foot socket wrench from the tools assembled on the platform and proceeded to remove all but one of the four bolts securing the horizontal beam to the vertical supports. The fourth bolt he loosened and tapped back through the hole until it barely engaged the two beams together. The horizontal beam squeaked as it slipped away from its support, unstably tied by a single thread of the last bolt.

Miras tucked the other three bolts into his jeans' pocket and drug the burlap sack over to the open end of the platform, tying it to the rope encircling the beam. Tugging at the ropes to test their sturdiness, Miras fecklessly kicked the bag off the edge of the plywood floor, sending Maria over the edge, precariously swinging in the wind from three feet of half-inch twine.

Mark arrived at the Olympic Stadium from the opposite direction of a convoy of two dozen concrete mixers, slowly spinning their barrels in unison, waiting to creep past the gate. He slammed on his brakes and slid to within inches of one of the trucks, further inflaming the already white-hot shoes of his four-heel disc brakes.

"Hey! You can't leave your car there!" the security guard yelled at Mark's back. "Hey, you there! You can't go in!"

Paying no attention to the guard, Mark frantically scanned the horizon searching for some sign of the thirteen year old among the confusion. Sparks danced at his feet from nearby torches at work.

Mark sailed up a ramp to one of the mobile trailers, bursting through the door to find six or seven annoyed faces shoot up from a set of blueprints. Without a word, be bolted back through the door, knocking down two men with long rolls of plans under their arms.

From the top of the ramp, Mark furiously scanned the enormous foundation being poured from the contents of the parading trucks.

"Hey you!" A red-faced foreman in jeans and heavy boots called. "You can't be in here without a hard hat!"

Mark scooted around a pillar.

"Hey, you son of a bitch! Stop right there or . . ."

Mark darted through an archway and headed toward the area where several cranes screamed under the weight of enormous steel beams.

The bustle of workers was chaotic, and Mark feared that Maria was already lost. Oblivious to the freezing air, nervous sweat stained his shirt.

"Get outta the way, asshole!" a disgusted worker yelled, teetering an eight-foot six by six on his shoulder.

Mark collided with men coming at him from every direction, bumping him into piles of lumber and shoving him against giant spools of cable. Where could she be? If he could just see the entire site.

Suddenly, he tore around a series of cement footings and ran toward the nearest construction elevator. About ten feet from the rusted angle-iron shaft, he skidded to a stop against the loose gravel under his wing tips.

A dark-skinned man stood leaning against the elevator framework, his arms folded across his chest, wearing a yellow hard hat and a rancorous smirk.

"Quite an impressive project, wouldn't you say, Mr. Townsend?" Miras did not bother to disguise his accent.

Mark took heavy steps toward him and grabbed the chest of his shirt.

"Where is she?" he demanded. "If you've hurt that kid . . ."

"Now there, there, Mr. Townsend," Miras admonished. "No need for a show of emotion. I assure you, all is quite well."

His eyes were like none Mark had ever seen. Their opaque blackness seemed to absorb every particle of light. Finally, he relaxed his grip.

"That's much better," Miras said, calmly sliding open the elevator door.

THE PROCESSION OF CEMENT TRUCKS continued its methodical advance as Darryl skidded his Accord parallel to Mark's car, angled in front of the north gate with the driver's side door standing open.

"Stop right there! You can't go in there!" The security guard charged at Darryl with his hand on the butt of his holstered gun, determined not to be slipped a second time.

"I'm with AOC insurance, mister," he said, flashing his AOC contractor's card as if it were FBI identification. "There's trouble at this site."

"I don't care if you're Ted Tur—"

"You get your ass on the phone and call the Atlanta PD here now!" Darryl's lips scowled as he spit the command.

The unsure guard hesitated.

"I mean now! Mister!" Darryl shoved the man with his enraged hand and hurried on his way to he didn't know where.

Following a trek similar to Mark's, Darryl ran through the arched entrances that would lead to the finished stadium. To his right, he glanced toward the cement trucks lined in a row, spewing their contents around heavy wire reinforcements housed inside massive steel forms.

Darryl ignored the inherent urge to yell Mark's name amidst the clamor and continued straight ahead, scooting past another guard posted at a secondary fence barricading the inner field of the stadium. The excavation for the footings and subfield drainage system had produced an enormous crater in the middle of the stadium, and cranes stood in the center of the hole lifting beams to workers who bolted them together into suspended spectator stands.

Darryl shuddered under his wool flannel suit coat as he stumbled over the lunarlike terrain. Against gusts blowing cold dirt in his face, he hurried across deep serrated ruts in the red soil, casting his eyes along one of the dinosaurian extensions supporting pulleys and cables.

Quickly, Darryl cupped a hand near his eyes to block the wind. He squinted hard to focus. Yes, there, on a platform.

Mark.

TWENTY-NINE

Mark stood alone with Miras on the small covered platform overlooking the interior construction of the stadium. The dark-skinned man ambled toward the edge of the platform and leaned against the open railing, tipping his hard hat back above his hairline.

"Hard to believe people from all over the world will be here this summer to watch the best athletes in history compete for precious medals." Miras did not look at Mark, but kept his eyes surveying the work underway.

About twelve feet under the platform, three men in hard hats walked the tightrope maze of steel, securing pieces of the giant metal skeleton for the upper decks. The men talked incessantly to one another, moving about the network of girders with seemingly madcap steps. Just above them, girders dangled from cables as crane operators waited for the high-rise artists to signal for another beam.

Controlling his rage, Mark followed Miras to the railing, bending next to him and gazing below. "I came for the girl," he said, with forced steadiness. "Where is she?"

Miras grinned, keeping his face straight ahead.

"In your line of work, Mr. Townsend, I am sure you have learned things are rarely as they seem."

"Where is the girl?" he yelled again, overwhelmed with vehemence to throw the bastard over the two-by-four railing and watch him flail in the air on his way to becoming a divot in the clay soil.

"Mr. Townsend," he said. "You surprise me. I expected more from a former Secret Serviceman. An expert in your field surely would have noticed this site has *two* construction elevators both leading to platforms like this one here."

Miras pointed toward the second platform about a hundred feet away.

"Near the that platform over there," Miras continued. "You can see a brown sack hanging from one of the girders, no?"

Mark wiped his eyes and blinked against the howling wind. He could see the blurry outline of a tool sack or something draped over the side of the distant platform.

"*You low-life scum!*"

He grabbed Miras at the neck and began bashing his face.

"*I'm gonna kill you, you miserable son of a bitch!*" Mark fumed, as he continued beating Miras, who lay on his back near the edge of the platform.

"Then, she will die!" the killer spat, blocking blows with his forearms.

Mark stopped.

Miras coughed blood and rolled onto his side. "She will die," he repeated, his face rubbing against the dirt-covered plywood.

Mark stood panting over the fallen hit man.

Miras slid his knees under his body and stood like a dog on all fours, coughing blood onto the platform.

"The beam . . ." he began, then broke into a flux of coughs.

Mark approached Miras and jammed his fingers into the man's hair, jerking his head back so the bleeding from his nose trickled down the front of his neck.

"Tell me, now!" he demanded. "What about the beams?"

Miras defiantly spit blood across Mark's shirt.

"The beams . . ." he rasped, still wearing the hollow stare. "The beams will fall." Miras coughed. "And so will she."

Frenetically, Mark dropped the disgusting head and jumped to the rail, trying to see a flaw in the beam.

Miras laughed slowly on the platform behind Mark.

"You can not find why they will fall," he teased arrogantly.

Mark whirled around and furiously punched the "down" elevator button, smashing the coating into plastic rubble.

Miras roared hysterically. "You fool! You will not make it. There isn't enough time to ride this elevator down, run to the other lift and ride to the top before the steel crashes into a tangled heap of wire on the ground."

Mark peered out over the beams.

"And such a sweet girl she was," Miras said.

Mark swung around and kicked Miras in the chest, ramming him into the thin wall along the back of the platform.

THIRTY

Almost like Chicago, Janis thought, buttoning his gray herringbone overcoat against the early winter front. Two steps at a time, he climbed a set of temporary wooden stairs leading to the future site of the corporate suites.

The long-awaited day had arrived, the culmination of planning and perseverance, of excelling within a bankers' suffocating bureaucracy, of surpassing scores of insolent superiors who bridled his creativity and stymied his genius out of a false commitment to conservatism.

Having reached the pinnacle of responsibility, Janis had proven himself worthy of an elite autocracy, wielding power with cautious deliberation, strategically maximizing returns while eliminating only those cretins who good society would not miss.

Standing in what would become an outrageously expensive suite for some corporate giant, Janis marveled at the grid work rising into the sky. Regrettably, his time to relish the ornate coliseum would have to wait several years, until the search for him withered from public apathy.

The focus of work was on the concrete and steel stands far on the opposite side of the field. A rush of power pervaded him like a narcotic-induced euphoria.

"I like it," he said approvingly.

In his degenerate mind, a fantasy fluttered of the president and first lady seated comfortably beside him sipping Schramsburg *Crémént* while game seven of the World Series entertained them all.

The corners of his sordid mouth rose to pitchfork points.

Searching for a place to sit and watch his engineered plight unfold, Janis found an empty wooden crate that had held a gross of two-inch steel bolts. He slid the giant box near the concrete wall at the front of the roughed-out suite and settled himself comfortably at the edge of his own twisted world.

THIRTY-ONE

What the hell is he doing? Darryl stood paralyzed, gaping up at his friend who swayed side to side, balancing himself across the four-inch girder leading to a sack invisible to those on the ground.

Darryl stepped closer to the foundation of the stadium wall just as one of the cranes next to him lowered its cable to pick up another beam from a nearby trailer. The screeching machine swiveled on its alloy treads, swinging dangerously close to Darryl, who dove to the ground to avoid being decapitated by a jagged angle-iron bumper.

He hit the dirt slope and tumbled down a ten-foot embankment below the level of the cranes. Getting up, he grimaced at the pain in his right shoulder and scaled back up the bank.

For the life of him, Darryl could not figure why Mark had ventured out onto the beam.

MARK DID NOT let his focus wander from the red steel under his leather soles. Staring at the small metal plank, he fought to keep his eyes from shifting, even for a second, to the peripheral scene of miniature workers and Tonka-sized trucks on the ground below. Halfway across the span, he had little choice but to proceed.

Gusts of wind threatened to knock him off his perch, but he maintained his balance out of sheer determination; his soul glued him to the steel.

MIRAS SLIPPED the third bolt from the beam.

The squeak of metal sliding against metal caught the attention of three workers, who shot their eyes to the beams above them.

Miras pushed against the fourth bolt, but the tremendous weight kept it wedged in place. He returned to the tool bin and found a ball-peen hammer. Leaning over the edge of the platform, he reached under the beam to give himself access to the threaded end. With heavy, but awkward, swings, he pounded on the end of the bolt, flattening the threads as it pushed through the hole.

After two dozen swings, Miras rolled back onto the platform, resting his aching arm. On his back, he savored the upside-down view of Mark teetering in the middle of the trestle.

At that moment, Mark slipped from his feet and smashed his chest against the unforgiving iron; his face blanched as the blow punched air from his lungs.

Miras sat upright and grinned at the security executive hugging the steel lifeline and swinging his legs to catch his heels again on top of the beam.

Miras quickly resumed his gawky crouch, pounding the bolt millimeters closer to catastrophe.

MARIA GOUGED THE BURLAP COCOON with bleeding fingernails. She managed a small tear in the scratchy fabric, opening a view above her and a little to one side, but she lacked sufficient bearings to decipher her position.

She could not interrupt the reflexive clattering of her teeth that scarred the raw sides of her tongue and embittered her mouth with a bloody tinge.

It was so unbearably cold.

Every muscle twitched in a jittery randomness as if playing different scores in the same melancholic orchestra.

She pressed an eye to her tiny window.

The ensconced sun began its descent behind a heavy wintry guise. All she could see was a strangely green sky. Her white incisors bit at the tight knots binding her wrists.

THIRTY-TWO

Miras could see light around the bolt, but it remained intractably lodged in the two beams, the threaded end now flush against one side, rendering the hammer useless in forcing it further out of the hole.

He searched the tool bin for yet another implement to help complete his mission. To one side, lying wrapped in its factory-packed cellophane and cardboard, the perfect solution for his dilemma—a shiny new twelve-inch punch—twinkled amongst the odd assortment of oily wrenches, cutters, and files.

Miras snatched the punch rabidly from its package and jumped back to the near boltless joint in front of the platform. His black eyes glanced down the beam in anticipation.

With his steady left hand resting the punch's narrow end on the bolt, with a surgeon's accuracy, his right hand smacked the hammer against the broad end, prying the mutilated bolt from the hole and rocketing it downward like a supersonic missile. Robbed of only a fraction of its speed, the hot bullet plunged through the hard hat and into the skull of an unsuspecting laborer below.

The man fell dead from his roost a fraction of a second before the dropping beam, released above by the unknown man wearing a yellow hard hat, slammed into the backs of his two compatriots.

The crushing momentum of the descending steel snapped a series of bolts tying the huge framework together, folding the red girders in on themselves like an imploding building detonated for demolition.

The collapsing trestles hurled Mark thirty feet through the air, miraculously landing him on his back on the free end of a lower beam precariously cantilevered from the stadium wall.

At the base of the far construction platform, the solitary bolt Miras had earlier left intact now refused to buckle and continued to hold the strain of the girder, now swinging vertically from its booby-trapped joint. Maria's bundle skydived the beam's length, catching at the last second on tiny broken fragments of bolts and knurled edges of steel.

A hundred feet below, the worker shot in the head by Miras' unintentional bullet hit the ground, crushing his face into an unidentifiable composite of flesh and white splinters on bone. The two workers struck in the back by the beam were sent free-falling, their horrified screams unmistakable, surviving the unthinkable flash in time when death is imminent and inescapable. Their twisted bodies lay grotesquely segmented under three or four beams that had pursued closely on the heels of their plummet.

Darryl stood nearby, staring aghast at the calamity, while all around him, workers fled for the safety of distance. Crane operators abandoned their machines and ran toward the exterior openings in the stadium wall.

The havoc kicked dust into the swirling breeze and a plume rose high above the stadium, as if a nuclear blast had struck the site.

Janis rose in awe, applauding cynically.

"Spec-tac-u-lar!" his lips formed

MARK STARED ABOVE HIM at the jagged ends of bent beams and fractured bolts. His legs dangled off the end of his support, still nearly a hundred feet above the tangled destruction on the ground.

Panicked, his eyes searched for Maria.

He winced from deep shooting stabs caused by broken ribs and split vertebrae, but he worked to swing his legs into a straddle over his sagging seat. Giant spots blotched his eyes and he listed dangerously to his left. Unconsciousness teased his brain before the sudden sensation of falling jolted him sensible.

Mark clutched his underpinning as scratching metal preceded another crash of beams tumbling onto the rubble below. Clouds of dirt from the aftershock cleared, and Mark squinted toward the second platform.

Through the haze, Mark scoured the top of the beam hanging beneath the second platform . . . but, below the wood floor . . . frayed remnants of yellow rope blew lonesomely from a mangled torn knot . . .

Mark's eyes bore on the second platform, then darted wildly around the site. Where was it! He could not find it anywhere . . .

. . . the sack was gone.

He thrust his face into his forearm and clenched his teeth. With disconsolate thoughts of plunging himself onto the heap below, he lifted his head again just as the wind parted the fog of debris and opened his view to the free end of the beam. There, swaying limply from the lone slipping bolt at the base of the foreman's platform . . .

"Maria!" he cried, cracking more ribs in the process.

Bracing his side, he managed to stand on the sloping beam.

"Maria!" he shouted again.

His head spun upward then down, right then left, calculating a way to get to the sack.

At the base of the pier, where it joined the stadium wall, he found a foothold and climbed up to another intact beam running at an angle toward a vertical support about twenty-five feet away. Mark searched, but no girders remained connecting his side of the stadium with hers.

Undaunted, he jammed his knees into the cold metal, cutting his fingers on the edges of the "I" shaped steel.

As he climbed, he fashioned schemes for crossing the canyon between them, combing his memory for scenarios taught in school or covered in his countless hours of continuing crisis training.

On the ground, where the construction site had become a ghost town of abandoned machinery and gusting wind, Darryl coughed the dirt from his lungs and searched the rubble in hopes of finding his friend still alive. With adrenaline-induced strength, he pulled pieces of beams from the pile and shoved drifts of clay away from the corpses.

Repeatedly, he shielded his face from the ghastly sights, nauseated by the gruesome mangling, but at the same time empowered by the absence of anything resembling Mark.

Lifting the end of a beam, broken and bent in several places, Darryl slipped on loose dirt that had been plowed up by a tunneling piece of steel. He stumbled onto his back, cracking his head against the excavated site. Stunned, he remained on his back for several seconds gazing unfocused on the churning sky.

THIRTY-THREE

Mark's footing slipped, tumbling his bruised body ten feet onto the beam he had just left. He swung over the side and hung upside down from his knees, clinging to the frigid steel.

Fearlessly determined, he righted himself and scaled the beam again.

Here and there, bits of broken bolts offered unstable footholds, but just enough for him to arrive twenty feet or so above the bent strut that had saved his life.

He stood on a six-inch ledge, hugging a vertical support and surveying his next assault of the man-made cliff.

"Maria!" he shouted again, now closer to the sack.

She jolted downward suddenly another two feet.

"Maria!"

Only a few threads of nylon remained.

Mark leapt to a frame three feet overhead, grabbing it with outstretched arms and swaying unprotected over the heap on the ground.

Like a special forces Marine, he threw one hand ahead of the other, coursing the beam with weak fingers, slippery

with blood. His feet swung forward as he flung his body
side to side, surging along at a reckless pace with no regard
for his own safety.

He reached the next vertical support where his arms
and legs hugged the beam. Exhausted muscles screamed
for rest, but passion pushed him up to the next horizontal
strut. Imbalanced by irregular frozen gusts, he fecklessly
ran across a fifteen-foot stretch to the final vertical strut remaining adjacent to the vast hole in the construction.

Maria's sack continued to slip, dipping closer to the
ground. Yellow threads popped into space like tiny coiled
springs.

There was no way to span the thirty feet between him
and the falling bag.

The girl slipped downward again.

"MARIA"

Blood warmed his throat.

THIRTY-FOUR

Darryl sat in the operator's chair peering over the seemingly random series of levers. Inside his chest, the seething fist of muscle pummeled its cage, each vicious throb clamping his temples like a vise. With hands shaking wildly, he thrust the largest stick forward and the powerful engine roared, immediately swinging the crane's cab to the right and the giant steel boom away from the torn girders.

Flakes of enamel split from his molars.

He grabbed the stick again and pulled it toward him. The beam hanging from the crane's twisted cable swung back toward the hole, but overshot its target, only a breath away from ramming into the last remaining struts standing beneath the far foreman's platform.

With a tense, gray face, he looked up at Mark holding onto the vertical girder, thirty or forty feet higher than where he had landed.

"Crazy son of a bitch," Darryl cursed. "Going up instead of down."

Another crash suddenly sent a host of beams hurling below, pounding the earth around Darryl's crane and further sealing the tomb of the dismembered workers.

Seeing colossal hunks of concrete ramming toward him, Darryl flung his arms over his face, realizing the flying pieces of stadium would surely flatten the cab.

The excavated site quaked under the tremendous impact from the tons of cement dropping from the walls.

Maria's rope lost more of its few shreds.

Choked by the dirt heaving into the tormented sky, Darryl violently jabbed the largest lever forward until the swinging beam finally aligned with Mark.

He moved to another line of levers and pushed one forward. The beam began to rise. Instinctively, he tapped the lever until the beam raised to Mark's height.

Amidst the wind and the raging waste, Mark had been unaware of the beam rising on the crane's cable, now almost within his reach. Mark could not see the cab of the crane, only its black boom rising out of the dense cloud of dirt.

Darryl raised the beam closer to where Mark stood.

Though at his height, the beam still oscillated twenty feet away from his perch. Darryl puzzled the last row of levers.

"Lord, you gotta show me the one!"

He pushed forward the one closest to him.

The crane creaked and swung the beam toward his intended target.

"Hallelujah!" Darryl screamed in the cab, mopping sweat with his sleeve.

He turned to the second row of levers and tapped the one he had learned spun the cable shorter. The beam rose to within six feet of Mark.

Without hesitation, Mark leapt to the teetering beam, landing the full weight of his body near the end of the twenty-five-foot girder, but inadvertently tipping it downward.

His tired hands slipped and his legs slid off the end of the beam, standing it straight up and down.

Darryl shouted, "Hold on!" as he tapped the second lever away from him, beginning the beam's slow descent to the ground.

Mark turned toward the crane cab, shouting, *"No!"*

He waved one arm wildly. *"UP! BACK UP!"*

The beam continued its gentle drop.

Mark madly pulled himself up the beam in front of Darryl's gaping eyes.

"Just stay put, Mark!" he shouted at the windshield.

Mark finally reached the crane cable and stood on the beam, holding the cable with one hand and fiercely waving the other.

"*Up*, you bastard! *BACK UP!*"

Neither man could hear the other's raging commands.

Mark grabbed the cable and began scaling the twisted steel wires with bleeding hands. He pulled himself higher, leaving the safety of the beam behind.

Darryl stopped the cable pulley, watching his friend climbing the cable.

"He must be insane!"

Shaking his head, he pulled the second lever toward him.

The beam rose a couple of feet, and Mark turned excitedly toward the cab and waved his arm over his head.

Darryl pulled the lever again.

Mark waved like a madman, and released his grip and slid back to the beam.

"Man, I ain't got a clue of what you're doin', you crazy son of a bitch," Darryl complained out loud. "But if you want to go up, I'll take you up!"

Mark stood at the cable, intent on the burlap bag slipping toward the ground. He laid down on the beam and crawled toward the end closest to Maria. The beam tipped down a few degrees, keeping him from continuing farther out.

He waved at the operator and pointed toward the sack.

Darryl tapped the first lever and turned the crane in the direction Mark indicated.

"Maria!" Mark shouted. He was within ten feet.

The girl jumped inside.

"Mark! Mark! In here! *IN HERE!*"

Her movement tugged at the rope and split it in two.

Just below his outstretched hand, she plunged toward the ground.

"NO!" Mark cried, slipping further from the beam as he tried to catch the bag before it fell.

Mark pinched his eyes, the scene of the bag slipping away just under his fingers replaying over and over.

"Damn! He's after that sack," Darryl realized, watching his friend dangle from the rocking beam.

"Mark!"

The frail voice was barely discernible.

Mark cursed the lying wind.

"Mark!"

He looked through the swirling dust. About twenty feet below, the sack had caught on a concrete pillar. The bag had ripped open, and Maria clung to torn remnants of burlap.

With vengeance, Mark signaled to the operator. "Down!" he shouted. "Down there!"

He pointed repeatedly to the child.

"My God!" Darryl yelled. With his eyes on the skinny girl kicking desperately, his hands shook even greater than before. "Don't let that kid fall!"

He jammed the second lever forward, dropping the beam instantly ten feet and spilling Mark over the edge.

Frantically, he pulled back on the stick and slowed the pace of the fall.

The beam began rotating, twirling Mark's end of the beam *away* from Maria.

"Hold on Maria!" Mark cried. "I'm coming! Just hold on!"

The burlap ripped again, leaving a thin six-inch piece suspending the child.

Darryl stopped the beam precisely where the child hung, but Mark still could not reach her.

The two men waited anxiously.

The beam slowly turned clockwise in the cloud of dirt.

The wind cut its icy tongue at the two, stinging their hands and weakening their grip.

Mark crawled closer to the end of the beam, anticipating its return to the girl.

Again, it canted under his weight, tipping further, lower.

Mark rose on his knees, gripping the steel with bony shins.

He reached, fingers outstretched, bleeding, numb, weak.

Without provocation, the burlap suddenly split in half horizontally, bearing the edge of Satan's hand.

Maria screamed and flailed her arms.

Mark lunged forward, slicing the skin over his knees to bone. His fingertips caught the child's wrist.

The weight of the two pulled the beam vertically straight up and down.

Mark hung to the steel, uncaring if he would ever walk again, but refusing to loosen his hold of Maria.

"If we go, we go together."

Darryl's hands trembled uncontrollably. He grabbed the second lever and pulled it toward him as far as he thought he could without shaking the two off the beam.

Sweat poured from his face and his hands slipped off the levers he struggled to control.

Mark yearned for strength to hold on, just a few more seconds . . .

Thirty-Five

An entire twenty-five-foot section of struts broke loose from its massive concrete footing and timbered toward the two survivors clinging to life's thin thread. The tremendous force knocked Mark and Maria off the beam and pushed the crane over onto the roof of its cab, uprooting its tanklike treads and wheeling them upward until they faced the sky.

Mark plummeted the last fifteen feet and hit the frozen clay on his back.

The skinny girl fell on top of him.

He threw his arms around her and rolled his body between her and the crashing steel storming down around them.

The gusts and demolition unearthed tons of soil, sweeping large chunks a hundred feet into the air. To those just outside the stadium walls, nothing could be seen through the impenetrable storm.

Inside the cab, Darryl tumbled against the walls and ceiling of the cartwheeling crane, struggling to brace himself during the unexpected assault. He grimaced in pain as his separated shoulder slammed into the control panel. Everywhere, flying glass slashed his face and arms as he tried to steady himself with bloody outstretched palms.

Janis held one arm over his head, gesturing pontifically from the edge of the blowing torrent, oblivious to its biting cold, intoxicated in the throes of suffering.

From the twisting pillar of dirt sailed the "I" beam from which Mark and Maria had fallen, hurled from its cable as the crane rolled end over end and cast free like a gigantic lure from the end of the whipping boom.

Turned on its side with its end cutting an "H" through the air, the beam flew parallel to the ground as if carried by an omniscient hand of supreme justice.

Janis turned to face his praise, both hands raised high to the sky, his head lifted up, basking in dark glory. The beam met him squarely in the chest, impaling him with its immense cross section which carried him off his feet and into the concrete wall behind him. His mashed torso hung monogrammed with the initial of his fate.

Instantly the wind died.

Mark covered Maria with his arms as enormous clods exploded into dust atop frayed steel and broken cement.

The only sound in the strange calm was the low rumble of two diesel engines still running in the abandoned cranes.

Mark rose slowly, gazing at the destruction surrounding him.

He lifted Maria to her feet, her deep innocent eyes looked into his face and she threw her arms around his waist and sobbed quiet tears of overwhelming relief.

Mark squeezed the girl tightly.

"Are you okay?" he asked.

"Yeah!"

She laughed and cried at the same time.

Far away sirens and shouts of workmen rose outside the broken walls, while Miras disappeared in the opposite direction from the few brave souls creeping carefully into the stadium.

"Ah, shit!"

Mark and Maria quickly looked at each other, surprised by the voice.

"I'll be damned if it ain't broken!"

Darryl's voice came from inside the mutilated cab.

Mark let go of Maria who followed him closely over the mangled heap and onto the bottom, now the top, of the overturned crane.

Mark crouched on his bleeding knees and leaned over the side of the floor, peering into the crumpled operator's compartment. Darryl lay on his back with his legs sprawled above him, resting an injured arm across his chest.

Mark smiled and chuckled.

"Think you're gonna make it, buddy?"

Darryl gleamed back.

"Sure good to see you in one piece, Mister."

Mark let himself down into the cab. "Likewise, friend. Wouldn't be here without you, my man."

Darryl's face turned serious. "Did the kid make it?"

Maria laid down on top of the upside-down cab and hung her head over the side. "You mean me?"

Her thin face was caked with clay and framed by a knotted mass of black hair.

The two men looked at Maria then at each other. Delirious laughter erupted from their indelibly united, but for the moment thoroughly expended, spirits.

THIRTY-SIX

W hy, you're Darryl Clements, aren't you?" the grizzled man behind the counter at the mini-mart said. Though he'd been getting more used to it, Darryl still cringed. His picture had graced the front page of *The Atlanta Journal* nearly a dozen times in the last two months, extolling his bravery and persistence in recovering the more than seventy-five million dollars stolen from the 1996 Olympic Foundation fund.

"Yeah," Darryl admitted, wincing as he reached for his wallet, the ligaments of his arm still tender. He was picking up some chips for tonight's concert. He avoided all the fat-free varieties, just to bug Esther.

"No, no, no," the man said, waving both hands. "It's on the house, Mr. Clements. I'm just damn proud to shake your hand."

The man leaned over the counter and extended a worn, callused hand. Darryl hesitated, uncomfortable as a first grader in a new Sunday suit. But he did finally accept the warm, vigorous handshake.

"That's what this country needs," the clerk said. "More fine young men like you. Reminds us all that there are still heroes out there."

"Why, thank you, sir," Darryl said, darting his eyes at the door for a quick exit. "Thank you very much."

Just outside the door, Darryl heard the clerk's booming voice. "See that man there. That's Darryl Clements. The man who saved the Olympics."

Darryl picked up his step when he heard the spontaneous applause break out behind him. That was really going a bit far, he thought.

Darryl hurried on to his office, looking forward to a busy day. He especially anticipated a phone call to a certain young lady in Panama City, Florida. On his desk was a check made out to Miss Ruby LaRouge. He planned to ask her if she could use eight hundred twenty-seven thousand dollars.

THE FIRST GLIMMER of constellations twinkled above a rolling Southern landscape, awakening from its leafless hibernation. Spring folded winter back with delicate white-and-pink dogwood lace and brilliant multicolored azaleas, trumpeting the arrival of another new beginning.

The Rockdale County crowd of about ten thousand murmured anxiously throughout the open-air arena of the Georgia International Horse Park, anticipating Elton John's benefit appearance at the host site for the Centennial Olympic Equestrian Events. Among those squirming in their seats were teachers whose innovative programs awaited badly needed funds raised during the ceremony for the Rockdale County Public Schools Foundation.

From a choice spot in the grandstands, Esther bent over the carriage and loosely tucked the corners of a light cotton blanket around her cherub's perpetually moving thighs. The rosy-cheeked infant grinned and gurgled at the beaming face overhead.

Esther gently rocked her newborn in a carriage fortified with a new mother's arsenal, ready for any unforeseen circumstance arising during the child's first night out. The many compartments of the stroller, field-tested under the scrutiny of the Swiss army, bulged with at least a month's supply of diapers, four changes of sleepers, a half-dozen neatly folded spit-cloths, individually wrapped pacifiers, and six pasteurized, sanitized, and sterilized bottles of a soy-based formula that only an infant's primitive taste buds could love.

Down on the front row, Darryl struggled to hide his self-consciousness. Sitting next to Victoria Milton, who had just this morning earmarked funds for a certain recently closed Miami orphanage, Darryl gazed every minute or so over his shoulder toward his wife and baby.

Darryl gave them a jerky nervous wave and nod. Sitting next to his wife, Maria nodded and waved back at Darryl, then tightly clasped the hand of her newly adopted mother.

Wild applause broke out when the international music superstar and part-time Atlanta resident bounded shyly on the stage. He took a deep bow at the waist before sitting down behind the grand piano. Tonight there would be no accompanying musicians, just Elton and the audience. After thanking the committee and the crowd, he opened with one of the more recent additions to his countless string of tender, heartfelt ballads.

And it's no sacrifice, just a simple word
It's two hearts living, in two separate worlds
But it's no sacrifice, no sacrifice, it's no sacrifice at all.

Maria's other hand found Mark's, sitting on her right. Hero and savior were titles he had waved aside, but Maria knew that he was her friend now for life. A dear, precious friend. She looked up at the side of his handsome face. If only she were older . . .

As the three-quarter moon rose high in the night sky, Elton's soothing voice seemed to paraphrase the myriad of emotions Maria had known in the last few months. Mark looked down at her and smiled and squeezed her hand.

His gift to her, comfort.

NOTES

1. Hertwig Middle School was modeled after a school within the Rockdale County Public Schools. Information may be obtained about the concepts used at Salem High School by writing its principal, Robert Cresswell, 3551 Underwood Road SE, Conyers, Georgia 30208.

2. Other suggested reading about public education:

Sizer, Theodore R. 1992. Horace's School. In *Redesigning the American High School.* Houghton Mifflin Co.

Finn, Chester E., Jr. 1991. We Must Take Charge. In *Our Schools and Our Future.* The Free Press.

Toch, Thomas. 1991. *In the Name of Excellence.* Oxford University Press.

Odden, Allan R. 1992. *Rethinking School Finance.* Jossey-Bass Publishers.

3. The continuing consternation over how to teach children values in public schools has somehow overlooked the method used by past generations to gird children with a solid moral foundation: a rich and thorough exposure to literature. Boards of Education should adopt a canon of core literature just as colleges and universities do for their students. Upon completing the twelfth grade, students would have read and critiqued the entire canon. One suggested list might include the works from *James Madison Elementary School. A Curriculum for American Students* by William J. Bennett, U.S. Department of Education, 1988.

4. How this country chooses to deal with the ever controversial issue of race relations is pivotal to the health of democracy. For a masterful reflection of this challenge, please read *The Disuniting of America* by Arthur M. Schlesinger, Jr., W.W. Norton and Co., 1992.